THE PEABODY LIBRARY
Columbia City, Indiana

Goodwin, Suzanne
Daughters

Daughters

SUZANNE GOODWIN

St. Martin's Press
New York

Library of Congress Cataloging-in-Publication Data

Goodwin, Suzanne.
      Daughters / by Suzanne Goodwin.
          p.   cm.
   ISBN 0-312-01414-7 : $16.95
   I. Title.
PR6057.0585D3   1988
823'.914—dc19   87-27368
                                                                           CIP

First published in Great Britain by Michael Joseph Ltd.

First U.S. Edition

10 9 8 7 6 5 4 3 2 1

Part One

CHAPTER ONE

Freesias grew wild in the gardens that April but nobody tended them. Tamarisks and the odorous eucalyptus were in full leaf, the hidden alleys noisy with birds who perched fearlessly on the bronze heads of animals. It was a garden of the Midi, costly and formal and all overgrown. Much the crowds cared. They wandered on the lichened terrace, sat smoking on the marble steps or walked towards the ballroom through wide-flung doors. It was hot as summer, Provence in peacetime. The hideous nightmare was over now. It was 1919 and girls and men embraced with no death in their goodbyes.

The Villa Roumaniev had belonged to a Russian grand duke in the rich yesterdays. When the war's freezing wind scattered the crowned heads and fantastic fortunes from the Riviera, the Russians disappeared. The villa lay deserted and dusty for two years until the French authorities bought the great house and turned it into a convalescent home. Since then hundreds upon hundreds of wounded men had come here: some had died in the long, elaborate rooms, some returned to the trenches. Now the house was celebrating its last night as a place of shelter for soldiers.

> 'Come, come, I love you only,
> My heart is true.'

The treacly tune was being played by a group of elderly musicians from the Cannes casino; they had patriotically offered their services free.

'Come, come, what does it matter?' sang Sara, dancing with a French general. He kept nibbling at her ear and she had to bend sideways to get out of reach.

3

'You are very beautiful. I would like to pay court to you,' said the general, meaning something different.

Sara couldn't help laughing, which hurt his pride. He was much decorated, had been wounded in the second battle of the Marne, and was fifty-three years old.

Sara knew the Villa Roumaniev as well as she knew her own home, twenty minutes' walk away through the pine forest. She had wanted to nurse here, but her mother had flatly refused and so Sara had to settle for visiting the sick men, reading to them, writing their letters and playing endless games of cards. Bending her head with its weight of coiled red hair out of reach once again of the general's hungry bites, she thought how strange it was to realize all these men in uniform would be gone tomorrow. Where will I go? What, oh what, will there be left to do?

The Roumaniev party had been in full swing for hours; it was long past midnight. The dozens of tall lamps, branched like Paris street lamps, which stood in the gardens had been dark since 1914, but tonight they shone like moons among the masses of trees. The dancers waltzed to the syrupy music. Many of the girls wore fancy dress – to the delight of men accustomed to women in starch and white veils.

Sara waltzed in a pierrot costume which Patou had designed for her mother in 1910, bell-skirted, patterned with black and white diamonds. A mask covered her eyes. Her lecherous partner kept trying to strip it off. Eventually one of her friends, Jacques Césaire, who could not dance because of a damaged knee, gave her a reason to escape.

'*Un grand ami – gravement blessé*,' muttered Sara in her American-French. Adding thousands of apologies, she moved out of her partner's arms. Trying not to look pleased.

Supper had been arranged in what had been the Officers' Mess, and before that the grand-duke's music room. The ceiling was painted with girls crowned in flowers, clashing cymbals and singing; their youthful faces, vacuously smiling, seemed for the first time since the war to be in harmony with the times.

Jacques Césaire and Sara collected some food from the tables against the wall. A waiter in uniform filled their glasses with vintage champagne. Food and wine were gifts from the still-rich families who had given money and time to the work at the Villa Roumaniev. Sara, wondering just how little her own mother had managed to contribute, sipped her champagne pensively. Her companion was silent. He was thinking how exhausting it was to limp after six months of convalescence, and how it slowed down one's reactions. Even one's pleasures.

They talked idly as they ate their meal. Sara had a talent for friendship and had been good to this man. In return he'd given her as much affection as he could manage. But he looked haggard and pale.

'Well, Jacques?' she said, smiling. 'And shall you miss me?'

'Yes. But I shall be returning to real life. Convalescence is a waste of time.'

'How can that be? You've been spending time getting strong.'

He picked up her hand and looked at it for a moment. The costume sleeve came to a point on her knuckles: below was the white hand of somebody young, the skin thick as a gardenia and without a mark. He let the hand go.

'*You* don't need time to get strong,' he said.

She heard the weariness and recognized it.

'Jacques, I don't know why you're still up. Why not go to bed? Tomorrow's going to be so long. Thirteen hours in the train.'

He did not look grateful for her concern but said in the disgruntled voice of the invalid, 'All this noise will only keep me awake.'

She laughed.

'If you don't get to sleep, you aren't really tired. Anyway, you once told me you used to manage to sleep when up to your thighs in mud.'

Now that he saw the chance of escape from the gaiety, his manners returned.

'It's the last time I shall see you, Sara. And in any case, I don't think I should leave you alone.'

'We've said our goodbyes, haven't we? And do you really imagine,' she added dryly, 'I shall be alone for long?'

5

She watched him limp across the room. At the door he turned to give her a ghost of a salute.

Just then a man sat down in the seat Jacques had left. Sara glanced at him and did not recognize him. He wore the high-buttoned uniform of an American army officer; she'd known a few of her compatriots since 1917 when the United States had come into the war; but most of the officers here were French or British. The man who had coolly taken Jacques' place was tall, olive-skinned, with dark eyes. He was very self-possessed.

'That French friend of yours must be out of his wits,' he remarked in a drawling American voice.

She was irritated and said nothing.

'Did I offend you? Sorry. Difficult to know what a girl thinks when she wears a mask. I guess it's a waste of time to ask you to take it off?'

'I'm afraid so.'

'What beauty are you hiding under it, might one ask?'

'Perhaps I have a squint.'

'No you don't. I can see your eyes. Very pretty ones.'

Silence.

'Compliments bore you.'

'Yes. Most Frenchmen pay so many.'

'And you're an American girl. Bravo.'

'I wish,' said Sara impatiently, 'you wouldn't address me as if I were ten years old. I really don't know why I'm sitting here. This place is full of my friends.'

'And I'm not one of them. By the by, when I said your French captain was out of his wits – sure, I know you dislike compliments – what I meant was that only a crazy man would leave the girl every man in the room wants to talk to.'

Men weighted their voices when they said things like that to her. They fixed her with meaning looks and, if they could, they touched her arm, hand, shoulder. It had taken months to get the convalescent officers to drop all that, but in the end Sara made them treat her differently. She'd heard that weighted tone, been given those sexual looks, since she had been thirteen. Now at twenty-two, she seemed to have been aware of her attraction always. Her manner was light, practical, rarely flirtatious. Compliments and invitations to bed were part of her life in Provence, like the air which smelled of rosemary or the dark sea which lapped the rocks.

'Dance with me,' said the American, 'and let's thank God it isn't a waltz.'

The ballroom had been Saint-Simeon Ward yesterday. Nurses, and nuns from a convent in Antibes, had rustled about speaking in low voices. Now the beds had disappeared, the floor shone with chalk and the orchestra were attempting something which Sara recognized as American ragtime.

'They're not up to it,' said her companion.

'But isn't it a wonder they are managing at all?'

'I guess so.'

He put his arms round her. He danced well, but differently from the French and British partners of earlier this evening. Faster. And with odder unexpected steps. The music stopped.

'That wasn't bad,' he said, and 'Good. They're starting again.'

Sara loved to dance and through the war had rarely done so. Her companions at the Roumaniev were always sick or recovering very slowly, and she disliked the parties given by her mother's friends at their homes on the coast. The Roumaniev was real and they were not. She enjoyed the unfamiliar sensation of dancing with this American who led her with authority, and taught her unfamiliar steps. Once, following him, she burst out laughing.

'You dance like a leaf,' he said, as the music stopped again. 'I scarcely knew I had a girl in my arms.'

They were both slightly breathless. The tempo had been fast.

'Mademoiselle Sara, now it is for me,' said a voice. It was the general, coming up on cue. She had known him for some time. He had waxed moustaches, a severe look and many medals. She had played chess with him, and he fudged the game to let her win.

'The lady has one more dance promised to me, *mon générale*,' said the American politely. 'Then I will surrender my prize.'

7

The Frenchman looked him up and down, hesitated, bowed, and left them with a sharp, 'I shall return in ten minutes.'

Sara and her companion danced again. But ragtime was over and it was a sad English tune.

> 'And when I tell them
> How beautiful you are,
> They never believe me . . .'

He danced her to the far side of the ballroom, at the furthest distance from the general and a group of officers, all of high rank, talking energetically by the bar.

'I bet ten dollars they're discussing strategy. God, how *can* they?' he suddenly exclaimed and before Sara, startled, could reply he said quickly. 'Take no notice of me. I'm sorry. It's just that any man's army, U.S., French, British, makes me sick right now. Time I got out of uniform. Look, shall we take a walk? Or sure as hell that friend of yours is going to nab you. What do you say?'

'Yes, please.'

In the rich Russian time the grand duke had bought forty acres of pine forest leading down to the sea, and had created the extraordinary gardens which Sara and her companion walked towards down the white marble steps. There were lawns and high hedges, French gardens, Italian gardens, fountains long since dried, lily ponds which had become circles of stained marble. The rosemary bushes had lost their clipped forms, the huge cactuses were split by drought. Everywhere was carpeted with pine needles.

'Where are you taking me?' said the American, as they went down a path towards a distant expanse of sea, 'For a swim?'

'Would you?'

'Yes. If you did as well.'

'Not me. I'm Provençal in my bones now. I expect my Puritan ancestors rejoiced in cold water, but it gives me goose pimples. I like the sea warm as milk.'

'Damn. I thought I'd found a way to make you take off your mask.'

'If I swam, I'd still wear it.'

She led the way through the pine trees and citrus bushes dotted with white flowers to the remains of a terrace which overlooked huge scattered rocks. An olive tree, bent like an old man, hung its branches over a marble bench. Around them where the pine forest had been thinned was an undergrowth, rough, prickly, of tree heather, juniper and myrtle. There was a scent of resin.

She sat down, spreading her diamond-patterned skirts. He sat beside her, put his arm round her shoulders, and violently kissed her. She had wanted that. He attracted her. She liked the feel of his hands, the shape of his face, and the way when his mouth touched hers his tongue opened her lips. As he continued to kiss her, pushing his tongue round her mouth, pressing her closer, she thought – shall I let you make love to me? Half of her said – are you *mad*, is this what's happened to you? That you're willing to behave like a whore? It was true she was not a virgin. She'd had a lover, her first, two years ago. He had been young and English and horribly sad, not physically ill but mentally in ruins after Passchendaele, haunted by nightmares. He had relatives in the South and they had arranged for him to be at the Roumaniev. Sara had gone to bed with him in a sort of passionate pity. He told her that often the faces of living people – her own – turned as he watched into the faces of his dead friends. Sometimes he saw them lying all round him on the ground. He had been her lover, and then had been sent north again and she never heard from him. Perhaps he was dead . . .

But tonight. Oh, tonight it was different. The war and the sorrow were gone, the Roumaniev itself was finished and she thought, do I want this stranger? Her body melted and moistened and answered yes. He pushed his hand into the deep neckline of her dress, caught one of her nipples between his fingers and moved it up and down. She felt slightly faint.

He took his hand away and looked down at her in the checkered light of a moon shining through pine branches.

'Take off your mask.'

'No.'

He put up a broad hand and touched the mask, exploring it. He ran his fingers along its hard satin edge, tracing it on her forehead, over the slits through which her eyes shone, along the back where it was attached by elastic across her hair.

'What makes you think I shan't drag it off?'

'You aren't that sort.'

'What sort is that, Domino?'

'A ravisher, I suppose.'

'I'd like to throw you on your back and ravish *you*.'

'I know.'

'And you'd like it too.'

'Would I?' she said, with a slight echo of her matter-of-fact self.

He said nothing but stood up, lifting her by her elbows. After embracing her for a long moment, he picked her up and put her down on the ground on the pine needles, pulling up her skirts. She was frightened, excited, half out of her wits. She scarcely knew what she was thinking or doing. She did not want to be taken like a raped city. She began to fight the big heavy body which moved on top of hers, pushing him away and moving to avoid his kiss. But she could as well have fought a thundering wave breaking over her. He opened her legs with his and entered her, not harshly but slowly, claiming her without effort, pushing into her, owning her. It was useless to fight. She was lost. And she lay under him, responding and knowing a kind of exquisite hurtful joy. He waited until her climax came so that they finished together. When they rolled apart, they were wringing with sweat. They lay in the half light, kissing sometimes. After a while they made love again.

'What's your name, Domino? Hell. Forget I asked.'

Taking her hand, he sucked each finger in turn.

'You taste good. Scent?'

'Rosemary. I put my hand along the top of the hedge.'

'They say the folk here eat roast lamb with rosemary.'

They began to laugh, and still laughing fell again into each other's arms, to kiss and embrace and gasp and desire again. How many times?

'Do you know you're the first woman in my life I've had who wore a mask? I've gotten used to it now. Don't think I want you to take it off.'

'Oh good.'

They lay quiet. Faintly in the distance they could hear music. And people laughing and calling to each other. The sounds came from the other side of the world.

'And what's *your* name?' she said at last, pressing her masked face against his chest.

'No. We won't say. We won't know each other's names. That's best, isn't it?' he said.

'Not really . . .'

'What good would it do us, Domino? What in hell good would it do us to know who we are?'

She did not remember how she returned home except that it had been in a motor with a lot of people, and her nameless lover had not been among them. Before that they had gone back to the villa and drunk champagne. Walking crazily, worn out with love, half asleep, a little drunk, she had fallen into bed still in her pierrot dress. She was woken by a thin sword of sunshine striking her face through the curtain.

For a moment, a few hazy seconds, she remembered nothing. Vaguely looking down, she saw she still wore the satin dress, it was creased and crushed. Then everything came back. Her stomach gave a drop as if she'd fallen from a height. She knew why her body glowed, why it felt sore, why she felt sore, why she felt serene, damp and tired. It was love-making. Not the way it had been with poor Philip, so desperate on his side, so pitiful on hers, but with a lover who gave nothing but pleasure. Long, continuous, thudding, unbearable pleasure. Who was he? When would she see him again? When, oh when, would she have him again?

Rolling over on her stomach, she groped for the clock by her bed, and looked at it for a moment without believing her eyes. Oh God, it was half-past one. He'll be gone, she thought. He doesn't even know how to find me.

All the well-being left her in a tense unspeakable haste as she stripped off the ruined dress, splashed her face with cold water and threw on the first dress she tugged out of the wardrobe. She did not ring for her maid but, cramming her untidy hair under a large felt hat, rushed out of the room.

At the top of the stairs she heard her mother's voice, gaily talking in the dining room. There must be a luncheon party. Tiptoeing down, nodding to one of the servants, Sara crept out through an open French window into the garden, taking a path which could not be seen from the dining room. She ran to the garage – her mother's limousine was not there. The chauffeur must have been sent on some commission or other. There was nothing for it, she must walk.

Through the pine forest Sara made her way running, changing to a trot, then a walk and then starting to run again. It was breathlessly hot. She saw nothing – not the tawny trunks of the pine trees, the fragments of azure sky, the herbs in lilac flower; she simply ran, the blood beating in her head, slowing down only to get back her breath.

At last she reached the drive and hurried up to where the Roumaniev lay blazing in the sun.

It was not the same place. Gaiety and music were gone. A khaki-painted lorry was drawn up by the steps, it was filled with men in uniform. When they saw Sara they shouted and waved their caps and she waved automatically in reply. She craned to see a certain face among those smiling at her. It was too late, the engine was starting up and as she stood there, the lorry trundled away down the drive.

Indoors, the huge rooms were empty. Beds which had been taken to pieces were in piles, their black iron bars sprouting wheeled feet. Mattresses went by carried on the backs of the few remaining troops, or were dragged off by hospital staff to be loaded into a second lorry which drew up just then.

In the great echoing house everybody was hurrying, intent on their tasks. Desperately Sara went to find the matron, Mrs Kestelmann. There was no sign of her. A young officer whom she knew came down the stairs, carrying a bulging valise.

'Christian. Hello. I'm looking for Mrs Kestelmann . . .'

'I'm afraid I have not seen her, Mademoiselle Sara.' He gave her his worried smile. She had known him for weeks, he had a back injury. He was brave and painfully thin, and much too young to look like that.

'I believe she went to the Mairie,' he said. 'To fill in yet more documents. She was quite angry, she wanted to stay here until we'd all left. Is there anything I can do for you?'

'I'm looking for a friend,' she said, in her accented French. 'He is American. A major.'

And she thought – *I don't know his name.*

'That was the last lorry of troops which went just now,' Christian said, blessedly incurious. 'Most of them went at dawn. It seems you have no luck, Madamoiselle Sara.'

'It seems I haven't.'

'The men going to Marseilles to take the ship left hours ago,' he said, adding, 'I only remain as I am to be collected by my family. I am sorry I cannot help.'

He still looked anxious and sad. He had his own troubles.

'Good luck, Christian,' she said suddenly, and put out her hand to grasp his own.

Her voice, her smile, were light. Her heart like lead.

CHAPTER TWO

'Why is it,' said Sara to Carl Bauer, 'that when two people stop laughing as one comes into a room, it is so infuriating?'

Bauer, sixty-five, small and thin with a long inquisitive nose, was cleaning his Napoleonic medals. Sara had called at his tiny house on the ramparts of Antibes. They sat in the petit salon which brimmed with his collection. The chairs and mirrors, the marble-topped tables, display cases, carpet, every bunch of roses embroidered under Sara's feet, had not been altered or much dusted since 1900. The sun slanted through heavy curtains and set Sara's hair on fire.

Carl polished the Emperor's profile.

'You are referring to your mother and Monsieur Tournamy?'

'Now who else would I refer to, Carl?'

'My dear Sara, I am not a visitor at the Villa des Roses.'

'It isn't for want of being invited. Don't bother to make excuses. I know you won't come.'

She picked up a curiously-shaped pearl earring which was in a velvet box on the table. 'Did these really belong to Josephine? They're not beautiful enough.'

'They are baroque pearls, which explains their uneven shape and are of very good grade. Of course they belonged to the Empress. I have the provenance,' was the reply. His voice was thin and dry. The Midi sun had sucked up the juices both of his voice and body, but not of his soul. He looked at the girl sitting upright in a dusty gilt chair.

It was over a year now since the terrible war, which people now curiously called The Great War, had ended. Carl had begun to notice an increasing restlessness in his youthful

14

friend. Bauer had lived all his life on the Riviera and never been part of its brilliance, but he had seen the war darken the bright south. The conflict had been hundreds of miles away in lakes of Normandy mud, it had spread across the maps of Europe, but remained far away from Provence. Yet everybody had been affected by its hideous presence. Death's hooded figure stood at the table at mealtimes, and pressed against people on railway stations. Sara once told Carl that when she was on Nice station saying goodbye to soldier friends, she did not dare to turn round. That was all over now. Yet the Riviera had not recovered its splendour. It was shabby and in part deserted. Few of Sara's American friends had crossed the Atlantic again, and her mother's Russian acquaintances, poor creatures, were gone for ever. Sara de Grelle's present state of mind bothered Carl; he discerned a savage boredom.

Not yet twenty-three, tall for a girl, with tawny red hair and a skin of radiant pallor, the texture of a gardenia, Sara looked clever, with her straight nose and a way of looking directly at people when they spoke to her. To be beautiful and clever, he thought, was difficult.

'You are asking,' he said, putting down the medal and picking up another, 'why it angers you to enter a room and find Madame de Grelle and her new friend laughing. And then, seeing you, they stop. That is because you are excluded.'

'But I don't want to be *in*cluded, Carl! When Mother occasionally gets possessive, I feel I'm being suffocated in her sables.'

He continued to polish, his hands covered in powder. He studied the medal, inlaid with brass laurel leaves, at a distance, then picked up a toothbrush to work more thoroughly.

'I sometimes wonder if you've forgiven your mother, Sara, for stopping you from being a nurse.'

She said impatiently that that was history. It was true that when war began she had wanted very much to nurse. Many of her friends trained and went into uniform, except those whose families had nervously managed to get home to the United States. Sara had been ill just about then. Later, she had been refused when she applied to a training hospital in Nice. It was only towards the end of the war that by chance she discovered the truth. Her mother, who had a number of high-ranking admirers, had pulled strings.

'By the time I found out, Carl, I was at the Roumaniev,' she said. 'Though lord knows why she stopped me. It isn't as if we get on.'

Sara's mother, an American heiress from New York, had married the owner of two very successful auction houses, one in Paris, the other in London – Alexander de Grelle. They had divorced years back. But Louise de Grelle never returned to the States, she remained living in style in a large house her husband had built for her among the pine forests of Antibes.

Poor Madame de Grelle, thought Carl, who had a weakness for middle-aged beauties, even one who had made it obvious she thought him of no account.

Sara leaned back and stared round the room. The past stared back. Carl's collection of what he called '*mes petites choses commemoratives*' filled the room, and every single object was connected with France's great hero: Napoleon. There was a marble bust by Canova of the most handsome man Sara had ever seen, with sensual mouth, noble profile and hair cropped like a Roman patrician. Had he really looked so? There were snuff boxes with the 'N' in pearls, bas-reliefs of battles where horses reared and heroes fell. A huge silk flag of Louis XVIII's was draped across one wall, embroidered with oak leaves and printed in gold with the King's speech to the '*braves hommes*' who stayed faithful to him. '*Brave*' was much used in paintings, cartoons, silhouettes, engravings. '*Honneur aux Braves*' was traced on a ribbon held in an eagle's beak. The bird represented Napoleon, wore a crown on its feathered poll. Below its mighty wings staggered his soldiers, armless or bandaged or on crutches, supporting each other. All were cheering and wearing in their black hats the sprigs of victorious laurel.

Few people knew of Carl's collection, it amused him to think how unknown it was. He had been collecting all his life, having inherited the basis of his treasures from his father. Joseph Bauer had been twenty, in the infantry of d'Erlon's

First Corps, the first soldiers at Waterloo to attack on that fatal day. D'Erlon's troops had marched and sung to *The Triumph of Trajan*, Joseph told his small son; they had charged up the slope with fixed bayonets, only to be driven back by enemy cavalry. . . .

How Joseph had worshipped his Emperor. The collection had started with the young soldier's own bayonet, the buttons cut from his uniform, and a medal awarded him after a minor battle in 1814 . . .

Carl, the child of Joseph's middle age, born in 1860 and had been taught about Napoleon before he could read. When Joseph died, Carl simply went on with the collection. He worked as a teacher; inherited a little money from a patron. He never married. He continued to buy, or to sell so that he could buy something better, rarer.

Over the years that he and Sara had been friends, Carl had shown and explained the history of every one of his treasures to her. She often said it was Napoleon, not Carl, who occupied the house.

She had met him when she'd come to Antibes to do some shopping, left the chauffeur waiting and run to the ramparts in a high wind to look at the rough sea: the Mediterranean had been in an interesting rage that morning. Suddenly it began to pour with rain. A little man short as a gnome, wearing a battered hat, hurried up to offer her his umbrella. Stooping, she was a good five inches taller than he was, Sara had been escorted 'for one moment until the worst of the rain stops, I beg, mademoiselle,' into his house.

That was how the friendship had begun. Louise had been presented to Carl later when, by chance, he met them both in Antibes. Her mother's manner on that single occasion had been cold to the point of rudeness.

When Carl had bowed and left them she had said, 'What can you possibly see in that little creature? He looks to me as if he needs a good scrub with Marseilles soap.'

'He is clever and kind, and an expert on Napoleon.'

'And since when have you developed a passion for Napoleon?' said Louise. What did not interest her annoyed her.

'His collection is magnificent. Father would be fascinated by it,' said Sara to tease.

'Why your father drags you to auctions and lets you mess about in his galleries with all that old stuff,' said Louise, 'I simply cannot imagine. He does not think, I suppose, that it will make you more attractive to men?'

Diplomatic when she wished to be, Sara held her tongue.

At the time she had met Carl Bauer, Sara had recently returned from a Swiss finishing school where she had learned long narrative poems in French, how to sing, and to row on the lake of Geneva. As the war began to smear its unspeakable suffering across France she – like everybody else – was tremblingly conscious of it all the time. It shocked her to be safe in Provence. With nursing denied to her, she threw herself into the task of visiting, amusing, caring for the officers and men convalescing at the Roumaniev. It was a sort of war work. And it kept her away from home, and from watching – with unenjoying eyes – her mother's love affairs. Since her early teens she had been aware of those, and there were moments when she was passionately sorry for Louise. But it was insulting to pity anybody so beautiful.

Yet she did not respect her. She ignored Louise's contemptuous dismissal of Carl, and the elderly man and the girl became close friends.

Today he sensed a difference in her. She did not fidget or make jokes. She simply sat not looking at Josephine's earring which was still in the palm of her hand.

'That will do for today,' he said, replacing the medal and taking the pearl from her to put it in its box. 'We need tisane. Margot will give us some. She's waiting to be called.'

He went out, returning to sigh that Margot was angry again; she said her *tarte aux pommes* should have been eaten half an hour ago. A big Provençal woman with shoulders that once carried a yoke and milk pails came into the room with a tray of tisane brewed from lime flowers and an apple tart shiny with melted sugar. She and Sara exchanged formal greetings in French. When she had gone, Sara poured out. She suddenly remarked, 'I don't know how you put up with me.'

'And I do it so well.'

'Yes. You do. I sometimes think you're my only friend left on the Riviera. Most of the girls are married or gone to London or Paris or something. And as for men friends –'

'There are a lot of those.'

'Carl, they're not fun. French ones who think I shall have a large *dot* from my father. And the English are just as bad.'

'What about your own compatriots?'

'I don't meet any,' she said disinterestedly. 'Then – going to Montreux with my mother. It's so drear, Carl. Last summer I spent my time longing to be here with you.' She looked round the room which smelled of lavender and dust. 'Instead of changing my dress six times a day and fending off men whom Mother will call my "beaux".'

'But that's a charming expression. American from the ancient times.'

'How she'd hate to hear that,' said the girl, heartlessly laughing.

'More tisane, Sara?'

'No, thank you. It's delicious, but no.'

A pause.

'Come along, Sara. What's the trouble?'

Before she could speak he added in his pernickety voice, 'Don't bother to deny there is one. You may as well tell me. Better to speak out, you know.'

'I had no idea it showed,' she said after a moment.

He waited with a certain curiosity.

Glancing at her, Carl wondered what she was thinking. Why was it that the eyes of some women, slightly sleepy, slightly swimming, were so evocative of sex?

'I suppose I miss the Roumaniev. How disgusting. To prefer the war.'

'Not the war. Only you were being useful then.'

'Yes. I was. And now I'm not. Things are changing, Carl, I can feel it. Can you? I'm turning into an anachronism, tied to Mother like this. Women worked during the war, rich and poor alike. The life she lives, and makes me live, is out of date.'

'She wishes to return to the old days. That's very understandable. She was a great beauty.'

Sara thought – yes, she was. She remembered the times, unreal as Ancient Greece, when her mother had lived here in a society entirely absorbed in pleasure. It was taken for granted that 'you simply must' spend part of each year on the Riviera. American millionaires had fallen in love with Louise, and driven her to gamble in Monte Carlo. 'Oh, it's so pretty,' Louise told her daughter smilingly. 'To see the roulette tables just shining with piles of golden louis!'

The money washing the Mediterranean shores, the round of pleasure in the company of princes and grand dukes, all, all was gone as if it had never been. Those whims of the enormously rich. One of Louise's Russian friends had employed forty-eight gardeners, and the flowers in his gardens had been changed every night so that he could enjoy a different sight each morning. Sara marvelled to remember things like that.

'During the war I never thought about the future,' she said. 'It was too sad and too frightening. I just imagined something would eventually happen to me.'

'A man, for instance.'

'Must it be a man?' said Sara impatiently. For a moment, the nameless lover of the Villa Roumaniev, an image forcibly pushed away for a year, rose in her thoughts.

'I don't know what I imagined,' she went on, 'but it certainly wasn't being stuck at the Villa des Roses.'

'Madame de Grelle needs you.'

'Of course she doesn't, Carl. She'd rather I wasn't around. Why does she make me stay, I simply can't understand it? I suggested going to New York to see my Great-Aunt Goodier, now it's safe to cross the ocean again. She turned me down flat.'

She sighed.

'It's my birthday soon. I shall be twenty-three. She detests my birthdays.'

'Time frightens her because she was so beautiful.'

'She still is,' said Sara, and was piqued when he did not agree. He asked instead if the presence of Monsieur Tournamy upset Sara?

She scratched her nose. Her mother's love affairs were nothing new. But they had been very respectable. The loose

Riviera morals never touched Louise with scandal. She still officially behaved like the good American niece of Miss Emily Goodier. During the war there had been staff officers who courted her. Even an occasional general. But surrounded by admiring men, propriety was part of Louise's household. It was different now. Jean-Claude Tournamy was twenty-five years old, and the words 'young enough to be your son' were in the faces of all Louise's friends.

Sara had met him at a charity ball in Menton. He asked her to present him to Louise.

'I so long for the honour. To meet a legend, you know.'

'Don't call her that for heaven's sake!'

'Why not? She is straight from the *Roman de la Rose*.'

Louise, waving a spangled fan, was gracious when Sara introduced him. For the rest of the evening they scarcely said a word to anybody else. That had been the start.

'My mother's never invited one of her lovers to live with us before, Carl. Everybody disapproves. Of his age too. And that's not all. They drink champagne.'

'But surely –'

'No, no, I don't mean now and then, I mean all the time. With luncheon. For *goûter*. During dinner and afterwards with coffee. Imagine, this morning I saw them having some with breakfast.'

Carl was silent. Limiting himself to two glasses of *vin de table* a day, and for high days and holidays an occasional glass of a fine Chablis, the picture of a river of champagne was intriguing.

'Do they get drunk?' he mildly asked.

'They don't pass out. As a matter of fact Jean-Claude has a head of iron. He's exactly the same at midnight as he is at ten in the morning. Not Mother. She looks stupid. Blurred and stupid,' repeated Sara, pouring herself more tisane with a steady hand.

You're a cool one, he thought. Daughterly love was shallow rooted in Sara; pull it up and she would not miss it. Would Louise de Grelle? From all he had heard, he doubted if either of them deeply cared for the other.

'I suppose,' he suggested in his fluting voice, 'you might

21

try to stop it. You could speak to her very tactfully. I've known you to be delicate when you want to be.'

She looked slightly, not very, amused.

'Mother can't stand criticism, she's never had it in her life since I can remember. And she'd be furious if it came from me. I get on her nerves all the time.'

Because you are young, and extraordinary to look at, he thought.

'Then speak to Monsieur Tournamy.'

'Jean-Claude would tell her afterwards and make it into a good story. They'd laugh. Carl, I am beaten. I don't even know why he encourages her. Except that people who drink usually prefer a companion until they are too far gone.'

'Such wisdom is disturbing at twenty-two.'

'So,' said Sara, 'is living at the Villa des Roses.'

There was a moment's silence.

'There is one thing,' she continued. 'She won't let me go to New York, but I can't see how she could stop me going to see my father, do you? He will be in London at the end of this week.'

'Of course she cannot stop you. You're of an age. Go and buy yourself and your maid a ticket, my dear Sara.'

She grimaced.

'If it were that easy. The fact is, I haven't a franc. A sou. I spent Father's allowance months ago and although Mother pays my dress bills (she quite likes spending money on my clothes) she never actually parts with real cash. She can scarcely bear to take it out of her wallet.' She sighed. 'Imagine Montreux again! Worse than ever, with popping corks on the train and . . . and she doesn't even try to hide that she's having an affair. It's the first time she's not bothering to keep up appearances.'

'I thought you were a modern young woman. Interested in a new freedom.'

She met his eyes with her direct, hard look.

'For the young. For me. Not for Mother. She was raised strictly. This affair is bad in every way. For her. For Jean-Claude wasting his youth. And very bad for me. Hell, why do I land you with my troubles? You're too sympathetic. I must go. But thank you for listening.'

She gave him the smile inherited from Louise, which enslaved people.

They walked through the narrow hall to the door. Across the cobbled roads were the ramparts built by Vauban in the 18th century, which dropped down into a sea lit with the silvery mid-afternoon light. Sara held out her hand and Carl, taking it, mildly said,

'I forgot to tell you my small piece of news. I have decided to sell the collection.'

She started as violently as if she'd been scalded.

'*What do you mean?*'

He looked delighted to see her blush crimson.

'But – you never said – you let me maunder on about myself and all the time – why, that's *awful*!'

'My dear young friend, I see you think I am in a financial difficulty. No, no, I promise you, it's nothing like that. What has happened is far more fascinating. Perhaps I should have told you before. It has been in my mind for months, but I decided not to speak until I had made the great decision. The truth is, I find I know my little collection too well. It is something that can happen, you know. I've no doubt your famous father has many times profited by it. *Mes petites choses* no longer have anything left to say to me. We have talked ourselves out. It is time for us to part.'

Sara gaped. Carl and his Napoleonic collection were so much part of each other that she did not know where Carl's personality ended and the powerful presence of the Emperor began. It seemed to her that without his collection, her friend might take to bleeding internally.

'But you could not *bear* to sell them!'

'Of course I could. They should be with other people, who feel as I used to do. Perhaps with a museum? Who can say. I am making a few enquiries. I am in no hurry. The letters I have received are so very entertaining. I quite look forward to the post. And I have already chosen the subject of my new collection. The Emperor himself was responsible. His son, Count Walewski, was the beautiful creature's lover for a spell. My choice, Sara, is Rachel.'

'Wasn't she an actress?' Sara had a strong sense of anti-climax. From Napoleon to an actress was a pretty steep descent. How could Carl –

'An *actress*, Sara? She was France's great tragedienne. "Born from classical times, her pale skin seemed made of Greek marble" ' he quoted caressingly. 'I saw a portrait of her by Etty and frankly, my dear, I was lost from that moment. So pale. Such profound dark eyes. The more I learn of her, the more I need to make my collection of the *belle Rachel*.' He sighed in contentment.

'She died not far from here, you know. She was brought to the coast in the yacht of her lover – carried ashore on a stretcher by two sailors, –'*une femme très pâle, les yeux profonds*'– and taken to the Villa Sardou at Le Cannet. On her deathbed she wrote seventeen letters to her friends . . .' he paused and murmured, 'the lovely creature was thirty-seven years old.'

His voice had the old ring she remembered when he used to talk about Napoleon.

'There's too much to tell just now,' he said, kissing her hand as she was leaving. 'Goodbye for the present, my dear Sara.'

Her mother's motor car, the old pre-war De Dion-Bouton limousine, was waiting for her by a deserted sandy beach where waves broke with scarcely a sigh. The elderly chauffeur saluted, and opened the car door.

He drove slowly up an avenue edged with tall wind-bitten palms.

Soon they were among the pines, and at a turn of the road which steeply rose were the locked gates leading to the Roumaniev's deserted gardens. Every time she passed, Sara had a stab of memory. I must have been mad, she thought. But that night of love-making with a stranger which had deeply affected her was in the past now. She no longer had the frightening sensation of being haunted. A year ago she had so wanted her nameless lover that she thought of nothing else. Sexual longing woke her at four in the morning. Every time she saw a figure in uniform she had a crazy moment of thinking it was him. It was the same when she heard a man's American voice. She dreamed about him and woke in tears.

24

She lost weight and looking at herself in a long glass despised her own reflection. If you are so indiscriminate, she thought, you should have the courage to match it.

But the haunting was over now. Only the smell of the pines, sharp and resinous, brought him back; and she remembered his body plunged into hers as they lay on the pine needles. And wondered for the thousandth time where he was.

CHAPTER THREE

The Villa des Roses, as with many houses in what Queen Victoria had called 'this paradise of nature', had been built upon a love affair. Unlike the Roumaniev, which imitated Italian palazzi with elaborate decoration and classical columns, Sara's mother owned a house which was pure Provençal. It was square and tall and plain and the colour of a tea rose. Tiles like halved flower pots covered its broad roofs, and under the eaves were painted, in swags and loops, trailing blue ribbons tying together thick garlands of pink and brownish-yellow roses. In the nineteenth century most Provençal villas had these under-the-roof paintings, and the artists who travelled from one new building to the next never repeated themselves. A young painter from the Haut Var had been hired for the Villa des Roses. He thought Louise a vision, and sat on the scaffolding in the broiling sun for many days, painting his interpretation of the house's sentimental name.

Louise's husband Alexander de Grelle had built the villa when he had been passionately in love with her.

She had come to Europe from America like many another wealthy young woman in the 1880s, in search – of what? A coronet? Love? Preferably both. Louise Goodier's parents died young, leaving their only child two dangerous gifts: beauty and money. She wore the things lightly, unconscious of their ominous weight.

'She is charmin',' said English duchesses.

'*Ravissante*,' said French countesses.

Louise Goodier was a beauty in the American style. Her hair, thick, coarse and richly black, was more luxuriant than the hair of most European women. She had high cheekbones which gave her face the mystery of a Red Indian, and almond-shaped violet eyes. When she smiled, which she did often unthinkingly, men went weak at the knees.

She travelled to Europe on the steamship *Umbria* accompanied by her aunt and only surviving relative. Emily Goodier, a thin stiff-backed New York lady, was fond of the girl and felt that perhaps Louise should travel, although she herself disliked foreign countries, foreigners, and disliked sightseeing more. She was abruptly polite to the people whom Louise collected round her wherever she went. But Emily wondered piously how soon they could take ship for home.

Louise, on the other hand, thought the other side of the deep Atlantic an enchanting place. Of course it was weighed down with the stupidest rules. People over here were proud of things that back home would have been pushed aside. Who in America thought more of a dead great-grandfather than a present employer? Yet Europe amused and pleased her. And she amused and pleased everybody she met. She spent a great deal of her parents' money on her luxurious self and luxurious surroundings. At their hotels, the Goodier ladies took enormous suites. Louise wore gowns which an Empress would not despise, and extraordinary furs. She was the acme of fashion, but fashions seemed transmuted by Louise. It was decreed that women's bodies should be imprisoned in boned corsets: somehow hers looked soft and supple under her gowns. 'A positive *Eugénie*,' Frenchmen said. She had a kind of retinue which beautifully suited her. A group of good servants were hired by Miss Goodier to accompany them across Europe as if the two ladies were princesses.

Louise could well have been royal. She swept up and down enormous marble stairways, took lessons on making her curtsey to the old English Queen.

'How many curtseys must I make?' she asked the dowager who was to present her.

'Nine, my dear. It is the most brilliant Drawing Room of the Season.'

Emily refused the honour of going to the palace, and sniffed.

But Louise took to it like a swan, as two Gentlemen of the Court gathered up her train after her curtseys, and draped the weighty silk over her arm. She backed out of the royal presence as if, remarked the dowager later, she had never walked forward in her life.

Wherever she was, in Parisian ballrooms, open carriages at Goodwood, the terraces of Roman gardens, the girl was radiantly at home. She seemed to have lived always in over-decorated houses under ceilings painted with kissing cupids, where men fell in love with her as if she brought with her some inescapable plague.

Louise met her destiny at an English house party in the summer of 1895. She had been invited to a Gloucestershire manor because of her fortune and her looks: in English society she was called 'the pretty Goodier gal'. The place, vaulted, Victorian and famous, hummed with life, and during her first evening Louise looked the other guests over with lazy good nature. They were all seated in a massive dining room lively with conversation, and Louise noticed that one particular man was much fussed over by her hosts. He was big, broad-shouldered, with a certain resemblance to the Prince of Wales emphasized by a sandy silky beard cut in the same style. He had an easy manner and penetrating, small eyes. During dinner he was the centre of attention.

'Who is the man with the ginger beard?' murmured Louise to the young man on her right, her host's eldest son and already under her spell.

'Alexander de Grelle. The owner, you know.'

'The owner of what?' enquired Louise idly.

The young man chuckled.

'It would do Alexander good to know he isn't as famous as all that. He owns *the* new auction house in Paris, don't you know? Now he's started one in Mayfair. They say Sotheby's and Christie's are not best pleased. Alexander likes to annoy.'

'Why does owning auction houses make him important? If he is important. Is he?'

'To a lot of people, very. He has so much knowledge and taste. The great thing, Miss Goodier, is to *know*, and Alexander does. He knows everything about objects of art.'

Louise didn't. She'd never been to an auction in her life, and to buy the sort of things all round her, paintings and marble, furniture and silken screens, silver, gold even, would not enter her head. The big brownstone house in New York that had been her home was a sad place now. Its old-fashioned furniture was all shrouded with dust sheets like lumpy ghosts. She avoided it. When she spent money in her lavish way, it was on clothes. They were interesting. Furniture wasn't. But the man sitting at a distance in the glow of many candles did interest her. She wasn't exactly sure why.

Later, in the Music Room, he was presented to her. He took a chair too small for his bulk and, between performances on the harp by a nervous girl in white, made conversation.

'I have been hoping for the pleasure of talking to you, mademoiselle. I met your father in New York once. I liked him tremendously. But could not get him, alas, to share my particular folly at that time. A passable collection of Chinese jade.'

Louise thought his manner and his French accent rather pleasing, but noticed that he did not seem to take much trouble to please *her*. He was simply himself: confident, easy, powerful. She did not see any consciousness of her beauty in his narrow eyes. That was a new sensation.

'I suppose my Papa didn't wish to buy the jade, Mr de Grelle. He wasn't interested in the past, you see.'

She missed the look he gave her.

'And do you feel the same, mademoiselle?'

'I guess I'm not much taken with the past either.'

'That is because you are so essentially the present.'

The harp tinkled away tediously.

'Are you laughing at me?' asked Louise.

'Now how could one laugh at a young lady who is such a success?'

During the weekend Alexander de Grelle seemed to be at her side a good deal. His rather plain serious wife, Lady Verena (who reminded Louise vaguely of a younger version of Aunt Emily), did not accompany them when Alexander took Louise strolling in the grounds. In the dusk he showed her the lake where water lilies were closing too fast. Lingering on a rustic bridge they watched a flotilla of moorhens. Then walked slowly back to the house through the fragrant garden. It was the time of day when men paid her compliments.

'Before the dressing bell we have time to go to the picture gallery,' said Alexander de Grelle, steering her into the house.

Louise's heart sank. If he wasn't going to make pretty speeches, she preferred to go straight to her room and choose her gown for the evening. Looking at paintings bored her deeply; she could not count the times her elderly hosts (it was never *young* men) had taken her to stare at portraits of sour-looking ancestors, or at alarming mountainsides where avalanches hurtled.

'Let us visit the Stuarts,' said Alexander, 'and pay our respects to the Martyr King.' He showed her the portrait of a delicate-looking man astride a horse too large for him.

'A failure as a king but I'm told an excellent husband,' said Alexander humorously. 'And here is his wife, with the angel holding a crown over her head. My countrywoman, Henrietta Maria. She did the English crown no good at all, by the by. Ah. Here's the fellow I want you to meet.'

He indicated the portrait of a man with a red beard, who had a faint look of himself when much younger. Twenty, perhaps. 'He died in glory on the battlefield, within sight of Charles,' said Alexander, while Louise, for once, looked at the painted face with interest. 'Charles made some inane remark about the debt of kings. What do you suppose happened, mademoiselle? The fellow's family (our hosts this weekend!) were made lords, when Charles's son came keenly back to the English throne.'

He burst out laughing.

On Sunday he played croquet with her, and did not let her win. The whole party assembled to take tea on the lawns, and Alexander quite shocked Louise by teasing his hosts about their family chapel.

'The pews are simply opera boxes,' he said. 'I'm afraid you had most frivolous ancestors.'

Discussing him later with her aunt, Louise said she was sure he was a member of the French aristocracy despite being in trade.

'I daresay, my child, since titles are a dime a dozen. Counts and such live on their wits.'

'Aunt, that isn't true! Why, one must be a Somebody to be invited to the manor.'

The little New York lady refrained from saying it was only Louise's supply of Goodier dollars in a sound Manhattan bank which had made the girl herself into a Somebody.

Louise thought about de Grelle and was intrigued. He hadn't treated her with any kind of homage, and it quite astounded her that her beauty had not obtained its usual devastating effect.

There had not been a sign on Alexander's broad and enigmatic face to show that in an instant, an hour, he had fallen so violently in love that he suffered unbearable pain. Like the women who hear the perilous music played by the god Krishna on his flute, Alexander had become helpless.

It was Alexander's desire to pursue and possess which had started his career. He hadn't a drop of the noble blood imagined by Louise. He was working-class French, the only child of a middle-aged couple from Alsace and the joy of their lives. Marc Grelle (his son added the 'de' years later) was a shoemaker; his speciality was dancing pumps for the gentry. He lived and worked on the first floor of a seventeenth-century house in the Marais, a narrow tumbledown building occupied by other craftsmen, a gilder, a worker in leather, and a man who restuffed mattresses. Marc made the pumps at his workbench, and visited his customers for fittings, in their houses of unostentatious wealth in the avenue Matignon and the rue de Castiglione. Lines of chocolate-coloured cardboard boxes were ranged along shelves in Marc's workroom, each labelled in his slanting handwriting. The names of the gentlemen upon whose feet the pumps would be placed were a roll-call of nobility: the comte de Noailles, the Baron Ghilain. English titles too (these customers were called upon at the Ritz): the Marquess of this and the Honourable that. The pumps were made in leather soft as silk and thin as gloves, and the crest of each customer stamped in gold on the inside sole. Some were brown, some glittering patent, some a rich bronze.

They had chased silver buckles and flat watered silk bows. The pumps were poems, and Marc Grelle was the poet.

But Alexander, to his father's contempt and his mother's regret, didn't have the gift. A fattish graceful young man, he was clumsy. Too careful to drop things, he couldn't shape and cut a piece of leather, sew a thin seam, arrange a lining any more than he could fly up to the gargoyles grimacing above Notre Dame and roost up there with them.

Due to the *Loi Falloux* by which in religious orders priests with no qualifications could teach, the boy's education had been sketchy: he was clever and ignorant. He was eleven when Paris was besieged, and famine stared his parents in the face.

But peace came. Marc began to make his slippers for the wealthy. What to do with the boy? Deep in their hearts, Marc's entirely French, Anny's Franco-Alsacienne-Jewish, was the belief that a son follows his father. Cuittier the butcher along the street taught his son the trade when the boy was twelve. It was the same with all their friends. But Alexander appeared one evening and said he had obtained work. He was a porter.

'A porter!' repeated his mother, shocked.

'At Chaumontel's. The auction house, *maman*, in the rue de la Paix.'

His father, hearing the news, exploded. But since the salary was not bad and teaching the boy to make pumps impossible, Marc accepted what he couldn't change. In any case, the boy was odd. He poked about in markets, climbed filthy stairways, spent his evenings on the *quais* or in God knows what slummy buildings in Montmartre. He collected things for a few sous. Any money left over after paying his mother for his keep was spent on this pathetic hobby. He returned home with parcels under his arm, and carefully placed their contents on the kitchen table for his mother's inspection.

Anny, to whom it had been a holy miracle that at forty-three she had born a child and a son, looked with fond attention and concealed stupefaction at the things on which he wasted money. Tiny landscapes in filthy mounts. Etchings of a statue, a fountain; rubbish like that. A child swinging on a gate. A peasant woman milking a cow. There was a broken gilt clock. Even a handfull of semi-precious stones, amethysts, a striped onyx.

'Lovely, my son,' muttered Anny. She wished he'd remove the things. She was cooking.

'What shall you do with that mish mash?' asked Marc, when this had been going on for months. The parcels were getting bulkier. Anny told her husband, 'One can't brush under his bed now. One simply cannot believe . . .'

'I shall sell them, papa.'

Marc, slipper spread on his hand, looked at the plump young man in derision.

'To whom? One of your schoolfellows as thick-headed as you?'

'Not exactly. To Monsieur Fabri, rue de la Belotte. He is an *antiquaire*.'

'Monsieur Fabri is one of your father's customers,' exclaimed Anny, alarmed. And of course Marc began to shout. Had the boy had the gall to approach one of his clients, a man of consequence, had Alexander had the impertinence . . .

Alexander waited respectfully for the shouting to stop. It was a trait of his, from some subtle Jewish ancestor, that he knew when to be quiet. When the noise died down, he replaced some etchings in a tattered folder and went quietly out of the room. The Grelles stared at each other.

The next evening he told them that Monsieur Fabri had been delighted with the etchings and had paid him three times what Alexander had himself paid for them.

Marc was thunderstruck. And later, amused. He was too French not to accept the reality. Anny was proud and still mystified. Within a year their red-headed son was making as much money, hanging about in the evenings and on Sundays, poking through broken trunks spilling on to attic floors and squatting on pavements going through heaps of yellowing bundles of drawings, as he did as a porter at Chaumontel's. And more than Marc made from the best dancing pumps in Paris.

Alexander loved the work he had invented, more even at a surging time of youth than sex. His passion to succeed blended with a similar passion to handle and in a way possess

33

the objects of his discovery, the pictures and bibelots, tiny clocks, broken bracelets. He learned at Chaumontel's, watching, asking questions, noting names and methods. And in the evenings he would find and buy a river scene, a racing horse, dragged out of a rickety drawer or a discarded portfolio. He bought books tied with rope and took them back to the rue des Cordeliers. Money mattered. But so did the things he found. And he had discovered more than that – his *métier*. His calling. Now it was simply a question of turning from porter and amateur into a real auctioneer.

He was energetic, ambitious, and romantically in love with yesterday. Paris in the 1870s was full of a discarded and carelessly despised past. Everything now must be *à la mode*, over-gilded frames for paintings, over-stuffed furniture, over-elaborate rooms matching the furbelowed present. Hands in his pockets, his lively face and neatly cut beard making him recognizable, he walked miles through the ancient Parisian streets, looking and bargaining and discarding and returning. He had an instinct to buy and sell as natural as that of a canary who bursts into trilling song. He never paid the price scrawled on the base of the vase and the flyleaf of the book. He offered half, smiled, walked away. Sometimes, not always, he returned a week later. He enjoyed the game itself and had not a frisson of conscience that some poor devil who sold him a drawing or a piece of ivory needed the money more than he did.

One evening an old woman shuffled up the stairs of the apartment. Somebody had given her his address. She carried a basketful of rubbish.

'You can have it for five francs,' she said, slamming it on Anny's scrubbed table.

Both parents were in the kitchen. Dumbfounded.

'I'll give you three,' said Alexander pleasantly.

She grabbed the money and went wailing down the stairs.

'Three francs!' snorted his father, 'Why, I have to work for hours for that. What's she sold you, eh? Bits of string.'

'A lottery is amusing,' said Alexander, tipping the dirty contents on to the table while Anny exclaimed, 'My God, keep away from the bread!'

Alexander rubbed his beard and began to arrange his

lottery. There certainly was string. Two plaster frames, gilded and broken. A necklace of sorts. Two books with no covers, one with bloodstained pages. A buckle which might be silver but surely wasn't. And a dirty clouded glass with mouldings round it. Alexander picked it up, looked at it, and put it under the tap. He polished it carefully with his handkerchief and took it to the door to hold it in the sunlight. He had seen a glass cup like this before. There was a message running all round the rim, and the decoration was of chariots and horses. It was Roman. A mould-blown circus cup of the first century.

After the cup had been sold, for the highest sum Alexander had earned until now, he made enquiries about the old woman. He never found her – but he did not look far.

Soon he had rented a small studio in Montmartre, dividing it into two with a curtain bought from discarded theatre props. On one side of the studio was his storeroom, each object catalogued. On the other, with a natural eye for display, a taste inherited from Marc, he hung his pictures, his scattering of semi-precious stones, a clock or two. Some jewellery. Some porcelain. Within a year there were dealers who thought it worth their while to call at the studio. Alexander met people. Made friends. And finally decided to hold his first auction. The catalogue was copied on the typewriter by his devoted mistress, Marie-France (she happened to work at Chaumontel's). He delivered twenty catalogues to twenty carefully chosen prospects. Half were from stolen lists he and Marie-France had memorized at Chaumontel's. The other half were the richest of his father's customers.

He and Marie-France, a worried-looking dark girl with big breasts which wobbled under severe white blouses, cleaned and cleared the studio, borrowed trestle tables from a vegetable shop and covered them with starched white cloths. Marie-France polished, scrubbed, unpacked, arranged. She was in love with Alexander and knew he was out of his wits.

Alexander, much spruced up, was ready at the appointed time.

'It is nine o'clock. You set the auction for half-past eight,' said Marie-France.

'People of consequence are not punctual in our business,' said Alexander. 'Ah. I think . . . yes . . . don't you hear a carriage?'

There was the thunder of wheels on cobbles, the slam of a carriage door. A handsome man carrying a walking stick and wearing the unmistakeable look of money came into the studio.

'Monsieur Grelle? I believe you sent me your catalogue? Good. Let me just take a look . . .'

Ten minutes later there were four carriages. Alexander, as cool as the red-faced Marie-France was not, postponed the auction for twenty minutes, if the gentlemen did not object? The gentlemen, thoughtfully walking up and down, examining, handling, absently agreed.

Alexander sold everything on display, and made a profit of two-hundred-and-fifty per cent.

Of course the romantic beginning could not last in its gim-crack way. But he was learning. He left Chaumontel's, hired a larger studio and regretfully got rid of Marie-France, replacing her with a girl he paid to work all day. He met the dealers, the experts, and the rich. He was out and about day and night, and within two years, at the age of twenty-one, was already in a degree respected. 'To be watched,' people said in the trade, half cautiously, half jealously.

At twenty-four Alexander took a steam packet to England. The Grelles saw their son's rise with astonishment, followed by pride. Marc Grelle did not resent it; he observed that the weight of success was heavy, despite his boy's broad shoulders.

'Such anxiety would give me no pleasure,' he remarked, taking a pump off its last. He carved his wooden lasts from solid beechwood in his own perfect measurements (he despised plaster casts). He absently caressed the wooden shape which was lettered 'Monsieur de Crèvecoeur'.

To Alexander's father, the gambling, the need for a constant and sharp-edged judgement, the knowing that other cleverer men waited to pounce, seemed an alarming sort of life. Risking money. Risking ruin. And Alexander of necessity had to deal with the high world. Marc, who fitted their dancing slippers so respectfully, despised all aristocrats. He often said to Anny that the boy would lose every penny and return to the rue des Cordeliers. 'He'll be lucky if he gets his work as a porter back.'

But Alexander's star was rising. One good introduction led to another, to three more; one bookseller or medallist met him at a sale and knew that here was a man worth cultivating. Alexander's studio-saleroom flourished; and London attracted him.

It was at a London sale of rare books, including a number of French chivalry romances, that Alexander met William Thornbury. Neither man was bidding, the prices were too high, but both were keenly interested. They were seated next to each other, it was early spring and cold, and Alexander's neighbour went to a window and slammed it shut. Alexander approved.

When the sale was over they got into conversation.

'What about a bite of luncheon?' said the man. 'My name's Thornbury, by the way. How do you do.'

'A great pleasure. Alexander de Grelle,' said Alexander. He added the 'de' on impulse, the chivalry romances put the idea into his head, and automatically changed his first name to its English version.

'But where shall we eat?' he enquired, looking with Parisian helplessness down a long street broken only by the discreet windows of galleries showing a Rembrandt etching or a Florentine incense-burner.

'Leave that to me.'

Thornbury steered him down a cobbled passage, round a corner and into an eating house. Fires burned, waiters hurried, brass winked, and over a spitting grill were lamb chops lined up like soldiers. The place was crowded but Thornbury had reserved a table. The meal was first-rate.

The two men ate juicy chops and talked of books. These, Thornbury explained, were his hobby.

'I took the morning off from my work. I shall have to repay it by working throughout Saturday. But I wouldn't miss a good auction like that one today.' He told Alexander that he was a clerk in the accounts department of the P & O office. Figures amused him.

'You can make 'em say or do anything you like. They often remind me of a troupe of acrobats.'

He was knowledgeable in an amateur way about books; through his work at the P & O he'd met the agent of the Earl of Lytchett.

'As a matter of fact I've been asked to catalogue his lordship's library,' said Thornbury with a certain satisfaction. 'I go down to their place in Sussex at weekends. First-class fare paid. Thought I'd start as I intend to go on.'

He had been cataloguing at Lytchett Manor for six months; most enjoyable.

'It's quite a fine old house really,' he remarked.

Alexander, who was getting the hang of English, guessed that Thornbury meant the Earl's manor was very large, rich, and stuffed with treasures. The dessert appeared just then. To Alexander's horror it was a pudding wrapped in a sort of towel. But it proved delicious, smothered in syrup. He had two helpings.

It was during the second that Thornbury came to the reason he had invited this foreigner to share his luncheon.

'The Earl,' he said, 'wishes to sell his library, which is why I'm doing the catalogue. First he wants to see just what he's got. Then he can get its worth calculated.'

'Why should he sell? To buy other books?'

'My dear fellow, he's as rich as Croesus. He isn't a collector,' said Thornbury, with a downward smile. 'That was his grandfather. It's the usual story. Collectors spend their lives getting wonderful stuff together. Their descendants can't wait to sell it. Heartbreaking – except for chaps like you.'

Alexander smiled slightly.

'His lordship hasn't approached either of the big auction houses, Christie's and Sotheby's, you know. He's as mean as muck,' said Thornbury. 'And they take a good percentage. Why not? It's a deal of work. But . . . well . . . from what you've told me it seems you're new to the game. Suppose, I am not promising anything, but suppose I wangled you an

38

invitation to look over the library. The Earl might prefer somebody just starting up, instead of the big guns. Could be an opportunity for you on this side of the Channel. You'd need my help, of course.'

Alexander played with his beard. He loved the unexpected. He visualized an English castle (to Alexander the wealthy English all lived in places which looked like the Tower of London), possibly thousands of precious books . . . and, quite as unexpected . . . the possibility of a colleague in his business. Working alone was the one thing about his career which he did not enjoy.

'We would collaborate over this?' he enquired.

'That might be possible.'

'And if we succeeded?'

'We'd draw up a partnership. In time I might manage to leave the P & O.'

They exchanged looks and both, in their different ways, grinned.

'You'll have to learn French.'

'I doubt I could manage *that*,' said William Thornbury.

Three days later he had arranged for Alexander to be invited to Sussex.

The two men spent an enjoyable weekend in the Lytchett library, sitting on the top of library ladders or on the window-seats overlooking an exquisite Tudor garden. The library contained many thousands of books and William's catalogue was now two thirds completed. His arrangement of the volumes made the task of studying the collection easy. Alexander had a gift he used all the time: an extraordinary memory. It was the basis of his early success in a career where knowledge can mean money. When he wanted it, memory spread out for him like a long scroll to be consulted. With his nose in illustrated monastic manuscripts, some illuminated in pure gold, spotting a four-hundred-and-twenty-seven-year-old Caxton folio, a fifteenth-century Ovid, a book of poems bound for Henry II, the facts he'd stored in his memory lay before him. He sat in the Earl's library, intent, absorbed and – when he let himself be – excited.

At half-past four a servant in livery brought tea. Wafer

39

sandwiches, almond cakes, éclairs. William opened a latticed window and the spring sunshine shone on the two young men.

'I think I like castle life,' said Alexander, licking a finger with traces of chocolate upon it. 'The books are impressive. What do you know about the milord who collected them?'

'Flaxman, the Earl's agent, knew him when the old gentleman was in his eighties. A passionate bibliophile. His wife died in childbed and apparently the Earl replaced her with books. Visited Florence, Rome, Paris, Madrid and so on. This library was his consolation.'

'Rare books are often the pastime of wealthy noblemen,' said Alexander, lifting a tea-cup so thin that the sun shone through it. 'This could be the book sale of the decade. Do you think his lordship would actually give it to us?'

'Not to us. To you. It will be up to you,' said William Thornbury with decision.

Alexander met the Earl that evening. He was big, hook-nosed, white-haired, despotic in manner; he glared from under thick eyebrows like an eagle looking out of a thatched house. Alexander wore evening clothes far better than any of the guests lounging in the drawing room. The Englishman decided he looked a gentleman, which Alexander was not. But he had the confidence of European men. And he used his charm mercilessly.

The auction took place in a hired auction room in Mayfair in the autumn, lasted a week and 20,000 volumes came under the hammer. William employed a practised auctioneer for the event; Alexander would have enjoyed taking the rostrum but his English was still uncertain.

The sale, with its rich profits, created a stir and some ill will from the leading auction houses. It made the two young men enough money to go into business together. And Alexander met the Earl's only child, Lady Verena Lytchett.

By the time Louise Goodier met Alexander, the 'de' was so much part of his surname that he'd forgotten the aristocratic prefix was an invention. William Thornbury had found a banker, and some excellent premises in Paris, in the rue

Royale. William's French was bad but his business acumen was brilliant. They also took smallish London premises in Bruton Street. William had started speaking hideous French, and Alexander alluring English.

As their success in both capitals steadily grew, Alexander widened his scope. He auctioned Italian majolica and Indian ivories, French armour and English clocks – he loved clocks. He auctioned coins and medals. He began to collect a team of men, each an expert in his field. There was one man whose domain was the seventeeth century with its golden faith, another who specialized in the eighteenth with its bewigged Age of Reason and sardonic gatherings in coffee houses. One man came to work in de Grelle's only when there was a sale of weaponry and armour. It had been to take a preliminary look at two fourteenth-century shields, inlaid with scenes from the Bible, that Alexander was invited to the Bethell's manor in Gloucestershire.

Alexander had been married for eight years to Lady Verena Lytchett when a young American heiress came into the library on the day after his arrival and changed his life.

A scent of box in sunshine drifted into the room with Louise, who wore white with blue ribbons, her olive skin and thick shining hair set off by the ridiculously virginal draperies. An American Madonna. She looked up at the big Frenchman seated on top of a library ladder.

'Lady Bethell says why don't we play croquet,' she said in her lazy American voice. She wanted to make him come down from the ladder.

'Alas, mademoiselle, I do not play croquet.'

'Well, I just can't imagine how you can stay up there reading when it's so much nicer out of doors.'

He shut the book, privately disagreeing. Everything that mattered took place indoors.

The girl was too beautiful. He was so physically conscious of her as they walked towards the open French windows that he began to sweat. In the distance across the lawns he saw the grey-clad figure of his wife talking to their hostess. It was like looking at a phantom on the other side of the Styx.

Nearby on a marble plinth was a bronze, a sentimental

mid-Victorian thing of a young woman, her hair upswept, tendrils escaping on her glowing neck. The bronze head shone richly dark; immortally young, immortally fixed, she was bent over a flower.

He put his hand out and touched it.

'Do you see this rose, mademoiselle? It is exactly, but precisely like you.'

CHAPTER FOUR

A year later, in 1896, society heard of the marriage between Alexander de Grelle and Louise Goodier. The divorce had rocked the English nobility, and had been angrily refused by the outraged Lytchetts for months until it was learned that Louise was pregnant.

Six months later, at the Villa des Roses, Sara was born.

The child scarcely remembered her parents living together. She dimly recalled London in a winter full of fog. Flares in the streets. At some other time they had an apartment in Paris overlooking a park with statues of many queens. That time, it was spring, she had seen her mother cry.

It was in Paris that her mother first told her she had a sister. Louise took Sara on her lap and Sara played with her mother's gold chain belt.

'You have a little sister, *chérie*. A half-sister. She is the child of Papa's other marriage,' said Louise.

'I don't understand.'

'Of course you don't. It is grown-up nonsense, isn't it? But you must know you have a sister, d'you see, because Nursie might tell you. Or you could hear the nurses talking in the park. And then, Papa's picture and mine are in the illustrated papers sometimes.'

They certainly were. The de Grelle auctions, both in Paris and London, were reported at length in the newspapers and shiny magazines. And Sara would see pictures of Louise and Alexander at the races at Longchamps or on the lawns at Ascot. The nurse who took care of Sara was English – they were so chic, Louise thought – read the magazines assiduously.

'There's your dear little sister,' said the nurse one morning, showing the child a picture. It was months since Louise had told her daughter the meaningless news, but Sara said carelessly, 'Oh pooh. I know about her.'

Nurse Pritchard who loved the upper classes said, 'She's not much like you. Pretty, though. Look at the picture properly, child.'

Sara peered. White-clad ladies, one in an enormous hat, standing about in a garden. A little girl also in white.

'Lady Verena de Grelle with her daughter the Honourable Catherine at Lytchett Manor,' read Sara. She liked to read aloud. 'What's an "Honourable"?'

'It means she is aristocratic. I hope you will meet her one day.'

'Nursie. Can I water the plants?'

The sisters met that year for the first time. Up until then, although he wished this to happen, Alexander was prevented by his love for Louise. She quite changed when jealousy stung her. The lazy sweet-voiced American girl screamed and battered him with her fists and once she seized a bread knife. He rather liked the displays of fury which flatteringly proved such passion. For the first six years of Sara's life Louise succeeding in preventing the two children from meeting.

Alexander visited London a good deal, the sales and profits of his auction house there were interesting, and there was also the piquancy of great rivals. When he came alone to London he always insisted that Verena should send their daughter up from Sussex to stay with him for a short time. He bought a too-large house in Park Street, so that he could receive the child whom he loved and did not understand. Besides, the Park Street house was useful for entertaining business colleagues.

It should have been a sign to Louise, still in the high summer of believing love and beauty lasted forever, when Alexander finally had his own way. He decided to take Sara to London one early summer when there was an important auction coming up.

Hearing what he was going to do, Louise was speechless. Then burst out in a trembling voice.

'How *could* you! You know how I feel about your hideous first wife!'

'Oh yes, little one.' He touched her nose. She started back and began to sob. Unlike most women she looked glorious when she cried. Alexander pursed his lips and smiled. He did not offer her his handkerchief.

It was her first defeat.

She returned to the attack many times, using different weapons. She sulked. She had hysterics. She coaxed. She was angry. Twice she tried to dissuade him after they had made love. He patted her nose. Finally realizing she had lost, she had a private word with Nurse.

Miss Pritchard listened with respect, saw what her employer was getting at, agreed and did the opposite. She had no intention of setting two children against each other.

Sara and her nurse travelled to London on the Mediterranean-Calais express, which was called the train of trains to be compared only to the Siberian Express and the Chicago and Empire City Vestibule Flyer. It was palatial. Plush, satin, fresh flowers, silver, and white-gloved attendants. The train roared its way up the map of France to the sea which, summer or no summer, heaved. The child was very sick.

She appeared in her father's drawing room on the afternoon of their arrival, distinctly greenish and not at her best. Nurse had rashly dressed her in mauve with purple stripes and Sara was told she must go into the drawing room alone. Pale and valiant, she entered the room – looked towards her father, then at somebody beside him.

Tiens, thought Sara, so that's her.

Seated on a large embroidered chair, grave as a judge or an owl, was an elderly ten-year-old who stared at her. Neither child said a word.

Alexander lit a cigar and looked quizzically from one daughter to the other.

'*Alors*, Sara, so here is your big sister. Say good afternoon to Catherine.'

'*Enchantée*,' said Sara and made a bob curtsey.

He roared with laughter.

'You don't make obeisance to your sister, my child, you kiss her. Catherine, embrace the little one. Come along. You heard what I said.'

His voice became sharp.

Catherine got down from the chair, came across the room and gave her sister a sort of peck. Sara smiled amiably.

'We came in a boat. I was sick four times. Have you crossed the ocean? It is very disgusting.'

'No, I haven't,' said Catherine and added, seeing her father still looking at her, 'I've been on the lake at home.'

'I also. But lakes don't show their teeth.'

Now that he had his daughters with him, Alexander became bored, rang for the nurse and told her to take them upstairs. They could dine with him later.

'*Dine*, sir?'

'Too late, is it? Very well, very well. I certainly don't wish to share breakfast with them. Shall we say luncheon tomorrow?'

From that time, yearly visits were arranged, shared by both children. They stayed with Alexander for four weeks, accepting each other's company with the philosophy of the young. The two girls made a curious contrast, noticed by all Alexander's friends and mentioned to him by nobody but William who was deeply interested in his friend's family and foresaw trouble. Alexander had married the first time from ambition, the second from passion. Both unions failed. And neither would have happened had it not been for the de Grelle success.

His first wife, Catherine's mother, Lady Verena, daughter of the old Earl, had been twenty-seven when she fell in love with Alexander. She was her parents' only child, they had expected a brilliant marriage, but at eighteen Verena had fallen unsuitably in love with the wastrel third son of a small land-owner. The Earl called the family petty gentry and forbade the match. After that Verena began to wane, quite gradually, into an old maid. She'd almost arrived at that state when Alexander appeared at Lytchett. She fell in love with him more deeply than she had ever loved the third son. She was dazzled by the self-confident Frenchman, so amusing and stylish and caressing and clever. And he saw in her a pleasant charmingly tempered girl who was his passport into the great Edwardian world. The Lytchetts raised great objections. But he won.

Verena was short and fair and inclined to plumpness, a busy little person, popular with friends and servants, indeed with everybody. She was thoroughly liked. She was rather pious, and people in the eighties, growing frivolous and immoral and taking their colour from the Prince of Wales, respected her the more. Poor Verena. She went on loving her sexy and enigmatic husband long after he developed a passion for Louise. She never spoke a word against him, and continued to love while she was suffering.

In her serious way she was ashamed that her love would not die. She hid it from her family, who positively hated de Grelle. He was a jumped-up nobody coming from God knows where. (Alexander had told nobody of his poor beginnings in the rue des Cordeliers.) De Grelle, said the old Earl, was a tradesman who should never have been allowed inside the house. They'd been off their heads to let Verena marry him. He viciously refused to permit the divorce.

But Verena, struck to the heart, was incapable of intrigue. She did not know how to save her marriage, to keep a man who was sleeping with another woman. In her years of marriage, she had spoiled Alexander as if he were a grown-up child and he'd taken it as his right.

'He will come back,' Verena said. Her parents exchanged looks. They wished she had the spirit – the guts – to hate de Grelle as they did. Verena came home with her daughter to Lytchett. The child grew up in the ancient house, her roots deep in the Sussex countryside.

Catherine inherited her mother's oval face but not its gentle charm. Although nobody recognized the fact, least of all the child herself, her strong will came straight from her father.

She was not unhandsome in a small neat way, with eyes of English blue, hair soft and fairish like Verena's and a short straight nose. Her mouth was firm, not to say thin. Beneath the understated manner there was rock. She loved her mother silently and too much. She shared with her grandparents the belief that Alexander was a villain. But she was the daughter of a celebrated man and he impressed her just the same.

Catherine was austerely brought up by the Lytchetts. The grandparents, shattered at having let their daughter marry a man who ruined her life, were over-strict with the child but Catherine thrived. The Lytchetts were wealthy; de Grelle was making a great deal of money, and his elder daughter was brought up like a princess.

When the sisters met for their yearly visit to their father, there was much in Catherine that the adaptable Sara found hard to take. According to Catherine nothing French was any good and everything English magnificent. When they were alone, Catherine turned into a shocking little snob and Sara had to listen to a hymn on the British aristocracy. At first Sara was puzzled by the titles. Catherine said she would make a chart. United for once, Sara was eight and Catherine twelve, they lay on their stomachs in the playroom while Catherine drew a pattern of precedence.

'That means order of rank and importance. First we have the King and Queen.'

'Edward and Alexandra. *I* know. He comes to Cannes quite often and he belongs to the Cercle Nautique.'

Catherine ignored that and continued the lesson.

Sara accepted Catherine's oddities, her satisfaction in putting her sister down, her contempt for things American or French. One could not *love* Catherine, of course, but the two might have been friends had Catherine not kept her at arm's length. When Sara made overtures, from grace and not affection, she made them to the air.

Early on in their time together she innocently asked about Catherine's life at home. What was Lytchett like?

'Do tell. And I'll tell about Antibes.'

'There's nothing to say,' said Catherine and changed the subject. It was a paradox that she showed off about English titles, English houses, talked of a world strange to the American-French child, but was dumb about her own family and home.

'Why won't Cathy tell me about her mother?' asked Sara to her nurse one night in London. 'Is she a cripple? Or perhaps mad?'

'*Sara.*'

'Why are you going all red? If people go mad they are made to live in the attic, aren't they? Or they go to places like the maison de la Sainte-Baume in La Californie. I suppose that's why Cathy won't say.'

Deeply shocked, Nurse Pritchard said Sara had seen in *The Bystander* that Catherine's mother was Lady Verena, very pretty, and what's more the daughter of an Earl.

Sara grimaced. She'd forgotten *The Bystander*.

If Catherine was dumb on family matters, Sara wasn't. She chattered about her mother, the Villa des Roses, and Provence.

'She's American, my Mama, you know. So am I.'

'No you're not. You're half French.'

'Oh sure. But I feel American.'

'One can see,' said Catherine.

Sara missed the sarcasm. She was kneeling on the window-seat in the playroom. Her nose was against the pane, their father had promised to be home for tea.

'In any case you're partly English now,' said Catherine, her eyes bright as they always were when she was being unkind. Sara turned in surprise.

'Silly. I can't be.'

'Papa said yesterday that England is the country of his adoption,' quoted Catherine, 'which means you have to be English too. You ought to lose that accent. It's not at all the thing.'

Sara was about to defend herself but a hansom drew up at the kerb. Her father's figure, broad, handsome, in exquisite clothes, emerged. As he stood paying the fare he looked up, saw her, and waved his walking stick.

As the years went by, the sisters, so foreign to each other, grew used to their annual month together. It was invariably arranged to suit Alexander, at the time of some important sale in London or Paris; he never saw either daughter alone. It was as if, thought Sara as she grew up, he was under the pathetic delusion that they were fond of each other. I suppose he prefers to think that. It would bore and bother him to know the truth.

Earnestly trying to make a slender link between her sister and herself, Sara found the task grew more difficult. During the war they met only in London; Catherine refused to go to Paris, it would interfere with her war work. She was a V.A.D. in a hospital in Lewes where, she said, staring at her sister, every pair of hands was needed. Catherine also reduced her visits to her father and only stayed a week.

During the four years of the war it was Sara who was forced to make the sometimes near-impossible journey to England. She travelled in crammed trains from the south; huddled on the decks of steamers crossing the Channel on a sea under which the menace of death lurked. She was jostled and thrown here and there across troop-crammed stations. When she finally arrived at Park Street and her father welcomed her it was like paradise.

It was during the London weeks in wartime, after Catherine had left to return to Lewes, that Alexander decided to teach Sara a little about auctioneering. He called his career 'dealing with history which we sell in fragments'. For the first time in years of fatherhood which despite pride in the girls had bored him, he was alone with one daughter. A lively girl full of curiosity. She looked at him with eyes like his own, asked him scores of questions. He took a fancy to instruct her.

Three sorts of people, he said, inhabited his world. Those who owned and then disposed of the fine things of the earth. Those who coveted – and bought them. 'And us, my child. We are between the two.'

He told her legends about auctioneering. Of fake master-pieces which fooled the experts, and wonderful prizes which, unrecognized, sold for ten shillings. The oldest legend of all, 'which I daresay they told in Ancient Greece' said Alexander, was that of the man in the saleroom who scratched his nose unwittingly or twitched his catalogue. Down came the hammer and he heard the dread words: 'Yours, sir. For five hundred guineas.'

It was true, Alexander told her, that there was a real danger of catching what was called auction fever. People in the auction room could turn into gamblers as obsessed as those who cannot leave the roulette table. When he'd been young in Paris, a book had appeared: *Les Petits Mystères de L'hôtel des ventes*. It contained sixty hints that a collector would be wise to follow.

'Oh, Father. Not sixty!' cried Sara.

'Sixty,' said Alexander. 'Alas, I only recall a few. Let me see. All subjects must be banished from the mind but that of the man's actual collection. He must not read books, be interested in politics, he must never go to the theatre. According to the author, Champfleury, he must "scorn the pleasures of family". Ah yes, he must also wear very plain untrimmed clothes at any auction and never forget the smelling salts. He must avoid highly-spiced meals, they are too stimulating. He must have cold baths to keep in trim. And he must never forget a bar of chocolate when he goes to an auction, to fortify the system in the afternoon before the bidding begins to get really hot. If you follow his rules, he says, you will become a real collector.'

'Oh Father!'

'Laugh away. There's sense in that preposterous advice. Particularly about concentration. As for the cold bath and the chocolate – *pourquoi pas?*'

Free from the thorny company of her sister Sara was with her father from morning until night. He took her to auctions at rival houses, introduced her to dealers and clients – telling her to look her prettiest and hold her tongue. He allowed her to sit in when he himself was on the rostrum in the de Grelle Galleries in St Charles Street.

In the past, Sara had sometimes tried to get her mother to tell her about her father's profession. Louise was always sarcastic. What was auctioneering after all to give itself such airs? It was no different from huckstering. A man at the door of a tent selling Doctor Prendergast's cure for alcoholism in plain bottles. This was Louise at her crossest and Sara only laughed.

But when Sara first began to watch her father on the rostrum, she remembered the word 'huckster'. It was like describing a silver goblet as a tin cup. When Alexander called the sums of money offered, an incantation of figures, he seemed to have a sort of hidden power, to be in tune with the particular object being auctioned, to understand it. When the things were beautiful and valuable, the saleroom crammed, his ivory hammer lifted, Alexander had a quality of grandeur. She felt when he looked towards some cold-eyed bidder that he could actually make him ashamed to call too low a bid. She had the idea that the auction-goers wouldn't like Alexander's ill opinion. His manner, enthusiastic, not exaggerated, was infectious, his voice almost caressing. She knew that collectors took pleasure sometimes in telling each other that it was due to de Grelle that they'd paid double what they intended for a seventeeth-century New York bowl by Kierstede or a long-necked hunter by Stubbs.

Alexander could be a tyrant on the rostrum sometimes. Like a brilliant teacher he demanded total attention. He loathed people to fidget and had once ringingly declared, staring at a restless dealer, 'Is that a bid, sir? Or are you saluting a friend?'

The manner of bidding seemed mysterious and sometimes invisible to Sara, apart from bids made in advance, with a ceiling beyond which the bidder was not willing to go.

'Yes . . . bidding arrangements are a little complicated,' Alexander said, amused. 'One dealer last week told me he was bidding when his arms were folded, but not if his arms were loose on his knees. And worse still, a private owner, a most substantial man, recently told me if his pencil was in his mouth I could sell below the reserve. Suppose he had dropped the pencil? Or swallowed it, perhaps?'

The riches of the centuries flowed into de Grelle's galleries. Masterpieces by Chippendale or the craftsmen who had worked in Philadelphia, jewelled stained glass from a French cathedral, a ring Queen Elizabeth had given her lover . . . value, like a halo, shone not only on the things made by the great artists and craftsmen. It shone too on things owned – even touched – by the famous. Collectors were excited by a gilt button cut from Nelson's tunic, a polished pair of boot-trees belonging to Abraham Lincoln, a crested chamber-pot of Louise XIV's or a wig of David Garrick's. Provenance was all. Faded letters and documents were pored over at de Grelle's long before the auctions.

'You are learning,' remarked Alexander, when he and Sara went into Christie's to look at some jewellery, and she at once recognized the difference between Regency and Georgian necklaces.

'There's so *much*, Father. I'll never keep people and facts and history in my head the way you do.'

He laughed, lowering his heavy eyelids as he did when he was pleased.

For the first years of the war, Sara never asked Alexander why he wasn't in uniform. Perhaps he was too old. He was simply his clever, bustling, charming and probably pitiless self. But in the shortened periods when Catherine also stayed in Park Street, Sara noticed that her sister was colder than usual. She and her father were being judged – they were still civilians. Although Catherine could scarcely appear at Park Street in her striped cotton Ward dress, she wore nothing but the heavy navy-blue uniform overcoat and unbecoming gaberdine cap when her father took Sara and herself out to the Ritz or anywhere else.

Despite the mute disapproval, Sara went on trying to spin a thread between Catherine and herself. Sara threw it. Catherine let it fall. Sara asked about the Lewes hospital: Catherine never mentioned Antibes. Sara talked of England and Catherine, despite the terrible war, did not speak of France. Now and then Sara managed to make her laugh. But the boastfulness had not gone; it was a kind of wonder to hear, at a time of death and grief, Catherine's conversation filled with titles.

Looking at her sister in the uniform coat down to her ankles, Sara thought she could be attractive if she gave herself the chance. With her own white skin, she admired Catherine's rosy cheeks and soft fawn-coloured hair which had lilac lights in it. She amused herself by wondering if Catherine fell in love. This was in 1917 after Sara's first love affair; the idea of a sexual life for somebody as reserved as Catherine was titillating.

But her sister, mistress of herself, was silent about her home, her mother and her private life. Slim, oval-faced, her hair screwed into a knot, she had an air of elderly dignity. One could imagine her, thought Sara, as lady-in-waiting to the Queen.

But Catherine looked at a too-lively, too-bright-eyed, red-headed American girl who was given too much of their father's attention.

And somebody should tell her to remove those freckles with lemon juice.

CHAPTER FIVE

Her sister came into Sara's mind when she returned home after visiting Carl Bauer. It was the second time in her life that she envied her. The first had been after Louise refused to let Sara be a nurse, while Catherine was in uniform all through the war. Sara made the best of it: she worked at the Villa Roumaniev. But she knew there was a difference.

Now for other reasons she envied Catherine all over again for the life about which her sister kept a smug silence. It must be a steady life, in which you knew where you were. Sara had sometimes quite pitied her English friends their prim upbringing and middle-aged chaperones. She knew they thought her, an American, rather shockingly free. So did Catherine. Now the situation was ironically reversed. It was she, not Catherine, who had lost her liberty. She was tied to a mother who drank too much and went to bed with a boy of twenty-six.

Going into the large cool house she went straight up to her room. It was the afternoon siesta, that time when she presumed Jean-Claude and Louise made love. In Provence the lazy heat of the afternoons thrumming with the sewing-machine noise of cicadas was for sex and sleep. She closed her door, took a book and sat by the open window. She must possess her soul in patience.

She remembered then that her father had sent her a package of new catalogues. To take her mind off her coming interview with Louise, she put away her book and began to study them instead. But the room was too hot and she had to close the shutters. In the striped half dark, as if she herself were in a seraglio, Sara read of Shiraz and Isfahan carpets 'with figures seated in a garden', and 'stylized vines, exotic birds and fishes.' She looked at a collection of Oriental fans. 'One' said the catalogue, 'dated 1776 is in a remarkable state of preservation. It opens from right to left as well as the usual left to right.'

Soothed by thoughts of de Grelle's, she dressed for dinner and put on her pearl necklace, a recent gift from her father.

He had made her grate the pearls against her teeth.

'You see? They are rough, not smooth. And that means they are real. Always bite your pearls, Sara, before accepting them.'

She and Catherine had spent four weeks with him in Paris in December. It poured with rain every day but Sara didn't care. The de Grelle galleries, overheated and over-decorated, were the place to be. Even Catherine was interested in the auctions at which smart Parisians crowded and her father was a figure of authority on the rostrum. As for Sara, she relished every minute. The hush. The tenseness. The deliberately blank faces of the bidders. The bang of the ivory hammer. The auction room had more excitement for her than a theatre.

Alexander and Sara, having seen Catherine off at the Gare du Nord when the four weeks were over, then dined at the restaurant at the Gare de Lyon where the ceiling paintings filled Sara with gloom. A hymn to the warm South. Sapphire seas, colonnades, seductive women with armfuls of carnations. Her father had his arms full too, of expensive magazines, Fauchon chocolates and Parma violets. He loaded his daughters with gifts when parting from them. 'God bless you, *mignonne*. Keep the windows shut. Currents of air do good to nobody.'

The next morning when she looked from the train window and saw the pink-tiled houses, the rocky coast and olive groves, Sara groaned. It was like going back to prison.

Now was the moment to slip through the prison bars, she thought. It was dinner time as she opened the double doors into her mother's drawing room. The marble floors shone like water, Persian rugs glowed here and there. The room, designed by Alexander before Sara was born and never altered, was richly French. Mirrors for reflecting Louise's beautiful face; chandeliers like suspended drops of water; paintings by Watteau in which girls frolicked and men wooed.

In the setting chosen for her long ago, Louise lay *à la Recamier*, in a gown of greyish-green taffeta. Sara noticed that she also wore the swimmy look of a woman who had just made love. Jean-Claude, with his customary air of waiting to enjoy a joke, was sitting at her feet. He rose as Sara came into the room.

'Sit down, *adoré*,' said Louise pettishly, 'Sara, Jean-Claude has poured you a drink.'

Sara smiled and shook her head, thanking him but saying she'd wait until dinner. It was a bad move and she thought – God! am I expected to drink as well?

Jean-Claude glanced at her in a friendly way. He knew she disliked his affair and rather agreed with her. His own family found it literally impossible to understand. When he thought about it, Jean-Claude didn't understand it either. But love made no sense. He liked Louise's daughter and admired her spirit. Seeing Louise looking at her so coldly, he asked her about Carl Bauer.

Sara told him about Josephine's baroque pearls.

There was a small pause and she thought – now for it.

'Mother . . . I wonder if I might ask a favour. Nothing important. Just that I'd quite like to go to London for a week or two. To see Father.'

'I didn't know you'd heard from him.'

'I haven't. Some catalogues came from London.'

Louise ignored those.

'If he hasn't written, why should you see him? You were in Paris in December.'

'The London sales sound so interesting,' murmured Sara.

Louise sipped her champagne and said nothing.

'There is something else,' ventured Sara. 'You'll be going to Montreux again soon, I suppose –'

'Indeed we will. What does that mean, pray?'

'Well. I do know Switzerland rather too well, mother. Being at school there for so long. I thought I could go to London instead.'

She glanced at her mother with a deference she was far from

feeling. She had begun to be angry; it was humiliating to ask like this in front of Jean-Claude.

'What you're saying is will I pay for you to go to London uninvited? Certainly not.'

'But surely –'

'I have said no. There's an end to it.'

The girl did not blush; she went even paler than her usual beautiful pallor. A few freckles across the bridge of her nose stood out like scars.

'Sara, *chérie*, all your mother wants – ' began Jean-Claude but she interrupted harshly.

'I am talking to my mother. I should have thought it more becoming if you would leave us alone.'

The young man blushed as red as she was white. Louise's face snapped shut.

'How dare you speak to Jean-Claude like that! In my house. My drawing room. He is our closest friend.'

'That's very obvious,' said Sara – and could have bitten out her tongue. Too late she saw the mistake of losing her temper.

'I didn't mean that.'

'Apologize to him,' said Louise, beside herself with fury.

'I'm sorry, Jean-Claude. I am very sorry,' said Sara at once, bitterly regretting her idiocy. 'Please forgive me. Of course you're a family friend, which is why you'll understand that I'd like to go to London or Paris more often to see my father.'

And you surely prefer me out of the way, she thought.

'You were there in December as I said –' began Louise.

'Lou-lou, let her speak,' murmured Jean-Claude, very touched by the apology and preferring a peaceful life. He thought Lou-lou outrageously selfish but doubted if poor Sara would get a centime out of his mistress. He agreed with Sara that she should get away; what was more boring than being forced into the company of lovers? But Lou-lou was so mean. She liked to buy things. A gold watch for him. A wonderful Vionnet dress, Persian blue and green, for Sara, champagne, out-of-season flowers, train tickets. But all the time he had loved Lou-lou he never remembered her giving

Sara or himself actual cash. She hated to part with money. He was not without means – his father owned vineyards in Condrieu. He disliked Lou-lou's meanness and did nothing about it.

'Very well,' said Louise, holding out her hand to him. 'Since Jean-Claude asks, I am willing to listen.'

He kissed the small rather plump hand. The atmosphere relaxed.

Sara was reasonable. She explained that she would very much like to see her father for a while and added a white lie, saying Catherine had invited her to Ascot. So . . . if Louise would be very kind and pay her fare on the Cannes-Calais express? A single fare, naturally. Her father would pay the return.

'He can pay both ways.'

'But Mother. He's in New York right now. He won't be back until tomorrow or the next day. Surely it is a little . . .'

'A little what?'

'Unreasonable to telegraph his office for money.'

'What's unreasonable about it? Send the telegram to William Thornbury or someone.'

Louise dimpled. She had returned to her usual indolent good nature. She knew it was impossible for Sara to send such a telegram – she'd never wired de Grelle's for money in her life. Louise was clearly determined to drag her to Montreux with Jean-Claude. From perversity? Or the idiotic idea that her daughter's presence would give the affair a false respectability.

Slowly waving her favourite fan sewn with spangles, Louise leaned back.

Beauty which is no longer in flower retains a heart-rending quality, and the signs of age in Louise's face enhanced it in a way. There were shadows under her eyes, yet the eyes themselves, almond-shaped, violet-coloured, were lovely. There was scarcely a thread of grey in her dark hair. Her cheekbones were mysterious, exotic. Her forehead was slightly lined, and below the fine jaw were traces of a double chin. Louise knew all the signs of her enemy, Time, with the wallet on his back. She studied her face in a looking glass which, like that of an actress, was ringed with bare electric lights.

Looking at her, Jean-Claude thought how fatal it was for a man to think not with his mind but with his guts. He could no more leave this woman than cut his throat. A wave of passion went through him. He said tenderly,

'Lou-lou. It would not cost much for Sara to go.'

'More than I can afford. And,' shaking a jewelled finger at him, 'it is no good joining forces with my daughter, adoré, I have made up my mind. I've said no before dinner. If necessary I shall repeat it during dinner. And even after dinner too. Now fill my glass, and give Sara one as well.'

Longing to throw it in Louise's face, Sara accepted the champagne.

Late that night, Sara sat by the open window brushing her hair. She looked out at the dark garden. How could she stay here? She was too old to be under her mother's thumb, humiliated from lack of money. There was no heart's reason to stay either, no war, no wounded men at the Roumaniev whose poor haggard faces altered when they saw her. And ahead was Switzerland in all its boredoms, made worse by Louise breaking unspoken rules and taking her lover with her. Sara had broken rules too, two men had possessed her. But the man in her mother's bed was twenty-six.

She tried to think of ways of escape. There were rich friends, established, celebrated, French, American, English. There was the baron who was Sara's godfather, there was Mrs John Adams III, there was the Grand Duke Osspasky; but he, poor man, had no money now. 'When I write cheques on the Imperial bank' he had told Sara, 'no roubles come.'

No, she couldn't borrow from Louise's friends. It would make her wealthy mother look ridiculous. Sara pulled the hairbrush down the length of her hair. In her thoughts a single friend stood out, like the Antibes lighthouse at the top of the Cap, from among all the men and women, middle-aged and old, whom she and her mother knew well. Carl. How could she ask *Carl* for money? She knew how carefully he managed on a small income, his servant was paid a pittance (and, devoted, had often declared she'd work for him for nothing). Sara knew, too, that before adding an object to his collection, he always sold something else. 'For the pearl of great price' he'd say. She could not ask Carl for a franc.

She wandered over to the marble-topped chest of drawers, unlocked the top drawer, took out her jewel case and tipped the contents on to the bed.

She scarcely slept that night. It was spring, but hot as midsummer and the mimosa tree outside her bedroom was thickly laid with flowers, their scent too strong. When dawn began to pale the sky, she got up, bathed and dressed as quietly as possible. By six it was daylight. She was excited but calm, she had had all night to make plans. She picked up her valise – she had packed almost nothing, she had no maid and must travel light.

Leaving her bedroom she crept down the stairs. The house still slept, none of the servants would be up until seven. There was a clear hour to get away.

She walked quickly out into a garden full of birdsong and the smell of mimosa, a morning in the Garden of Eden. The sun was not yet up, the air cool. Dressed in a pale suit and a little felt hat, she wore high-heeled suede boots and carried her valise, which was scarcely more heavy than the jewellery in a packet inside her handbag.

There was a horse-drawn cab at the corner of the Antibes ramparts. Sara had just enough to pay for the journey to Cannes. The driver, old and darkly sunburned, opened the door for her and glanced at her with the impassive eyes of a peasant. If he wondered why the lady had no maid, he did not show it. He chirruped to the horse and they moved away.

The sixteen kilometres along the coast took nearly two hours. Sara looked at the jewelled watch pinned to her lapel; Mother is still asleep. Good. They'll find my note when Thérèse comes into my room at half-past eight. Oh, but I wish you'd go just a little faster, thought the impatient girl. The horse and driver seemed to doze. But at last the road wound to a promontory and there, lined with tall palms, its villas nestling among the trees, was the long curve of the Croisette.

She had asked the driver to leave her at the Hôtel Gonnet et de la Reine. She paid him. He saluted and trotted slowly away in the sunshine.

Crossing the road, Sara walked fast towards the huddled houses and quay of the old town. At the back of the quai Saint-Pierre were alleys where jewellers and workers in leather had poky shops. The houses pressed close, smelling of the fish market. She and Louise had gone there to have a bracelet made by a solemn Spaniard called Gomis. Thank heaven the shops are open, she thought. Cannes wakes earlier than the Villa des Roses.

The Cannes-Calais express gave a satisfied hiss as it drew into Victoria Station in a cloud of smutty steam. Porters surged forward as the travellers stepped out. Voyagers with children, men in capes and tweed hats, ladies wrapped in furs against the damp London April, and two yapping Pomeranian dogs which had got on the nerves of everybody but their owners in the restaurant car. One burly porter, spying a young lady whose clothes spelled money, hurried up to her, hand outstretched for her valise. He was outraged when she shook her head, saying she would carry it herself.

'Just as you like, miss.'

As if one *liked*, thought Sara, I positively loathe carrying the thing. In her naiveté she had imagined the gold bracelets would provide enough for her train and sleeping car tickets, her meals, and still give her a generous amount for expenses. She had not enough to pay a bus fare let alone a motor cab.

In the long and wakeful night hours rocking towards Paris, when she watched the streaming flat landscape of Normandy from the train windows, when she stood leaning on the rail and staring at a roughish sea, Sara tried to sort out exactly what had happened. Did she mean to leave Louise for good? What did she hope? *Want?* That was the nub of it.

As long as the war had continued, its dark presence had

stopped her and every other young woman in Europe from seeing just how free they'd become. The times, the tragic times, had given them liberty. They had left their homes, nursed and driven ambulances, farmed, worked in factories, lived independently. And had discovered that their bodies, in the past kept inviolate by their parents until marriage, were their own.

That was why she was here. At nearly twenty-three and breathing the new freedom, she was still dependent on the whim of her mother. It wasn't to be borne. Which was why, without a dollar, a centime or a shilling, she set off in the bitter wind to walk to St Charles Street.

London was so dark after Provence. The pavements were wet from last night's rain, the trees still almost leafless. No colour anywhere. Her valise weighed a ton and her fashionably narrow skirts made it difficult to walk quickly. Grit blew into her face as she made her way in the direction of Mayfair where, she very well knew, her father's welcome was not going to be warm. Since she was a child she had never appeared uninvited.

Her father's life, crammed with work and with colleagues connected with work, had narrow partitions into which he fitted his daughters. His chosen companion, Sara supposed she must be his mistress, was Lee Becker, an American painter. Lee was fortyish, with enough private money to paint what she liked without being at the mercy of what she sold. Sara was fond of her. She was a little person with eyes like spoonfuls of the Mediterranean and wonderful American teeth. It's a mercy, thought Sara, dodging a blast of London dust, that Lee will be on my side. Are there going to be sides? Lee once said to her,

'I often think Alex only understands people who work.'

'And respects only them?'

'Sure. Of course,' added Lee, seeing what Sara was thinking, 'he doesn't feel like that about his daughters.'

'You mean we're allowed to be parasites.'

'What a word,' Lee had said, laughing.

Sara remembered the conversation and felt more dubious than before.

At last she turned into St Charles Street. The huge house of Portland stone had belonged to a Lord Faramond who died 'without issue' as they said in Debrett, years ago. William Thornbury bought the place cheaply due to its unwieldy size and lack of style, and Alexander turned it into his London auction house. Now in 1920 the St Charles Street galleries were as familiar to people who bought and sold objects of value as the Louvre to art-lovers and Buckingham Palace to social climbers.

At the top of the flight of steps Sara was bowed to by the doorman who had known her since she was ten, and made her way up a staircase to the left, to an office. The girl working at a very large typewriter was new to Sara: her father's secretaries never stayed long. She was young and nervous and wore a black taffeta bow at the neck of her modest blouse. Seeing Sara, she gave a start.

'Good morning,' said Sara pleasantly. 'I am Miss de Grelle. Is my father in?'

'Oh. Oh yes, that is, would you be seated and I'll just . . .'

The girl, flustered, disappeared into the further room. A moment later its door burst open and there was Alexander, arms outstretched.

'*Mon enfant.* The surprise! Such a surprise!'

He drew Sara close. She could smell the familiar scent of Alexander, expensive soap, cigar smoke, the fragrant pink carnation in his buttonhole. He pressed her to him and her forehead was against his beard.

'Come along, tell me why you have startled me like a jack-in-the-box.'

He took her into his office which was furnished exactly like an Edwardian drawing room. A coal fire burned briskly. The carpet was very thick and dark crimson, Alexander liked red, and the chairs were of green or brown leather with brass studs. Bookcases, tables and desk were Georgian.

Asking his secretary for coffee, 'hot, hot hot,' he settled his daughter by the fire, lit a cigar, 'May I?', and studied her with narrow, narrowed eyes.

He was not best pleased by this apparition. It was not his style to be taken unawares and besides he instinctively felt her presence boded no good. The girl was pale. Of course she always was pale, he himself had had that white skin as a boy, but Sara looked more greenish than gardenia today. And travel-worn. Her boots were dusty and when she peeled off her gloves he noticed they were none too clean.

Her face, however, was not travel-worn.

'You and your mother are taking a little trip to England?' he sociably enquired, deciding that come what may he would not see Louise. The secretary arrived with coffee. Alexander picked up the silver pot to pour out.

'I have left Mother,' said Sara.

One might as well get it over at once.

He paused, pot in the air.

'I beg your pardon?'

'I have left her. And the villa. I came alone.'

'What did she say to that?'

'She has no idea I am here.'

Positively intrigued, he handed her the cup and then leaned back, drawing on his cigar. He was more amused than he intended to show. He had a conscience about both his daughters. But work – thrusting, hungry, never-satisfied work – stopped him from being much of a father.

'How exactly did you achieve this escape?'

'I slipped out of the villa yesterday morning and took the express from Cannes.'

'To –' he looked at the ash on his cigar 'land yourself on me?'

'Something like that,' said Sara, and smiled.

'Might one enquire exactly why you ran?'

Sara had known this question would come up at once, and had given what was to be her reply much thought. She had decided against the truth. She could tell it to Lee Becker, but she could not insult her mother to the man who had made Louise suffer in the past. Louise never talked about any of her failures, and rarely mentioned her marriage. But it had been Alexander who had left Louise.

'It's very slow being a *jeune fille* in France,' Sara said casually. 'More than ever in the Midi. Most of my girlfriends seem to have gone. Or they are married. And as you know everybody leaves the Riviera in any case before the eighth of May. Mother goes to Montreux. Well. . . . I've lived in Switzerland such a lot, having been at school there, of course. Mountains and chocolates and rowing on the lakes. What else is there to do? Father, I don't want to spend my days waiting for a husband. Some French girls apparently don't mind doing it, even now.'

'You are half French,' he said coldly.

'Oh sure. And half American. And feeling,' added Sara to tease, 'more American with every birthday. So I asked Mother if I could come to see you. And when she refused I thought I'd come anyway.'

'What do you mean, refused?'

'Oh, you know Mother. She wouldn't give me the fare,' she said, laughing.

'Then how did you find the money? You have scarcely,' he added, conscious of the niggardly amount he allowed her, 'saved up.'

'I sold some jewéllery.'

'Any good pieces? I trust not the sapphire cross.'

He sounded very sharp.

Sara laughed outright.

'I wouldn't dare. I got rid of some old bracelets my American Aunt Goodier sent me. The man gave me a very bad price. Not enough for me to have breakfast on the train from Dover. Or take a motor cab here. I had to walk,' she finished in martyred tones, 'all the way from the station.'

Ah, thought Sara. A reaction. And about time too.

She enjoyed her father's horror and anger – was Louise mad? – his ringing bells, ordering breakfast, fresh toast, Oxford marmalade, more coffee. Where was her luggage, he asked. Had she travelled first class? Where was her maid? He had a passionate attention to detail. Sara began to feel that the whole adventure, which with lack of breakfast and porters had turned into a dusty mess, had been worthwhile.

There was a flattering bustle. The girl with the taffeta bow darted in and out, breakfast arrived; and just as Sara had graciously settled to the feast, and Alexander was watching her eating it with affectionate satisfaction, the secretary came in again.

'I am sorry to disturb you, Mr de Grelle. But Mr Hutchinson-Deluth has arrived.'

'Has he?' said Alexander briskly. 'Good. Well, now, Sara, I fear you and your breakfast must be moved. Miss Tomkins, ring for a porter. And look after Miss de Grelle for the time being.'

To Sara's annoyance a porter carried her tray out of the room, and she was taken back to Miss Tomkins's office. While she drank coffee, a balding man in a coat with a velvet collar was ushered in. Alexander was waiting.

'My dear fellow. Good of you to come all the way from the North. Such a journey. Come in, come in.'

Sara's breakfast ended with a strong sense of bathos. She had been supplanted. Through the closed door of his office she heard their voices. Everything had been exciting when she had been with Alexander. Now it had slowed down. She pushed away her breakfast and stood up.

'I think I'll go into the viewing galleries, Miss Tomkins. When my father's free again, perhaps someone could come and fetch me.'

'I'll come, of course, Miss de Grelle.'

Sara went down the corridor, across a wide landing from which one entered the main auction room and into the galleries which led from one into another like rooms in a Tudor palace. There was a sale at the end of the week and the 'Objects of the European Arts, 1870 to 1912' had been put on display to make them, as far as possible, look as if they were in the rooms of a mansion. People were in and out of the galleries, standing in front of glass cases, leaning over to study this or that, asking the porters 'May I take a look?' and briefly checking a silver or porcelain mark. Sara joined them. She looked at a brass baptismal jug with a handle like a gryphon, a tea-set patterned with bamboo branches, some fire grates of brass pierced like fine lace.

Gazing at the things soon to be sold, Sara had a feeling of wonder about the past. It was so silent. What hands had poured that teapot, perhaps nervous hands of a girl unhappily in love? What baby too small to howl had given a choking whimper when cold water streamed from that pious-looking jug?

Objects had more than a patina. They had a kind of magic, she thought. She forgot to be offended that her father had bundled her so unceremoniously out of his office.

Glancing up, her whole stomach turned over. There was a man standing by the open door, speaking to the hall porter. He was tall, dressed in elegantly dark clothes, and he turned and walked off in a way European men never did, with a loose-limbed graceful ease.

It was her lover from the Villa Roumaniev.

CHAPTER SIX

Every instinct rushed towards him. She almost cried out, almost ran to the door. But then she stayed still. How could she call out to a man whose name she did not know? To that sexually familiar, utterly unknown stranger? And even while she hesitated, wanting to hurry across the room, it was too late. She forced herself to walk in a leisurely way to the top of the staircase. The doors leading to the street were swinging. He was gone.

She went slowly down the corridor, back towards her father's office. It's for the best. What in the world would I have said to him?

In the office Miss Tomkins, who seemed in a permanent state of anxiety, said 'Your father asked me to say he will only be five more minutes. May I get you anything?'

'I'd very much like to look at the old bound catalogues on your bookshelf. May I?'

Miss Tomkins handed them to her, and Sara went back to her chair. Turning the pages, she tried to calm down. It had been an extraordinary shock seeing him again. And here in London, of all places. I won't think about him. He's gone, and we'll never meet. I wish I didn't feel like this. *It's ridiculous.*

'A fine pair of gilded fauteuils,' said the catalogue.

'A superb secretaire with full front and eight small inlaid drawers.'

She somehow succeeded in at least looking at the secretaire and admiring its flowing lines. On the next page there was the illustration of a clock.

'A spectacular Louis XVI clock, provenance impeccable, originally the property of the Empress Josephine.'

And just then, despite trembling nerves, she had her idea.

She closed the book and thought about it. Her pale face in repose had a look of Alexander. The same concentration, the same stillness the more remarkable for being rare on a countenance so lively and expressive. Miss Tomkins, who was stage-struck by her employer, saw the likeness and thought – you'd know she is a de Grelle the moment you saw her.

At last the door opened and Alexander and his visitor emerged, still in conversation. They shook hands, and Alexander said somebody called Buckingham would look forward to the visit.

He must be selling Father something, thought Sara. I suppose Buckingham is one of our experts. I must find out.

The elderly visitor turned to leave, briefly glancing at the red-headed girl in the corner. Jove, he thought, that must be the second daughter. What did they say about that second marriage? It foundered too. De Grelle is a rogue with women.

When he was gone Alexander said, 'Well, my child, now you may return.'

He stood back for her to enter the room first. Sitting down near the fire, facing him, Sara looked at her father. She read his thoughts which plainly said – what am I supposed to do with you? And since he only showed what he was thinking on purpose, she got up her courage. He was an alarming adversary. Heavy, fattish, his eyes almost Slav, his tawny beard showing traces of grey, he still resembled the late Edward VII but without a monarch's serenity. In its place was a kind of purring hardness. And he looked so foreign, thought Sara. He didn't even look French. He could have been a Russian noble in the days when they had been powerful before the Revolution. Above all, Alexander was impregnable. Nobody in the Villa des Roses looked like that.

Well. She must attack the fortress, and a direct assault would not do.

'So. Your mind is quite made up, is it, about not returning to the Midi?'

'I'm afraid so. I can't live with Mother any more. It was different during the war when I worked at the Roumaniev. There's nothing to do now.'

'Except dance and sing.'

She did not rise.

'I thought perhaps you might put up with me for a while. Then I could go and visit with Aunt Emily.'

'Emily Goodier? That piece of American starch.'

'She's fond of me. We write now and then. And there are some cousins in New York. Besides, didn't you say in December you might open a branch there?'

'My plans are scarcely a reason for you to land yourself on that elderly Puritan. She may not wish to be so landed. Few people do.'

A hit. A palpable hit, thought Sara. And didn't rise for the second time.

'When Mother and I were in New York in '13' she said sweetly, 'Aunt was quite pleased to see us. She was very kind.'

A pause. He hasn't refused to let me stay in London, she thought. He can't, can he? Now was the time to lead the conversation towards her idea.

'I've been looking at next month's catalogue. European objects of art, eighteenth century. I'd love to come to the auction. May I?'

'Enchanted,' he said as if to a stranger, adding in the same tone, 'naturally you like French things.'

'Not very much. I don't like buhl and all the tortoise-shell and brass inlays. Then there's Watteau. Such exaggerated courtliness and the satin clothes are as slick as the oil he painted in. Imagine living in his world, Father! Endless conversations in gardens, and, if you're a girl, men ogling and playing the mandolin. Of course I know the three we have at the Villa des Roses are very good ones –'

'They certainly are,' cut in Alexander, speaking for the first time with feeling. You'd like to put them in the saleroom, Sara thought.

'I suppose it's a sign of an untrained taste not to like Watteau,' she said casually. 'But I do like Napoleonic things. There's a clock in your sale catalogue which belonged to Josephine. I wonder if it's as good as the one which belongs to a friend of mine in Antibes. That's a pearl. Crystal and gilt and a chime like bells.'

He listened to this, slightly raising his eyebrows, and then said, 'What has your friend's clock to do with me?'

'Possibly quite a lot. I want to work for you,' she said promptly.

She began to speak fast before he had time to laugh and to prevent her.

'Please listen, Father, don't brush me aside or shut me up just yet. And don't say the only place for women in de Grelle's is to be a Miss Tomkins. And don't, most of all, say I know nothing about your business! That is more or less true *now*. But what did you know about Chinese porcelain or Russian ormulu or William Kent or Persian miniatures when you were my age? Or let's say when you started, which I know was younger than me. I do happen to know a great deal about a Napoleonic collection which a friend of mine wants to sell.'

'Indeed.' The girl amused him. Not the collection.

'De Grelle's might wish to handle it,' she added.

He shrugged.

'A few documents and two or three engravings. A helmet picked up on some *champs de bataille*. My dear Sara, we know all about such little scratching together of curios.'

It was her turn to raise her eyebrows.

'I'm sure you do. Carl's collection has taken all his life, he's over sixty, and his father's before that. His father fought for Napoleon and was at Waterloo. It's a complete record of Napoleon's rise to fame. There are portraits, manuscripts, letters (isn't Napoleon's writing *awful*? Carl can read it. I can't make out a word). Let me see . . . what else. There's a contemporary painting of the Emperor landing at Golfe Juan after escaping from Elba, and flags belonging to Louis XVIII, with oak leaves and fleur-de-lys, an address in gold to the people of Golfe Juan. And an inkwell of Josephine's, and the clock I mentioned. And her earrings. And a glorious chicken-skin fan of hers with painted chinoiserie sticks.'

Alexander smoked for a while. Sara waited. Once or twice during the pause her body remembered that a little time ago she had seen her lover. Seen him, and lost him immediately. But somehow she managed to keep his image at arm's length while she looked at her father, willing him to do what she wanted.

The silence began to last too long. He was doing it on purpose.

'I would like to work for you,' she repeated.

'So you said.'

'I wouldn't be a liability.'

'What makes you think so?'

'Because I learn quickly and I am not a fool. I wouldn't, for instance, use the fact that I am a de Grelle. I know quite a bit about French painting and furniture, although I dislike some of it at present.'

He did not miss the 'at present'.

'Perhaps I could start in the catalogue department.'

He gave a scoffing laugh.

'My poor child, my experts are the best in the country. On Old Masters, seventeenth- eighteenth-, early nineteenth century painters. Arms. Porcelain. Jewellery. Objects of Virtu. Miniatures –'

'One of them could use an apprentice,' she interrupted, seeing he was enjoying the litany and it could go on for some time. 'Particularly when I am doing the catalogue for my friend's collection. I would do it in French and English, of course. And naturally I'd do that one on my own, wouldn't I?'

'Ah yes. To change the subject for a moment, Sara. Perhaps it might be worthwhile for one of my chaps to go to Antibes and take a look at this precious collection you keep talking about. What did you say your friend's name was?'

Sara burst out laughing.

'Oh Father. You don't truly think I'd tell you, do you? Unless I'm to be the one to do the job. We must trade. Work at de Grelle's for me. An important sale for you. That's a fair exchange. No, now I come to think of it, it isn't all that fair. You get two things for my one. An interesting sale. And a new worker. Oh, I've just remembered. Carl also has a Canova marble bust of Napoleon. And some sheets dedicated to the Corporal Violette, illustrated with violets, you know. Secret sheets distributed to his follower after he was taken to Elba, saying "I will return when the violets bloom again." '

I am being glib, she thought.

Alexander looked at her reflectively. The Corporal Violette sheets were a rarity. So was a Canova.

He sighed.

'You drive a hard bargain. But I have always been weak where my daughters are concerned. You will be employed as a temporary – mark that – a temporary assistant to Gilbert Travice. He's my chap for the late eighteenth and early nineteenth century in Europe. You will be on a six months' trial and if at the end of the time Travice and I do not consider you are earning your salary, then *out*.'

He stood up, kissed her cheek, and gave her a look which, for the first time this morning, told her she was not looking her best.

Tired and triumphant, Sara was driven home in her father's Rolls to his house in Park Street. She was welcomed by the butler, Georges, an old friend. Small and dark, Georges never had a consecutive conversation with his employer or either of the de Grelle daughters. He was a reserved man and even with his wife Marie, the house's excellent cook, he was not voluble. But he made up for his silences with his expressive black eyes, and he beamed at Sara. He took her up to the room she always occupied when she stayed in London.

Taking off her coat and giving a yawn, Sara suddenly saw herself full-length in the looking-glass. She couldn't believe her own reflection. Creased, travel-stained, her gloves as grubby as her finger-nails, a strand of hair emerging from under the brim of her hat. That was the girl who had had the gall to bargain with a man conscious of the appearance of everything, from a woman's beauty to a silver spoon. It was astounding that he allowed her even to be seen at the galleries. He should have packed her straight home to take a bath.

She spent the afternoon asleep. Yesterday's dawn start after a night of wakeful planning, the long journey on a rocking noisy train, the rough Channel, had taken their toll. Just before she fell asleep, looking up at the ceiling's oval of plaster cupids, she thought – today I saw him. Today I lost him again.

When she woke it was seven o'clock. She had a long bath and changed into the only evening gown she had brought. The dress she'd thrown into the bottom of her valise had been the one, out of her large wardrobe, she hoped would travel best. It was a dull purplish silk with grey lights, low cut in the bosom, a Vionnet. With no maid to look after her in her father's bachelor establishment, she did her rich red hair herself. Looking at herself, she thought – I suppose I'll do.

When she went out on to the landing, she thought how quiet the house was. Except during the siesta, she was accustomed to the noises of Provence. Voices bursting into argument or laughter, down in the kitchens, out in the garden. Provençal people were as passionate as Italians. And the cicadas in summertime, the frogs croaking their love songs. Lately there had been Jean-Claude strumming American jazz on Louise's piano and sometimes she heard her mother's tender laugh. Those were the noises of life in the Midi, together with the winds, the Mistrale or the Tramontana, blowing through the pines with a sound like the sea.

Here in Park Street as she went down the thickly carpeted stairs the only noise was a horse trotting by in the street. She opened the drawing room door, wondering if her father was yet home.

Lee was standing, one hand on the marble chimneypiece, looking down at a newly lit fire. She spun round.

'The runaway!'

They did not kiss. Lee was not one for embracing. She held you, Sara thought, physically at arm's length while mentally folding you in her arms. Did that suit Alexander?

'I asked Georges to light the fire,' Lee said. 'It's so darned cold and this house is like an ice box.'

'You're always cold,' said Sara, smiling.

'It's this benighted country. Well, Sara? You look dandy. I congratulate you on that Vionnet. Now tell me what this is all about. Your father telephoned. Rather brief and rather *bouleversé.*'

'You surprise me. When I appeared he didn't bat an eyelid.'

'Of course he didn't. He's a salesman. But being descended upon by unexpected daughters wasn't in his diary for this month. Tell me the entire story. But don't bother with the end. I am *astounded* that he has hired you!'

This time Sara told the bald truth. She described her mother's lover. Attactive, twenty-five –

'And a drunk?'

'Lee, I don't know. I have never met one. They both keep drinking champagne but it seems to have no effect on Jean-Claude. That's what is curious. And one never notices when he drinks, just that when you look at his glass it is suddenly empty again.'

The story finished with Sara's penniless walk to St Charles Street. Lee chuckled.

'You did the right thing. Getting away. But why for crying out loud didn't you wire me for money? Don't bother to answer. Your stinking pride.'

Sara admitted that she had thought it rather clever to sell the bracelets which she never wore anyway. But it was odd how the money hadn't gone as far as she expected.

'It never does and it's time you found that out. And time you began to work too. Your father can't make up his mind whether to be tickled or appalled. You don't have to live in this barn if you don't want to, Sara. My mews cottage might be more fun.'

'Lee, it's very sweet of you but –'

'But you prefer it here. Can that be filial affection, or the instinct that it's smart to be near your parent now that you're going to work at de Grelle's?'

Before Sara could deny the accusation, which of course was true, her father came into the room. He always did this suddenly, noisily, as if in a hurry to move on to the next part of his day or his life. He looked impressive in evening clothes, and Sara decided that his resemblance to the late King was deliberately fostered. Nothing with Alexander was accidental.

'I should have telephoned you, *chère amie*,' he said, kissing Lee's hand in his rapid way with a gallantry that slightly reminded Sara of the tiresome men in Watteau's paintings. 'I did not tell you young van Rijn is dining with us. He is somewhat late,' he added disapprovingly, glancing at the clock.

'Why does that name ring a bell?' said Lee.

'Because you have seen it at the top of cheques. Which is just where I hope to see it. He is one of the New York banking van Rijns.'

76

Lee smiled. Alex never invites anyone here without a reason, she thought, whether it is someone selling up their priceless library or a banker offering his priceless services. Which am I?

She and Alex went to bed together. He was a passionate and satisfying lover. When their affair had begun years ago she had wanted very much to marry him. He had never asked, and she could not. It wasn't in her nature to try. They behaved circumspectly, as close friends. Everybody believed they slept together but nobody said so to them. There was a flavour of a late Victorian love affair about it. Lee enjoyed his love-making intensely, but often thought he had other women. Like the unspoken subject of marriage, his sexual life apart from her was never talked of either. Lee was rather sorry. The subject, particularly with a man of his generation, fascinated her. She had a strong female curiosity about the *maisons closes* in Paris which she had read about. In her imagination she saw Alex in claustrophobic rooms hung with red velvet, the beds with canopies, where plump-thighed girls in corsets, their stockings showing the tops of bulging thighs, embraced him, removing their white drawers tied with tape at the waist. White drawers! The idea made her smile. So did corsets, which were utterly out of date. A friend of hers, an Oxford don, had said that in human history, 'When the corset disappears, my dear Lee, promiscuity arrives.' There seemed a paradox there somewhere.

It would have shocked Alexander to the depth of his fifty-year-old soul had Lee asked for details of such places. What he did in Paris, what he had done in his lusty youth, remained a mystery. To Lee he gave a warm attention, a concern, a sunlight raying on her, bathing her in a golden light. When the sun went in, she was perfectly sure it would shine again. And in the meantime, his absences gave her the chance to get on with her painting.

While they were drinking madeira and Alexander and Lee talked, Sara was reflecting on her father's news that there would be a fourth for dinner. She never remembered an evening in Park Street or in Paris when her father had not invited somebody else to join them. Once during the war Catherine complained.

'I do think, Father, you might have dined with us alone on at least one evening.'

He raised sandy eyebrows.

'My guests are to do with my work, Catherine.'

'Exactly. Which doesn't make them very interesting or amusing, you know.'

'Work is always interesting. Your ancestors understood that.'

'My ancestors,' said Catherine, to her sister's admiration, 'fought for their country.'

'Of course they did. Working to get titles and land. *Voilà*.'

Interrupting Sara's thoughts, the drawing room door opened and Georges announced in his low voice,

'Monsieur van Rijn, sir.'

The young man who came into the room was profuse in apologies. Just as he had been leaving the house where he was staying, a cable had arrived from New York. He had been forced, he really was so sorry, sir, to reply at once.

Alexander welcomed him. Lee smiled from her sofa as he was presented. Sara looked at the new arrival. And froze.

It was her lover again.

'And this,' said Alexander, bringing him to her with somewhat mocking formality, 'is Mr van Rijn, Sara. Perry. My second daughter.'

She offered him her hand. When he touched it, it was freezing cold.

Perry van Rijn sat down beside Lee and the talk started easily. Sara scarcely said a word. She was suffocated by the thudding of her heart. How could she remain calm, seem calm? Her body knew this man: his tormenting attraction had worked the moment he entered the room. That second when she looked at him again, every violent emotion from the Roumaniev took possession of her. She remained quiveringly silent, while Perry van Rijn's dark face showed nothing but a smiling politeness as he talked to Lee and then to Alexander. Now and again from courtesy he glanced in her direction.

Georges announced dinner. They moved into the dining room where Lee had ordered another fire to be lit. Sara was placed with her back to the warmth.

'You may feel chilly after coming from the South,' Alexander said. 'My daughter, Perry, has only arrived from France today. And you from Southampton. How was the ocean journey?'

'Very crowded, sir. But I managed a good deal of deck tennis.'

He didn't know me, Sara thought, when she went to bed that night. The shock, fierce as a blow across the face, had worn off now. Real life had taken over from the fantasy they had made on a night filled with the last hectic urgency of the war. The young man tonight, talking to her father and urbanely smiling at her or at Lee, wasn't the man who had made her almost faint with desire. He looked the same. Tall, easy, dark-eyed, dark-haired, with an olive tinge to his skin and a deep cleft in his chin. When he laughed he looked young. In repose he appeared hard, rather cold, even formidable. It was extraordinary to realize that the man in the drawing room, drinking coffee and talking of painting to Lee, had pressed her down so savagely in the pine needles that when she had looked at her naked back in the mirror the next day, there were marks like whip lashes across her buttocks.

Van Rijn had not shown in a single way, not by a flicker, that he recognized her. Had possessed her. It was clear that he did not know who she was.

Why not? My voice is the same. And my hair.

But she had worn that stupid titillating mask. And when they had talked their voices had been lost by the music. Later, while they made love they had whispered.

Lying with wide-open eyes she suddenly thought – perhaps he *does* know. And thinks it won't do. He'll pretend and go on pretending, so as to get out of the situation. God! does he imagine I would chase after him and try to start it all again?

In her petted life as a beautiful girl she had never lifted a finger to beckon a man towards her. Men had been the pursuers. Could Perry van Rijn truly imagine *she* would run after *him*? Impossible. But suppose he made a move towards her himself, did she want him? No. She did not. What she wanted, or had done with exquisite pain for weeks and weeks after they had parted, was the man in the Roumaniev garden, the violent and demanding, the untiring and satiating lover. What had that man to do with the well-bred supercilious New Yorker making conversation with her father. She wanted the man who had existed when they lay together then, the emotions she felt, the physical bliss he'd given her then. Intense and sharp and with a taste of sin about it. But the man himself had gone. He was changed, and real life, money and business were responsible. I don't want this Perry van Rijn, she thought. The man I still thirst for disappeared in a lorry which drove to Marseilles.

It's my father who wants him now.

When Perry, and Lee who had shared a motor cab with him, left Park Street, Alexander walked with Sara to the foot of the stairs.

'And what do you think of my young banker?'

'I don't know him, Father. Pleasant enough. Clever, I suppose.'

'He wouldn't be where he is otherwise. His name is valuable, as you must have guessed. I am eager to open my new branch in New York. Van Rijn's is an investment bank. One of the best on Wall Street, it was started by his grandfather.'

'So you want something from Mr van Rijn.'

Alexander, usually perceptive, did not hear the irony.

'True. True. The something which I want, child, is *l'espèce*. Good Yankee dollars. And young van Rijn is here to make up his mind about my English and French businesses. Whether they are worth an investment. I have a battle on my hands, I daresay.'

'And will you win?'

'There's a foolish question.'

Sara slept badly and by the time she came down to breakfast, her father had left. Georges, serving her coffee and rolls with approval, he thought English breakfasts barbarous, said that 'monsieur leaves as the clock strikes eight'.

'How early, Georges!'

'He likes to be in his office before anybody else,' said the butler, thinking – Reynard has many tricks.

'Does he ever walk, Georges?'

'Never, Mademoiselle Sara. Harrison comes for him in the Rolls.'

Father might, thought Sara crossly, have given me a lift.

Before leaving for de Grelle's she telephoned Lee on the vexing problem of clothes. Lee exclaimed at the news that apart from underwear and a clean blouse, Sara had brought nothing but the Vionnet.

'We'd best go to Molyneux and send Alex the bill. Do you want me to meet you in your luncheon hour? Is an hour long enough to choose anything halfway decent?'

'Luncheon isn't exactly an hour, surely. We could take longer.'

'None of your Provençal siestas over here, Sara. You're in a Puritan city now. An hour means fifty-five minutes. Don't fret. Captain Molyneux is over from Paris and I'll see him and ask him to suggest some things for you. He's quite an admirer of yours. It would be better if we could get you something right away for working, wouldn't it? Alex said your travelling suit, to put it politely, was somewhat wilted.'

'I wish you'd stop laughing, Lee, I looked *awful!*'

When Sara arrived at the great florid building, a young man at a desk in the hallway said would she go straight to Miss Tomkins?

Along the corridor Sara passed many porters wearing the de Grelle green baize aprons with her father's emblem on the chest: a gold circle enclosing his twined initials and the date 1880 also in gold. Lee told Sara once that he would have given a fortune to have had his profile as part of the emblem; he was thinking of the Christie's sign, with James Christie's aristocratic profile above the date, 1776. But even Alexander couldn't compete with the only house in the world which had an unbroken two-hundred-year-old history of fine-art auctioneering . . . in the matter of emblems, anyway.

Miss Tomkins, with a fresh bow of pale blue, said good morning with a blush. Everything, thought Sara, made her blush. I bet Father turns her into a beetroot a hundred times a day.

'Mr de Grelle can see you at once, Miss de Grelle.'

Oh can he, thought Sara. He could have seen me at breakfast and brought me here in his motor.

Alexander was dictating to yet another secretary in discreet dark clothes. Exit of respectful girl. Both she and Miss Tomkins were very goodlooking and Sara wondered with a gleam of inward amusement whether her father had ever in his life employed a plain woman.

'Well, now,' he said, gesturing her to a chair, 'I have spoken to Gilbert Travice, one of our most distinguished experts, I hope you'll remember that. He will be good for you. And is willing to take on the task. No doubt it will waste some of his valuable time but *quoi faire?* You must be trained by somebody.'

Sara said nothing.

'He is away at present at the Exeter House Library,' continued Alexander. 'You can make yourself useful for the time being. I have asked Guy Buckingham to keep an eye on you. I will ring for him in a moment. Meantime, there is something I have to say. Those clothes are not suitable.'

He frowned at yesterday's travelling suit.

'Oh, I know,' said Sara hastily. 'I brought nothing with me. But Lee and I have fixed to go to Molyneux and –'

'I am not talking of clothes for your social life, Sara, but for your employment. You must wear something dark and unobtrusive. An overall would be best.'

She could not believe her ears.

'You must bear in mind,' he said as if to a child, 'that to employ a woman here at de Grelle's, one who is not in the position of a clerk, is revolutionary. Quite revolutionary. Gilbert Travice was somewhat shocked when I told him what I intended. You have doubtless noticed that my secretaries wear dark colours. Just as it should be. We don't wish the feminine element noticed or drawn attention to at de Grelle's. In your case it is more important still since you will be training on the professional side. The British Museum, I know for a fact, wouldn't think of employing a woman for anything but work of a clerical nature. I have always been an innovator' he added complacently. 'So. A well-fitting dark overall, if you please. You may have silk if you wish.'

Lee had already arrived chez Molyneux when Sara appeared, somewhat breathless. She ran all the way from St

Charles Street. The gallant Captain was out visiting a royal client, but he had conferred with Lee about Sara and together they had selected a choice of twenty frocks, coats and suits which might please her. Lee and Sara were ushered into a room of pearl colour and mirrors, with enough palms to fill the Promenade des Anglais. A sedate middle-aged woman of great composure said she would fetch the mannequins.

'Got your breath back?' enquired Lee, as Sara and she were given little gilt chairs.

'My father has taken my breath away permanently.'

Sara told the story of the overall. She got no sympathy. Lee tried to keep her face straight.

'I guessed that would come. Have you seen the two young women in the packing department? Extinguished in blue alpaca. And little Miss Tomkins very subfusc. I'm always waiting for Alex to stop the poor child from wearing those tabby-cat bows she's so fond of. Did Alex mention that women are banned from working at the British Museum unless chained to a typewriter? It's barbarous when you remember what they did during the war. Men were only too grateful then . . . never you mind, Sara. You're in the building. That's the great thing. And Captain Molyneux must design you a beautiful navy-blue silk overall. Ah. Here comes a masterpiece . . .'

A tall and beautiful mannequin had entered in black crepe which burst, here and there, into gigantic blue flowers.

Lee and Sara chose a number of exquisite dresses, including some satin evening gowns, and an afternoon dress of green patterned with grapes.

'But when shall I ever be free in the afternoon?'

'Think of Sundays.'

Before and after her expedition to Molyneux, Sara spent the day in a small high-ceilinged office with Guy Buckingham. He was de Grelle's silver expert, a burly, thick-set man with barley-coloured hair, heavy-lidded eyes, and a lazy manner. One expected him to yawn.

'I can't for the life of me imagine why you should wish to work in this madhouse,' he said. Near his desk was a table entirely occupied by a gigantic silver creation designed to fill the centre of a thirty-foot dinner table. It sprouted with palm trees, African kings and English military figures wearing topees. He pushed the centrepiece, which was very heavy, to one side, muttering 'So sorry there isn't much room,' and pulled up a chair for her.

'My father says you're the great silver expert. A wizard, he called you.'

'Don't you believe him, Miss de Grelle. He makes pretty speeches to oil the wheels. I am a fool at the game. I'm only here because he couldn't find anybody better. Sotheby's and Christie's swallowed all the good 'uns after the Armistice. However. Take a squint at these four. What do you think?'

He handed her some spoons. They were so worn and thin that on two of them the edges of the bowls were sharp as razors.

'Look at the finials,' he said, 'that's what we call the end of the handles.'

Sara saw the tiny figures.

'I suppose they must be apostle spoons. Those little people have a religious look.'

'Well done. They are a complete set. Matthew, Mark, Luke and John.'

'But where are the other eight?'

He arranged the spoons in a row. 'The whole set, twelve apostles and Christ as well, are much rarer. Sometimes the silversmiths made a separate apostle. Sometimes, like this, the four Evangelists. These were made about 1500. Pleasant things, aren't they?'

Sara liked Guy Buckingham from the first. Remarking how little he knew, piling the small surface of her table with books, he talked to her, taught her. During the day he showed her something of silver marks, asked her to check pages of a catalogue, gave her his notes, showed her cups and spoons, mugs and candlesticks, spoons, forks and candle-snuffers. They were in parcels, packed, unpacked, they were along the shelves, on top of the bookcase, and ranged over his desk.

'Do the de Grelle experts like you always have things all over their offices?' she asked. 'Aren't you worried when they're so valuable?'

'Can't sleep a wink at night,' said Guy. 'There are those bars across the window up there. But what about magpies? Suppose they came through and snapped up St Matthew and St Mark in their nasty sharp beaks?'

The April sun was still shining when Sara, after the first day in her life of paid employment, walked home through Hyde Park. Now that she was alone, the uninvited presence of Perry van Rijn came into her thoughts, claiming them by right. She tried to shove him viciously away. He was the past. She had never been made love to by that well-dressed New York banker. The man in whose arms she had lain naked had been sad and mysterious, she had felt it even in his passion. He and she had been part of a tragedy which was over and yet was in them still.

How strange. Nobody talks about the war now, she thought. We want to forget it. Just as, Perry van Rijn, I want to forget you.

In the thin sunshine the lilacs were beginning to bud, and a mass of flowering currant was the colour of raspberries. It smelled fragrant, not heavy as the mimosa outside her bedroom at the Villa des Roses had done. A girl rode by on a glossy horse. Two English nannies, slowly pushing magnificent perambulators, gossiped as they walked. And Sara was suddenly glad, glad, glad that she had left Provence for ever. She had written to her mother last night to tell her so – at Lee's insistence.

'But I left a note saying I was going to London,' Sara had said irritably.

'A note is not enough. Your father has telegraphed, by the way.'

Sara looked at her.

'You mean you did.'

'Do I? Just write and say you're safe and well and perhaps add you are working at de Grelle's. Make some graceful remarks to smooth her down. You're good at that.'

Thinking it over, Sara knew Lee was right. Viewed from the safety of Park Street, she was slightly ashamed of her dramatic exit. It was extreme, and Sara's instincts were for action after reflection, for diplomacy and not for force. She

wrote an affectionate and tactful letter. It would not be well
received, of course. But the letter was posted.

Georges opened the door, giving his guarded smile. Sara
often thought he was shy.

On the oak chest in the entrance hall was a furled black silk
umbrella and a pair of pearl-buttoned suede gloves. Something in the way these things were arranged, the gloves
smoothed out and parallel to the umbrella, told Sara to whom
they belonged.

'Your sister has arrived, Mademoiselle Sara.'

She wondered if she heard a ring of sympathy somewhere.

She opened the drawing room door and loped in, exclaiming
cheerfully, 'My dear Cathy, Father never said you were
coming today, what a pleasant surprise.'

Catherine put down her tea-cup. She managed to conceal
the fact that the bright-haired new arrival was most
unwelcome.

'Apparently Father did not inform either of us. When I
telephoned, he did not say you were expected in England.'

And Georges didn't tell you I was here, thought Sara. I
expect he preferred not to.

'Oh, I only arrived yesterday.'

Antagonism as sharp as pungent scent filled the room. And
she had come in full of good intentions. 'I'm staying awhile,
Cathy.'

She sat down, sprawling in a chair not designed for so
modern a pose, turning her American ease and Frenchified
charm on her sister. Catherine, upright as royalty, offered her
tea.

Sara hastily refused, having swallowed cups of what she
considered a disgusting English drink in the office. Catherine
was saying that she had come to town 'for her Ascot fittings'
when Georges re-appeared. She was wanted on the telephone.

After her sister had left the room, Sara grimaced and stared,
frowning, at the carpet. Why did Catherine get on her nerves
the moment they met? She blamed herself. She was like a
tiresome dog bounding up to lick somebody's face in spite of
being shoved constantly away. Sara never understood why
she went on trying to create a semblance of friendship

between them both. It was instinctive. She despised herself and then did it all over again.

In her father's study, Catherine picked up the telephone.

'Yes, Dudley. What is it?'

The slightly metallic voice was flatter than usual. She hoped he was not going to suggest changing their arrangements.

'Oh, it's nothing,' was the airy reply. 'Just that I want to go to your Pa's sale tomorrow. Coming with me? We can pop back to the gallery later, and if you're good I'll buy you some lunch.'

His slangy English grated, but she said mildly enough, 'Why do you want to go to that particular auction?'

'I called in to take a look just now. There's a pencil and water colour picture I wouldn't mind bidding for. John Thirtle, one of the Norwich school. Cotman's brother-in-law. He's not much in fashion at present.'

'Then how do you know you'll sell it?'

He gave his self-confident laugh and told her to leave his business to him. She agreed to meet him at de Grelle's the next afternoon.

To her relief, Sara had left the drawing room when she returned. Arranging her pleated skirts so that they should not crush, Catherine sat down. She was thinking about her sister.

Although they met little, it seemed to her that there was something in Sara which invaded her life. Sara took their intimacy for granted and it did not exist. When they were together with their father, Alexander paid too much attention to Sara, and she in turn had a confidence in her way with him which Catherine resented. Why should she feel sisterly towards Sara? Their mothers, even their nationalities, were different.

The consolation had always been knowing Sara lived a thousand miles away in the South of France. What was she doing here in London? Catherine had the uneasy feeling that she might be here for good.

Part Two

CHAPTER SEVEN

Catherine de Grelle liked life to be planned, and then kept to the pattern on which she had decided. She was still unmarried and had refused three proposals of marriage since she was eighteen. Privately she had decided that none of the young men pleased her. And besides, she disliked being pawed. She had inherited none of her father's sexual drive and thought very little about sex.

As a young girl living in a beautiful and famous house, the granddaughter of an Earl, she had been something of a catch. When the old Earl died there had been no male relative to inherit the title. This meant that the Sussex manor, its good farmland, woods and streams, not to mention a gallery full of pictures including two Rubens, were destined to belong to Catherine.

The elder of the two de Grelle daughters was pleasant-looking. Her narrow eyes, not unlike her father's in shape although an English blue, were charming when she smiled and meant it. She could be engaging. But since the war had ended two years ago men had stopped courting her, and although her body was relieved to be left in peace she was rather offended. It was shameful how girls ran after eligible men now, she thought. So many many young men had been killed in the war. Including two of those who had loved her. But these regrets were banished from her mind when they gave her pain, for her mother was now gravely ill, and it was Verena who claimed all her thoughts. The last thing Catherine wanted at present was the unexpected arrival of her half-sister.

Alexander had not missed the fact that both his daughters,

unalike in so many ways, would soon become women to be reckoned with. There was a certain look sometimes in Sara's eyes which amused him. And he noticed how Catherine's mouth grew thin when she was set on getting her own way. He approved when she behaved acquisitively. It showed a certain gumption which had been a quality poor Verena had lacked.

It would have surprised him to know that Catherine wanted a good deal. She wanted some kind of precedence over that tiresome American half-sister. She wanted to be sure that by rights she would inherit the major part of her father's empire. And recently she had begun to want a man. Dudley Forrest.

Her mother had been ailing for a long time and in recent years had been mostly in bed. She was very weak. But Verena took a tender, almost a passionate interest in everything to do with her daughter. She had heard of an invitation sent to Catherine by some neighbours whose lands 'marched' as the old saying was with the Lytchett properties. Verena insisted that her daughter should go to the dinner, although Catherine wanted to stay at home with her. Instead, Catherine found herself placed next to a man who made it very obvious that he was setting out to please her.

Dudley Forrest was nearing forty and although English by birth had spent many years in Australia. He had fought with the Aussies in Gallipoli, he told interested English friends. Since then he had knocked about the world. Catherine was not drawn to him. She rather disliked his colonial accent, so different from the clipped upper-class English she was accustomed to among her family's acquaintances. And his manner had none of their well-bred off-handedness, he was almost ingratiating. He was quick-witted, laughed easily and was slightly self-conscious.

His good looks were rather coarse. He had a straight nose and thick nonedescript brown hair, and there was no distinction in the rugged face and full, smiling mouth. But Catherine's hostess privately told her that Forrest had had a remarkable war. At Gallipoli where the Australian troops had been trapped for months on the beaches, shelled day and night with appalling casualities, Forrest, fearlessly risking his own life, had saved a comrade. He had been awarded the DSO. Despite her reservations about him, Catherine – who had the Army in her blood – approved.

After dinner when the gentlemen came into the drawing room to join the ladies, a young girl began to thump at the piano. Forrest came across the room and sat down by Catherine. He began to sing with the music in a soft, pleasant voice.

> 'Stumbling all around
> Stumbling all around
> Stumbling all around – my – honey,'

he sang. 'It certainly sounds odd to hear one of my favourite tunes played here. Do you like American jazz, Miss de Grelle?'

'Good gracious, no.'

He chuckled at the brusqueness of the reply, and that made Catherine smile as well. She had no idea why she had amused him. They exchanged commonplaces for a while, and then he said eagerly, 'I've been told that you have two pictures by Rubens in your gallery at Lytchett, Miss de Grelle. He's a wonder. A great genius who could paint a Venus or a Virgin and Child and make each work a positive hymn of beauty. Didn't I hear you have a study of his *Feast of Venus?* And a portrait of his wife Helen Fourment. I'm very impressed.'

'I should never have imagined that paintings interested you,' said Catherine coolly. 'Lady Willingdon said you spend most of your time travelling.'

'So I do. Or did until I fetched up back in Merrie England. But painting, my interest in it, is the reason I've been travelling, you see. You might call it my life's work.'

He explained that he was not a painter himself, but that before and after the war he had dealt in pictures. He specialized in water colours, engravings and mezzotints. Good oil paintings were beyond his modest means. But he'd had some success. 'The Aussies are starting to take a shine to culture. The rich ones, that is.' He added that he had been in England now for six months, and had rented a small gallery near Claridge's.

It was not long before Catherine found herself – she had

not intended to do so – inviting him to Lytchett to see the Rubens. Personally she thought the paintings hideous, but could not help pluming herself on owning them when the man was so impressed.

Verena was pleased when she heard Catherine had invited a new friend to the manor. She had been in bed for many months, fussed over by elderly servants, visited constantly by her mother, old Lady Lytchett who still lived in the house. The place was a world of women since the Earl had died during the first year of the war.

With thinning hair tied in girlish plaits and rings hanging on her wasted fingers, Verena looked frail.

'I'm so glad you've invited someone here, Katy. It will do you good.'

Catherine sat down and gently took her hand. The woman lying in the elaborate bed with its silk hangings patterned with Chinese figures, hills and animals, was the only person she had ever loved. Catherine did not flinch from looking at the truth, she knew Verena was dying. A feeling of revulsion came to her when she remembered her father, strong and virile, a sun king, and compared him to the wasted figure in the bed. Alexander was responsible for that fatal sickness: he had struck Verena down.

'Mama, Mr Forrest is only coming to see the Rubens.'

'Oh, of course,' said Verena, faintly smiling.

'I wonder if you would like him.'

'If you do, Katy, I would.'

Catherine's invitation to Forrest had been sufficiently vague but he telephoned the very next morning after they had met, speaking as if he were an old friend.

When he arrived, loud in admiration of the rambling Tudor house and fascinated by the paintings, Catherine introduced him to her grandmother who gave him tea. Lady Lytchett apparently approved. She was a big-bosomed down-right woman with more vitality than is usual for somebody of over seventy-five. She wore very large pearls, half hoops on most of her fingers despite rheumatic joints, and was the Queen of Lytchett. She had never relinquished the sceptre to Verena and held it in an iron grip.

'I like that man,' she said to her granddaughter when Forrest had left. 'He's common and he don't know how to put on clothes (he cannot have bought that jacket in England) but I like him. Cultivate him.'

Catherine said nothing. She never took Lady Lytchett's advice.

'Don't know why I bother to tell you what to do. But I make no doubt you'll see what's under your nose. *He* may take it into his head to run after *you*. You'll enjoy that.'

Her prophecy proved right, for Dudley Forrest telephoned again and appeared again. And again. When he was back in London he wrote to say he was coming to an auction in Arundel: would Catherine come with him? As weeks went by Catherine accepted his attentions complacently. She had no other masculine admirers and it was pleasant to be taken about. Her grandmother's approval removed the stigma of the Australian accent. It was also Lady Lytchett who suggested he might be taken up to Verena's room and introduced.

'Grandmother, I don't really think –'

'Stuff and nonsense. Your mother is interested. God knows the poor gal has little enough that does take her fancy. You present him to her. Tell him to talk quietly for once.'

When Catherine told Dudley Forrrest that he was going to be allowed to meet her mother he said, in an emotional voice, that it was a great honour. Catherine did not need to ask him to lower his energetic voice: he was gentle and respectful when she took him into the sickroom. Verena was charming to him and he made her smile.

Later she told her daughter that Dudley must be invited to stay for a weekend.

'Mother, you are not well enough for us to have visitors.'

Verena insisted. She remembered her own courtship and marriage just then. Inexpressibly tired, often feeling very sick, she lay on her pillows and thought for hours about Alexander. In her mind he was still the young man with auburn hair, skin glowing with health, eyes shining with life, who had taken her heart by storm. She remembered the first time he had chastely kissed her, pressing his lips three times on to hers. It had been a moment of bliss.

But when Catherine thought about her father she saw a different man. She never forgot that he went through the war unscathed, eventually in 1917 landing some kind of staff work in Paris which was clearly a sinecure. How had he managed to go from London to Paris and back so effortlessly, even despatching de Grelle catalogues to interested officers in the trenches? And when Catherine was commanded to London to see him, there was Sara newly arrived from the South of France and wearing fashionable clothes. She thought both her father and sister disgustingly unpatriotic and used to return to Lytchett, shocked, to tell her mother that Alexander was actually still running de Grelle's and that both the auction houses were carrying out *sales*. In wartime. Alexander, she said, was even cheerful. Her mother had smiled when Catherine said, 'It is dreadful. His being still the same.'

'But isn't that just what one treasures in Alexander? That he goes on.'

'He's heartless.'

'He's himself.'

'Whenever I mention you, he looks ashamed,' said Catherine tactlessly.

'Does he? Poor Alexander.'

'Oh Mama, you are just hopeless.'

Graceful, grateful, there still remained in Verena something of the girl who had married the young auctioneer against her parents' wishes; now on her deathbed she wanted Catherine's happiness with the same gentle passion.

So Dudley Forrest was invited to a house of sickness and behaved well. He stayed a weekend. A week. Soon he became an accepted part of the household. After Verena's death he waited awhile, and then asked Catherine to marry him. Catherine placidly told him he must speak to her grandmother.

This was early April in 1920, the same week that Sara had fled from Antibes. The rain was pouring down over a sodden countryside. Leaving Catherine to go for one of her drenched rides in the woods, Dudley went in search of Lady Lytchett, privately thinking the interview so much taradiddle. He found the old lady vigorously knitting, seated in what was called the winter drawing room.

'I – well – the fact is I just asked Cath to marry me,' he said, sitting down and giving his self-conscious grin.

'No surprise in that. She said yes, I take it.'

Dudley said that she had. In the talk which he followed he confessed that he would not, for the time being, be in a position to keep his future wife. He described his not-very-brilliant situation as the owner of a small London gallery, then added some boastful descriptions of his brilliant future. Nothing he said surprised Lady Lytchett, she knew it already, and nothing disturbed her. Men in the past had married Lytchett women and lived on Lytchett money. Clicking with the knitting needles she said, 'I am willing to oblige you as far as money is concerned. For the present, that is. What is more interesting to us all is that my granddaughter will one day be rich. She will inherit a large portion of de Grelle's. The only trouble there is that Alexander de Grelle will spite us by living to be a hundred.'

He burst into a loud laugh, then with a switch to solemnity said how much he appreciated all Lady Lytchett had said, spoke of the honour of marrying Lady Verena's daughter and so on. The old woman listened with impatience. I suppose he feels it's expected of him, she thought, studying his hair which had a satin quality, although he used hair cream which she abhorred. His good skin was rather pale but with a tinge like faint sunburn. He had excellent teeth. A masculine-looking male. Powerful shoulders, flat stomach, long legs. He should breed well. One of her ancestresses had been given the curious duty of being in the bedchamber, witness to a royal coupling. Lady Lytchett did not in her thoughts actually stand by her granddaughter's future marriage bed to watch Forrest heaving away. But stationed herself approvingly outside the bedroom door.

It was agreed that Dudley and Catherine should marry in about a year. In the meantime when not working in London, he could make his home at Lytchett, and stay there at any time and for as long as he wished.

Catherine much enjoyed her engaged state and discussed with Dudley and her grandmother when they should put the announcement in *The Times*.

'You would be very foolish not to speak to de Grelle first,' said Lady Lytchett. 'You need the ruffian on your side.'

Dudley laughed. He laughed a good deal at Lady Lytchett's remarks. They made an interesting contrast, the handsome cowboy of a man with his Australian accent and the big, jewelled, powerful old woman. When they played chess, she could not beat him. Old as she was, she was conscious of his sexual attraction. You can see it at once, she thought. Is Catherine in love with him? I suppose she must be. But Lady Lytchett had seen her own daughter fall in love like a woman throwing herself over a cliff. Catherine showed no such signs.

Dudley, at ease in his dealings with the old Countess, talked to her as if she were young and beautiful.

'I see you're wearing the pearls again, Lady Lytchett.'

She touched her neck, scraggy as that of a tortoise.

'I certainly am. They must be worn as often and as long as possible. I make my maid wear them when I don't wish to. Pearls must be used to look their best. And don't –' she added, her voice like the rap of a fan 'make an indecent joke. I can see it in your face.'

'I do apologize.'

'You lack taste, my dear. It shows in your choice of paintings.'

Ignorant as a peasant on the subject of art, living in a great house filled with masterpieces, Lady Lytchett's eyebrows were often raised to her hairline when Dudley showed her pictures he had bought at country auctions. Gloomy mountains. Farm carts. Broken windmills. Tumbledown cottages and farm children playing by dilapidated fences. Where, she enquired, were the Alma Tademas? Dudley's choice was stuff. But she liked to hear from Catherine that he had later sold the things in Davies Street, and always enquired at what profit.

Now Dudley was part of her life, Catherine came frequently to London and stayed with her father in Park Street. She introduced Dudley to him one evening; Alexander was in a hurry and it was no more than a brief greeting. Alexander accepted the appearances of his elder daughter without question; he was much occupied with a coming sale of considerable interest: a collection which had belonged to a German baron killed at the end of the war. Catherine seemed content enough, and he saw little of her. He left home early each morning, and spent the evening either at dinner parties with Lee, entertaining at home, or giving evening views to clients interested in future auctions. At other times he was in Paris, and more recently in New York. He and Catherine had a certain modus vivendi: live and let live. He had not changed his opinion of her since she was a stiff little thing of twelve years old.

The Lytchett family had not invited him to Verena's elaborate funeral in Sussex. Catherine wrote to inform him of her mother's death in four lines on mourning paper edged with black. She did not come up to London for some weeks, but when she eventually reappeared, she expected him to speak about her dead mother. He said nothing.

Ever since the divorce so many years ago, he had never spoken of Verena to Catherine or to anybody else, including Lee Becker. Locked somewhere inside him was a painful guilt at what he had done to the eager girl he had married for reasons of state. But he thrust into dungeons any emotion which had the power to hurt him. He lived in the present and slightly into the future. The fierce competition with other auction houses in Europe, the holding together of the coloured strings of his two businesses in his broad hands, these absorbed him. So did an idea which had first taken root in his mind during the war. He had heard of the famous New York sale in 1916 of 'Art Treasures and Antiquities from the Davanzati Palace in Florence'. Alexander knew that for years the palaces and ducal villas, even the churches in Italy had started to send their treasures, not to London or Paris but westward to New York. Among the most successful of these cargoes to come under the hammer of the legendary auctioneer Kirby was the Davanzati sale. Alexander, hearing the total netted at the sale, grew thoughtful. His banker friends in New York had also told him recently that in the last ten years, the United States' imports of antique works of art had risen from $78,000 to over $21,000,000. New York was again in the grip of auction fever. And where that fever raged, Alexander needed to be.

He was a man of French realism and Jewish energy, and he

was making daring plans. He was vigorous, shrewd, a natural impresario, a natural salesman. The objects he sold, the price he won for them, always excited him. But like a palette upon which some colours are simply missing, he lacked sentiment. Yet the imprisoned thrust-away guilt about Verena remained ... it forced him unjustly to give his elder daughter a very liberal allowance, whereas to his favourite and younger girl he scarcely gave enough for her to pay for her silk underwear.

Unlike her grandmother, cousins and other members of the Lytchett clan, Catherine bore her father no malice. *They* had never forgiven him, and as he grew richer and more notable, they disliked him the more. Catherine accepted her position as the daughter of an eminent man. She had her reservations, but no intention of cutting off her nose to spite her face.

It was now necessary to get her father's approval of her marriage. She and Dudley were both keen about this, and she planned carefully how she would break the news.

Catherine had always been a planner. She planned her appointments and her opportunities, her wardrobe and her social dates. She planned to meet this one and that. She planned her future. She was never *not* planning and Lady Lytchett once said that if she could manage it, Catherine would plan where she was going to sit in Paradise.

It was a serious and jarring blow when she arrived at Park Street to find her sister installed in the house.

With the pious hope that Sara would be out of the way, Catherine dressed for dinner. She rang for the parlour maid to help her, having discovered that Kitty was clever with hair. Kitty, thin, eager and elderly, dressed Catherine in black velvet, arranged the young lady's soft brown hair in becoming coils on either side of her cheeks and fastened the small diamond necklace. Catherine descended the stairs in a stately manner, the long skirts sweeping behind her. She had telephoned de Grelle's earlier, and asked Miss Tomkins to arrange that she should see her father this evening before he left for the country.

Yes, said Georges in reply to her enquiry, the Master was in his study. He was too old a hand to look curious.

Sitting at his bureau, Alexander called, '*Entrez.*' He stood up, greeting Catherine as if he had not seen her for weeks. It amused him to ask after her health: he knew she was as strong as a horse.

'Sit down, my child. There is something you wish us to discuss? Very well. We have twenty minutes,' he added, looking at one of his French clocks, a particular favourite on which a cherub seated on a swing moved the minutes merrily to and fro.

'Father. I would like to become engaged. I would like your permission to marry.'

She was nervous and her voice was more than usually metallic.

'Indeed. You gave me no inkling of this.'

Before she could speak, he held up his hand.

'Yes, yes, I know that's out of fashion. Young women these days, I am told, particularly when they are – how old are you? Twenty-five?'

'Twenty-seven.'

'*Tiens*. Women, as I say, begin to make their own decisions. Freedom is in the air. Tell me about this suitor of yours. I gather it is the young man I met the other evening. Forrest? Was that his name?'

Alexander looked at her with benevolence: the soul of paternal kindness.

Catherine relaxed and talked briefly about Dudley, placing him in a good light and mentioning the Mayfair gallery. Alexander nodded, pulled at his beard and said he would be happy to speak to the young man.

'Ask him to arrange it with Miss Tomkins,' he added.

He glanced covertly at the swinging cherub. Catherine was no conversationalist and had always bored him. After a pause he enquired about Lytchett. Although never speaking of Verena, even now she was dead, he invariably enquired about the house. It was as if he expected it to fall down.

'Your grandfather's death must have made a difference to the family, is it not so? That outrageous People's Budget as they called it. I remember what a shock it was to us all at the time. A blow to the nobility. Dreadful. And of course now it begins to show. People die. Great houses must be sold. Any time your family wishes to sell, my child – I recall some good pictures and *objets de vertu* – I would be honoured for this to be done through de Grelle's.'

It was something he had been unable to say when Verena was alive.

'I'll remember, Father.' Catherine's tone had a meaning as loud as a shriek. Her father was being vulgar. His eyes hardened. He was never put down by anybody, least of all by a chit of a daughter.

A more cheerful thought struck him.

'Have you told your happy news yet to your sister? No? Then we must tell her together.'

It was as good a reason as any for getting Catherine out of the room. 'You have already seen Sara, have you?' he asked.

'We had tea together,' said Catherine, which was not strictly true.

'Good, good. Let us go and surprise her.'

But the drawing room was empty.

'Aha, I think I can guess where she is hiding.' His manner had changed, he winked facetiously and tiptoed over to the door of the library, opening it with a flourish.

'Just as I thought. Pillaging my books again; just you put them back exactly where you found them. Come along out, Sara, your sister has something to tell you.'

Sara emerged, looking questioningly towards Catherine who, disliking her father's theatrical tricks, said nothing.

'The girl is shy,' said Alexander. 'What do you say to this, Sara. Our Catherine is to be married.'

Sara's face positively shone. She went over and took both Catherine's hands.

'How lovely! Lots and lots of congratulations. Oh, I know in England one isn't supposed to congratulate the girl, but in America we do. How lovely, Cathy, I am so happy for you.'

With a not very successful attempt at a smile, Catherine muttered something, relieved when her sister let go of her hands. How effusive Sara was.

'And Sara has some news too,' added their father, playing the role of parent for all it was worth. 'I have a notion she has not told you yet either. Secrets? Tut tut, we can't have those.

102

Your young sister, Catherine, has talked me into allowing her to work in my business. She began in de Grelle's this very morning. What we have to see now is if she has the stomach and the art for it. She is going,' he added heartily 'to be made to work like a dog.'

My sister, reflected Sara as she changed for dinner that night without the ministrations of Kitty, was distinctly not pleased to see me today. And why did she object to my working at de Grelle's? She's getting married, and she certainly would not want to be employed as I am. She would think it *déclassée*. Girls like Cathy don't earn their own living. That's what she still thinks ... Arranging her tawny hair, the thought came to Sara that there had never been any kind of news in the past concerning herself about which Catherine had not looked annoyed. It was as if Catherine wished her to stay in a sort of vacuum without a sniff of competition. Unreasonable, thought Sara. What with Mother in Antibes and Cathy in London ...

She deliberately took a long time to dress, not wanting to run into Catherine again. Her father had left, she heard the front door slam. However much Georges tried to see his master out in style, Alexander beat him to it and slammed the door so loudly that the house shuddered to its foundations.

Tonight Sara decided on one of her new Molyneux dresses, white satin edged with black. She thought she would call up Lee who would give her dinner of sorts, talk of painting and be amused to see the frock they had chosen. Sara was debating whether to bring Perry van Rijn into the conversation. Did she mean she wanted Lee to arrange for Sara to see him again? No, I don't, thought Sara almost fiercely.

She looked critically at her heavy red hair and fastened on some drop pearl earrings. When she left her room and came down the staircase, a young maid was crossing the hall.

'There's a gentleman called, miss. Said he would wait to speak to you,' said the girl, who was newish. 'Mr Vazin (she meant Georges) is out on an errand for the Master.'

'I am not expecting a gentleman, Rose.'

The girl indicated the drawing room, did not open the door for her, and vanished like a rabbit down the kitchen stairs.

Wondering which of her father's clients was going to be disappointed, Sara went into the room.

Perry van Rijn got to his feet.

'I hope you didn't mind my waiting. I only wanted a quick word.'

It was such a shock to see him that she felt quite sick. She needed every one of her five wits to manage a cool, 'You came to see Father? I'm afraid he left some time ago. For Gloucestershire. He won't be back until Sunday evening.'

'Yes . . . your maid said . . . perhaps I might call him up if somebody has the number? I could call him tomorrow, perhaps.'

'Of course. We'll get it for you. Do sit down, Mr van Rijn. May I offer you a cocktail?'

Her face, with its radiant pallor, was as calm as his. Her dress shimmered.

She rang the bell and the nervous Rose brought some drinks; Sara had been taught by Jean-Claude, and mixed the Manhattan herself. She put the frosted glass down beside him on a table.

He sat looking up at her for a moment, not touching the drink. Then he leaned back and said, 'You're the Domino, aren't you?'

Sara went scarlet. Her pale face was so suffused with colour that she looked as if she had been scalded.

'I thought you – you hadn't recognized me.'

'Did you?'

Slowly, slowly, the blush began to ebb.

She said, 'I can't imagine how you knew. It's a long time.'

'To you, perhaps. Being young.'

'You're so elderly, are you?'

She managed a smile.

'Considerably older than you, I imagine. Of course I recognized you the moment I came into this room. Your hair. Your figure. You could have taken off the mask, you know. One saw very well what you looked like.'

'I enjoyed wearing it.'

Silence.

It throbbed.

104

'I don't think' he said carefully, 'your father would be exactly overjoyed if he knew.'

She was about to say something impulsive, she had no idea what, when a chill went through her. She thought – I was right. He is changed, just as everything is changed; he isn't the soldier who made love to me. He's afraid his business will be damaged if Father found out what happened between us.

She twisted the stem of her glass.

'Oh, Father knows precious little about me, or my sister either. His daughters appear in his life only at intervals. I'm in London now because I am going to work at de Grelle's. But he still knows nothing much about my life and I certainly wouldn't tell him. He's easily bored.'

'Not by a daughter, surely.'

He's relieved, she thought with contempt. Her feelings were flags in a fiercely veering wind – they blew violently in the opposite direction. She sipped the cocktail: it was too strong.

'What interests my father is opening a branch in New York. What do you think about that, Mr van Rijn? Is it a good idea?'

He accepted the change of subject. The red-headed girl sitting opposite him had skilfully removed the tenseness from the air.

'Oh, he is naturally the best judge,' he said. 'Your father has tremendous flair. Everybody admires it so much; it is what he goes by. And needs all the time.'

'In this case apparently he also needs you.'

'Or someone like me.'

You have a poker face, Perry van Rijn, she thought. I don't want to play cards with you and I wish you would go.

'I don't understand much about banking . . .'

'Why should you?'

'Oh mercy! Please don't say it is not a subject for a woman. Things are different now. Hadn't you noticed? And women are different too.'

'I'm sorry. That was clumsy. I didn't mean . . . but what do you want to know about banking, Miss de Grelle?'

'Call me Sara.'

He gave a polite inclination, a sort of nod. They talked pleasantly enough, emptily enough. The negligent-seeming man described banking as: 'Tides of money, you know, which wash around the world looking for good strong harbours with stout walls.'

'Do you think de Grelle's might be a safe harbour in New York?'

'That's what we are considering, Miss – Sara.'

'So that is the message you want my father to have? I'll give it to him, if you like.'

He really laughed at that. No, he said, nothing so simple. It wouldn't do to leave messages about anything as complex and delicate as finance.

'But I thought,' said Sara, refilling his glass, 'I thought that was why you waited. To give us a message to give to Father. Oh no, you need his telephone number, don't you? I'll get it.'

She was about to stand up and ring the bell again but he said casually.

'That wasn't exactly why I waited.'

Oh God, thought Sara.

'You mean you waited for me,' she brightly answered.

'Yes.'

She said nothing.

'Domino –' Perry suddenly said and came across to her, lifting her by her elbows straight into his arms. He kissed her, opening her mouth with his tongue. As he pressed against her she could feel through the satin dress that he wanted her. She returned the kiss as hungrily as he. Her head began to swim. When the kiss, which lasted a long time, finally ended he said in a blurred voice, 'We can't – not here –'

'No, we can't,' she murmured, thrusting her hand into his thick hair.

'The house where I'm staying. Everybody's away.'

She was too far gone even to ask questions. She thought of nothing, nothing, but possessing and being possessed. He pressed himself against her again, then said in a different voice, 'Let's go.'

They took one of the horse-drawn cabs waiting at the corner of the street and Sara did not remember the journey, only the sound of the horse's hooves in the empty Mayfair streets on the spring evening, and Perry van Rijn's kisses which seemed to go on until the cab suddenly drew to a halt. They climbed out, into a square of tall plane trees and old houses dozing in the twilight.

He paid the cab and took her to a corner house. She faintly noticed it was very old and shabby. The steps were cracked, the front door paint blistered. Much she cared. She was so excited that she felt faint. He was silent. He opened the door and took her into a house which seemed as if it had never had another occupant – if her father's house was quiet, this one was in thrall. 'Upstairs, Domino. Don't look at me like that. Not yet.'

Bending, he took her in his arms and carried her up the winding stairs to a bedroom, a large bedroom heaped with books and silks, like a bedroom in an opera.

They undressed without taking their eyes from each other, Sara clumsily undoing satin buttons, van Rijn throwing jacket and trousers to the ground. When they were both naked she thought – how strange – last time in the Roumaniev gardens it was dark and I did not see what you looked like. His skin was pale honey colour, the muscles of arms and shoulders heavy, his waist narrow as an athlete's. She ran into his arms.

CHAPTER EIGHT

Perry van Rijn left for New York on the White Star *Olympic* three days later. Before that he and Sara visited the house in the square every day at lunchtime. Sara, like all de Grelle employees, had fifty-five minutes of liberty, from one o'clock until five to two each day. Perry collected her in de Grelle's reception hall. They scarcely spoke on the ride to the house. They sat silent, not touching. The drive every day was so exciting that she could scarcely breathe. It was the knowledge of what they were going towards, the tacit understanding between them which made her tremble. Part of her was terrified at the intensity of her desire for him, her entire feelings, her self, the self she had always owned and commanded, fell helpless in front of him. She wanted nothing but to be naked, sprawling, open, possessed. She was too far gone to notice that he told her nothing of himself, that he was silent after their sexual union as well as before. When they finished, gasping, sweating, the time was so little that she could only just pull on her clothes, pin up her heavy hair and – Perry was swift to dress and always ready before she was – almost run out of the house to where they knew there was a rank of motor cabs.

'Tomorrow?' he would say, bidding her goodbye without touching her, at de Grelle's door.

After three days he did not say it. Instead he murmured that he would see her tonight at Park Street for dinner. He was sailing with the tide, from Southampton, the following morning.

The dinner, one of her father's banquets for prospective buyers, went by for Sara in a meaningless haze of talk. Perry sat at the far end of the table, talking to Lee who was on his right. After the meal Lee played the piano, and the guests sat around drinking coffee and liqueurs. Sara thought Perry could come over to her, but he didn't. When he rose, from a long conversation with Alexander, it was her father who brought him over to Sara.

'Say goodbye to somebody who may well become an important friend of de Grelle's,' said Alexander, patting Perry's shoulder. 'I've always had, don't you know, a paternal feeling for my bankers.'

Perry laughed, showing his beautiful teeth. He took her hand. He did not press it, and scarcely met her eyes. In what seemed a moment, he was gone.

She wandered over to the piano where Lee, her rings and bracelets lying on the piano lid, was playing Chopin. Lee smiled at her, her intensely blue eyes very kind.

'You have been looking distinctly peaky in the last few days. Great black shadows under your eyes. Shocking. You could use some sleep. Is it old Gilbert Travice?'

'Don't you like him?' said Sara, trying not to think that this minute the space between Perry and herself was widening and widening. Inside, she sobbed.

'Who likes Gilbert?' said Lee. 'He's enough to drive one crazy. But he's as good an introduction as any to a rough world, Sara. Keep that handsome nose to the grindstone. That is the smart thing to do.'

Sara wondered, feeling the excruciating pain of heartache, how she could be strong enough to take the advice.

Why did I do it, she thought, as she lay in bed that night, why did I let him have me again, why feel that I'd die if I did not have *him* again? What happened to me? All her instincts told her, now that it was too late, that Perry van Rijn was dangerous. How do men manage it, she thought, how can they make love without emotion and only for the sensation? Behave with such sexual passion and simply take ship to New York? Having him in her body and her arms had meant too much to her, too little to him. She couldn't regret the love-making, but remembered it with a kind of disbelief. He was so demanding, so exciting, so exquisite, so intense a lover. How could he do it and not mean it? It was a question as old as the world and there was nobody to answer it for her. She felt inside her as if a child sobbed in a dark room.

With a different kind of fierceness now the sex was over, she put her mind and body to work.

The man Alexander had chosen to train her, the de Grelle expert in late eighteenth- and early nineteenth-century Europe, was Gilbert Travice. The moment Alexander introduced her to 'Your tutor – Mr Travice,' Sara's heart sank to her shoes. Travice bowed and smiled, but both pleasantnesses were only directed at her father.

Gilbert Travice was ageless: perhaps fifty, perhaps over sixty. He was rather stout, with crinkled yellowish-grey hair and the face of a disapproving prissy old woman. Through gold-rimmed glasses his pale eyes were enlarged, and when he looked straight at people, which he rarely did, it was a shock as if a fish were regarding you through a bowl. He was not popular anywhere in de Grelle's, and was brilliant at his work.

The office to which he took Sara on her first morning with him was larger than Guy Buckingham's. It was at the back of the building on the ground floor, overlooking a dark paved courtyard and a plane tree. Like Guy's the room had the air of moving-day. There were piles of boxes on shelves and tables, packets on Travice's desk and the floor, and along a bookshelf a row of Della Robbia plates decorated with dragons and roses.

Travice removed some parcels and allotted Sara a small table too close to his desk. Before she had time to fish out a pencil, he gave her a homily.

'I am sure you realize, Miss de Grelle, that the task you are to learn is not easy. One might say it is more than usually difficult. It needs ability, and first and last, and all the time, accuracy, accuracy and more accuracy.'

He beat on the desk with his hand.

It was fortunate for Sara that she had Carl Bauer's collection as the shot in her locker, for it was obvious that here was a man who had no intention of teaching her anything.

'Let me understand the position, please,' he said, when she mentioned that she was writing to Carl. 'You are familiar with the Napoleonic collection belonging to Mr de Grelle's friend, this Mr Bauer.'

'Oh, my father doesn't know him, Mr Travice. Carl is a great friend of my own.'

He digested this while arranging clean sheets of blotting paper, which he demanded should be provided each day by a lady clerk in some outer office.

'And Mr de Grelle has decided you are capable of preparing the catalogue? In French and English?'

'Only with your help. I shall need that so much. And be very grateful indeed for advice,' murmured Sara with the diplomacy that rarely left her. But whatever he was thinking, Sara could see, was not to her good.

In fact, Gilbert Travice had been so shocked when his employer told him of this young woman's arrival in his life that he had not slept a wink all night.

He asked Sara some searching questions about the collection. She answered promptly. He considered the replies and asked some more. She knew he wanted to nonplus her, to discover gaps in her knowledge. So far, he failed. Sara thought she heard in his voice a positive longing for her to prove an ignoramus forced to return to wherever girls like her came from. He looked at her over his spectacles.

'I hope you understand exactly how crucial this work is,' he said, relinquishing for the moment his game of snakes and ladders. 'A cataloguer has to be an expert. It is absolutely essential. Remember at all times that if you make an error it does not hurt *you*. The man it will damage is the auctioneer on the rostrum. A mistake in a catalogue description – well –'

He shut his eyes.

'It could be detected by a man considering a purchase. Somebody could go so far as to mention the error *aloud* during the auction! Do you realize what that would mean?'

'Whatever it was wouldn't fetch its price,' said Sara cheerfully.

'Miss de Grelle. We are speaking of something more than selling an object. We are dealing with knowledge and reputation. Accuracy and depth. The de Grelle name for scholarship, for absolute honesty, a record unblemished.'

Perversely because he praised her father's business, she wanted to contradict him. It wouldn't do, though. She wished to please this infuriating vain old man, who must have in his head things more valuable than all the books along his shelves. A hoard, a golden hoard. Besides, Sara did not meet her enemies straight on. She liked to negotiate and persuade, and thus to win. She respected and disliked the man.

At present meekness was all she could afford, and a quickness of comprehension which Gilbert grudgingly allowed. He did not find more than ten faults a day in the first pages of her Bauer catalogue, and these were of presentation and rarely of facts. He did not allow raciness and deplored adjectives.

'But don't we want to sell, Mr Travice?'

'All we do is to state what is offered at auction. A Regency rosewood mantel timepiece in a lancet-shaped vase, and so on. The style, Miss de Grelle' with a mixture of pity and sarcasm, 'has altered since James Christie was called the King of Epithets. We don't applaud at sales now. Nor do we praise in our catalogues.'

Sara never answered back. His sometimes-brilliant knowledge of some obscure point on Napoleon's France impressed her. She trained herself to bear it when he read her work in a disapproving silence punctuated by sighs. Travice was a door into de Grelle's, in a way.

But for all her imaginative understanding of men and women, she had no idea just what a shock she had been to him. Gilbert Travice was settled, self-satisfied and utterly absorbed in his work. To find a young woman cluttering up his office was the worst blow he had suffered since the Zeppelin raid destroyed a storehouse of rare books in 1916. Travice was deeply middle-class; women should not be allowed to work in de Grelle's even as typists. They were the softer sex, with whom he'd had little connexion since his mother's death. Through his work there spread the images of women . . . their billowing hair and swimming eyes, their rosy nipples and beckoning hands. They stared at him from painted canvases, thrust out their bronze or sculpted marble breasts towards him. He never connected such beauty with breathing, living women. *They* had no place in his world, let alone being allowed into his office. At auctions they were merely present to encourage men to spend money.

In the upper classes to whom his work was directed he was aware that women had power: often it was they and not their men who ruled. Gilbert was not interested. The nobility had never impressed him, and when he saw them crossing pavements spread with crimson carpets, towards distant music, he sniffed.

But horror struck into his soul when Alexander de Grelle decided to allow his daughter to work in Gilbert's office and to prepare the Bauer catalogue. He tried various tacks with his employer. He pointed out the impossibility of the catalogue not being written by a Frenchman.

'My girl is bilingual, Mr Travice,' said Alexander kindly.

Gilbert retreated to his second defence. Surely it was essential for the collection to be catalogued on the premises? A member of the Paris auction house should be sent down to Antibes.

'It is Monsieur Bauer's friendship with Sara which has brought us the sale. Without her he would not have placed it in our hands. And she knows the collection backwards.'

Gilbert did not know that Alexander had spent two hours cross-questioning Sara. He had slipped from French to English and back again; asked her questions which contained traps. She had not fallen into one of them and appeared literally unconscious of the change of language, running her American-English into her American-accented and idiomatic French. Later Alexander wrote to Carl Bauer and received a satisfactory reply.

He was sorry for poor Gilbert who accepted the decision that Sara should work in his office as if hearing of a cataclysm.

Carl's first consignment arrived on Sara's desk three days after she joined Gilbert. The parcel from Antibes contained pages and pages of tiny handwriting, some of it illustrated with grotesque caricatures, figures with balloons coming out of their mouths, and references to events discussed with Sara over the years.

'Yes, yes, don't waste my time. A catalogue in two languages! An alarming amount of work to be accomplished; please apply,' snapped Gilbert when Sara showed him her booty.

He was more vexed still when half an hour later the fattest of the de Grelle porters appeared.

'Message for you, miss,' boomed the porter, shattering the British Museum atmosphere into fragments.

'What are you doing here? Go away,' exclaimed Gilbert, making a shooing gesture as if at an intrusive bullock.

Harry stood his ground.

'Sorry, Guv'nor. There's a lady asking for Miss de Grelle most particular.'

'For me, Harry?' said Sara, who knew all the porters by name and liked them.

'Wouldn't go to Reception, straight she wouldn't. Guess where I found her,' said Harry confidentially, ignoring Gilbert's angry face. 'Poking about in the basement all among some silver of Mr Buckingham's. Took her out of there very sharp, I did. She's stowed away nice and tidy in the big storeroom. Wouldn't wait in the viewing gallery, miss. Friend of yours. Wants a private word, she says.'

With a hasty 'I won't be a moment, Mr Travice,' Sara went out with Harry who guided her down the stairs.

In the basement were the cellars, cleared and rebuilt and heated, where packing case after packing case, crate after crate, were stored and later brought up for the destiny which awaited them in the auction rooms. There were statues, vast paintings, ghostly-looking mirrors, even an Egyptian mummy case. In the largest of the storerooms, standing in front of a gigantic picture of a battle at sea, was a girl. She was dressed in black and white. Seeing Sara, she came running, arms outstretched.

'So it is you! Guy swore it was!'

'*Fay.*'

The girls kissed and burst out laughing. Harry, with a fatherly nod, left them to it.

Fay Nelson, blonde as a Scandinavian, resembled a slender fifteen-year-old boy. Her figure was thin, the way she stood gawky, her eyes were round and blue and a small hat covered most of her fair hair. She patted Sara's arm.

'I couldn't believe my luck when Guy said Mr de Grelle's daughter was working here. Of course I've known Guy forever, he's a sort of relation, Daddy adored him so one can't *tell* him anything because he gets that worried look. Oh, Sara, we can't talk here with those awful ships firing at each other. Look at all the sailors who've fallen in. Do you think they will be drowned? Can you creep out and have some coffee at Rumelmayer's?'

'Not possible.'

'But you're His Majesty's daughter!'

'To put it more exactly, I am his wage-slave.'

'You are a fool,' said Fay admiringly. 'Then if you won't creep, what about luncheon? Shall I come and get you?'

Sara said that would be nice and added, remembering a house in a lost square, that she must be back on the stroke of two.

'I shan't get you back until dawn.

"Three o'clock in the morning
We danced the whole night through!" '

sang Fay.

'Alas, no chance. I really do have less than an hour.'

'I'll be here on the dot of one. Can I be a minute sooner?'

'Not a minute.'

Fay giggled as if at a music hall turn, exclaimed it was topping to see Sara, and that she would be waiting.

When Sara went back to the office, Gilbert had gone out. She sat down, smiling to herself and thinking of the unexpected reappearance of her friend. She had known Fay Nelson for four years during the time they had both been at school in Montreux. Fay, somewhat younger, had been her favourite friend. She was incapable of learning French or putting her mind to any kind of study, and Sara let her crib her essays, and sat next to her at more difficult courses, prompting her like a ventriloquist.

'Why are you so nice to me?' asked Fay, smiling blissfully.

'Because one can't help it.'

'See? That's nice too.'

The grave German tutors, the temperamental French teachers, the art teachers, even the stately headmistress could not understand the combination of Sara de Grelle and Fay Nelson. The girls were as different as chalk and cheese. That was what Sara enjoyed. She liked, almost loved, Fay's view of the world, the way she skimmed its surface like the creatures on village ponds called boatmen. It wasn't possible to imagine Fay hurt or heartsick. Her parents spoiled her. So did Sara. Fay was always busy with a new dance and a new tune. She consulted Sara about everything: letters to her parents, which clothes to wear, which lessons to cheat at and – a favourite topic – her latest revenge joke.

'Do you think, since she split on me to Mademoiselle and I owe her for that, I might creep into the dormitory this afternoon when everybody's out and sew her nightie hems together at the bottom in tiny weeny stitches?'

During the last two years at school, strings of admirers lined up for Fay. She needed advice about those too.

Sara lost touch with her during the war.

'You know silly me, I don't write letters,' Fay once proudly told her. Occasionally, when visiting her father in London, Sara had telephoned the Nelson house in Chester Square. There was no reply. Then one time she did get through to be told by a butler: 'Mrs Nelson is indisposed at present, miss. Could you ring again in a month or two?'

But when Sara did, the telephone rang in what must have been an empty house.

It was extraordinary to think she had not seen her schoolfellow since before the war – eight years. And more extraordinary that Fay seemed unchanged.

The black and white figure was in the entrance hall as Sara hurried down the marble stairway.

'I've ordered us something at Gunter's. Let's walk fast,' said Fay, pushing her arm into Sara's. 'I do believe you meant it about having to rush back.'

'I'm afraid I did, but it is lovely to see you.'

'Much lovelier, *me* seeing *you*,' said Fay with what Sara thought a somewhat ominous emphasis. It made her wonder.

During the meal which Fay had already chosen, she had a

116

gift for small graces, they agreed that eight years were impossible to bridge. Sara suggested exchanging some basic facts. She told Fay she had left the Riviera, and come to work for de Grelle's.

'That's all about me, really. Oh yes. During the war I did work, of sorts, in Antibes. I visited a convalescent home every day, to try and amuse the officers. Chess, and writing their letters. Things like that.'

'I wanted to drive a lorry but it was too heavy,' said Fay. 'Mummy was ill, too. I was in the country a lot. We used to roll bandages. Both my parents are dead now, Sara. I'm an orphan.'

She paused, spoon in hand, from eating a strawberry ice cream.

'I don't feel like an orphan. But how to know? In the pictures it's usually Mary Pickford and she gets jumped on by huge men like that porter at de Grelle's and she sort of shakes and trembles.'

'I'm sure huge men want to jump on you.'

'Don't mock. Sara . . .' coaxingly.

'Mmm?'

'I suppose you've guessed I want a favour. You know silly me. I always did, didn't I, and you always helped with my French and all that.'

Sara was intrigued. What could Fay, materializing out of nowhere, possibly want so soon?

'Your father's place sells things. Guy Buckingham says they sometimes get big prices. I was wondering if you . . . I mean de Grelle's . . . might manage to sell this old thing?'

She opened a little flat black satin handbag on which was the initial F in diamonds and pulled out a packet of tissue paper. Undoing it, she produced a small ivory figure which she put into Sara's hand.

'Horrible, isn't it? A king or something. My father said it came from China and his grandfather brought it back centuries ago.'

Sara placed the figure on the table. It was wonderfully and elaborately carved, crowned, holding a spear so thin it could have been a thread of stiffened cotton. The king was in armour, even his miniature feet covered in elaborate patterned mail. The ivory was yellowish and felt like silk.

'Fay, I don't understand.'

Fay rounded her eyes.

'Of course you don't, darling, why should you? I know I'm a meanie springing it on you when we haven't met for a hundred years. When Guy told me about you . . . of course I couldn't ask him to sell it because of his being Daddy's friend . . . but when he said about you I thought – Sara to the rescue again. Do you think you could be? To the rescue, I mean.'

'But why –'

'Don't ask,' said Fay, looking ceilingwards. 'I'm broke. Utterly stony. Isn't it tragic?'

Fay told her in more detail about her family. Her father had been killed in 1916 in the Battle of Jutland. 'He was quite a hero, you know?' Her mother had been ill a long long time and had died last year. Fay waved to a waiter for more coffee. The gold sunburst clock on the wall of the restaurant told Sara she had fourteen minutes left. Fay ate a sugar lump dipped into black coffee. She had scarcely touched her meal.

'But I thought your family was rather rich, Fay,' said Sara, getting to the point.

Fay fidgeted.

'Who's rich? All those death duties and things. How furious Daddy used to get, saying it was as bad as Oliver Cromwell, I never understood what he was talking about. What I do understand, Sara darling, and it's staring me in the face, is that I'm stony. Everything's in trust. Everything's tied up. I mean, it's like that man outside theatre queues who's all covered in chains. But he always wriggles out. That's what I can't do. The parents left me that huge great house in Chester Square where I was born, it's so old-fashioned. I'd move out tomorrow if I could. Imagine the bliss of a flat. White satin cushions and being wafted up to one's front door in a silver lift decorated with cockatoos. But I can't move out. I can't do anything until probate and the horrible lawyers say not then. I'm stuck and I need money, darling, who doesn't? *You* must,' she went on guilelessly, 'or you wouldn't be working and having to run at the end of luncheon, poor you. If I can't get

118

my hands on the money in the bank, 'cos Daddy stopped me, the only thing is to sell some of the rubbish in Chester Square. When Guy told about you I thought – what ripping luck. Sara was always so kind. Darling, you will, won't you?'

The long speech ended and Fay fixed her blue eyes on Sara.

Sara did not return the look. She was studying the ivory king who was standing where Fay had now put him, on a hill of sugar lumps.

'I don't see why not . . .' she said slowly.

Some weeks later, having made a friend of the man who dealt in ivories and discovered, not to her surprise, that the king was very old and valuable, Sara had him inserted into a sale of such things. The king was sold for two hundred pounds. Fay was jubilant.

Sara began to attend a number of the auctions as the spring moved into early summer. She needed to get her father's permission to do this; she went to see him in his office. Alexander, looking like a large tortoise-shell cat playing with a mouse, said, 'Which auctions?'

'As many as I can.'

'I prefer my experts to keep away from the sales.'

'I know.'

The cat's velvet paw was in the air.

'Every auction I go to will make me cleverer,' said Sara reasonably.

He lowered his eyelids.

'Very well. *Allez*. Off with you back to Gilbert, if you please.'

Despite Gilbert's hostility to this decision, Sara went to auctions of drawings, musical instruments, cameos, armour, silver. She developed a dangerous taste for the sales, and often found it difficult to go back to her desk, or to sit down at work on Carl's cramped lists when she knew there was an auction in progress of oriental carpets straight from the *Arabian Nights*. She rationed herself to two auctions a week. Her figure darkly and expensively dressed, she always left her despised overall in the ladies' lavatory, her hair glinting, she became familiar to the de Grelle staff and to many of the regulars in the saleroom. She was very still, sat at the back, and left so silently that nobody saw her go.

One rainy morning at the beginning of June Sara slipped out of Gilbert's office and made her way to the main saleroom. She took her place, thinking as she'd done many times, that the big well-proportioned room with its high windows and skylights was like a conservatory. It was crowded today. The chairs in rows, ranged as at a concert, were all taken. Objects to come under this morning's hammer were distributed round the room on tables and in corners. There were some Waterloo chairs, an intaglio-topped marble table, an unusual glass clock like a vase, with ormulu mounts, and a row of white vases, south Staffordshire, dated by de Grelle's as 1755, the opaque glass patterned with oriental scenes of courtly ladies, exotic flowering trees, hunters and flying birds. The viewing had been on for ten days, and Alexander had given one of his elaborate pre-sale dinners to which he had invited two important dealers. Both were interested in the vases, painted in *famille rose* in imitation of contemporary Chinese porcelain.

As Sara watched people consulting their catalogues or simply staring into space, she noticed they never looked towards the things about to be auctioned. They had studied what they wanted days ago, pricing them, making decisions as to the ceiling beyond which they couldn't, even dared not, go. Like lovers, they now refused to catch the eye of the beloved.

Two people came into the room just then; Sara had a stab of interest when she saw it was her sister with a man. It must be Dudley Forrest whom Catherine was going to marry. The announcement had been in *The Times*.

'Catherine, daughter of Alexander de Grelle and the late Lady Verena de Grelle', her address merely Lytchett, Sussex. You couldn't, thought Sara, be grander than that.

She looked covertly across the room, curious to know what kind of man her sister had chosen. She saw somebody tallish, paleish, broad-shouldered. Sara had known young Americans with figures like that. I bet he could play baseball, she thought. There was something about him, she was not quite sure what, which did not seem to match her sister's style. Sara puzzled over it. In her mind she had imagined her sister engaged to some negligently well-dressed man with a kind of unselfconscious arrogance. Upper class. But the man with her sister, muttering in her ear and occasionally grinning, looked like a handsome bank clerk.

The auctioneer, short and fair and infinitely better bred than Dudley Forrest, took his place in the rostrum.

There was the usual total silence.

'Lot One. A pair of tiles.'

Porters in baize aprons, including her friend Harry, bore each object to the foot of the rostrum, held it up for the auctioneer who said 'Thank you'. Then the porter carried it to face the customer. Patterned medieval tiles. A looking glass. An enormous Majolica plate. Two tiny silver vases. The porter stood facing the buyers, as if the objects were on trial.

'Fifty pounds. A hundred pounds. More?' said the auctioneer.

Bang went the ivory hammer.

Infected as always by the mute tenseness and excitement of an auction, Sara's rationed half hour was soon over; she must return to work. She slipped quietly to the door, just as Catherine and her fiancé also rose. Outside on the landing, free of the religious hush, Sara went over to them and said cordially, 'Cathy, I didn't know you were back in town. This must be –'

She turned with a smile and the man stretched out his hand.

'Dudley Forrest. Glad to meet you, Sara. I'm engaged to Cath, as I'm sure you know.'

He was exactly as Sara had thought him at a distance, but more self-conscious. He had fine grey eyes which he fixed on Sara as if swearing eternal brotherhood. As they talked he laughed a good deal. Catherine listened, looking at Dudley and not at Sara. Catherine was dressed with her usual subdued good taste, in a pale suit and a high-necked white silk blouse. Her well-bred appearance was a contrast to her companion.

'I'm afraid we can't stay,' she said, breaking into Dudley's comments on *famille rose*. 'We're already late. We have a luncheon appointment.'

She never said with whom or where.

'Some of Cath's relations may be persuaded to buy a picture or two,' said Dudley, laughing. 'We're out to tempt them. I daresay Cath's told you about my gallery near Claridge's? I came this morning thinking I'd brighten up the place with a vase or two, but the prices are right out of my reach. The water colours too.'

'Dudley buys at country sales,' said Catherine. 'Now, Dudley, don't start to talk again, we must hurry. Goodbye, Sara. Come along, Dudley, you know how I dislike to be late.'

Catherine had broken her own rule about not staying at Park Street more than once during any week. Dudley had finally obtained an appointment with Alexander. Of course Alexander came across him at times in the house, but never for more than a few minutes. Catherine, for once, was nervous about the coming interview. She wanted Dudley to shine.

She was perfectly aware that he was not a gentleman, as she phrased it, but that was what she liked and disliked in him. His free and easy manner got on her nerves but she admired his cheek. Under the boyish forty-year-old charm he was ambitious, and she needed that. The old ways were dying, thought Catherine. Her grandmother agreed with her. To be prosperous one must move with the times, and those were out of joint.

People her mother would never have met in her life were welcomed at dinner parties. Conversations about sex were actually heard in drawing rooms. Girls smoked in public and drank cocktails. Dudley was Catherine's life-belt to keep her in the swim, in a river which was flooding and sweeping away the war and its heroes. To be brave, to have suffered, was no longer fashionable.

It would be serious if Alexander did not like Dudley. Although she had never been close to him, Catherine was impressed by her father. He was so wealthy and celebrated. She still held him responsible for her mother's death, but this did not come into her considerations. He was important to her. If he took against Dudley, the sun would go in. Fortunately there was no sign of Sara on the evening when Dudley was due to talk to her father.

She waited for Dudley in the drawing room. He came striding in, grinning.

'Are you sure that suit is all right?' she said, looking him up and down. 'Father notices everything.'

'It is the one we chose at Hawkes. I think it's very good.'

The suit was pale grey. His shoes were highly polished and brown.

'Oh, I don't know,' said Catherine dubiously. 'You look, well, frankly you look too well dressed.'

He laughed but his eyes were not amused. He was vain of his good looks. Catherine played with her engagement ring, diamonds and onyx in the newly-fashionable platinum.

'You will remember to let Father talk, won't you?'

Dudley walked over, pulled her to her feet and kissed her. She stiffened, not because she did not enjoy embracing him, but from nerves that Georges or the parlour maid would come in.

'Dudley, don't.'

'Passionate little thing, aren't you?'

He knew very well he could rouse her.

'Cool down, Cath. Do you imagine I haven't met people more important and a damned sight richer than your father? I can do this with my hands tied behind my back.'

'Don't be too sure.'

Georges appeared, to say the Master would see Mr Forrest in his study now, sir.

'You'd think I was going up for a hundred lines or a whacking, wouldn't you, Georges?' said Dudley to the butler. The Frenchman gave an unamused smile. Catherine was too fretted to notice her betrothed's bad taste.

Dudley swung into the hall in the wake of Georges's neat figure. Free of Catherine's nagging, he was filled with sharp interest and confidence. He liked difficulties. He enjoyed sailing when the winds were dangerous, excelled at games in which a quick eye and brute strength were needed. He liked proving himself strong and clever. It was a challenge to see the great de Grelle alone.

In his study, Alexander was looking along the bookshelves for a particular volume, and had just found it when Dudley was shown in.

'Sit down, Mr Forrest. I will be with you directly. I've been looking for this annoying book for a week.'

'English landscape painting. I have a copy myself, sir. It is not bad.'

Alexander, riffling through the pages, gave an automatic smile.

'The George Barret reached a high figure yesterday,' continued Dudley. 'But I put that down entirely to de Grelle prestige.'

The compliment was clumsy but Alexander didn't mind. He shut the book and said pleasantly, 'I like Barret. Romantic Irish landscapes . . . Wicklow mountains . . . he shouldn't be in this book at all. He was as Irish as the shamrock.'

'But they had no Irish school of painting then, did they? With respect, I thought the price the painting fetched was pretty ridiculous. Didn't Richard Wilson describe Barret's style as spinach and eggs?'

'I see you were disappointed at not getting the painting, Mr Forrest. Well, now. Shall we talk about my daughter?'

The interview developed a distinct chill when Dudley, using the same manly approach so successful with Lady Lytchett, spoke of his lack of funds. A few hundreds in Coutts' bank and that was all. Alexander pushed him: how much exactly? And how much had he paid for the Davies Street gallery? And how much did he owe? Dudley answered frankly. His position, his finances, were less than impressive; but Alexander couldn't help liking what the English would call his sauce. He also had something which all auctioneers admire: a fine memory, an aptitude not unlike an actor's for absorbing the flavour of another's man's taste and reflecting it back. Almost before Alexander recognized the trait, Dudley confessed to sharing his own strong liking for early nineteenth-century water colours of Arabia, for an American portraitist, Gilbert Stuard, who had painted in Dublin in the 1700s, and for the rare Chinese mirror paintings.

Yes, thought Alexander. He's worth the whistle. By the time a half hour was up – despite enjoying the man's company Alexander never wasted the treasure of his time – he decided Dudley Forrest would do. But Catherine's choice did surprise him. What could she possibly see in Forrest that *he* saw? I suppose, thought Alexander who did not know his elder daughter at all, it's sex.

When they parted, Alexander said he would see Dudley again.

'We will talk about my daughter's little financial affairs. No, on second thoughts, perhaps it would be better if you saw my colleague William Thornbury. He looks after that side of things. You and he must meet,' said Alexander. 'Now I must toddle.' It was a word he had picked up from soldiers in the war. 'Goodbye for the present, my friend.'

Dudley left him, and returned to the drawing room.

Catherine had gone up to change and he had the elaborate place to himself.

He rang the bell and ordered himself a Sidecar.

'It needs' he told Georges, 'plenty of Cointreau.'

CHAPTER NINE

The unlikely figure of Fay Nelson, getting in the way of de Grelle porters and replacing the smell of dust with Chanel No. 5 in the storeroom turned out to be a figure of destiny for Sara. Quite suddenly, Sara was possessed of friends, inundated with invitations to dine and dance, with letters inviting her for country weekends – and with men.

Fay was loud in delight at having found her again.

'Lucky me,' she said, telephoning Sara at work, to Gilbert Travice's chagrin, 'to have discovered my chum again.'

'Fay, I can't talk now.'

'Of course you can't. You're working. I only rang to say come and have cocktails this evening. Say yes, say yes.'

At the close of a wet working day, the rain had stopped and there were roses in Hyde Park, Sara, free of the hated overall, swung down the street towards Belgravia. London had a festive air as if the great city had taken a deep breath and begun to enjoy itself. And so had she, glad of the chance to be with someone of her own age who was not her own sister. Catherine was much at Park Street, but never had a proper conversation with her. She irritated Sara every time they met. I suppose I should ask Lee's advice about her, but advice to do what? – thought Sara. To get some kind of civilized friendship going between us? If Cathy doesn't want it, and she certainly doesn't, I must lump it.

There was another reason, loping along in the soft evening past the eighteenth-century Sloane Street houses with their thick black railings and closed faces, why she was glad to meet Fay again. She had been violently affected by the flare-up of sex between Perry and herself and anything, anything, was welcome to stop her desolate thoughts.

From the time she was a child she'd prided herself on not crying when she was hurt. Once in London Catherine had unwittingly slammed a door and squashed Sara's fingers. It had been the horrified Catherine, not Sara, who had wept. Sara had stuffed her poor hand into her mouth and borne it. She wouldn't cry now. It had been so unimaginably wonderful to have her lover again. When she remembered the fast-fading sensation of his body plunging into hers, she still had the feeling that she was plummeting down in a lift. Why should I agonize and mope now? I am behaving like my mother. I wanted him, and I had him as he had me. And now he has gone. She pushed him out of her thoughts as if she were shoving him physically out of a window to break his neck.

Fay Nelson lived in Chester Square in a large tree-shadowed pillared house in a square belonging to the Duke of Westminster. The houses had a grave air, like embassies. The door was opened by a middle-aged parlour maid with an embassy-staff look about her, who began to say Miss Fay would be down shortly when there was a scream from the top of the stairs.

A dragonfly in orange and red came darting down.

'Sara! I thought you'd forget, you have *so much more* important things to think about. I've been telling Bobbie how I found you, well, it was Guy of course but he'd have kittens if he knew I'd actually come to your father's place. I shan't tell him. He's a pet but he fusses rather. He reminds me of my old bear, except it's only got one eye.'

Fondly kissed, Sara was taken upstairs to the drawing room by her chatting hostess and introduced to a man who was florid, fattish and fair.

'My clever best friend,' said Fay pointing at Sara, 'and this is Bobbie who loves me madly.'

'Don't we all?' said Bobbie, pouring Sara a cocktail.

The evening began with the cocktails, went on to dinner at the Carlton with a number of Fay's friends and ended back in Chester Square where young men, by now collected into a sort of gang or orchestra to accompany Fay, rolled up the Aubusson carpet and played American jazz on the gramophone.

Fay's high spirits, her rounded eyes surprised at everything in the world from a compliment to a dearth of horse-drawn cabs at four in the morning, were infectious. People caught her mood. She had a kind of profligate generosity of spirit, invitations poured from her like paint from a tube. Sara soon found it was a mistake to admire anything Fay owned. She gave it to you. Within a week of their meeting again, Sara was part of Fay Nelson's life as if they had never separated.

To Sara, who had escaped from being a daughter in Antibes to being a different kind of daughter in Park Street, Fay's total lack of older people in her life was wonderfully simple. She epitomised the freedom in the air now. Of course Fay did not have a 'job' as people called it nowadays. She was free by chance. But she caught her liberty in both hands like a skilful cricketer seeing the ball shooting towards him. Fay matched the times.

Speaking about her parents, 'Of course I adored them and they quite liked me,' she described how they made her take a chaperone when she went out with a man. Imagine the fogeyish idea. Fay and her girlfriends went anywhere they chose with men. The air tingled with sex.

The Chester Square house she had inherited from her father had been built in the 1840s as 'a small residence for a gentleman'. There were twelve bedrooms, a high-ceilinged L-shaped drawing room and a library. The house was designed to be run by a regiment of servants, with maids to carry the coal and clean the brass rods of ninety-five stairs, and for the thriving, humming, leisured – or slavish – life of the past. In the dining room hung portraits of Fay's family, distantly related to England's heroes: admirals with predictably blue eyes, ladies with enviable pearls. The curtains were of a rich Admiralty blue and so thick that when pulled together they swung like curtains in a theatre. The library at the back of the house was crammed, shelf upon shelf, with volumes on the history of the British Navy.

Fay lived in her house like a bird who has flown in through a window: open it and the little thing will fly out again. Every time she visited Chester Square, Sara was surprised to find her still there.

'Here's my one chum,' said Fay when Sara called on a May evening after a particularly difficult day with the catalogue.

'One of these days I'll arrive and discover you've gone,' said Sara, sitting down on the bed.

Fay was fastening her suspenders, front and back.

'You don't think I don't *long* to, darling. But I've told you I am penniless. Hard up. Haven't a bean.'

With one leg bare, the other clad in the newest flesh-coloured stockings, she gestured at a tiny beaded handbag.

'Do you know what's in there? Ten bob. Just enough to tip Charles at the Carlton to keep our corner table.'

'Fay –'

'Which reminds me,' said Fay hastily, sensing she was going to be offered some commonsense, 'You see that really ghastly clock? I was wondering if de Grelle's . . .'

Fay's admirers, never less than two and usually half a dozen, appeared to be late this evening and Sara saw the chance to speak about Fay's growing passion to sell things. So far Sara had successfully sold the ivory king, and a week later Fay appeared at the auction rooms with an elaborate silver cigarette box. That had been Edwardian, and fetched little. Only Georgian silver kept its value. The clock Fay now pointed at, shaking her head in pity, was on the wall facing the window. Sara had often looked at it, enjoying its gilded curlicues and had noticed – she hadn't commented because Fay would yawn – that it wore like a star at the top of its head the gilded raying sun of *le Roi Soleil*.

'It must be Louis XIV' said Sara, going over to look.

'Daddy said so. I remember how I groaned that there's no minute-hand. I thought it was bust, but Daddy said they often didn't have minute-hands on clocks then. Daddy said they thought minutes didn't matter a bit,' said Fay, laughing. 'I think they do sometimes, mmmm, don't you?'

She gave Sara a naughty look.

Sara wasn't to be steered from the point.

'I'm sure it is valuable. Perhaps very.'

'Hooray.'

'But it is part of your home. Your inheritance. You can't go on selling everything in sight.'

'Just watch me.'

'*Fay!*'

'Oh dear, are you going to be serious? You're as bad as Daddy's lawyer, Mr Lavery. Or Guy. It's all my parents' fault anyway. My money' said Fay, sighing, 'Is tied in knots. How am I supposed to exist, I would like to know? And I've always hated that old clock with no minute-hand. If you'd be a saint and get rid of the horrid thing, I can put my collection on a shelf there instead.'

Sara grimaced. She knew that if de Grelle's did not sell the clock, Fay would dance along to King Street and offer it to Christie's. She agreed to ask one of the de Grelle experts to come and look at it.

Fay was immediately all sunshine.

Her friend's desire to get Sara to help her sell her possessions was the only flaw in their renewed friendship which, like a magical door opening into a garden, took Sara into enjoyment. Fay knew everybody. Her father had been a distinguished sailor, her godmother a friend of Margot Asquith's, her countless friends were the rich and the not-so-rich young. Her girlfriends flocked to London from their country houses for the Season; they all rather resembled her but they were none of them so vivid or filled with so volatile a gaiety. They were schoolgirlish, found life 'awfully ripping' as they clattered up and down the stairs at Chester Square.

One strange echo of the Great War sounded like a muffled bell in the appearance of the young girls. It was their passion for wearing beige. Beige silk dresses and suits. Beige evening gowns with ribbons and frills. Beige straw hats tied with trailing chiffon. The colour was a pale echo, a very ghost of khaki.

The young men who drove up to Chester Square in their Duesenberg Roadsters or Sports Rileys were as irrepressible and idle as Fay. Nobody seemed to work, and Sara's employment at de Grelle's was mentioned with a drawling, laughing '*I say!*' The men who were not helplessly in love with Fay were invited by their youthful hostess who would say beforehand, 'Jack will just do for you, Sara, as a spare.' Fay spoke of her men friends as if they were parts of the cars which often, with peals of laughter from their owners, broke down.

Men fell in love with Sara too. They were attracted by her extraordinary looks, her tawny eyes and red hair which, daringly, she was thinking of cutting short. Another stronger reason for the male admiration was that Sara seemed accessible. They guessed she was not a virgin. Yet for all the passionate embraces in cars, motorcabs or the slower clip-clopping horse-drawn growlers and hansoms which made their way gently down Park Lane, Sara did not go to bed with anybody.

She knew they continued to hope. She intended to go on refusing. What was that disgusting French expression, she thought, having escaped yet another desiring male at four in the morning, and slipped into the Park Street house to safety. *Allumeuse*. Is that what I am now?

Fay watched with approval, Lee with sardonic amusement, the procession of men chasing after Sara. There was Jack, the tall son of a baronet, who was a wonderful dancer, and Larry who made her laugh. There was Nicholas who knew about painting, and Pat Isaacson who was large and kind and almost speechless with love of her. There were young men with money and young men in debt. Not one stirred in her that longing, that restlessness, that hunger and thirst that had come to her simply sitting in the same room with Perry van Rijn. She liked her men friends, and loved nobody.

Coming into Gilbert Travice's office, buttoning on her dark overall one June morning after a crazy Chester Square party which had not ended until dawn, Sara felt distinctly frail. She swallowed a yawn which, together with the fatigue, vanished when she saw Travice was going through her work. He put down a sheaf of pages.

'I would like a word with you.'

She sat down.

'I think' he said slowly, 'No, I don't think, I have decided that you must give up this work.'

Sara felt as if he had flung a bucket of cold water in her face.

'What can you mean?'

'I mean that it will not do. Mr de Grelle informs me that the

Bauer collection is to be auctioned in the rue Royale next month. This –' contemptuously 'is due to go to the printers at the end of the week. What have you been doing with your time, pray? Certainly not working.'

Silence.

'I am sorry,' said Travice, triumph in his thin voice, 'but you must pass the whole thing to me. It is most inconvenient, considering the burden of my own work. But there it is.'

Sara's mind was racing. She had leaped ahead, seen her father's reactions, knew she could not count on his support. She was furious with herself. She hadn't a single argument to advance, and how could she throw herself on the mercy of a man so pleased to be rid of her?

'Packet for you, miss', said the post boy, swinging into the room and slamming a lumpy envelope in front of her. It was covered in French stamps.

The boy winked and swung out again. Sara picked up her paper knife and opened the parcel thinking – oh Carl! Please, please, send me *a real mess*. She tipped the papers out on the table in front of the watching Travice.

Carl's reply was not to one but four of her letters and Sara could not have invented anything so blessedly complicated and, to anybody but herself, incomprehensible. The lists, the comments, were in such chaos that nobody but Sara could have sorted them out in less than a couple of months. As usual the letter was full of information but peppered with private jokes, with references to the times they had spent together, to visits they'd made to museums or libraries, to objects about which she had questioned him and to which he replied in their secret language.

'Remember how badly our *general* was paid when he was commanding near Antibes that time? Don't forget Madame Mère doing the washing (may be in the Count's diary but probably not), and didn't the girl steal the artichokes? Or was it both girls? You'll remember because it made you laugh. That little silver helmet, now. It's Caroline's, not Pauline's, and don't forget I haven't either of their shields. Try page 117 of my notes, no, they'll be later. You'll manage, *ma chère Sara, because you always do*.'

Sara handed the letter to Gilbert. She was grown-up enough merely to look concerned.

After Sara wrote to Louise explaining that she was going to remain in London, Louise wrote crossly back, washing her hands, she said, of Sara's future.

'You may tell your father that he can cope with you, for I certainly won't.'

Alexander, to whom Sara gave a mild version of the letter, thought it amusing. Unlike the old guilt about Verena, he had no such feeling about Louise. He'd heard all about the procession of her lovers. He thought it might be entertaining to send Sara to Antibes for a spell of work with Carl Bauer, just to annoy Louise. Lee Becker dissuaded him: she thought the idea spiteful.

Although Alexander's two daughters were his heirs, up until now he had never had a deep interest in either of them. He was too busy, and in any case the role of father did not suit him. He liked the light to shine upon himself. But now his second daughter, who resembled him in a number of ways, was permanently in his London home. Working at de Grelle's too. They met for dinner sometimes and talked shop. The smell of her scent, the smell of expensive womanhood, had never been part of the Park Street house until now. Lee no longer needed to tug his sleeve to remind him he was a parent. Not to Sara anyway, although Catherine remained an indulged stranger.

While he was playing with the idea of sending Sara to Antibes, it occurred to him that now summer had begun to burn down on the Midi Sara's mother would have left and there would not be a fashionable soul in sight. More amusing still that Sara would have to live alone in the Villa des Roses, annoying the absent and money-minded Louise. He sent for Gilbert Travice.

'How is my daughter shaping up?' he enquired confidently.

Travice's reply was non-committal. Pressed by a now suspicious de Grelle, Travice said that he did not think she was exactly pulling her weight: she did not apply, he said. Alexander, now a thunder-cloud, burst out that if his daughter was not earning her keep she must go, and would Travice give him a report on the state of the catalogue at once.

Carl Bauer's long convoluted letter arrived in the nick of time. Sara's bacon was saved. But she'd had a fright. She realized only when it was almost snatched from her how much she wanted to go on working at de Grelle's. She liked the very shape of the building. She loved the auctions, they were like the theatre or bull-ring. It touched her lively imagination to know that hundreds of precious things poured into her father's galleries from all corners of Europe. Books with thick calfskin bindings, some with golden clasps. Suits of armour standing in the storeroom like phantoms. Boxes smeared with dust, filled with the love-letters of famous people and still, thought Sara, damp with their tears. At dinners and private views she was allowed to meet some of her father's business connexions, and learned of auction-room friendships. She met Alexander's friend Joshua Wolfe, an elderly bachelor, American, rich, whose main occupation was collecting.

Wolfe did not, like many collectors including Hearst himself, hoard the things he bought in warehouses and unpacked boxes after he acquired them. What Joshua bought he arranged in his New York house, his Paris apartment or his London chambers. He talked like a historian, and retained a certain glee at every new acquisition. One evening at Park Street he spent an hour talking to Sara about a set of eighteenth-century coloured prints of the *Cries of London* which he had bought at de Grelle's.

' "Knives, Scissors and Razors to grind," ' he quoted to Sara, his faded eyes twinkling, 'and there's "Hot Spice Gingerbread, Smoking Hot".'

'A man in Park Street sometimes goes by shouting "Muffins," ' said Sara. 'He rings a bell.'

'Well, young lady, I am glad to hear it,' said Joshua gravely. 'He sounds full of pep. But don't you kid me into believing he wears a tricorne hat.'

Sara met French dealers, English lords, German collectors – and American millionaires. In such company she was on her mettle: she glittered like her hair.

But now, alarmed by Gilbert Travice for the first time,

Sara had to forget even such pleasures as invitations from her father, let alone from Fay. She began to work in earnest. She worked long hours, stayed until after the rest of the de Grelle staff had gone home; Gilbert Travice privately said to Guy Buckingham, 'It can't last. Women have no stamina.'

Persuading the Head Porter to let her have a key to St Charles Street, Sara worked at weekends. The catalogue manuscripts grew thicker, Sara paler. At last both its French and English versions were ready. One morning an hour before Gilbert Travice arrived, Sara sent the packages straight to the printer.

'They've gone,' she said, as Gilbert came into the office.

'Indeed. You do realize Mr Bauer will go through every line. And if there are serious mistakes –'

'Off with my head,' said Sara. She was pleased with herself. Her first, perhaps her only catalogue. Her father had twice said she was only working with Travice 'to watch the wheels go round.'

This time, she thought, I pushed them.

With her desk swept clear she unbuttoned her overall, symbol of slavery, and went down the corridor towards the saleroom. As she arrived by the double doors they swung open and she heard the familiar 'Sold!' and the hammer-bang. A man came through the doors. He stopped when he saw her. It was Dudley Forrest.

'Why, Sara. May I call you that? We'll be related one of these days. Were you going to the auction? Not very interesting. Too much fancy furniture and not nearly enough paintings.'

'But the Constables. How did they go?'

'Too high for my sights. Do you like him?'

'Not much. Father said I'd best keep my opinions quiet when they are so ignorant,' she said, and laughed.

'Yes, one has to get one's eye in. Mine's getting better. There was a time in Australia when all I looked for was great big oils.'

'Who by?'

'Nobody in particular, it was size that counted. Stags on Scotch mountains. Waterfalls. Boats at sunset. Sheep on

135

hillsides. I even got hold of one of those Biblical scenes, thunder and lightning and thousands of souls in their night-shirts. I wanted them to cover the walls of a lot of the new houses in Melbourne and Sydney. Quite a scarcity at that time of man-sized paintings, I found.'

They exchanged looks of amusement, mostly at the souls in the nightshirts.

'I expect they're importing oil paintings as big as the sitting-rooms walls now I've started the fashion. Or maybe they're getting 'em painted specially. Did you know William Vanderbilt had his pictures custom-painted? One painter, Gérome, charged so many francs for each character in the picture, and so much for each feather in the king's hat. He got mighty rich!'

He laughed, out to please and amuse. Sara was willing to be friendly but thought him somewhat over-keen. She'd been curious about him since they had first met. Catherine never gave her a chance to talk to him in Park Street, she always hurried him away.

He asked her about the forthcoming Bauer sale.

'Father says I can go to Paris with him for the auction. Nerve-wracking in a way, as it's the first I've been part of.'

'More than that. You brought it to de Grelle's.'

'Sheer chance really. I happen to be a friend of Carl Bauer's.'

'Nothing more useful than a friend in the right place, eh, Sara?'

'Or a father,' she said.

'True. Particularly a de Grelle.'

When they parted she decided she quite liked her future brother-in-law, in spite of the egregious manner. It was surprising that her sister was marrying a man as tough and sexy-looking as Dudley Forrest. Catherine would kill me if she knew what I'm thinking, but I bet he improves her. She'll get softer. She might even be friendlier, thought Sara with twenty-three-year old optimism.

CHAPTER TEN

Catherine and Dudley had arranged to spend a long weekend at Lytchett; she had only visited London to order some clothes. They had both been invited to friends of her family in Scotland in August and Catherine decided she had no suitable tweeds. Nor, she pointed out, had Dudley. There was a good deal of visiting the Lytchett's tailor in Savile Row.

Like a magpie putting shiny things into its nest, Dudley picked up some of the upper classes' curious rules. Not only about the right club, Brooks's in St James's to which he must wait to be elected, but having his shoes made at Lobbs, and other, odder, regulations. One must remember not to shout for the servants ('what are bells for?' said Catherine). One must put up with the precedence at dinner parties, with people of rank at the best part of the table, the top, and people like Dudley somewhere near the bottom. Now entirely due to Catherine's dead grandfather, whom Dudley had never clapped eyes on, he noted that he was moved up a few places. It was rum.

Settled in an empty first-class compartment of the train, Catherine looked critically across at her fiancé. He was the best-looking man she had met for years, the cleverest and the quickest. She prided herself on her choice. She reflected that one of these days she would approach her father and suggest he gave Dudley a position at de Grelle's. After all, Dudley was an expert on early nineteenth-century water colours. And as Dudley himself somewhat vulgarly put it, 'I only need to get into the building. After that, leave it to me.'

Dudley was rather quiet, staring out at the woods in full summer leaf. Catherine would not have been pleased if she had known what he was thinking. It was about her sister. The thoughts were not sexual, although he admitted to himself that he would like that red-head lying under him on a bed. But he wasted not more than one hot fantasy over that. He was sizing up Sara as an antagonist. He knew his Catherine and Sara was nothing like her; it was scarcely credible that two women so dissimilar should have come from the loins of the same man. He thought of Lady Verena, so delicate and over-bred. The sort of women he was half sorry for, half awed by. Thank God Catherine had more spunk than that, though he had seen that her mother was a nicer, sweeter woman. He did not object to Catherine's core of hardness – he preferred it. But that other girl was too bright by half. She looked at home at de Grelle's, she behaved like an old campaigner. Of course she'd probably picked up some of her talk like a parrot before she'd been in the place five minutes. Dudley had the same knack himself. But . . . she bothered him.

Lytchett dozed in the late sunshine when the horse-drawn cab from the station set them down at the front door. Roses as bright as soldiers in a painting of the Crimea spread along the walls of the old house. Catherine rang the bell. Another of the rules Dudley had learned was that 'one does not need, or indeed wish to have a key'.

When the butler opened the door, a Dalmation, a Sealyham and two spaniels came rushing up, barking joyously. Catherine patted them without interest and said in a tinny voice would Parker please take the dogs back into the kitchen.

Lady Lytchett was out, and Catherine ordered tea in the summer drawing room. It was full of sweet peas.

'Home,' she said, sitting down with a pleased sigh. 'I don't enjoy Park Street very much.'

'Especially with your young sis knocking round the place.'

He sounded very Australian.

'She and I haven't much in common,' said Catherine indifferently.

'She's still your sister.'

'As you very well know, a half-sister.'

'Sure. Different mothers.'

'If it had not been for her mother, mine would still be alive,' said Catherine in a colourless tone.

'Not *her* fault though, is it?'

'Dudley,' she began. 'Ah. Tea. Thank you, Parker. Put it here. Yes, move that little table. None of Cook's spice cake? Yes, just a little . . .'

Parker disappeared, returning with the spice cake. He approved of difficult masters. Every time the young lady complained she scored a point with Parker.

When he had gone and she was pouring tea, Catherine resumed.

'Dudley, I really would prefer not to have conversations about my family. You know everything that you should know. But it is simply a subject I prefer not to discuss. Particularly since my mother has died. So – if you don't mind.'

Dudley helped himself to a piece of bread and butter.

'Sorry, Cath, but this time you'll have to lump it. Discussing your family, to be exact your sister, is what we've got to do. Hasn't it occurred to you that she's getting a darned sight too popular with your father?'

'What do you mean?'

There were times when Catherine's voice was like steel.

He smiled.

'What I mean is that your Dad is changing his mind about her. Remember you've sometimes said that when she turned up from the Riviera she played at being keen on the auction business but you didn't think he would be taken in. People must do that with him all the time, you said. *You* thought she was sucking up. It isn't like that any more. Sara has been working her guts out –' Catherine gave an involuntary frown at his language, 'for that Napoleonic sale that's coming up. And she's been a useful connexion over it too, putting it right on her father's plate. She told me –'

'When have you seen her?'

'Jealous,' he said, grinning. 'We met at de Grelle's yesterday when I was prowling about. She hove into view and we talked a bit. Good thing we did from all I learned. Just you give her half a chance, and who do you suppose will inherit that wealthy business we've both got our eyes on?'

'That's impossible. I am the elder. The heir.'

'But you're not working there in a blue overall, are you?'

* * *

Dudley was a man who knew when to move fast. He could gauge when a small dark shadow in the distance was going to turn into a tornado. It was the same when he sailed, which he did skilfully. He would judge the weight and danger of a wave. In sex he never wasted time on women whom he could see would refuse him, and his *amour-propre*, a fierce thing, would wither at a No. His instincts were strong, and when they warned him he listened.

Catherine took what he had said with a flinty face and became very quiet. During dinner with Lady Lytchett she scarcely spoke a word except when questioned by her grandmother about the visit to Scotland.

'Know how to shoot, Dudley, do you?' enquired the old woman, being served by Parker with a slice of treacle tart.

'Oh yes. I shot in Australia.'

'Kangaroos?'

'Occasionally.'

'Did you eat them roasted with onions? I hear the aboriginals do,' said Lady Lytchett who liked to goad him.

'They were mighty tough,' said Dudley not to be outdone, and yes, he could shoot. He had shot a hundred pheasants at a shoot with the Trobeville's last year.

Lady Lytchett had begun not to believe Dudley's stories. She put her attention to the treacle tart instead. After the meal Catherine excused herself. She had a headache and would prefer to go to bed. In actual fact she had suggested to Dudley that he ought to talk over the matter of Sara with her grandmother.

'Good idea. She may think of something. She's not near as ladylike as you are.'

Catherine did not reply to that, but offered a smooth cheek for a kiss and retired to her room, where she nagged her maid. Dudley had worried her. What he'd told her about Sara rang true. She was annoyed with herself for not having seen it and then, in reverse, congratulated herself for never having liked her sister. There was something vulgar about her; it must be that awful mother. Still in her imagination the wronged Verena lived, an accusing ghost, and the unknown Louise who had stolen Alexander was a painted whore.

Lady Lytchett and Dudley drank coffee and she told him to

pour himself a brandy. She picked up her *petit point*, working at it for a while in stitches so small that an onlooker would think it a miracle she did not need spectacles. But Lady Lytchett took off her glasses to look closely at things. Threading her needle, she said, 'And what's the problem?'

'How did you –'

'My dear man, credit me with some commonsense. I know Catherine had a slight headache, her eyes were strained and she went that nasty colour. But if she'd been in rude health she would still have left us. You arranged it between you. What do you want?'

Her face, haggard with the years, looked pleased at the prospect of trouble.

He swirled the brandy round his glass.

'What do you know about Sara, Lady Lytchett?'

'De Grelle's other daughter?'

'That's the one.'

'Never clapped eyes on her and don't want to.'

'She's not half bad-looking.'

'So was her mother. American, of course. Couldn't help that, though, could she?'

'Did you like her?'

'*Like* her? I detested her. Still do. Louise Goodier ruined my girl's life and I'm not inclined to ask her progeny to tea. Somebody or other who was fool enough to visit the Riviera told me Louise Goodier has begun to drink. Doesn't surprise me. No breeding.'

Dudley nodded in the manner of a man who shared with the Lytchetts the honour of high birth. She cocked an eye on him, putting down her sewing.

'What has that girl to do with us?'

He spoke in a rapid, even voice.

'She's begun to work at de Grelle's. She's hand in glove with her father and turning, or soon will if I'm any judge, into teacher's pet. Seems to me she's taking to the auction business like a duck to water. She's not a fool either.'

Lady Lytchett said nothing. She digested what he had said. Dudley waited.

'I'm not going to have that again,' she said at last. 'It isn't to be considered. The Goodier girl stole my daughter's husband. It was a disgrace. The Earl never got over it. I'm certainly not allowing her brat to start stealing my granddaughter's inheritance.'

Dudley looked at her with respect. She's a tough old bird, he thought, she could be an Australian. Now that he had met a number of these upper-class Britishers, he saw why they'd got their positions and why they held on to them. He decided to keep silent. She picked up the embroidery again.

'What's de Grelle like these days?' she asked after a pause. 'I haven't seen him since he was young. The Earl liked him. I never did.'

'Middle-aged but has kept his looks. Impressive.'

There was an unconscious ring of reverence in Dudley's voice.

'Impressive?' repeated the old woman. 'That jumped-up auctioneer.'

'He's a long way beyond that, Lady Lytchett. He knows everybody, and *they* know and respect him.'

'Everybody?' she said satirically.

'Of course. It's his business to know 'em, isn't it? And convenient for them to know him. Bankers, politicians, international collectors, dealers. Every man jack who has bought or sold at de Grelle's.'

She gave him a hawkish look.

'Envious?'

'Very.'

'Good. With enough envy, up you'll go. So in your opinion de Grelle has taken it into his head to teach that girl the business. What does Catherine think?'

'She doesn't like Sara.'

'My good man, I should very much hope she doesn't. But does she see what you see?'

'She never talks much to her, and certainly never had a chat about de Grelle's the way I did yesterday.'

'Mmm. So the girl's worming herself into de Grelle's and her father's encouraging her,' said Lady Lytchett. She picked up her embroidery and sewed for so long that the listening man grew restless.

Finally she said, 'This wants thinking about. I shall sleep on it. I will let you know tomorrow what I decide. In the meantime nothing more to my granddaughter, if you please.'

Dudley, thinking she could sleep on the problem until Christmas without it making a blind bit of difference, said goodnight and lounged upstairs to his bedroom. Along the corridor was his virginal betrothed. Much good her proximity did for a healthy man with a liking for sex after a good dinner.

Lady Lytchett believed that only lunatics and the hot-headed young acted on impulse. She went to bed, gossiped with her maid who was as old as she was, and slept for her usual seven hours. At half-past six in the morning she rang for her tea, propped herself more comfortably on her pillows, and settled down.

In the spacious four-poster bed hung with embroidered curtains, she resembled the ageing Queen Elizabeth. She had the same strong nose and high forehead, the same haughty carriage of the head. She turned the problem over in her mind. She recognized in Forrest a man who could be useful indeed. Now and then she saw the slightly blank look in his eyes which meant he was thinking of ways and means. He was greedy for power and success. She liked that.

It was illogical for her to hate de Grelle still with all her soul, yet regret that Catherine had inherited nothing of his selfish artfulness. Catherine had determination, but at present that wasn't what was needed.

Years ago she had come into possession of a fact about Alexander de Grelle. She had tucked it away as if locking it in a safe hidden behind a painting of the Lytchett armorial bearings. There it remained like money or a sword. It might be useful one day while she was still alive; and if not the information was contained in her will.

From the moment Dudley talked of Sara's position in de Grelle's, she thought of the knowledge and considered whether she would share it with him. Sipping strong tea, she reviewed the position. And made up her mind to open the safe.

She sent for him in the mid-morning. Dudley was in the summer drawing room, growing steadily more irritable from inaction. Catherine was somewhere down a passage on the telephone to a dressmaker. Dudley thought of all he could be doing with this time limping by. Outside the windows spreading as far as the Downs and beyond was Sussex. A few miles away he could well find some dusty shop where an ignorant trader would sell him a painting for a couple of pounds without knowing its value. There were country pubs where he could hear useful gossip and have the luxury of drinking alone. There was liberty. But the old woman had said she would see him so he was stuck. When she finally sent for him, he jumped up and moved fast.

She was in her husband's study looking bright and beady. She waved him to a chair.

'Shut the door. That habit of leaving doors open will be the ruin of you.'

'I expect that's because I have no secrets,' he said, shutting the door too noisily.

'Everybody worth their salt has some.'

He threw himself into a chair facing her.

She looked at him.

'We have to stop any possibility of Catherine's inheritance being in danger. That's all there is to it,' she said.

He gave a slightly incredulous laugh.

'Of course. But what can we do about it?'

'Hold your tongue, Dudley. I have something to say. This is what you are to do. Go to London and see that tailor's dummy William Thornbury. Do not, I repeat do not attempt to see de Grelle. Thornbury's the one you must deal with. He'll agree to a meeting since you are marrying into the family. When you see him, tell him you have in your possession certain information.'

Dudley stared. He simply could not imagine what was coming next.

'My own daughter does not know what I'm going to tell you,' she continued, 'and I certainly don't intend to disclose how the information came to me. It was many years ago. It couldn't have done Verena any good to know it; it would have humiliated her. As for Catherine, I will not allow you to share it with her either. Not for the present. It would be unwise to fuel her dislike for that girl.'

Dudley was fascinated.

'The fact is,' said Lady Lytchett coolly, 'the plain fact is that de Grelle never married Louise Goodier. People speak of her as his second wife. But after Verena devorced him he did not re-marry. He had no wife but my daughter. That brat of hers is illegitimate.'

Dudley and Catherine had arranged to drive to Brighton in the afternoon to visit one of Dudley's favourite haunts, the twisted alleyways and passages where all the antique dealers had their shops and storerooms. There, among a good deal of junk and cobwebs, he often picked up a bargain: some discarded etchings only his sharp eyes would discover, a portfolio of water colours, pencil sketches, even. Catherine also enjoyed poking round the shops, often literally stirring objects with the end of her parasol and wrinkling her nose.

They had luncheon at the Albion Hotel where the broad windows faced a shining Channel and the decorative entrance to the Palace Pier.

'Your grandmother thinks I ought to go to town and see William Thornbury about one or two matters,' said Dudley during the meal. An orchestra was sawing away at ten-year-old operettas. Dudley looked confident and cheerful, his eyes on the girl sitting on the other side of the table. She wore violet: it suited her.

'It's something to do with Sara, isn't it?'

'Oh, just odds and ends. A brief chat about your father's will might be a good idea.'

'Grandmother doesn't imagine he'd *change* it, does she?' said Catherine, scoffing. 'Father may be showy and foreign but he has a very strong sense of family.'

'So have you.'

'That's different,' she said. 'Our family has tradition. Father has nothing of that. But he is French and they have their own firm ideas about property. He would never pass me over in favour of Sara.'

Although she was so positive, he could see she was uneasy and even angry.

'So the matter may as well be brought out into the open right away. While your father's comparatively young and the

145

inheritance is years ahead. It just needs clarifying.'

He didn't add – 'before Sara gets her claws in the business.'

'Don't let's talk about it any more, Cath. You're looking very pretty and I shall buy you a present. What do you say to those opal and diamond earrings?'

'But they're much too expensive,' she said, brightening.

Dudley pondered a great deal about the information his future grandmother-in-law had handed to him. He thought it resembled one of the current cartoons in which some bearded Bolshevik (there was a good deal of talk about Russian spies in the newspapers) was depicted holding a bomb with smoke coming out of it.

He was flattered that Lady Lytchett had told him the secret and relieved that Catherine was not to be involved. He was being treated like a Lytchett; and besides, he liked plots. Pleasant, easy, companionable, he was naturally devious. He did not admit to himself that he told lies. He regarded himself as altering the truth rather in the way illuminators had set to work to improve tedious pages in the Bible.

Before Lady Lytchett dismissed him this morning she gave him a warning.

'Don't underestimate William Thornbury. He's a strong one.'

'Another?'

'Don't fish. I was not going to refer to you.'

William Thornbury arrived at St Charles Street at nine o'clock every morning. His secretary, a flighty girl from Balham with sparkling black eyes, set the wall clock by her employer. She was ravishingly pretty and flirtatious, but efficient. William, like Alexander, never employed plain women and de Grelle's had a bevy of good-looking secretaries, modest in dark colours. Recently (to William's private amusement) they had begun to shorten their sombre skirts; they now showed some inches of silk-stockinged leg.

From the quiet, awkward and keen young man who had shared a luncheon of grilled chops with Alexander all those years ago, and negotiated Alexander's invitation to Lytchett,

William had thickened, toughened and mellowed. He looked like a seal. His hair brushed flat on his head was still plentiful and a silver grey; his face, although narrower than those of the pleasant sea animals, had the smooth lines of a creature in its element in the ocean. Business, de Grelle business, was the sea in which he effortlessly swam. He knew the strong currents, the places of ease and danger, how rich or useless, nourishing or not worth the dive were the harvests in the sea bed. The auction business thrived, and Thornbury thrived with it.

He accepted that de Grelle's success was due first and foremost to Alexander. His friend had daring, took risks, had a cool French head and great moral courage. He was morally as brave as a lion. Not physically, though. In the war Alexander had been terrified that he would be called to the front. As the carnage went on, the lists of the dead and missing tolling like some awful bell across the newspapers, Alexander became very quiet. When William Thornbury was called up in 1916, Alexander was shattered. How could the London business manage without him? But it did. Alexander looked after it. He also, rather suddenly, blossomed into staff uniform in Paris and much of de Grelle's most profitable business at that time was in France. In the trenches, Thornbury often spent hours writing business letters, teased and approved of by fellow officers. He and Alexander discovered that collectors did not lose their passions to buy because they were fighting a war. One English lord wrote long letters to Alexander arranging a sale of miniatures, while being shelled for twenty-four hours.

All this was in the past. At present William Thornbury was deep in new complexities about opening a de Grelle branch in New York.

He was at his desk on a fine summer morning, having arrived as always on the dot. His room was sober, with few of the spoils of de Grelle's which enriched Alexander's office. William had a single painting, a view of his home city Bristol, on the plain grey walls. A thick Turkey carpet covered the floor but not as far as the walls; a band of parquet was polished by the charwoman every day before he arrived. In winter the open fire was replenished by the pretty secretary, who in summer brought sweet peas for his desk from her Balham garden.

She had just given him his post and retired to hammer virtuously at her elderly typewriter (William disapproved of money spent on office machines). Looking through his letters, he found one with 'Private' on the envelope. He slit it open with a silver paper-knife.

It was scrawled in large writing with a thick nib, was untidy and brief.

Seeing the embossed blue coronet at the head of the page and the signature he raised his eyebrows. He had not seen Alexander's mother-in-law since the Lytchett wedding in 1886.

'I'd be glad if you could spare ten minutes to talk to Dudley Forrest, who is the bearer of this letter. Doubtless you are by now aware that he is betrothed to my granddaughter. I take it you are still in your position of family trustee. If this has changed, would you be good enough to inform D.F. with whom he should be in touch.'

There were no regards or sincerelys. Merely the initials C.F.L.

William rang the bell for his secretary.

'Is there a gentleman waiting?'

Yes, he was in her office said the girl, slightly simpering. She thought Dudley handsome.

'Show him in, Miss Collins. And I do not wish to be disturbed.'

Dudley strode in, William's hand was wrung as if they were close friends.

'Surprising we haven't met before but Cath hasn't yet fixed her engagement dinner,' said Dudley. 'We'll hope to see you then.'

William gave the sort of nod he reserved for strangers who spoke to him in railway carriages.

'Of course you're wondering what the deuce I'm doing here, Mr Thornbury. It's simple, really. Lady Lytchett wants me to talk to you about Cath. Her prospects, if you see what I mean.'

'I don't think I do, Mr Forrest.'

'Well, of course, we're referring to her father's will,' said

148

Dudley with engaging openness. 'To put it bluntly, we're bothered.'

'And why should that be?'

Christ, thought Dudley, he's a cold one. No wonder de Grelle has kept him all these years. He'd take, thought Dudley relapsing into Australian, the pennies off a dead man's eyes.

He decided to put his cards on the table. If he didn't, they could both sit for half an hour saying nothing, or rather he would talk and the man on the other side of the desk would look surprised or pretend he didn't get the point.

'I realize I'm speaking of the future, Mr Thornbury. But the fact is that Cath's sister appearing, as she's done, changes the picture, wouldn't you say? I mean until now it's been straightforward. Two daughters. Inheritance divided in some way between them, but more of course to *the heir*. I'd consider that right and proper, wouldn't you?'

William shot him a glance.

'I cannot discuss anything as completely confidential as my partner's will, Mr Forrest. Is that the only reason for your visit?'

Dudley, who'd never thought he would get a word from him about the will, smiled.

'Well, no. Not the only reason. Something else rather delicate as it happens.'

William Thornbury was silent. What was the fellow up to? He smelt trouble. The old loyalty, steady as the flame in a sheltered oil lamp, burned in William still. What could the 'delicate' business be. For one ludicrous moment it came into his mind that Catherine de Grelle was pregnant. But he remembered her proud virginal face which he had always admired, and knew this was out of the question. Despite the changing times.

Dudley leaned back in the uncomfortable chair. He was playing for big stakes and enjoying himself.

'Mr Thornbury. I'm afraid what I am going to say won't please you. But it has to be said. I represent my fiancée's interests. Sara de Grelle is working here now, and from what I've seen and judged she's a chip off the old block. I am a salesman myself in a way of speaking, I own a gallery near Claridges. If we look at it fairly, here's young Sara up to her neck, or soon will be, in her father's business. And here is my future wife who has nothing to do with it at all. Indeed, wouldn't wish such a thing. What Sara de Grelle can do in selling and so on, Cath couldn't do in a month of Sundays.'

'Yes?' said William Thornbury. The man was too reasonable; nobody spoke like that without ammunition.

'Mr de Grelle could very well change his mind about his daughters,' continued Dudley in the same tone. 'You must see that. One so useful and bright, the other a mere passenger. A taker. Sitting there accepting de Grelle cash and giving nothing back. But she *does* give something back by existing. She is Alexander de Grelle's daughter.'

'Mr Forrest –'

But Dudley was in full flood and talked him down.

'In plain English, Catherine is his only legitimate child. She is his heir.'

There was a pause.

William Thornbury did not blink an eyelid.

'Where did you hear such a story?'

'From an unimpeachable source.'

'Have you told Catherine?'

'Let us say – not yet.'

Thornbury thinned his lips. His face, the seal's face, showed nothing. Dudley admired him for being able to blank his features so. There wasn't a sign whether Thornbury knew the story, believed it, or thought it poisonous nonsense.

Dudley waited with a glittering interest.

'You realize,' Thornbury finally said, 'that repeating such a thing is actionable?'

Dudley rubbed his chin. He still couldn't make out what his opponent was thinking.

'Of course. And I've no intention of repeating it. If you mean to Sara, by the by, I wouldn't be such a fool. I mention it to you now because of my natural concern, and Lady Lytchett's, for Catherine's future.'

It was diplomatically spoken.

William Thornbury said slowly, 'All I can say, Mr Forrest,

is that my partner has strong feelings about inheritance. Catherine as the elder will certainly be the person to have precedence. You and Lady Lytchett may set your minds to rest about that.'

It would do for the time being. Dudley stood up.

'I'm glad we've nothing to worry about. Thanks for seeing me.'

'Good morning,' said William Thornbury frigidly. And rang for Miss Collins.

When he was alone, William sat lost in thought. So it was out at last. He did not bother to ask himself how the Lytchetts had got hold of the secret. After the divorce they probably used private detectives; the upper classes never minded underlings dirtying their hands. He sat thinking of the past, once so passionate, now diminished into a sordid story used by that mischief-maker who had just gone.

He thought for the first time in years about Verena when she had been young. How often in the past he had asked himself if she might have weathered the storm of her husband's obsession with another woman if she herself had not been a person of honour.

Alexander was a sensual man. He had always known his power to attract as he knew his power to succeed. His business proved him of high consequence. With hands metaphorically filled with sovereigns, his male allure at its most potent, his violent love impossible to refuse, he won Louise Goodier. It astounded William that his friend bedded the virginal American heiress out of wedlock: another proof of Alexander's irresistible force.

When the divorce, savagely refused by the Lytchetts until the shameful fact of Louise's pregnancy was common knowledge, became final, William and Alexander had luncheon together. They met at a beefsteak house near the Law Courts. They sat, as on another momentous day when they had first met, on a wooden settle. The inn smelled of meat sizzling over an enormous grill set above a bright fire. William was hungry but Alexander, an unheard-of occurrence, ate almost nothing. William never remembered seeing him so disturbed. He drank some champagne and said for the third time, 'So it's over. Settled.'

'Apart from one or two points about Lady Verena's money.'

'We must be generous, William. Very generous.' Alexander drained his glass. 'I've told you that, haven't I?' He paused. 'Louise is now very *enceinte*.'

William made a mutter more of agreement than sympathy.

'Her aunt has gone. Left for New York. Says she'll never see her niece again. Did I tell you that too?'

'You mentioned something.'

'Louise was heartbroken. But the old lady's hard as nails. I don't mind telling you she shocked me. Louise has gone to Cannes, by the way. Staying at the Carlton until all this is done with.'

'Very sensible.'

'We've been quarrelling a good deal,' Alexander said broodingly, 'and I received a letter – of a fury! – today.'

'But why is she angry?' William was surprised.

'Waiting for the divorce, and all the trouble with her aunt, has made her dreadfully nervous. I also.'

'My dear fellow, that's all in the past now. You and Louise can forget the unpleasantness and leave the details to me. I will keep you informed of anything important. From what we've discussed, the Lytchetts will have no cause for complaint. You will see Lady Verena now and then, I daresay, to talk of your daughter's future.'

'Good God no! You'll have to do all that.'

The response was so violent that William was shocked. It offended his sense of what was right.

'But you will naturally wish to see the little girl sometimes,' he said, with reproof in his voice. It had been a grief to Alexander and Verena that their child had been a girl.

Alexander said irritably, 'Yes, yes,' and then, with a change of tone, 'Louise is sure she's bearing a son. When a woman is *enceinte*, you know, if she carries the child high . . .' In his French way, offensive to English reserve, he indicated a bulge under his own waistcoat.

'Have you both arranged the date of the wedding?' said

William. 'I expect it will be in France.' Then, to the waiter, 'A little Stilton and some celery. And black coffee.'

The waiter went away in the direction of an outsized Stilton wrapped in a snowy napkin and festive vases of celery. Alexander said, 'I am not going to be married.'

William gave a positive start.

'You're chaffing.'

'Oh no. I shall not marry Louise. In fact, I cannot. That's the reason she is so angry. But she'll get over it. Because,' he added, hooding his eyes, 'she has to.'

'But I don't understand what you are saying! What earthly reason have you for such an appalling decision?'

'So you're on Lou-lou's side, are you?'

'*Sides*, Alexander! Are there *sides?*'

William was almost speechless for a moment and then went on indignantly, 'You break up your marriage after a mere four years, you desert your wife, member of a celebrated family, and her child. You seduce a young American who is now to bear your second child – and *you refuse to marry her*.'

Alexander pursed his lips. His friend never criticized him and always used an approach which had a gentlemanly affectionate discretion about it. He knew that William admired him.

'I am sorry. The decision is made.'

The waiter arrived with the cheese. The two men were silent for a minute or two.

'I take it you are going to give me an explanation,' William finally said in a very flat tone.

'As I've given one to Lou-lou until I am blue in the face,' replied Alexander with a martyred sigh. 'It's perfectly simple. I am married. And my wife is living.'

'You *were* married. Until this morning.'

'Oh, don't talk such stuff! How can those lawyers who charge too much and wear fancy dress have *un*married Verena and myself? You recall our wedding day in Sussex. You came to the church. We said nothing about a certain matter which the Lytchetts thought an insult – but the truth was Verena and I had already married early that morning in a fusty Catholic chapel in Ditchling. We had to creep out of the house like burglars,' said Alexander, slightly smiling at the recollection. 'Old Lady Lytchett was furious lest somebody, one of the guests, should see us. In my faith' he added, 'a Protestant wedding is null and void. I had to get a special dispensation to go through that Protestant ceremony, after we had married in Ditchling.'

William knew little about Roman Catholics and was astounded that his partner was devout.

'And?' he said.

'And nothing. I am explaining that my wife is Verena. I cannot have another while Verena lives. It is plain enough.'

Plain, thought William. What's plain about it? The man is talking trash.

'I had no idea you felt so strongly about your Roman Catholic religion,' he said, looking down his long nose. He intensely disliked everything about this conversation. Most of all Alexander's questionable motives.

His friend sighed loudly and drank another glass of champagne, noticing with surprise that the bottle was almost empty.

'I don't practise my religion, I haven't done since I was twelve years old. What has that to do with it? I am a Catholic – not a "Roman", if you please. There are only Catholics, the word means universal. I am a Catholic, and in my faith a man can have only one wife. If Verena should die I would marry Lou-lou the same day. As it is – I cannot.'

'And what about Louise? Do you mean to sit there and tell me you'll subject that unfortunate young girl to the humiliation of – of –'

'I shall love her all my life,' said Alexander gravely. 'She is everything to me. The most beautiful and enchanting creature I have ever seen. I am the world's most fortunate man to have found her. But there is the matter of my immortal soul. Living with her, it's true, I am in mortal sin. But how do we know what will happen? Destiny is full of tricks. If I marry her I shall commit a sin of infinitely greater proportions. I shall be excommunicated. No, I will not do it, William. Nobody will know this. I've told Lou-lou so again and again. She can call herself my wife and yes, I will call her that also.

154

Officially, we will be married in France. Nobody will know,' he repeated, 'but you, me, and Louise. It cannot harm her or my son-to-be. And now, my dear chap, let us go back to St Charles Street and forget this conversation. The best thing to do with a secret.'

'Suppose it does not remain one?'

'It will. You and I will never breathe about it, you because I trust you with my life, I because of Lou-lou. As for her, poor *mignonne*, she has a wonderful American capacity to forget the things that hurt her.'

Part Three

CHAPTER ELEVEN

Important sales make international news, and Carl Bauer's sale caused advanced, fascinated comment in the American press, the English and German press, as well as in passionate leaders and learned dissertations in *Figaro* and *Le Monde*. Sara's two versions of the catalogue, the English and the French, were sent to Carl well in advance. Poring over them in his room in Antibes, Carl found few mistakes. The catalogues were printed and distributed both in Europe and the United States. Weeks before the sale Alexander and his head of the Paris office, Lucien Molinard, had so many meetings, private viewings, conferences and disputes that the pace would have sent two weaker men into hospital.

Sara had been informed by her father (who wore the air of conferring a special favour) that she might come to Paris for the auction. She pretended astonishment, banishing from her face the knowing look of somebody who had given him this great big plum in the first place.

Catherine did not suggest attending the Paris sale. Anything even slightly to Sara's credit – such as in the past the allure of living in the Midi – was ignored by Catherine if possible. To attend an auction of which her sister had been the instigator was not to be considered. Alexander may have guessed this. He invited her and accepted her refusal without comment.

The person loud in dismay when hearing that Sara was going to France was Fay.

For a girl whose telephone rang from morn until night, and for whom Chester Square was cluttered with open cars, motor cabs, growlers and hansoms at all hours bringing admirers and friends, Fay was outraged at losing Sara for two weeks. What would she do without her? All those parties which had been planned, Sara could not be absent! Larry, Tommy, Bobbie, Eddie, Joey were counting on Sara. Fay's men friends all had names which sounded as if they were in the chorus of a Gaiety musical comedy.

'I'll be back the moment the sale is over,' Sara said, kissing her friend's painted cheek; Fay used make-up as thick as an actress on stage and did not need a speck of it.

'That's forever. I suppose I shall have to give you up for the beastly auction. Well. I promise not to groan . . . if you'll sell the Sèvres. You will, won't you?'

'The Sèvres! You don't mean that huge dinner service,' exclaimed Sara, half shocked at her friend's rashness, half excited at the exquisite china going to de Grelle's galleries.

'Hideous stuff,' was the characteristic reply. 'Thousands of plates and dishes all covered with views. All those mountains and castles and rivers and bridges. I hate eating my roast beef bang in the middle of the lake of Geneva, don't you? Daddy said it belonged to our revered and far-distant relative Lord Nelson himself. Specially made for him or something. Daddy even liked it. He and Nelson had the most drear taste in china. You'll have to get it to de Grelle's in deathly secrecy, Sara darling. Suppose Guy found out? Well, when it's sold that doesn't matter but until then . . . I know you'll manage it,' went on Fay with beautiful confidence. 'Now let me show you something you *will* like. Joey bought it for me in Brighton.'

It was a coloured postcard by Fay's favourite artist Donald McGill, showing a man and woman both wearing bathing costumes. The man was ruefully gazing down at his own gigantic stomach.

'It's as big as a zeppelin,' said Fay, her eyes brimming.

Under the picture was printed: ' "And how's Willie?" '

' "Wish I could tell you, dear. Haven't seen my little Willie for years." '

Lee Becker was coming to Paris with Sara, to see the fun, she said. They were not staying at Alexander's apartment but at the Crillon.

Years ago, Sara's father had bought a modest four-roomed apartment in the rue Chauveau-Lagarde and furnished it in the Parisian style of the 1890s. His parents, after their son's rich success, had been able to move back to Alsace twenty years ago. They had been invited to stay in the apartment once or twice. But he introduced them to nobody. The apartment was always kept in readiness for him and was two steps away from the rue Royale where de Grelle's Paris house stood among noble shops, facing the romantic façade of Maxim's. Alexander never appeared in his Paris galleries for very long; they were run with great flair by a man he had chosen in 1914 at the beginning of the war.

'Fortunately,' Alexander said to Lee at the time, 'he is a cripple.'

'My dear Alex, what do you mean?'

'He will not have to fight for *la patrie*.'

'Are you saying you don't love your country?'

'How can you ask? I am a son of France. Lucien Molinard has been mutilated by life. It's a fine action for me to provide him with the work for which he was born. So he will be able to serve France in his own way.'

Alexander knew a good thing when he saw one. Molinard was a tall stooping man whose hip had been misplaced at birth; there had been operations but they made his limp worse rather than better. He had the air even when young of a diplomat, and now in his late forties of a senior minister. His thick greying hair was brushed back in two wings on either side of a thin and sardonic face. When not on the rostrum he never stayed serious for more than five minutes, and even grave business talks were shot through with a deflating humour centred on himself and everything else. It did not surprise Lee – or Sara either as she grew to know the Paris galleries – that Alexander was less involved with the rue Royale than with St Charles Street. The answer was Lucien Molinard. Alexander visited Paris, discussed, suggested. He never took over. And it was Lucien who would take the rostrum at the Bauer sale.

Auctions were part of French life. Since the 1850s there had been auctions every afternoon for nine months of the year at the vast Hôtel Drouot where the contents of private houses were sold. People could buy anything there, from a broken perambulator to a Louis XV commode. Dealers, collectors, big crowds of sightseers jostled together, the atmosphere was raucous and the noise indescribable.

Dramas happened at the Drouot. One dealer, Jacques Helft, desperately wanted a rare ewer coming under the hammer. Too wise to bid himself, he asked a friend of his, a diamond dealer called de Haan – sharp as his own diamonds – to bid for him. The first lot was a collection of battered saucepans and the auctioneer suggested twenty francs. De Haan bellowed forty. He went on shouting, bidding against himself and paying ludicrous prices for ten lots of valueless rubbish. Nobody wanted to bid against a madman. By the time Lot Twelve, the precious ewer, came up, de Haan bought it for a tiny fraction of its value.

The de Grelle galleries had none of the rumbustiousness of the Drouot but the auctions were certainly fiercer than at St Charles Street. Frenchmen could show their feelings and often decided on that luxury. Whether at the Drouot or the rue Royale, art experts by government decree had to be present at every auction, to agree if requested the authenticity of anything sold. If the buyer could later prove these omniscient men wrong, there was a special fund to give him his money back.

Carl was diverted at the prospect of experts mulling over his collection and heavily pronouncing their opinions. In his many letters to Alexander (Carl detested the telephone) his attitude was a schoolboyish, 'Just let 'em try to prove me wrong, that's all I say. Just let 'em try.'

They did. They niggled over an ugly gold bracelet which was said to belong to Napoleon's oldest sister, Elise. They demanded proof that her husband Félice had given it to her. Carl produced a faded letter from Jérôme Bônaparte, who had watched at Elise's bedside when she was dying. A letter from Jérôme was not to be doubted: he was France's final link with a glorious past.

But if the experts were eventually satisfied about Carl's collection, France herself was not. The Paris press was full of comment. 'The collection is one of the most splendid ever brought together – started by a hero of Waterloo,' trumpeted the newspapers. 'A true witness to French history and her glory.'

But rather too early for comfort the news that Carl was auctioning his *petites choses commemoratives* was a fire which began to make patriotism come to the boil. Alexander had feared just that. Were not these objects of importance to the soul of France, cried one newspaper. They were things which had belonged, portrayed or were connected with the most astounding man in modern history? Following many articles on these lines a movement began – to force the French government to buy the collection outright. To the relief of Carl in Antibes and Alexander and Lucien in Paris, the movement failed.

Public comment, though, continued to be vociferous, and Carl, Alexander and Lucien decided to put on an exhibition at the rue Royale for three weeks before the date of the auction. Distinguished de Grelle clients, of course, would have private viewings. But the public exhibition was arranged and announced.

For three weeks, Frenchmen who had never entered an auction house, even the noisy Drouo let alone the hallowed de Grelle's, shuffled into red-carpeted rooms and stood reverently gaping at the Canova marble of their hero, his incomprehensible letters, at the flags and banners, the caricatures and one lock of grey hair imprisoned inside a locket of gold and pearl.

The exhibition, meant to cool things, made them worse. Another movement was started, this time to buy outright the choicest items of the collection. The public were captured on the very steps of de Grelle's by eager young men who enjoyed a cause and asked to sign a petition. One wealthy landowner, an ex-colonel in the artillery with the *croix de guerre*, travelled to Paris from Bourg-en-Bresse to interview Alexander and Lucien Molinard. *He* wanted to buy the entire collection and present it to the Musée de Versailles. Or better still to a specially prepared gallery in Les Invalides.

'But you have not yet seen the collection,' said Lucien.

'I have studied the catalogue and consulted many authorities. The pleasure of viewing is yet to come,' said the colonel. 'I sincerely hope that Monsieur Bauer will agree with me . . . at all costs we must save our Emperor from the hands of the Americans.'

Lucien and Alexander looked grave.

'Alas,' said Lucien, 'we can promise nothing, *mon colonel*.'

Their visitor was perfectly furious.

As a matter of fact both owner and the two auctioneers knew that some of the collection would inevitably go to America. In France prices had quadrupled since the beginning of the war, and as the franc declined the dollar rose. Even a modest sum of dollars would pay for an American to live comfortably in Paris now. A windfall would make a Grand Tour possible, with the added delight of bringing home some booty. Americans were now the new rich pilgrims. A single greenback would buy a Frenchman's supply of bread for a month. Such changes were reflected, day after day, at de Grelle's . . .

The afternoon of Sara's arrival in Paris she went to meet Carl's train at the Gare de Lyon, standing on the crowded platform eagerly watching the express draw in with its sigh of steam.

'My dear Sara, I did not expect such a compliment,' exclaimed Carl, picking his way down from the high steps of the *wagon-lits* to be welcomed by a vivid figure in turquoise and black, her charming pale face enhanced by a great black straw hat.

'Oh Carl! I couldn't wait to see you! Everybody is in such a spin, you can't imagine, people coming to see Lucien Molinard and my father, and on the telephone just begging for information. All the famous greedy collectors. The dealers. It's thrilling. Look, shall we leave your luggage at the Crillon first and then I'll give you tea at Fauchon's. Fresh *millefeuilles*.'

On the ride through Paris she chattered and he listened with amusement. This was a different being from the dissatisfied girl who had wandered round his house on the ramparts. She was more beautiful. Harder?

De Grelle had not yet met his daughter's friend, despite rivers of correspondence. The two men, one large and florid, the other diminutive and elfish, took to each other. At dinner Carl spoke of the offers he had received.

'Every day letters come through my letter box. So many they fall like stones. And so amusing. Angry, beseeching, tempting. The good Colonel Renan offered me a surprising price indeed.'

'Why did you not accept?' enquired Alexander.

'Well, that would not be interesting, would it? I know many people wish to keep the collection permanently together. But what has been for me, and for my father before me, of such fascinating interest ought to go, I feel, as de Goncourt put it *"aux héritiers de mes goûts"*.'

'Many people wished to save your treasures from the hands of ignorant millionaires,' said Alexander, who liked to tease.

'Monsieur de Grelle. Millionaires who come to your auctions or send their minions to bid for them are never ignorant.'

'But the Musée de Versailles?' murmured Alexander. He was perfectly safe to argue. The auction was tomorrow.

'Yes. They spoke of renown to continue after I am dead. You know, that does not stir me. What does is the idea of some excitement, and some francs of course, *now*.'

'Tomorrow's auction,' said Alexander, 'is going to give you both.'

The sale was to open at two in the afternoon, but crowds began to gather at dawn. Many of the ticket-holders, afraid there might be a mix-up or danger of their not being able to get in, arrived before midday. Seeing the favoured ones allowed to enter, the crowds shouted insults. Sara, as she and Lee were dragged almost off their feet on their way to the door, thought the noise was like the start of a small revolution. De Grelle's harassed staff, guarding the doors and taking tickets, managed to shove them through and prevent the indignant surging patriotic mob from getting in.

The seats in the saleroom were on three sides of a square, the rostrum high as a pulpit on the fourth side. Sara and Lee, battered by their entry – Lee's hat had been knocked over her ear, sat right at the back. The room began to fill so fast that soon men and women were standing behind them pressed against the wall. You couldn't, murmured Lee, put a pin between them. They saw Carl and Alexander at the front to one side. Alexander was not taking part in the auction.

The room was packed, the voices buzzed, people nodded to each other without warmth. Lucien Molinard came slowly to the rostrum, leaned forward and looked coolly at his audience. There was an immediate silence.

'The Bauer collection,' he said, 'was begun, ladies and gentlemen, in 1815. Monsieur Bauer's grandfather fought for the Emperor, was wounded but not mortally, and this formidable collection began, literally, with his sword. It was started by a man whose devotion to the Emperor burned steadily until both his own and Bonaparte's death – the humble soldier, the exiled eagle. During the years of Napoleon's reign France was a nation of heroes. In a particular way the young Bauer was one of these.'

A minute later, when everybody thought Molinard had decided to make a long speech on the shining authenticity of the things to be auctioned, the porter entered with a gold-framed picture. Molinard called 'Lot One.'

Sara sat still as the bidding began without Lucien Molinard needing to ask. His manner was *dégagé*, his voice never loud. There they were, the paintings and sculptures, tattered flags, swords ploughed up among the skeletons buried in fields once screaming with battle, jewellery which had shone on the necks of the great-for-a-while. Prices were very high. In almost all cases they were above the estimates. Two elderly men, with tough expressionless faces, stood near the rostrum: the experts. But they were never called upon to give an opinion or estimate a value.

Nothing was heard but the monotonous repetition of figures and Lucien Molinard's 'More?' looking from one familiar face to another. He knew two thirds of the people present; some had given him bids in advance. A head briefly nodded. Someone slightly raised his catalogue. It was astonishing how quickly the things which had taken a century to amass were sold. Occasionally Lucien could not resist a remark. A letter about Jérôme Bonaparte when he met – at last – his American son.

'The boy,' said Lucien, 'was homesick for the United States and did not wish to stay in Europe. Many people agree with him. He adds in a postcript "everyone of the Bonapartes is living above their means, the only exception is my grandmother." '

Sara recognized the man who bought that letter. He was a thin-faced American collector, Phelps Martin Schreyer; she had met him in Park Street. So did Lee who whispered in her ear, 'Jérôme's son is going back to the States again.'

There was a slight frisson in the room when Lot 168 was called. It was a hitherto unpublished letter of Napoleon's to Marie-Louise.

'*You are in my thoughts. In my spirit. Your nature is as beautiful as you are.*'

'One wonders if the poor Empress ever read it,' remarked Lucien, 'considering the fiendish obscurity of her husband's handwriting. Am I bid a thousand? More . . .'

The figure rose. The procession went on.

Now and then Sara looked in Carl's direction, but he was so short she could not see her friend over the heads of the audience. Only once during the sale did the silences, the litany of figures, the bang of the hammer, alter. Many minor contestants had stopped bidding. Some had left. The field steadily narrowed until all that remained were a Parisian dealer, André Grimault, and the American Martin Schreyer. The lot – Napoleon's hair in the gold locket.

The bidding started high. And rose. And rose again.

Like people circling the main table at Monte Carlo everybody was hushed and unmoving. Neither man stirred. The bidding went on.

'Five thousand. More?'

'Six and a half. Thank you.'

Up it went. The porter who held the locket aloft unconsciously made it swing.

'More?'

Lucien looked enquiringly towards Grimault. The Frenchmen sat like a stone.

A pause.

'Twenty thousand? More?'

A longer pause.

'*Sold.*' The hammer slammed down. Napoleon's curl of greying hair had become American.

'*Traitor!*' shouted somebody.

At the celebration dinner late that night at the Crillon, when Alexander announced the total of 350,000 francs, Sara's composed little friend looked stunned.

'Carl!' exclaimed Sara, laughing.

'Yes. Yes, indeed,' said Carl. He did not know what he was saying. It was quite some time before he could eat a thing.

After the meal Alexander led Lee on to the ballroom floor for a foxtrot, remarking that he wondered where the waltzes had gone. Sara stayed with Carl who was pensively adding sugar to his coffee.

'What are you thinking about, Carl? All that astonishing money. Or were you remembering the letter. "Your nature is as beautiful as you are". You were so excited when you made out what he had written . . .'

He looked up at her absently. She was sure he hadn't heard a word she'd said.

'I saw a crayon drawing in the rue de Seine yesterday, Sara. I must buy it in the morning before anybody else gets it. It catches some quality that must have been in her face. Ah. *La belle Rachel.*'

She laughed but she was shocked. He was as pitiless as a Don Giovanni moving on to the next bed companion.

'Did you know,' he went on dreamily, 'that Rachel possessed a singular and most dreadful ability? She could stop her heart from beating. You don't believe me? It's true. When she was playing in *Phèdre*, she literally fell into a faint and had to be revived. The audience, seeing that mortal pallor, worshipped her the more. Those triumphs killed the lovely creature. To bring on fainting fits, arrest the beating of her heart, damaged her health irreparably. She was thirty-seven when she died.'

He sighed.

Then added briskly, 'One of your Papa's friends says he may be able to trace some of her costumes. He knows a dealer in theatrical antique things. And did I tell you I have bought the charming little piano on which her sister – your namesake – used to play . . .?'

Sara smiled. She sat with Carl and he talked like a lover about Rachel, the small ignorant Jewish girl whose father had been a pedlar, whose mother sold needles and pins, and who had become France's greatest actress. 'More soul than flesh,' he said. 'When you come to Antibes again one of these days, my collection may be worth looking at.'

On her return to London Sara went to see Miss Tomkins and asked for an appointment to see her father – 'early in the morning, please.'

She wanted to catch him when he was fresh – and still in his post-auction glow.

'Well, my daughter?' he enquired as Sara arrived five minutes early.

He looked with complacency at the glowing girl in her dark silk overall, 'And what have you come for? To ask about your commission?'

'*Quelle joie*. Do I get some?'

'Of course not. But you did quite nicely. I heard a compliment or two about the catalogue.'

'So did I.'

He lowered his eyelids and said nothing.

'I was wondering, Father, if the time has come for me to make a move? Now the Bauer sale is over, I might perhaps be more useful . . .'

She looked at him with mild enquiry.

He pulled his beard. He was thinking that Gilbert Travice had done her some good, but no daughter of his could stay much longer with that old crotchet and not strangle him.

'We'll see,' he said annoyingly. The tone was dismissive.

Wanting to push her case Sara decided not to do so. Which was as well since in the afternoon she received two lines from her father, personally delivered by Miss Tomkins who also bore a letter for Gilbert. He opened it, fussed. His employer rather frightened him. But both he and Sara read their letters with concealed relief. Sara was to be moved and would work in future under the tutelage of Guy Buckingham.

Clearing her table, packing her things, Sara made Gilbert a small speech of thanks.

'You taught me so much, Mr Travice.'

He nodded, hoping she would not continue. Saying goodbye she thought – you did teach me useful things. But you criticized every word I wrote and almost got me pushed out of de Grelle's. However, Sara never left enemies behind.

Alexander was away from London a good deal that summer, and after spending time in Paris went straight to New York for a start, only a start, at laying plans for the new auction house.

'Of course nothing may come of it,' he told Lee. But his voice was falsely modest.

With her father absent, the autumn was lit for Sara by Guy Buckingham. He welcomed her into his office as if she were a long-lost cousin. He was shy and warm. Silver had been his subject, his passion, since he had been a very young man. He loved silver as some women love diamonds. Sara saw him handle it, study it, run his fingers round the lid of a two-hundred-year-old tureen tracing its wreath of flowers. The lid was topped with the figure of a dog, paw in the air, straining forward . . .

'Silver is like music or the alphabet, Sara,' he said. 'Nothing can be new. Yet look what people do with an octave of eight notes or the twenty-six letters of the alphabet. Silver was used as payment in Babylon. All the embossing and casting with flutes, gadroons, chasing, high relief, have been known and used for thousands of years. It is the same. Yet wonderfully new.'

He patted the silver head of the hunting dog.

He was a man whose affectation was to be lazy, know little, move slowly. 'I must be mad to take on this,' he would say yawning as they set off for a country house. In his car he drove as if racing round Brooklands, whirling Sara out of London in his open Sunbeam along empty roads where yellow leaves were tumbling down.

They were taken to the cellars and silver vaults of old, old houses. They peered into enormous cupboards or sat at tables groaning with silver amassed over generations. They spent days examining, dating and listing the shining harvest. It was like being assistant to Merlin.

The date ringed on a page in Sara's diary finally came when Alexander was due back in Park Street. Sara left work early to be home when he arrived.

With Lee in attendance he came into his house like royalty, the cabman staggering under a cabin trunk and every member of the staff, down to a shy kitchen maid, in a nervous bustle.

Georges went up the stairs with a particular valise of his master's which, thought Sara noticing the way the butler carried it, must be filled with gold bars.

Signalling the hero's return, every light in the house shone, from the French chandelier in the hall to candles in silver sconces on the chimneypiece in the drawing room.

During dinner Alexander talked to both his women at once, turning from Lee to Sara and back again. The burden of his song was the American market, and his new auction house.

Like everything else in that great continent, he said, de Grelle's venture would be riskier, with larger rewards if it succeeded. The auction business in the United States dealt with vast fortunes, and some vast frauds as well. In the past (possibly still) there'd been what he called 'the deplorable traffic' in Old Masters. Some of the people who dealt with them were ignorant and 'aboundingly optimistic'. Some were deliberate deceivers.

'Before the war, I gather, there was one auctioneer, by the name of Theron Blakeslee, who sold a positive ocean of Thomas Lawrences, Joshua Reynolds and Romneys to upper-Class America,' said Alexander. It seemed Blakeslee produced experts to verify the pictures.

'Happy collectors hung their prizes at home, showing them to envious friends,' he said sardonically. Of course there were other, cooler and detached eyes who could have spotted that a Reynolds which had undoubtedly come from that painter's studio consisted of the master having painted only part of the lady's pink dress. He hadn't laid his brush once upon her ill-executed face.'

'Is Blakeslee still auctioneering?' asked Lee.

'The unfortunate man put a gun to his head years ago. Sitting by a large so-called Rubens.'

Alexander turned to his own affairs. New York was the thing, he said. Sad to say, Europe was impoverished by the Great War, so what to do? Turn to the New World.

'Paris, London, New York. My three galleries will be the most celebrated in the world,' he said, 'greater than my London rivals, or the Drouot or Charpentiers. But there are great obstacles in America. Great obstacles.'

He spoke as if these attracted him. Brushing aside tales of frauds and fakes, he said there were some hugely successful auction houses, 'their reputations nearly as good as mine. Perry van Rijn tells me there are up to a thousand firms dealing in some kind of art in the States. New ventures can start brilliantly. And fall dramatically (I am quoting van Rijn). Of course that's the merchant banker speaking. His colleagues were just the same when we were talking – what is their expression, *mignonne*?'

'Turkey?' said Lee.

'Precisely. When we talked turkey. But I still made a sale.' He spoke of what he called 'the vital spirit of New York'.

'You have become an admirer of our country all of a sudden,' said Lee.

'I have always adored America.'

Lee gave him a very dry look indeed.

Sara tensed at the sound of Perry's name, listened only to that.

'Of course New York's a leading international centre of banking now. It is banks which maintain a country's stability,' said Alexander who had the actor's trick of absorbing something of the people with whom he'd spent his time. 'How brilliant those men can be, doing their tricks with other people's money.'

Not only with their money, thought Sara, what about their hearts?

With her father back in Park Street, activity returned to the house. He was up betimes, leaving in the Rolls before eight each morning and, as was his custom, never offering Sara a lift. She breakfasted alone and walked to St Charles Street to

172

be welcomed by a paradoxically punctual Guy Buckingham.

'Here's the girl I need. Lots of work. Can you bear it?'

One morning when he was out of the office Fay appeared, charming in a high fur collar and a coat the colour of an emerald, looked round like a burglar and whispered, 'Is it safe?'

Laughing, Sara asked what she was talking about.

'Guy, of course. I've brought this!'

She produced, from a fur muff pinned with violets, a little package. When unwrapped, she put on to Sara's desk a small gilt-edged plate on which was an exquisite scene of a castle on the top of a rocky promontory above a rushing river.

'This is a bit of the Sèvres. Just for one of your wizards to look at. If they think it's worth de Grelle's putting it in an auction, they can come and look at the whole service in Chester Square. Piles and piles of it in a cupboard. I shall just hope and pray it will sell,' said Fay. 'I *need* some money. You're peachy to help me.'

Sara did not have time to answer for Guy reappeared and she just managed to shove the plate in a drawer. He would find out in the end, of course. By which time Fay's Sèvres would be in a sale catalogue and it would be too late for him to do anything. One hoped.

'Hello, Fay, what are you doing here?' drawled Guy when he saw the bright green-clad figure. He smiled lazily.

She ran over to kiss him.

'Isn't he sweet, Sara? The only man in my life who blushes.'

Sara's London life that autumn was very full. Her work with Guy took up much of it, they drove out of London sometimes for two days at a time, there were houses to visit, silver to appraise. And when she returned she was snatched up by Fay. She was always racing back to Park Street to change into evening dress.

There was still no sign of Catherine who remained in Scotland.

'I suppose she and Dudley Forrest are staying with a duke. That'd suit your sister down to the ground,' said Fay who – rarely meeting Catherine – always declared afterwards it was impossible that she could be related to Sara.

One evening when the leaves had begun to cover the pavements and stick there because of autumn rains, Sara called on Lee in the mews cottage. Lee was standing in front of a finished painting which she covered at once with a cloth.

'I know. If I say I like it you'll go off it,' said Sara. She began to wander along the far end of the studio, poking about in Lee's books for something on Cellini.

'Sit down, Sara. You're fidgety. I had a letter from Catherine today. She will be back from Kyle of Localsh next week.'

'Will she?'

'You don't sound very interested.'

Sara came over to sit near Lee, with a massive book on the Renaissance in her arms.

Lee raised her eyebrows.

'Work? You never stop. You're as bad as Alex.'

'I don't eat and drink and breathe it, Lee.'

'True. When not with Guy Buckingham (whom I do approve of) you're out dancing with that Nelson girl, whom I don't. Approve of, I mean.'

'What's wrong with Fay? She's cute.'

'She hasn't an idea in that dizzy head except what to sell next from that dam' great house. Yes, I know all about that and so does Guy. He pretends not to because he is so fond of the child. I can't think what you see in Fay Nelson. However, that's a pointless remark. What *is* to the point is the subject of your sister. When you came rocketing to England last year I was sure you'd see more of each other.'

'How can I see more of Cathy when she doesn't see more of me?'

'Try.'

'Face facts, Lee. You do on other things. Take a look at us, will you? Her mother was English, she was educated over here. Mine's American and I was dragged up in Switzerland. Why, we practically talk a different language. And she's never liked me. I don't blame her. I wouldn't like me if I was her.'

'Why?'

'I'm not her sort. We're chicken Maryland and boiled beef and carrots.'

Lee, more serious than usual, said that Sara was the one

174

who should bend. She was flexible. Catherine wasn't.

'Besides, to be crude, your father did leave *her* mother for *yours*.'

'Ancient history.'

'Centuries ago to you, I suppose. But it's still the reason why you are both the way you are. How can you have nothing in common? You have Alex. Catherine is an important part of your life. Perhaps more important than you guess.'

Sara suddenly looked up, wondering what that meant. It's to do with Father's business. She's thinking that when he dies we'll snarl over de Grelle's like two dogs over the same bone. But that won't happen for years and years, and Cathy and I will be old by then and I –

Her thoughts stopped short.

She was driven home in the slowest of horse-drawn cabs; clip-clopping through the deserted streets of Sunday evening, Sara returned to the uncomfortable thought. Not about de Grelle's which simply wasn't to be worried over. But to her own future. What is going to happen to me? I will soon be twenty-four. Mother would call that old. She remembered Louise liked to say 'I was scarcely eighteen when your father married me. Such a child. Why, I just knew ab-so-lutely nothing!'

By nothing Louise meant sex.

That was not the way it was with Sara and Fay and many of the girls who danced the night away in London. They did know about sex. One evening Fay had asked Sara, when they were in Fay's bedroom which was decorated with pierrot dolls, 'Sara . . . have you . . . *you* know . . . with a man? I sort of feel you have.'

'And I sort of feel I shan't tell,' said Sara, laughing.

'Oh, you're so cool and collected. I bet you're a fire of passion underneath like in that naughty Elynor Glyn book Tommy lent me. *His Hour*. She fainted and then came to, and didn't know if he *had* or not!' Fay gave a little scream of laughter.

'What I mean to say really,' she added, licking her finger and smoothing her eyebrows, 'is that I have.'

'Was it very thrilling?' asked Sara, thinking how could Lee disapprove of this girl.

'Not the first time. I didn't like it much. It was Bobbie. I hadn't told him I'd never done it. It was during the war and poor Bobbie was going back to the trenches, and do you know, when he kissed me he *cried*. Sara it was so awful, a man crying. I thought I'd die. Of course I cried too, and Mummy was out that night and he came up here and that was it. He was *horror-struck* when he found it was my first time.'

Looking through her jewel case, she picked up a diamond bandeau and put it across her forehead.

'Golly, that tickles. Of course,' confidentially, 'I had to pretend I'd liked it and after that we did it a lot during his leave. I got quite good. I could go on for ages!'

She caught Sara's eye in the glass and giggled. Adding with a sigh that it was mean of Sara not to tell.

'I love secrets.'

'Maybe I'll tell you another time.'

'And maybe you won't. I think you fell for whoever it was. I've often thought that about you, darling. Do you still see him?'

'Not telling. Not telling.'

'I shall goudge it out of you one day. Anyway,' said Fay, changing the subject, 'about me – there's someone at present who's wonderful, darling. I haven't seen him lately because he's away, but he's back this week and then – boy!'

She put her arms across her thin bosom and hugged herself.

'He'll go on and on too. Much longer than Bobbie. When he does it, this special one I mean, I always think I'll just faint. I almost did once. Went all dizzy. I wish I had swooned away. Wouldn't he have been pleased?'

A chorus of male voices came from downstairs shouting, 'Have you both died? Can we come up? Will you come down?'

Fay, fastening the diamond bandeau, scampered out of the room.

And Sara found herself envying her. A feeling of bitterness, strange to her youth as the wing of a cold reptilian creature, touched her spirit.

It was nearly winter, and she had thought she was free of Perry van Rijn. After their three visits to that house in the empty square she had felt she had some mortal illness. He'd left her, left London, and her physical memories made her feel ill. She shook when she thought of him, dreamed he was making love to her, woke sick with want. It was exactly as it had been in Antibes: she was haunted by him. But time, feared and hated by the poets, had its blessings too. And as the weeks went by the ghost of Perry's love-making began to leave her. She was young and strong, de Grelle's filled her life, the ivory hammer struck and the great game of each auction unfolded. Slowly the fact that her body had been so possessed, her spirit so thirsty and not sated, began to fade. The only thing she feared was that when, inevitably, they met again she would not be able to resist him. Her thoughts which accepted such a slavery disgusted her. When she envied Fay's sigh of remembered pleasure, Sara shuddered.

Alexander was going back to New York. He gave Lee and Sara luncheon at Claridge's and kissed them impartially.

'I am much welcomed on board,' he said. 'They tell me business people are the most cherished by the steamship companies. Very right and proper. I sat at a table on my return last time with a buyer who has crossed two hundred times! I feel I shall be doing just the same. Weaving across the Atlantic, a shuttle in a mighty loom.'

When he had driven away, Lee began to laugh.

'The more he sees of New York, the more he wants to stay,' she said. 'Do you think he plans to move us all there? I wouldn't put it past him.'

Park Street was dull, and so was de Grelle's, when Alexander was away. Catherine was still in Scotland, which was a relief.

'You don't imagine that duke has started enjoying her pouring out tea, do you?' said Fay. 'Your sister has poured so much tea she could launch the *Aquitania*.'

Ten days after her father had left, Sara was telephoned in her office by William. He had received a cable from Alexander, who would be back again by the end of the week.

'Topping,' said Sara.

'It's nice to hear you say that,' was the pleased reply.

Sara smiled when she put down the telephone. William's

feelings for her father did not change. She remembered
Louise remarking on that once. With sarcasm.

'You seem to like William Thornbury, I can't imagine
why. That loyalty of his – to my erstwhile husband of all
men. He'd sell his grandmother if he got a good price.'

Guy was out with a prospective client, and when he came
striding back, a yellow scarf round his neck, Sara thought he
looked just as if he were off to the races. Only the binoculars
strung round his neck were missing.

'Hungry?'

'I am, rather. Shall I pop out and get our sandwiches?'

'No sandwiches. I'm taking you to the Ritz.'

'Goodness. What's happened? Are we celebrating?'

'It's a day of mourning, actually. My birthday. I am forty-
five. And don't tell me you imagined I was older or you shan't
have any pudding.'

They walked down St Charles Street in the cold sunshine.
London was pleasantly crowded and the autumn sales had
been busy.

'We're in for a post-war boom,' he said. 'Don't think it will
last, though. Do you?'

'Yes I do. I feel it will,' said Sara.

'That's because you are twenty-three, my poor child.'

The Ritz was also festive and during the meal Sara persuaded Guy to talk on his favourite subject. It always fascinated her, she could never hear enough. He told her about the
great goldsmiths of southern Germany in the sixteenth century, of their fantastic and grotesque silver cups. Moving over
the centuries, he talked about the Restoration in England and
the 'carefree silver'.

'Everybody wanted some silver at that time. If you were an
aristocrat you had family silver weighing down your dinner
table. If you kept an inn, you had a line of silver tankards on
the counter. And if you were a blackguard and hadn't any, you
shaved some off the coins and melted it down.'

Sara laughed and listened. As Guy was calling the waiter
for more coffee, she glanced idly across his shoulder.

At some distance away, sitting at a table by the windows
overlooking the park, was a girl. She wore the ghost-khaki

satin which was still the rage, and a tiny hat was pulled down over her lint-fair hair. It was Fay.

In that moment of recognition when, seeing somebody one knows very well, one views them as a total stranger, Sara was struck by the childlike quality of the girl. Her melting expression, a schoolgirl sexuality. Fay threw back her head and went into a peal of laughter. And then with a pang so sharp it took her breath away Sara saw the man who was with her. He sat with his back to Sara, but she knew the shape of those shoulders, the dark glossy hair into which she had thrust her hands.

CHAPTER TWELVE

When Georges opened the front door on a cold night a week later, Sara heard the sound of a piano. He took her coat, murmuring confidentially. 'The Master telephoned. He will be home this evening. And the *demoiselle* has arrived with Mr Forrest' (he meant Catherine). 'Also the American gentleman'.

Stripping off her gloves Sara said.

'Which gentleman, Georges? My father knows dozens.'

'Mr van Rijn. I have served,' added George with French revulsion, 'the Martinis.'

'Oh, poor Georges,' said Sara, smiling with nerves.

It was useless to escape up to her room. And in any case she was not a girl who ran away – except on that momentous day when she escaped from the Villa des Roses.

Three heads turned as she entered the room. Catherine swivelled round on the piano stool. Dudley and Perry stood up. There were greetings and commonplaces and Catherine, in her hostess's voice, offered her a cocktail.

'Cath's been giving us some jazz,' said Dudley, walking across to the piano. 'Go on, Cath. Sara will like *Swanee*, and I know the words.'

He bent over to pick out the tune with one finger, and Catherine began to put chords to the music. Dudley started to sing in a pleasing baritone, breaking off to say, 'Follow me, like this. *Da* da da da, *da* da da da, that's it.'

Catherine played with a light expressive touch and Sara turned casually to Perry.

'Hello. How long have you been over?'

'A week or so. I was to travel with your father in the *Orcades* but needed to come sooner. Bank matters.'

'Impressive.'

'Not at all. Banks have their rivals too. We have to move very fast sometimes, just as auctioneers do.'

The tone was as meaningless as her own.

They sat down, not close, and talked to the accompaniment of *Swanee*.

'How I love you, how I love you,' sang Dudley.

So this is how it is, thought Sara with a dreadful lack of surprise. We wanted our liberty and we've got it, and they treat us the way we deserve. He is in love with Fay, just like every man she meets. Who can blame him?

'Alex asked me to dine this evening,' he said. Does he feel he has to explain, she thought, her nerves bleeding. Does he imagine I am such a fool I don't know what he is really saying?

'Your father has a surprise for the family, he told me.'

'Oh, that's easy to guess,' said Sara. 'The New York venture's going ahead. Congratulations. I'm sure you and your bank are the reason it's all fixed up. Business things like that must be run of the mill to you.'

'Of course they're not.'

'Banks can't get the thrill out of it that my father does. All the money van Rijn's handle. And make, I suppose. I bet you often find yourself looking at people and simply thinking how greedy they are.'

She stared straight at him, telling him that she was greedy no longer.

His expression slightly altered. He looked easier and, with the perversity of the male sex, very slightly put out. Get used to it, she thought, this is how you want it and how it's going to be. You and I are through. Don't expect me to show I care a cent for you. And thank your stars that what you did wasn't to a different kind of woman who broke her heart. Mine hurts. But I suppose the way to cope with that is to meet it head on.

Catherine was playing with more assurance, and Dudley repeated the refrain, 'How I love you, how I love you, my dear old Swanee.'

'People seem to believe,' Perry said, 'that if one deals with money, one gets to resemble the stuff.'

'Bright and hard, like the gold used as stakes in Monte Carlo before the war?' said Sara, smiling.

The door opened, Catherine's music stopped in mid-phrase, and Lee and Alexander appeared. Lee was laughing.

'Jazz, Cathy. You're full of surprises. Perry, Dudley. Good to see you.'

Alexander spread out both arms as if to say, 'I am here.'

Both daughters went to him to kiss his cheek. Lee ordered more cocktails, at which Alexander groaned as if she'd pushed a thorn into his finger.

'Must you, *mignonne*?'

'I'm afraid I must. We are moving with the times, my dear. I guess I am. Your girls, and Dudley and Perry, are *of* the times. But if you want to stay in aspic, that's your look-out.'

Soon Sara managed to leave and go upstairs to change. The rest of the party were already in dinner clothes.

She sat down on the bed and shut her eyes. She thought of the great city outside the windows, and other cities, the sparkling towers of New York at night, the leafy boulevards of Paris. Among the teeming millions of souls how many, like her, wanted a man or woman who had rejected them? What an extraordinary pain it was, this yearning, this starving, shivering thing. Why Perry? Why not one of a hundred men she had met or would meet while her beauty lasted. She changed into a white dress, brushed her hair fiercely until it shone, coiled it, and returned down the stairs.

Catherine was playing again. But with Alexander at home it was Offenbach.

Bars of pungent cigar smoke lay in the still air, the talk was animated against the background of nineteenth-century songs written for theatres haunted by cupids. Lee and Dudley were discussing aquatint-engravings, Perry and Alexander business. Looking up, Alexander noticed the unguarded expression on the face of his younger daughter sitting at a distance from him.

He broke off and raised his voice.

'Sara, come and sit by me. Catherine –' speaking above *Orpheus in the Underworld*, 'you shall go on playing later. Silence, everybody, if you please. I have something to say.'

Everybody looked expectant, including Catherine. Dudley had set her mind at rest after visiting William Thornbury; her sister was no danger to her after all. She felt almost benevolent towards Sara.

Alexander, drawing on his cigar, enjoyed the pause.

'Of course,' he said, after an interval which only an actor would have dared to use, 'you have all gathered by now that with the help of this young man –' looking at Perry, 'we are to have a branch in New York. Arranging this has not been easy. At times it has been a battle. One might even say a bloody one. However we have won through. And the van Rijn bank are giving us long- and short-term loans. Entirely due to our friend Perry here.'

'That isn't true, sir. It was your own reputation.'

'Well, perhaps a little . . .' allowed Alexander. 'De Grelle's in New York are to have fine new premises. In the most fashionable part of the city. The *new* fashionable district, Madison Avenue.'

In full flood, he liked to talk of what absorbed him, he told them that in the old days it had been Madison Square which was the pinnacle of fashion for auction houses. That was over. He talked of the legendary auctioneer, Thomas Kirby, who headed the American Art Association.

'Kirby was called The Million Dollar Voice,' said Alexander, and Sara thought it was a nickname he'd like himself. But Kirby, it seemed, was a very old man now and things were moving on. To Madison Avenue.

Part of Alexander's hard-won victory had been the loan for new and handsome premises . . . 'They're good, aren't they, Perry? Of course a good deal of work has to be done on the building, alterations and so on, to give it the de Grelle look.'

'Of course, sir,' from Dudley, eagerly listening.

'It comes to me more and more,' continued Alexander, nodding pleasantly in Dudley's direction, 'that America really is the new world for us auctioneers. We are going to open in February. I shall return to New York before Christmas, and will not be back in Europe until after the opening, of course. So. Now to my surprise. I want both my daughters, and Lee of course, and you, Dudley, to be there for the great day.'

He listened smilingly to the thanks and exclamations. Interest, admiration, strong attention were what he savoured more than anything in the world except the challenge of the rostrum.

The van Rijn bank's decision to finance de Grelle in New York was strongly influenced by his timing. New in the United States, Alexander was already one jump ahead of the formidable leader, old Thomas Kirby of the A.A.A. The Million Dollar Voice was ill and getting old. 'He is running,' said Alexander simply, 'a losing race with time.'

And the A.A.A.'s famous galleries on 23rd Street, once called the most beautiful building in the world, were outmoded. The building, opened in 1883, was in sore need of repair. The skylights rattled when the rain hammered against them, frightening the stenographers. Rats had been known to chew the account books and one daring rat appeared among a display of oriental rugs. It was true that the galleries with their red plush walls and polished floors could have been repaired and made to shine again, but Madison Square itself was no longer smart. Fashion had shifted and the fine arts trade was moving northwards.

Gustavus Kirby, old Kirby's son, had bought some land at Madison Avenue and 57th Street, where he planned to build a positive palace covering the entire block front on the east side of the avenue from 57th to 56th Street. Alexander knew all this. He also knew that Gustavus hadn't yet started building. And he himself had his eye on a spacious and pleasant house in the same avenue . . .

Alexander met his leading rivals at the smart opening of a new gallery while he was in New York. The gallery's owner, who valued what de Grelle's in Paris could do for him, said when he arrived, 'Now, whom do you wish to meet, Mr de Grelle? Just say the word and I'll introduce you.'

'If there are some gentlemen from the American Art Association?'

He was promptly presented to Thomas Kirby and his son. Neither man was pleased to meet the large confident bearded foreigner. After the briefest of remarks, the frail white-haired

Kirby, whose expression was almost ludicrously severe, turned away to talk to Gustavus.

Two men nearby, however, welcomed Alexander hospitably as if greeting a valued friend and not an invader. The tall grey-haired Major Parke, who had run A.A.A.'s subsidiary, the Parke Gallery, until 1918 but was now in the main house, gripped Alexander's hand.

'A pleasure, sir. A real pleasure.'

Beside him was a plump and positively Pickwickian figure, Otto Bernet. He, too, greeted Alexander with warmth. The three men talked of French furniture which was the new gallery's speciality. What did Mr de Grelle think of this? And that?

Alexander knew the reputations of both the men treating him with such charm. They were considerable, despite being in the shadow of the white-haired old tyrant, the Father of Auctions, at present on the other side of the room, irritably refusing a glass of champagne. Major Parke had an uncanny flair for predicting the value of even the most difficult things coming into the A.A.A., and as for Bernet, who'd worked there since a boy of fourteen, he, too, had the expert's flair and strong sense of values. Curiously, neither man had had any kind of education. Otto had been hired at fourteen to polish furniture and run errands; Parke, who had the air of being of good family (he was born in west Philadelphia), had left grammar school to work on the drummer's wagon belonging to his father, a dry goods salesman. While Otto, passionate for self-improvement, stayed in the saleroom at night, climbing on to the rostrum to imitate Kirby and shout to lines of empty chairs, 'Do I hear eleven thousand?', Hiram Parke charmed his father's customers, learned to ride to hounds, and developed a liking for the wealthy and the gold-dust of their manners. He had the air of a country squire. The term Major had come from his time in the National Guard. It stuck for life.

It was these two and not the delicate angry-looking old man who interested Alexander. He noticed as they talked that it was they who asked him questions.

When he left the gallery he was thoughtful.

Next morning at the bank, he pushed harder.

Even before the deal went through, before he'd chosen his new premises, Alexander was planning his first auction. It had to be impressive. He must show the de Grelle authority, and persuade the influential New World that his was a firm to be reckoned with. He wanted to see that light in the faces of the crowd.

It looked as if he would succeed. For he had beaten the other established auction houses already in being awarded the sale of Henry Benjamin's collection.

Benjamin was railroad rich, over eighty, and lived in seclusion in a huge brownstone house to which nobody was invited. Alexander had been fortunate enough to meet him twenty years ago when on one of his American forays. He had always been attracted to auctioneering in the United States. He'd taken with him some choice sixteenth-century Italian paintings, 'mostly angels and saints' he called them, and a single Alfred Sisley of a road in Normandy after the rain. Sisley was fetching no sort of price, but Alexander liked the painting and took it on impulse.

Henry Benjamin heard about Alexander through a man he hired to go about in the art world. He sent for him. Alexander was received in a lofty, stuffy room by a thin little man with sparse white hair, rheumy blue eyes and a shirt which seemed too big for him. His voice was hoarse, his manner dry as a biscuit. Alexander propped up the Italian pictures against a row of chairs. Monks bowed in prayer. Beatific visions, holding chaplets of roses, hovered above them. Angels with curiously smiling faces blessed kneeling princes. Or, cheeks inflated, blew silver trumpets. Benjamin studied the images of the ages of faith. There they were, figures with a joyous gaiety in religion. He bought them all.

'I'm not haggling – this time,' he said.

'You have purchased nothing that will not rise in value, Mr Benjamin.'

'I know that, man.'

The interview was not long. Alexander was very curious to see his collections, but wasn't invited to stay. Just as he was leaving, the elderly man said, 'What's in that packet under your arm?'

'An Alfred Sisley. I don't know whether the painter would interest you.'

'He does. I was at the A.A.A.'s exhibition of the French Impressionists, sir, back in 1886. I was younger then. In my forties. But I could afford to waste money and that's what the clever ones told me I was doing. There were forty Monets, you know. Some of the Manet paintings were listed as by Monet – James Sutton should have been ashamed. And the Renoirs . . . enough to make your mouth water. The press called 'em 'coloured nightmares'. Humbug. Well, every auctioneer knows the story of *that* sale by now. But I bought fifteen of them. Monets. Two Renoirs. Our friend Sisley, and some Pisarros. I paid seventeen thousand dollars and was told I was off my head. Come and take a look.'

Alexander did.

He looked, too, at the other galleries in a silent stuffy house meant to buzz with life, to the sound of voices and slamming doors and children's clatter. Alexander was taken through a gallery of Florentine carved walnut furniture, of glass cases containing fragments of painted stained glass, where Christ's face looked gravely up, or a hand clasped a Madonna lily. Renaissance paintings glowed on the dark walls. The house was filled, not with living noisy children, but with the seething centuries.

Benjamin, a lonely, avid collector, did not forget Alexander. They had something in common for Benjamin's grandmother had been French. The old man took a fancy to the visitor, almost a fellow countryman. Alexander actually persuaded him to talk a little French. The two men corresponded over the years, and Benjamin was Alexander's first regular American client.

With no family to love (rumour had it there was a son he had disinherited, but that disinherited son was always a legend of the rich and lonely), what Benjamin lived for was his collections. But like little Carl Bauer, whose passion for Napoleon finally wore out, the old man was no longer in love with the Italian booty which filled his furthest galleries. He fell in love, instead, with French painting.

The affair began when he startled the experts by wasting

his seventeen thousand dollars. Benjamin, a despot in the past, never paid heed to other people when, as he said, his bowels told him he was right. He hung his French pictures and visited them daily. During the war in 1916 he bought another Pisarro and paid more for it: five thousand dollars. Although, as one dealer waspishly said, he could have had other paintings by the same artist a month later for a thousand dollars a canvas. Benjamin didn't listen. He chose some sumptuous, bursting Renoir nudes during the war too. And a dark-faced woman at a piano, by Manet, in 1920; she cost him seven thousand dollars. 'Far too much' said the art world. Benjamin, whom they never met, annoyed them.

But every time Alexander went to New York he was invited to the brownstone house, and the two men went to the gallery of French Impressionists. Hung on the walls, immortal, moving, was a world of exquisite simplicity. Houses huddled along a village street, the soft muddy track reflecting the rain. Poplar-tall roads. Canals. Old, old churches. There was the Seine with its tugs and rowing boats. Smiling girls dancing with their men under the plane trees. A sky floating with clouds blown by a fresh spring wind. Alexander and Benjamin stood and looked. They never said a word.

During one of these visits the previous year Benjamin showed signs of failing health. He said suddenly.

'What'll happen to them when I'm dead?'

Alexander knew who 'them' was.

'I'm sure we needn't discuss the eventuality yet, sir.'

'You're too polite, that's your trouble. I won't last much longer, young man.' He always called Alexander young. 'So my beauties will be sold, won't they?'

'You could leave them to one of the museums. Or a university?'

'Why? I don't owe anybody anything. Sell them. Didn't you tell me last time you wanted to start up in New York? Sell them then.'

Alexander, whose heart had swollen, answered that he hoped to open his new galleries very much sooner than the sad event of his friend's demise.

'Can't be sure, can we? Yes, I'd like you to be the one. You understand them.'

A pause.

For a single moment, the old man looked quite young. He gave a goblin smile.

'I'd sure like to be there and hear what price you get for 'em all.'

Henry Benjamin died that winter. He'd added a codicil to his will and, to the baffled rage of the great American auctioneers, Alexander was awarded the rich prize.

As in Paris, newspaper comment was hot on patriotism. 'One wonders why a visiting foreigner, a newcomer on the scene, is to have the privilege of handling such an important American collection,' said one leader. But Henry Benjamin's Impressionists had all come from Europe.

Catherine was gratified at the idea of the long costly sojourn in America. It pleased her to think her father was paying hundreds, perhaps thousands, of pounds to transport the family on the *Aquitania* and she had the pleasant glow of reflected extravagance which wasn't costing her a penny. Catherine's instinct, which came from her father, was for knowing the right people. There would be some of those in New York, useful to Dudley as well as to herself, society people, very possibly with 'old' money, too. She looked forward very much to the coming journey. Unlike Sara, she had never crossed the Atlantic, never been abroad at all.

Dudley was amused that his betrothed was such an inexperienced traveller.

'You'll be seasick', he said to tease. 'You'll spend the entire time flat on your back in your stateroom with a stewardess bringing bowls of water.'

'You enjoy making things sound unpleasant,' said Catherine coldly. They were spending Christmas at Lytchett and walking in the woods. He took her gloved hand. She snatched it away, thinking there were times when he was a boor. Pulling her roughly to him, he put his arms round her and kissed her lips chilled by the frosty afternoon. He shut his eyes and, for the first time in their chaste exchanges, tried to force his tongue into her mouth.

She started violently back.

'*Don't.*'

If she offended him he never showed it. He grinned.

'If you say so.'

'I do say so. Let's enjoy the walk. Grandmother said she saw a snowdrop.'

That's what you are, he thought. Ah well, can't have everything. I don't know why not, though, some chaps do. And his thoughts went to Perry van Rijn whom he'd seen, one evening in Mayfair, in a horse-drawn cab. It clopped by slowly, and he glimpsed van Rijn and a blonde girl. A sexy-looking girl, pop-eyed and silly, he knew the sort. He'd had an affair with a girl who looked like that in Sydney. Dandy, her name was; hot as Hades in bed.

Catherine broke in with more charm than usual.

'I know you didn't really mean I'd be a bad sailor when we go to New York. I'm afraid I'm not good at being teased. That's because I'm an only child.'

Neither of them noticed the omission.

Dudley was also looking forward to the trip and thought it unexpected of de Grelle to invite him. Lee Becker told them that Alexander had rented a palatial house on Rhode Island for a couple of months. They were all to be his guests. Dudley decided to get up some connexions in the art world when he was in the States: it was a perfect opportunity. Although Catherine was a valuable part of his future, things weren't happening fast enough. He'd once said that to Catherine, she hadn't known what he was talking about. For Catherine, things went at the speed she chose. Her way of running her life tickled him. He privately nicknamed her 'Planny Anny'.

Of the four people about to cross the Atlantic to attend what it was hoped would be Alexander's New York triumph, the one who would have preferred to go to the South Pole was Sara. She told herself that seeing Aunt Emily, seeing New York where in the past she had been happy, re-meeting old friends in the city where she'd felt most herself, would be wonderful. But before that she must find a way to get over the wound, deep – it sometimes seemed mortal – which Perry, so courteous and well-bred, and hideously cold, had just given her.

The first time they had made love, in the Roumaniev gardens, it had been a kind of miracle to snatch at happiness after years of tragedy. But it hadn't been like that when he had reappeared in London. She blushed inwardly to remember what she'd done. She could have refused him then. Instead there had been three days when for a rationed hour they had gone to that house in the deserted square. She hadn't looked at what she was doing. She hadn't thought at all. She had simply felt she would die if they didn't fall on a bed and do it again and again.

What had she imagined? That here was her nameless lover, who by wonderful chance had come back into her life and this time they were starting a real love affair which would last. She hadn't thought that or anything else. She had only lain down, thinking Perry would somehow own her body, and she his, for always.

He had not once written to her after he had left England. Now here he was treating her as a social acquaintance and in love, she supposed, with Fay. What could she do about that? You couldn't force a man to choose you rather than another girl, and she disdained the idea of trying to 'get him back' as predatory women called it. Although she often felt so hurt that it was as if she had been stabbed, she loved Fay.

I must avoid him in New York, she thought. And he'll be glad when I do.

Fay telephoned the day after Perry dined at Park Street.

'Guess who's appeared in my life. The man! When he walked in I just went groggy at the knees. You wait till you see him. Not sure I want you to, though. Wouldn't it be awful if you became my hated rival?'

Fay telephoned with the usual eager invitations, but Sara managed to keep away from Chester Square until Fay announced that she was giving a party. She'd found a thrillng black pianist and a drummer and it was all going to be the greatest fun. 'We'll dance in the drawing room and right out on to the back terrace. I'm having it hung with fairy lights.'

'Fay, it's December. We'll freeze.'

Sara already felt cold at the idea of the party.

'Rubbish, darling. Sex will keep us warm.'

Sara knew she couldn't possibly avoid accepting, and she and Guy decided to go together. They spent the day in the country, examining and listing a collection of snuff boxes, the property of a country squire recently dead. His daughter wished to sell them at once.

'The old story,' said Guy. 'He must have loved them. She can't wait to get rid of them.'

Some of the little pocket boxes were of gold, some enamelled, one set with almost black opals, one in the shape of a silver shell. One rich-looking gold box encrusted with pearls which Guy opened made him bark with laughter.

'You'd best not look at this one, Sara. It is *very* rude.'

After the long day and the shared pleasures of work, Sara felt armed. By her kind companion. By the crowds at Chester Square. By the thump of music. She knew she was going to see Fay and her own onetime lover and felt as if she were waiting to have a tooth dragged out.

She saw him the moment the front door opened. There was Fay at the top of the stairs hanging on to Perry's arm, while he looked down at her with an expression of smiling indulgence.

'I think the clever thing would be to eat,' said Guy, surveying the press of people. Some couples had begun to dance up and down the stairs. 'At parties like this people fall on the food like wolves.'

Sara scarcely saw Perry during the evening except once when he waved to her across the heads of the dancers.

The party had two miserable results, Fay confided to Sara when they met one Saturday afternoon for tea at Rumelmayers.

'Isn't it dreadful. Every one of my little liqueur bottles is gone.'

'Oh, poor Fay. Did somebody lean on the chimneypiece and smash them?'

'Smash them, darling! They *drank* them. I could have cried. But Perry cheered me up and we've started a new collection. Perry says when something bad happens, always start again at once.'

Charming, thought Sara grimly.

She loved Fay, was touched by her, envied her talent for slithering along the top of the water on skis. But by an effort of will she had to avoid thinking of Fay and Perry in bed together. How horrible sexual imaginings were.

Fay toyed with an éclair and pushed it away.

'Oh look. There's your big Sis and that cowboy.'

'Why do you call him that?'

'I can imagine him riding the range and lassoing people. Has he lassoed your sister?'

'Perhaps she lassoed him.'

'Perhaps she did. Catherine's sort of determined. Like you, darling, in a way. But then not a bit like my one chum. You're a mystery. Catherine isn't. Anyone can see what she's up to. Even silly me.'

She sipped her tea, then pushed that away too.

'Sara, something much worse than my collection has happened. My pearls have gone.'

'*Gone?*'

'I know,' agreed Fay, accepting the shocked tone. 'It was at the party. Bobbie said I must go to the police, he even started walking to Gerald Road station, I had to run after him to stop him.'

'But – but –'

'No buts, Sara. How could I go the police and say arrest Eddy Bryant. Poor Eddy, he hasn't a –'

'Fay, you are being *ridiculous.*'

Fay piled lumps of sugar on the tablecloth, there was no girl in London who made more mess when she was in a restaurant. 'You know me,' she said, sharing the problem of her own character with Sara helplessly.

Sara argued. She could see she was wasting her breath. Fay had the maddening habit of agreeing when you criticized her. Of course Eddy Bryant must be stopped. And she did love the pearls, especially the emerald clasp. But there it was, and she repeated it as if it were the refrain of a song – how could one go to the police and say, arrest Eddy Bryant?

Two days later a jubilant Fay telephoned Sara's office. Perry was wonderful, wouldn't Sara just guess that? He'd seen Eddy and actually managed to get the pearls back.

'Perry's lending him a wee bitty to tide him over . . . poor Eddy. They say,' confided Fay, lowering her voice, 'he's going to become a half-commission man.'

When Sara asked Guy to translate this later Guy said dubiously that they were hangers on. Messers in the City. They sold shares. They were seedy sorts of agents and got half the proceeds. 'Don't have a thing to do with them, Sara, I beg.'

Perry was soon gone from London, loudly lamented by Fay. 'I'm a sort of widow now.'

But when she received the extremely handsome cheque for the Sèvres, she looked radiant.

'Oh goody, Socks and I can go on the tiles.'

'I thought you were a widow.'

'Oh, I am. Socks is only a spare.'

'Poor Socks.'

'Don't be silly, Sara, he adores me.'

Fay had come to Park Street to hug Sara goodbye before she left for New York.

'It'll be so boring when you're not here. You won't take a fancy to New York and stay, will you?'

With her trunks packed, her engagement book a blank for the next two months, her work with Guy tied up, Sara went early to bed. Guy, like Fay, had earnestly said he hoped she wasn't going to desert England and remain in the States. Sara wondered why they both thought that possible. When she lay in bed, looking at a gleam of light from a street lamp which came through her curtains, she thought – I shall see New York again. Can I be happy there?

The *Aquitania*, berthed in Southampton, lay like a huge hotel along the quayside – a hotel with slanting gangways, up and down which scurried porters loaded with luggage and travellers heavy with furs. It was bitterly cold. Lee had gone down to Southampton the previous day to supervise the freight of her paintings. Catherine and Dudley were arriving by motor from Sussex. So Sara took the boat train from Waterloo alone. She looked out of the smutty window at the back gardens, tiny houses, bare apple trees, and for a moment remembered, like a thin scent, the Riviera at this time of year. The mimosa would be beginning; in the Villa des Roses Louise had it changed twice a day so that the flowers were always covered in soft yellow down which, thought Sara, was rather like Fay. Fay. Perry. I'm getting used to it at last. Perhaps in New York I will meet someone . . . but then the memory, sexual and shudderingly painful, swept back. I haven't recovered yet. How long does it take for, God's sake?

The porter, giving her a grubby numbered ticket, vanished with her trunks and Sara went to have her passport stamped. The porter reappeared at Customs where a pinched-looking man chalked her trunks without interest. Sara walked up the gangplank into the ship.

It was crowded not only with travellers but with their relatives and friends, and as she made her way along the embarkation deck she saw stewards loaded with boxes of flowers, packets of letters and telegrams and parcels of books. In the distance a military band was playing *Oh I do Like to be Beside the Sea.*

A stewardess took her to her bedroom. On the *Aquitania*, and the other great ships, it was not called a cabin. The room, much decorated in rose-pink, was spacious. Not the colour for me, thought Sara. She was pulling off her hat when there was a knock on the door. A telegram and a small box of flowers were delivered.

The telegram said 'Hurry back' – it was from Guy. The box contained a bridal bouquet of white gardenias and a card scribbled 'Fay' with a line of kisses.

Another knock. Lee peered in.

'Here you are. I've been waiting for you. Catherine and Dudley came aboard hours ago. They're having tea. Would you like some?'

'I'd rather chat,' said Sara, sitting on the bed.

Lee wandered about, opened wardrobes, sniffed the gardenias.

'What romantic friends you do have.'

'Jolly ones too. That's what you look,' said Sara.

'Well, that's just how I am. Guess whom I met in the main lounge. Perry van Rijn!'

Sara paused only for a moment, then said what on earth was

he doing in Southampton? She'd thought he was in New York.

'Sure, he did go back, but he returned on the *Orcades* only last week. The poor man must be bored with the ocean, but Alex begged him – something to do with money, don't ask me what. Capital investment? You know what your father's like. Van Rijns have men in their London office, but nothing will satisfy Alex but having Perry involved. So back poor Perry came. He jumped at the chance of being with us now.'

'For tea, you mean?'

'No, addle-pate! He's sailing with us,' said Lee, and burst out laughing.

The look Sara gave her was bright and hard.

'You don't seem very pleased, Sara. You're not too nice about Perry, I notice. He's always charming about you. Alex is devoted to him, can't get over finding a man who is clever *and* young. You know how he can't abide people he can fool or bully.'

'Which is why he chose you,' said Sara, desperately changing the subject.

'He didn't choose me. I chose him. Get that right.' Lee was sniffing the gardenias again.

Trembling inwardly, scarcely able to concentrate, Sara said the first thing that came into her head.

'Why don't you marry Father, Lee? I'd love you as a stepmother. And perhaps you'd quite like me as a daughter.'

The moment she'd spoken she could have bitten out her tongue. Lee looked stricken. But recovered at once and said in her usual matter-of-fact tone, 'Don't forget Catherine. Another daughter.'

'You don't seem all that struck with Cathy,' said Sara, more tactless, more nervous.

Lee grimaced.

'Don't you know me yet after all this time? I'm very fond of Catherine, more than she knows; and more it seems than you do either. As for your question, of course I shan't marry Alex. How could I paint if I did? Alex is French and Jewish in his soul. He thinks women of our sort should stay at home arranging the flowers and supervising *la cuisine*.'

196

'But I don't do either,' said Sara, clutching at a second change of subject.

'Oh *you*. You forced him into letting you work at de Grelle's, and don't let's pretend the Bauer sale wasn't part of the deal.'

The *Aquitania* sailed with the evening tide, the ship's sirens hooting, the lines of people on the quayside passionately waving. Sara, wrapped in furs against the cold night wind, went out on deck. She leaned on the railing and the figures on the quay grew smaller and smaller until they were a blur. Lines of lights winked in necklaces through the mist. A man came and stood beside her: without turning, she knew who it was.

'I wonder why watching the land disappear is always sad,' he remarked. 'Cigarette?'

'Thank you. No.'

'I forgot. You don't smoke.'

'And Fay smokes too much,' said Sara casually.

'Sure. She never finishes one, though. Usually only lights up to try and blow smoke rings.'

There was a pause. A girl and a man went by, the girl was saying, 'I had boxes and boxes, did you see them, Harry? The stewardess could scarcely fit them into my bedroom.'

'Fay sent me some gardenias,' said Sara, thinking, perhaps I should go. Why is it so hard to move?

'There's a big dinner on the first night out,' he said, seemingly ignoring the gardenias. 'Well, you've crossed often, you know all about it. Your sister is the one who finds everything quite a thrill. The shops and swimming pools and the Palladian lounge ... it's the first time I've seen Catherine impressed.'

'I shall hear about it at dinner, then,' said Sara. She thought this unlikely; in an hour Catherine would behave as if she'd crossed the Atlantic a dozen times.

The shore was only a band of lights now and the mist was thickening.

'Sara.'

His voice had a deeper note. She recoiled.

'I must go. I have to dress,' she said, and before he could speak hurried towards the companionway.

The night was cold, the mist almost veiled the stars; there was a slight swell, but nothing strong enough to disturb the well-dressed passengers pouring into the enormous pillared dining room. Above them was a ceiling painted with a passable impression of Tiepolo's *Apotheosis of Aeneas*. He soared heavenward to meet his mother Venus, naked upon the clouds. All round them were cherubs diving through the air like small, stout and dimpled swimmers.

The first-class passengers all appeared to be solidly rich; most were Americans returning from visits to Europe and the orchestra was almost drowned by their cheerful talk.

Catherine, wearing her favourite brown satin, looked bright; this was the life she preferred, with people of 'her' sort and every luxury provided. To make things perfect she had a handsome man as her companion and wore his ring on her left hand. Dudley was in high spirits. He was unimpressed with the vast floating palace, and the first time had been in the position of giving Catherine some social advice.

'Don't forget,' he said as they came on board, 'to tell the stewardess exactly what you want. Which frocks you'll wear and when you want them laid out. What time she is to draw your bath, whether you want breakfast served in your bedroom and so on. Everything, in fact. She's your personal servant.'

Catherine took this in. When they sat at dinner, with diamonds shining on the necks or in the hair of many of the women, Catherine shone too. It pleased her that Sara was quiet tonight; her sister had moments of American showiness and it was a change to see her subdued. Perhaps, thought Catherine charitably, Sara might even make a good marriage. She wasn't bad-looking if one admired that sort of thing.

During the meal Lee amused the party with talk of Atlantic crossings in the past. Of the passenger who travelled with a hundred-and-forty trunks and the South American beauty who never crossed without ten maids. She talked of gamblers and scandals. Of the girl for whom the ship's orchestra was assembled to serenade her outside her stateroom. 'The

Captain knew she enjoyed music while she was having a bath.'

Catherine listened and smiled. Sara, still uncharacteristically silent, ate almost nothing.

When coffee was served and the dance floor began to fill, Perry said,

'Will you dance, Sara?'

She couldn't think of a single excuse. On the glassily polished floor they danced to American music filled with the nostalgia of city dwellers for their faraway homes. 'Omaha, I'm coming back to you!' was the refrain.

'I don't know about that tune,' remarked Perry, leading her into a turn. 'I think I'd prefer the old stuff they played at the Roumaniev. It was more cheerful. Do you remember your admirer, the general?'

'Of course. He went to Algiers, I think.'

'Did you see any of your friends from the Roumaniev again, Sara?'

'Not one. They all left on the same day.'

'Were you sorry? Did you miss them?'

'Of course.'

'What about me?'

The music stopped. People clapped. The night was still young, the first night at sea. The orchestra began again.

He put his arm round her and they danced.

'I asked you a question, Sara.'

'I know. And I don't want to answer it. It's all forgotten.'

'Are you sure?'

He swerved, taking her with him. She was suddenly and angrily nervous.

'Listen. I know how it is between you and Fay. She's crazy about you. Stop this.'

'Stop what?'

'You know very well. This.'

'I'm only dancing with you. Nothing to that.'

'How stupid of me. I thought there was.'

He looked down at the top of her glowing copper-red hair. He could not see her face.

'You're very cool. Well, perhaps there was supposed to be . . . forget it. I apologize.'

'Oh good.'

'Don't be so cold. It sure doesn't suit you.'

'You'd be surprised,' she said fiercely, 'how cold I've become.'

CHAPTER THIRTEEN

The Atlantic weather, often cruel and always uncertain, was kind to the seventeen hundred passengers settling down for their five days at sea. Cunard over the years took more and more trouble to make them enjoy themselves and gaiety was the order of the day. Deck games, shuffleboard, deck tennis, even tugs of war and childish potato races were in a daily programme of ship's sports. There was the swimming pool, where the emerald-lit water washed beneath Roman pillars. There was a music room, a library. And the exquisite elaborate food, eight courses-long for luncheon and dinner. The regiments of servants, dining stewards, deck-chair stewards, were there to help and wait upon the travellers. The purser was himself a celebrity; his name was James Spedding and Mayor Jimmy Walker of New York was his friend.

The de Grelle party spent their time in different ways. Dudley taught Catherine billiards at which she proved surprisingly skilfull. Lee, a sketchbook on her lap and a rug round her knees, sat in a sheltered corner on A deck where she could draw. She sketched the passengers striding on their walks, with the long lines of decking planks under their feet, divided by shining bands of tar. She drew the sheerwaters, small tubby black-and-white birds with enormously long thin wings held out stiffly, sheering just above or in the trough of the waves. Sometimes she sat for hours, headbent, absorbed in a novel or a biography. But she never minded when Sara came to sit with her.

Privately she thought the girl seemed troubled. Lee wondered if Perry van Rijn was chasing her and Sara fending him off. Sometimes when Perry came lounging up to sit with them, Sara's pale face would go pink, and when the colour ebbed she had a pinched look. This happened one morning when Sara was with her and Perry came towards them, a thick scarf round his neck flying in the wind.

'Perry,' said Lee, 'we need coffee. Scalding hot. That wind has a bite in it. Could you . . .'

'Of course. Back in a trice.'

Sara wrapped in furs and gloves, a little woollen cap over her hair, snuggled close to Lee for warmth.

'Sara. Might one ask without being too nosey what's going on between you and that man?'

Sara's thin face, with its scatter of freckles, blushed again. Paled again.

'Nothing. What makes you think there is?'

'Oh, I don't think anything. But you're never exactly welcoming. Does he bore you? Talking about money and that curious merchant-banking world? Perhaps he thinks as a de Grelle you'll be interested.'

'But I like hearing that –' began Sara vehemently. Just then Perry reappeared followed by a steward, adroit as a rope dancer, carrying a tray.

Lee, holding the steaming cup in both hands, asked the two young people what joys were in store tonight. Concerts? Chess tournaments? Fancy dress? Privately she thought the round of pleasure on the great Atlantic liners a curious phenomenon. The latest craze was organized pillow fights.

'I ask myself what happens when the weather worsens, Which of us three will get seasick first?'

'Me,' said Sara, thinking, then I can get away from him.

'Mmm. You don't look the sickish sort. I am. How Alex dislikes it when I disappear to throw up. And he marches round the deck filled with conceit because of his steady stomach. How's yours, Perry?'

'Up until now, okay.'

'You don't look the sickish sort either,' said Lee, glancing at him with brilliant blue eyes.

How attractive he was, she thought. Seductive, even. She couldn't imagine why Sara kept him at arm's length. But there was a mystery in sexual attraction and a greater mystery in motives. Even her own. Why after ten years was she still Alexander de Grelle's complacent mistress? There had been a time when she loathed the fact that he had not asked her to marry him. She had thirsted to leave him. Now she was used to it. He visited her in her mews cottage, took her when he had the fancy, was passionate, satisfying. They lay together as married people do. But he had not become her next of kin. Yet how could she have fooled herself into thinking she could leave him; his hold on her, his hold on life itself, was so strong.

Lee was right in her guess that the weather would deteriorate. The *Aquitania* became, as her Captain called it, 'pretty lively in a sea-way'. With the result that a number of passengers retired and were missing for dinner on the second night. Catherine was among them, sending a message via a steward. Dudley sent back a bunch of red roses from the shop on deck, and a card full of concern. Privately he thought she was making a silly fuss. She'd only looked pale; he'd seen crossings where people were so ill they appeared near to death.

The next casualty was Lee. The de Grelle party was now reduced at dinner to three. Dudley decided to enliven the meal with stories of the card-sharpers who travelled on the big liners, his favourite being one who dressed like a curate. Sara was glad of his talk, glad to laugh and let Dudley take the stage. When the meal was over he stood up, saying he was meeting an American for billiards.

'He's by way of being president of a steel corporation,' he said. When he had left them there was a marked pause. The waiter came up, wheeling a trolleyful of liqueurs, green and golden and colourless and sickly yellow. They reminded Sara of Fay's collection of miniature bottles. She suddenly saw her scatterbrained friend, eyes shut, speaking of Perry with a kind of bliss. She turned her eyes involuntarily to the man opposite her and something in her face made him say, 'Do you want me to go?'

'Not particularly. Anyway, where would you go to?'

'I could have a Turkish bath,' he suggested, smiling.

'Do you like them?'

'No. They make me feel stupid.'

Her pettish manner amused him.

'I might go and join Dudley for billiards.'

'Perhaps you should as he's playing with somebody important. That's known as making useful friends.'

He was still not offended. Music filled the space between them. It was very sentimental.

'Do you object to making useful friends?' he finally asked.

'I'd be a fool if I did. De Grelle's must have been founded on Father's talent for liking people and their liking him. People do like him enormously. They even trust him.'

'Why "even", Sara?'

'Because I'm sure he's a fox. But not one who sinks its sharp teeth into people. Do you think he does that?'

'Sometimes.'

'So does everybody,' she said, before she could stop herself. There was a silence.

'Cathy's not averse to a few useful friends either,' she said. She regretted her last remark.

'And what about you?'

'Have I any? My useful friend, I suppose, is a good memory. I need that all the time when I'm working.'

She had slightly thawed.

'Come and dance, Sara.'

'I don't think I want to.'

'Not true. You were made for dancing. Come on. Let's see what it's like to dance on a floor that's never in the same place twice.'

The floor tipped up, then down, as the ship dived and rose. To dance was like skating and Sara's shoes seemed soled with glass. Once she slid out of his arms and he only just caught her. The ship steamed on. The music ended and the few brave dancers applauded. Sara, still supported with his arm round her waist, looked up at him. He was staring at her mouth. With the hand not holding her, he put his fingers across his own lips.

They went out of the ballroom in silence. She was beyond thinking. The *Aquitania* lifted its bows fifty, sixty feet high, then down it came, dipping and diving as it cleaved through the enormous waves. Every beat of the ship's engines, heartbeats, cruel heartbeats, took her and Perry further away from

Fay. I'm a bitch, she thought. Then thought of nothing. They went down a passage to his bedroom, he unlocked the door which swung so heavily that it almost crashed into her. When they were inside, it slammed and he locked it.

The lamp in the ceiling swung to and fro. On the dressing table his brushes fell against each other, clattering. The ship thudded like her heart.

They took off their clothes in hurried silence, dropping them on the floor, not looking at each other. She thought of nothing but what awaited her – her conscience, her common-sense, her self-command were gone like pieces of veil in a fire. He walked naked towards her and she saw the familiar body, creamy, pale, and his swelling muscles and that part of him which was going to give her what she thirsted for. She wrapped her arms round him and pushed hard against it.

For lovers who knew each other's bodies the act of love was not the hasty, violent, unskilled act of a couple at a drunken party. There was time to savour, to move slowly, to take each part of the loving in its own exquisite time. Until the end when it grew fiercest, and they finally parted, breathless and silent.

He said nothing. Neither did she. They had not spoken a word since they left the ballroom. They lay, bodies separated, until at last he said, 'A penny?'

'Not for sale.'

He turned, leaned on his elbow and tweaked the red hair lying in strands across the pillow.

'Ow. That hurt.'

'I meant it to. Tell me what you're thinking.'

'You won't like it.'

'I guess it's something uncomplimentary,' he lazily said. In his voice was the slightly laughing note of a man who knows he has utterly pleasured a girl. God, she thought, almost hating him for that satisfied music, do all men think what they do to us is so unutterably clever? But her indignant thoughts were at odds with her swooning, satisfied body.

'Well?' he said, pulling her hair again.

She sat up, covering her full white breasts, the nipples the colour of a wild rose, with the sheet. Because she and Perry

205

shared nothing but sex, because no word of love with its poetry and sadness was ever spoken between them, a kind of fierce modesty came to her the moment it was over. She tucked the sheet behind her back. Then, 'I was thinking about Fay.'

'I know.'

'Then why did you ask?'

She did not understand him. He hurt her. With her body still actually able to feel his inside her, he hurt her.

'I wanted you to say it aloud because you sure as hell have been repeating it in your thoughts. And in your eyes. You brought Fay along as an extra member of the party. Stop it, Sara.'

She was quiet for so long that, raising himself and leaning on his elbow, he looked down at her again. She lay flat on her back, looking at the ceiling. The bunk, the cabin, the ship, heaved up, then down. The engines throbbed.

'You're very quiet. What is it?'

'You know perfectly well.'

He began to stroke her face and by that touch she knew he wanted her again. He'd done this before, had her, and had her again so quickly. He did not touch her now with affection but with rising desire.

'Sara, Sara. Don't you *know* you're the most exciting woman I've ever made love to?'

Dudley's teasing about Catherine was wrong. Like her father and sister, she was a good sailor. Her headache and slight nausea were only due to rich food after the somewhat Spartan menu in Lytchett, where her grandmother believed in things wholesome but not elaborate.

The morning following her absence from dinner saw Catherine in one of the small dining rooms, eating a large omelette.

'I slept like a top. One could have been in Sussex,' she said, while the ship heaved and slid and she had to save her coffee cup from disaster. Dudley was attentive. His fiancée was looking her best in a white woollen suit buttoned up to the neck and enhancing her rosy English complexion. He had spent a successful evening, having won five pounds from the steel corporation's president, and made an appointment to meet him in New York.

Hearing this, Catherine approved. She was in a sunny mood. Dudley found her attractive this morning. Her little air of cool self-satisfaction was a sexual barrier he would soon break down.

'What's on the cards today, Cath?'

She took a tiny appointment book from her handbag. Planny Anny even made arrangements when at sea. Coffee with Mr and Mrs Somebody, swimming with Somebody Else, and luncheon with a prince.

'What kind of prince?' enquired Dudley with a loudish laugh.

Catherine said repressively that he was Russian. Dudley didn't imagine he would be an English royal prince, surely.

'I never sort out the handles, Cath. Except that a Russian swell doesn't hit the target any more.'

'Blood is blood,' said Catherine.

'Oh, you've got scads of that,' he said on cue. 'But nobody's falling over themselves to know the poor old Russians any more. Sara said her mother knew loads of them on the Riviera before the war. Hundreds of people at dam' great parties, and the crowned heads dead drunk. Now they're hard pushed to earn a quid or two. Sara's mother was thinking of having a Russian princess for a lady's maid.'

Catherine did not continue this line of talk, which glowed with Sara's French past. She had a curious, obscure jealousy of her sister's girlhood which had not been nearly as happy as her own.

By chance the sisters met that afternoon at the hairdresser's. Due to the rough sea, the salon was almost empty. Sara's red hair was swathed in a turban when Catherine arrived. Later both girls emerged with shining hair and manicured nails. Sara said in a friendly voice, 'Let's have tea.'

'Without the men?'

'Definitely without the men.'

She had slept deeply. Woken as she'd done in the past as if every nerve in her body had been caressed, looked at herself in the glass and seen her own swimming eyes and the dark shadows under them which meant an overdose, a delicious, exhausting overdose of sex. This well-being, this gentle indifference so at odds with the dark heaving sea, had made up her mind for her. Until they landed, just for these four and a half days, she *would not* think about Fay. She'd done wrong. Excuses thronged into her head, begging like suitors to be accepted. That she'd been Perry's lover first, two years ago. And again in London before, she supposed, he and Fay had been together. But he'd chosen Fay, hadn't he, instead of herself? And Fay had fallen desperately in love with him. God knows, thought Sara, if he loves her. Perhaps he does. But I am with him now. A poem came into her mind.

> Then talk not of Inconstancy
> False hearts and broken vows.
> If I, by Miracle, can be
> This live-long Minute true to Thee
> 'Tis all that heaven allows.

That's Perry, she thought. I suppose his heart is false. All I know is that I can't resist him. If what I feel is love, I don't want any part of it – after the ship docks. But there are four and a half days left. They seemed to stretch into infinity. All those hours. All those opportunities to repeat the one blissful, unbearably exciting, hungry, thudding, meaningless act.

It is sex with Perry which makes me feel friendly to Cathy, she thought.

They sat in the Palladian lounge and Catherine ordered tea. When the waiter had gone, she turned to her sister, 'How are you enjoying the trip? Dudley likes being with us so much. It was good of Father to include him. But of course he is a member of the family now.'

'So he is. He was telling me about his plans for the gallery,' said Sara good-naturedly. As usual there was to be no mention of herself. She didn't mind. It amused her that Catherine should pour tea and eat bread and butter as daintily as a sparrow, and be unaware that Sara was having a fierce love affair a few cabins away. She'd say I am taking after Louise. *Am I?*

'I've been thinking Father might take Dudley into de

Grelle's,' said Catherine. 'He's so clever and he knows everything about early nineteenth-century painting. So knowledgeable.'

'I'm afraid there is somebody . . . Alban Tucker is the de Grelle man for that period.'

'But Dudley is family,' repeated Catherine.

Gazing at her sister's face, Sara remembered searching there in the past for some physical resemblance to their father. She felt the old desire to please. She did not know why Catherine whom she didn't love and often didn't respect should affect her like that: ties of blood were the devil. But because of her own melting, hazy happiness just now, she was willing to reach Catherine, even through her sister's egotism. She chose subjects to please her. Dudley's gallery. His potential success. She spoke of Catherine's first visit to the States.

'I wonder what you're expecting, Cathy?'

'Dudley has warned me,' said Catherine, with no trace of humour, 'that it will all be very American.'

'But aren't you used to that? What with Lee and me.'

'Oh yes,' Catherine was not listening, 'but he says American men – I don't count Mr van Rijn – are entirely different from us. They have a passion for money.'

Sara was so thunderstruck that for a moment she couldn't think of a word. Catherine! The one who on the rare occasion when they had lunched together at Gunter's, had divided the bill so exactly that she had practically sawed a penny in half.

'Perry van Rijn deals in money too. A merchant banker. Why not count him?'

Why did she encourage Catherine?

'Mr van Rijn is from one of the old New York families. Do have an éclair, Sara. These little ones are quite good. Devonshire cream, too. I don't know how they manage it. But Dudley says Cunard pride themselves on their pastry cooks.'

The four days, so endless in Sara's hot imagination, so filled with expectation and encounter and the luxurious aftermath of sex, were over. The ship was due to dock in New York harbour at six in the evening. The rough seas had calmed as they drew nearer to the continent and many passengers who had retired, to be ministered to with ice packs and weak tea, emerged. Interestingly pale, they were all set to enjoy the ball on the last night at sea, and the drama as the ship approached the towers of New York.

And during the four days and four nights Sara and Perry made love. What is it about sex that the more you had the more you wanted, the more your body hardened or moistened, for man and for woman? There was a magical anonymity about the ship. It was too large and too crowded for them to worry that they would be noticed when, in the afternoon, at night, even once in the mid-morning, they went to Sara's room or to Perry's to repeat, over and over again, the act that left them gasping. Not once, not ever, did he say a word of love. He was passionate, skilful, exciting, silent. And Sara never spoke an endearment to him either. She didn't dare. It was as if they had made a pact, a devil's pact, which allowed them only to do this, just this. It was brimful of pleasure, running over, spilling across them when they were naked. How dared they want anything else?

She was too dizzy and dazzled by the continual sex to ask herself what would happen when the voyage was over. Once Fay glimmered into her mind and she thought – perhaps Perry will marry her? But a moment later she saw him walking along the deck in search of her, his easy figure silhouetted against a background of almost black waves. And every thought but desire went out of her head.

It was getting dark as the *Aquitania* approached New York, and the towers across the water one by one turned into oblongs of diamonds. The sky was pure aquamarine without a cloud. The passengers crowded on deck as the city drew nearer, ferry boats whistled and tramp steamers went by loaded with cargoes from the four corners of the world. We are cargoes too, thought Sara. Perry stood beside her as the huge continent came nearer and nearer.

It is seven years since I was here, she thought, staring at the huge buildings soaring raising up to the sky – she could count over a dozen rearing up dramatically. They seemed strange to her. Will the city be changed, she thought.

She forgot how much she was changed.

Part Four

CHAPTER FOURTEEN

Alexander met the family on board ship, and drove with them to the hotel: he had chosen the old-established and expensive Ellsworth Palace overlooking Central Park. When Perry said goodbye to Sara he pressed her hand so hard that her amethyst ring made a dent in her finger which lasted for hours. She watched him go.

At dinner, Alexander who found prohibition both extraordinary and tedious, said he only wished he could order champagne.

'Why? Are we celebrating all the arrangements being perfectly fixed?' enquired Lee, drinking orange juice.

'Not exactly. I would like to have proposed a toast to Hope, I think.'

She put down her glass and said at once, 'Something's happened.'

'I'm afraid it has.'

Four pairs of eyes were fixed on him, and Alexander who relished the dramatic told them that he had had a shock: of the kind every auctioneer dreads.

It seemed that the dusty legend had been true after all and Henry Benjamin had a son. There had been great difficulty in tracing him after the old man died, but he had eventually been discovered working as a teacher in a small town in South Carolina. He was married, with two grown-up sons.

'Don't say he's going to cancel the auction!' exclaimed Sara in horror.

'No, no, Henry Benjamin wished things to be sold. He was rather flattering about me . . . as it happens. Men make jokes in their wills sometimes,' he added dryly. 'But Lorin Benjamin is not an easy customer . . .'

He described the man. For whatever passionate Jewish reason Lorin and his father had quarrelled, he'd spent years pinched for money. He'd made his way, as good Americans did, married, raised children. But when Alexander showed him his father's collection his indifference, said Alexander, 'gave me frostbite.'

'Yes, yes,' was his only response, 'I suppose they're pretty valuable.'

Lorin Benjamin was tall, haggard, not unhandsome, with a mop of greying hair and an irritable face. The fortune pouring down on him in showers of gold gave him no joy, nor the beautiful emotion of wonder. It simply fussed him. He was anxious over the inheritance, the future, the attention of the newspapers, the auction, – and the paintings. The day before the *Aquitania* arrived the executors telephoned Alexander to say that Lorin was withdrawing the two Renoirs. They were being sold privately – at sixty thousand dollars.

'But Henry Benjamin said *you* were to auction them!' said Lee, shocked.

'My dear *mignonne*, to sell them through a dealer is scarcely breaking the terms of the will,' said Alexander, sighing.

He was sharply aware that Renoir's value had taken a strong upward turn after the painter died in 1919. Five years ago you could buy a Renoir for fifteen hundred dollars. But at a sale last year, the *Canotiers à Charenton* sold for twenty-seven thousand dollars. He had looked forward keenly to auctioning Henry's Renoirs, they were two of the stars of the show. He and the old man had loved those pictures. The women were so beautiful, so stupid, so fleshly, so immortally young. Alexander had thirsted to be the man to sell them – he felt as if he were to be the seller at a disgraceful and titillating slave market. And of course, there was the profit.

During dinner his family were shocked and sympathetic, and he did not pretend he hadn't had a blow. It was not surprising that he could do with some champagne.

But his delight in the future reasserted itself when he took the family to see the new de Grelle galleries. They were in one of the handsome brownstone houses which, despite building plans, still lined Madison Avenue. Alexander had managed to buy the house at a perfect time, had been able to enlarge it and now, elegant and opulent, it was a mansion which was part of the city's exclusive new art world. The main saleroom had been converted, two large rooms knocked into one to resemble the largest at St Charles Street, even to the skylight and the floors of polished mahogany. The viewing galleries were filled with Benjamin's furniture, mingled with French pieces which had been shipped over from Paris. Two of the galleries housed the old man's Renaissance treasures. In the furthest gallery were his French paintings.

Catherine and Dudley walked round together with much observant interest, then she went over to speak to her father.

'I have the ghost of a headache and want to be at my best for tomorrow. I'd like to go to bed, and have some tea in my room. Tea always does the headache good.'

'Of course, *mon enfant*,' said Alexander. He had been talking to Sara of Alfred Sisley, 'Do you realize his parents were *English*! It is impossible to believe!' He broke off to look kindly at his elder daughter. 'I am sorry for the headache. But you will be clever if you obtain tea in New York.'

Catherine smiled. A travelled friend had warned her and she'd brought a stock from Fortnum and Mason. It only remained to send instructions to the hotel kitchens.

The Bauer sale in Paris had been newsworthy. So was the New York opening. Comment had been growing in the American press for months, one scarcely opened a newspaper or magazine without seeing the word 'de Grelle'. Tales of disaster and triumph, the disasters naturally being more accentuated. Alexander was used to the press but this was the glare of a Sahara sun. He was fortunate in having as his colleague the cool and worldly Clarke Cheritree Spencer who was to be head man in de Grelle's in New York. Spencer merely said that press comment added brilliance to the opening. 'Good or bad' he added.

Clarke Cheritree Spencer was a prize and Alexander had wooed him from a successful rival. Spencer had decided to accept because he liked the idea of a new American auction house with French and English connexions. He was a good-looking, compact, confident man with a light manner who had come into the auctioneering world by mistake, back in 1911. The famous A.A.A. had auctioned his own father's collection of American things for which a vogue had just begun – American glass, pewter, eighteenth-century silver, some beautiful colonial furniture. Spencer thought the auctioning of his family's collection was carried out somewhat badly and remarked that 'he bet he could do it better'. Some rivals who admired the young man's moneyed background of culture invited him to try. To his surprise, Spencer found himself working.

Now, with a new and fascinating gallery under his command, he welcomed the press's attention, even their waspish attacks. And one kinder commentator wrote, 'De Grelle's are already, without doubt, one of the magnetic attractions in the world of fine things.'

The saleroom was rapidly filling up when Sara, Catherine, Dudley and Lee arrived well before the time of the opening. Sara looked round with intense interest, comparing these people to the crowds in London and Paris. She thought they looked richer and – did she imagine tougher? The women's furs were a uniform, the men looked as opulent as they. She wondered if her impression was due to the mixture of nationalities in her own country, which made for a stronger, fiercer, more considerable physiognomy. She saw eagles in the audience. Or men who, negligently leaning back, had the air of being about to spring up and shoot from the hip. I look at my own countrymen as if they were strangers. So they are, because I've been away so long.

Guy Buckingham once told her he estimated that a crowd at an auction was made up roughly in thirds – a third were dealers, a third collectors, and a third (as Lee had said in Paris) came for the fun of the thing. Sara recognized some of the dealers, both European and American. All the distinguished American dealers sat more or less in a block together. But the continental dealers found their reserved seats (to their annoyance) scattered through the house. It was a tactical device of Alexander's, to control them if he considered their bids too low.

216

At the back of the saleroom was the dark-clad over-thin figure of Lorin Benjamin. He came in just before the auction, and remained like a statue all through it, scarcely budging.

The warming-up session in the afternoon was to be conducted by Cheritree Spencer, his first appearance on the new mahogany rostrum. In the evening, Alexander would take the stage.

As Sara looked round, an impressive befurred figure approached her. It was an old friend of her mother's, Mary Drexel II, wearing the largest pearls Sara had ever seen.

'My dear child,' said Mrs Drexel. 'A joy to see Louise's daughter. You must come by and meet the family soon. My girls will be crazy to see you again.'

Sara replied suitably, introduced Lee and Catherine, Mary Drexel was gracious, and then went back to her seat. And you, thought Sara, are one of the third who has come to watch and not to buy.

Who can foretell the results of an auction, Alexander often said. He had conducted a famous auction in Hampshire only the previous year at which, despite some fine *objets d'art*, the thing had been a dismal failure . . . because the sale was in a marquee and it poured with rain all day. It was this uncertainty, this anxiety, which added a flavour of danger. Alexander was aware of the shocks which might come, or – in an owner's case – the baffled rage of disappointment. He had planned the sequence of the Benjamin sale carefully. Those children dear to the old man's heart, the French Impressionists, would be auctioned by Alexander himself late in the afternoon. After their interesting success, with the buyers warmed and enthusiastic, the real stuff for which they were hungry – the treasures from Italy – would come under the hammer. The auction would thus go from strength to strength.

A number of people had seen him before the sale to give instructions on how how they would bid or in which way they would indicate whether they wanted to continue or not. Usually without even a nod of the head, since most of them wished to hide their interest in case it became infectious.

There had been some elaborate bidding arrangements

beforehand. 'If Mr Behrens is sitting down, he's bidding. If he stands up, he's stopped.' All the other variations of the 'Yes' and the 'No' were added. Every one of them was connected with the Benjamin Renaissance collection. It was for those that the room was full of dealers and collectors, eager for more treasures from the golden Italian past. Not a single man had indicated interest in the French paintings.

But Alexander was an optimist. And wasn't New York rich and daring?

Sara was nervous when the auction began. She admired Cheritree Spencer's cool rostrum manner, and the lots, porcelain, early Victorian water colours, some furniture, sold very quickly. Spencer was cool and so were the prices.

At last her father came to the rostrum. He wore a black braided suit and his inevitable pink carnation. With his greying but still auburn hair and beard, his brilliant eyes sparkling and narrowed, Sara saw why people nicknamed him 'the French Fox'. Watching him as he opened this part of the auction, she thought he was like a celebrated conductor. He stood with legs slightly apart, his slender ivory hammer ready to beat sharply down. A porter in a dark green apron with the gold-encircled DG entered, carrying a painting which he placed on the velvet-draped easel – Utrillo's *Neige dans les rues de la Butte*.

Alexander did not open with a roll of drums. But his affection for the painting warmed his fine voice. Somebody made a bid. One hundred and fifty dollars. Sara bit her lip.

Alexander was a gambler and it was thirty long years since the famous débâcle of the A.A.A.'s auction when *The Impressionist of Paris* had burst on baffled clients, and received an avalanche of scorn. He was sure taste was changing. He could smell it. As a young man in Paris he'd met Victor Chocquet, the small-time customs official who bought oils from Gauguin or came home to his wife to say, 'No chicken today, dear, I've found a little Daumier.' Chocquet told Alexander that at a Drouot sale in 1875 (when he'd bought Manet's *Paysage d'Argenteuil* for a hundred francs), 'some of my friends' canvases were slashed, my dear de Grelle. Oh, how they were detested!'

And that had been long before the A.A.A.'s disastrous sale. And now Alexander had strong hopes for these visions of exquisite France. Taste *was* changing. It *must*.

He was horribly, magnificently wrong. It hadn't. Nobody wanted Benjamin's beloved pictures. A Raoul Dufy went for seventy dollars – (Sara was also wrong, it was bought by Mary Drexel). The Sisley went for no more than old Benjamin had paid for it, and a Bonnard for less – four hundred dollars. The only picture which created a distinct interest was a Cézanne – *his* prices had dramatically risen since his death in 1906. The painting was a study of the artist's particularly loved subject, the Mont Sainte-Victoire, until the last. Cézanne had painted it when the sun was setting, lighting its western face. The mountain dominated the landscape, like a leading actor centre-stage.

When the picture was on the easel, Alexander said a word or two.

'The French author, d'Arbaud, calls this mountain, "The spirit of Provence. Majestic. A living face which ennobles all who see it". This is what the great master shows us . . .'

The bidding began slowly, rose steadily. Seven thousand. Eight thousand. 'More?' said Alexander in his warmest voice.

Finally the contest was between a stout dark-eyed New York dealer and a quietly elegant man in pale grey, John Israels, a lawyer from Philadelphia. Alexander knew Israels, a courageous collector whose opinions were his own.

Up went the price, thousand by thousand.

Israels won Cézanne's mountain for twenty-one thousand dollars. The price made the crowd, and later the press, gasp.

Alexander slammed down the ivory hammer.

'Sold to Mr Israels. And worth,' he said, aware of the audience's feeling for the Impressionists, 'three times the money.'

There was a pause. The crowd talked in low voices. Shifted. Then the auction started again.

A porter in his white gloves carried in a Carpaccio, one of his paintings of *La Légende de Sainte Ursule*. Sara thought – ah, we're back in the past now. Not France twenty years ago, but Venice in the fifteenth century . . .

And even as this thought came to her, somebody broke into spontaneous applause.

When the auction ended that night, every piece of Renaissance art, the furniture, crucifixes inlaid with pearls, the great heavy carved tables, the glass, all was fiercely bid for, fiercely won. Alexander's angels and saints were destined to bless the walls of galleries, the homes of the fabulously rich.

The auction continued the next day. And the total, when the first de Grelle sale in Madison Avenue ended, was $927,850. Lorin Benjamin heard the news with a dark, tense face. He took the train back to South Carolina next morning. He had neither congratulated nor thanked Alexander – who did not expect it.

Alexander gave a celebration dinner, of course. It went on far too long. Both Sara and Catherine were tired and even Lee looked pale. Not Alexander, he was stimulated by excitement. Sometimes, thought Sara, he's like a jockey who's won a race. Sometimes like an actor. Sometimes like a king . . .

She lay, wakeful and restless, in her luxurious room, remembering the crowds and silences, her father's 'More?' and the short hard rap of the hammer. She slept at last, but woke before seven. The sound of the auction had faded from her thoughts now. They came to Perry. He had not sat with them during the sale, but her nerves had told her he was there; then she had seen him right at the back of the room, standing. He had slipped away and not dined with them last night.

So it's over again, she thought. Should I be humiliated at being used? How can I be, since *I* used *him*? But something inside her wept just the same, the child in the locked room.

The family was only to remain in New York four more days while Alexander and Spencer worked through the myriad details following the auction. Lee was seeing friends and going to a gallery which sold her paintings. Catherine and Dudley wanted to shop and sight-see. Sara telephoned Aunt Emily Goodier. The voice which replied was as sharp as she remembered, if perhaps slightly hoarse.

'No cablegram or letter? You're as sudden as your mother. Very well. Come along if you wish.'

No impulsive welcome there. The cool reproach gave Sara a feeling of security. She felt in need of rules.

The little lady who answered the door of the sedate house on 96th Street looked older than Sara remembered. But there was the same bright glance, the same high cheekbones, and the same kind of blouse with a high boned collar and lines of tiny tucks.

'Well, well, quite a surprise,' she said, allowing Sara to kiss her cheek. 'I read about the fuss in the newspapers. And saw your name.'

She took Sara into a sitting room which had not changed since 1880. The painting of two Puritan men sitting at a table was over the mantelshelf. Three fans were pinned over a glass-fronted case filled with the thinnest Japanese china. There was a fish made of silver mesh. A photograph of Emily's father, standing beside a spindly table which emphasized his solid bulk, was in an elaborate silver frame. And the antimacassars which Emily had crocheted in the pattern of stars and stripes were pinned on velour-covered chairs which, thought Sara, probably did not often have a man, let alone one with oily hair, seated on them.

'Sit down, my child, take that chair yonder.'

'I should have written, Aunt Emily. Will you forgive me?'

'I don't expect so. Your mother never writes except to send Christmas cards in French. What do I want with those? Will you take coffee?'

It came, hot and black, in a heavy silver pot.

The old woman and the girl talked in the accepted way of exchanging news, each one putting her cards, one by one, on the table. But with the old and the young, Emily only placed a mere three cards, Sara had a score.

She had forgotten Emily Goodier and how she liked her. Had forgotten her aunt's severity and humour and flat New York voice. Sara admired her precision, admired the house in which every ornament was dusted every day.

'So your mother's husband is spreading his wings here in New York, is he? It was in *The Times* this morning. A deal of money changing hands, and much of it landing on him.'

'Ten per cent, Aunt Emily.'

Her aunt gave a bark of laughter.

Sara did not stay long. Emily made no bones about friends being due for luncheon, and did not invite her great-niece to join them. One knew where one was, thought Sara.

'It's time to take yourself off,' said her great-aunt, 'But before I say goodbye, I suppose I must ask after your mother.'

Sara was ready for that.

'Just the same. In the Villa des Roses. You know how she is.'

'I know how she used to be.'

'She doesn't change, Aunt. She's settled on the Riviera. And goes to Switzerland every summer when the south is too hot.'

Emily examined the vivid girl opposite her.

'Hmm. Do you visit with her?'

'Not just now. I work for my father, you see.'

'So you do,' said Emily, apparently reading in Sara's face the answer to various questions. Not particularly happy, thought the old woman, for all that glowing paleness. She looks more like her father than her mother. There's little Goodier blood there.

'I read today that you're off to Newport,' she said, standing up, 'to live in a French château of sorts. Do you know Newport?'

'No. I am told it's thrilling.'

'What language. It is not thrilling at all, but it is certainly curious. Our wealthiest families settled there after the Civil War. Their taste has to be questioned, I myself consider the palaces they built quite ridiculous. But the Belmonts and the Vanderbilts were pleased with them and I have never been invited as a house guest. It surprises me that your father found a place empty.'

'He said it's a little château, owned by the Adams family. Built in 1880.'

'La Pallice. I like the description "little". How many guests are invited? Fifty?'

Sara kissed her cheek and Emily stood at the door waiting until she saw the girl safely into a taxi. Then she went back into her house.

During the remaining days in New York, which were turning steadily colder, Dudley and Catherine were out a great deal. Lee took Sara shopping. Sara had thought she knew the city she'd so enjoyed at sixteen, but it wasn't as she remembered. She had believed life was casual and one's time was one's own. But one invitation led to twenty, the telephones never stopped ringing, beginning at eight in the morning – New Yorkers rose early – and calls, messages and floods of flowers continued until midnight. Hospitality and welcome were extraordinary.

'You seem *bouleversée*, Sara,' said her father at dinner. 'Has it not entered your head that you are the daughter of somebody celebrated? But you can forget the young Americans languishing for your *beaux yeux* tomorrow, I want you to come to de Grelle's to look at the latest shipment from France. Silver to make Guy Buckingham's mouth water.'

Neither Alexander nor Sara noticed Dudley Forrest's expression. He was looking from father to daughter and back again.

Next morning when Sara and Alexander left for Madison Avenue it was cold enough to take their breath away. A few flakes of snow were drifting down from a sky far off in between the cliffs made by the skyscrapers. Sara forgot the weather during a day of absorbed interest. Not only in silver but in Louis XVI furniture. But when she and her father were driven home, they saw that it had begun to snow in earnest. There were drifts along the pavements over three feet high.

'Everything American is so sudden,' said Alexander, peering out with amusement. 'Sunshine on Monday. Antarctica on Tuesday. Stimulating. Have you brought enough furs?'

After too much food and too much talk that evening, Alexander eventually allowed his three women to retire, kissing the hands of mistress and daughters and bowing to Dudley who laughed and bowed back.

Sara trailed down the hot, thickly-carpeted corridor to her room. She yawned as she shut the door. Wrenching off the diamond bandeau worn across her forehead, she saw in the glass that there was a long red mark on her skin. Fay had complained of the same thing.

The telephone broke the rich silence. Outside, far down in the street, the snow had laid a carpet, turning Central Park into the Russian steppes, decorating the turrets and the towers of the city, muffling the world.

Sara lay across the bed and picked up the telephone.

'It's me,' said a man's voice.

Her stomach dropped.

'Sara. Are you there? Or am I addressing a total stranger?'

'Not exactly. Hello, Perry. Goodnight, really. It's late.'

'I won't keep you long. We haven't seen each other since the ship. My fault.'

'No, mine. Lee and I – Cathy too – are always out. Such a lot of invitations.'

'Good,' he said annoyingly. 'I called up to tell you some news. I'm invited to Newport at the end of the week.'

Silence.

'Sara? Have you gone to sleep?'

'No. I heard you. How – how nice.'

'Nice for me. I shall see you. A lot of you.'

A pause.

'A good deal of you. All of you, come to think of it.'

Knowing exactly the effect he'd had, he laughed when he said goodnight.

Alexander hired an enormous car to make the day-long drive to Newport. He was interested in the falling snow. During breakfast in the hotel dining room, he stood up two or three times to go to the window and report on the weather. He enjoyed that. Lee and Catherine looked disturbed, Sara and Dudley less so.

'Alex,' said Lee, when he came back with news of crawling cars and pedestrians like Eskimos, 'are you sure it's wise to drive today? We could get stuck in a drift.'

'*Mignonne*, I have talked to the chauffeur. He's bringing a second man in case of difficulties. All that's needed is to get chains fixed to the wheels. They do it in Switzerland and Austria. I remember, before the war, my Delage *clanking* me into Salzburg for an auction. You must trust me. When have I led you into a snowdrift?'

'There is always a first time.'

'We need rugs. Hot water bottles – the hotel must supply them. Brandy. Coffee in thermos flasks. The chauffeur is Polish and an excellent man. We should be in Newport before dark.'

There were times during the journey when Lee and Sara, huddled together, remembered that. They left a city unbearably beautiful in the snow, and at last the streets turned into country roads. Gradually the track began to vanish. Gentle, inexorable, the snow continued to fall. It dropped veils ahead and behind them. To stare into it was to look into the heart of a white chrysanthemum. The hot water bottles grew cold. They needed the brandy.

Lee and Sara said little but pressed against each other for warmth and company. Dudley, sitting with Alexander behind the two chauffeurs, talked knowledgeably of driving on difficult surfaces from ice to desert sand. All three women were muffled in fur rugs. The only person who said nothing (Alexander gave much encouragement to the drivers) was Catherine. Dressed in dark green with a huge fur collar and a muff as large she sat with her eyes shut in a stoic silence. That comes from English breeding, thought Sara. They stagger off to the South Pole and die, but they never grumble. Lee and I would grumble ourselves into safety.

At last the crawling journey, the freezing journey, came to an end. Dark shapes of houses glimmered through the snowstorm. Sara made out the cupolas of what looked like a Venetian church, the drive of some palace dimly shining through trees monstrous with heaped snow. Alexander was jubilant.

'I told you to trust me. We are in time for dinner. Congratulations, Tomascewski! Now, let me show you exactly where to find La Pallice.'

He spread out a map.

After many wrong turns (every landmark was obliterated), the car drew up at last by the steps of a huge château.

The door opened – doors always did for Alexander – and servants hurried out. The three women, half frozen, tottered up into light and warmth.

The Château de la Pallice Saint-Symphorien, named after a château in the Auvergne, had been built in the early 1880s by Selby Adams, the railway millionaire. Like many of his enormously wealthy friends, he took a fancy to Newport's mixture of country and sea, its invigorating air. In winter there would be sleigh rides, in summer sailing and boating. His friends were creating the sort of life they had seen in Europe, and he determined to join them.

Selby Adams already owned a Park Avenue mansion destined years later to be turned into a museum of Victorian splendours. He proceeded at Newport to build the replica of a château he'd seen as a young man when he had travelled, with critical curiosity, round the Old World.

Near the River Allier in the Grande Auvergne he had fallen in love with a seventeenth-century fortress, a moated, twin-turreted threatening castle built to subdue the countryside. Adams decided that was the house he would create on the other side of the Atlantic – it would not be for power but for a leisured magnificence. He approached the elderly owner of la Pallice Saint Symphorien. France was still suffering from the defeats of her 1871 war with Prussia; she'd been forced to pay huge indemnities and had lost Alsace and Lorraine. The château's aristocratic owner welcomed the prospect of American dollars pouring into his depleted French bank. He received the team of well-known New York architects hospitably. The seigneur, as he would once have been called, dug out parchment plans of his château which were works of art in themselves. He found details of the very stones and where they had been quarried. The architects were taken up huge stone stairways, peered through arrow slits, walked the battlements. The seigneur ushered them down to the dungeons, and made excellent jokes about his ancestor, who imprisoned men when they made a mistake in architectural plans.

The Americans – French wasn't their strong suit – leaned on their interpreters, worked very hard, sat in turreted rooms overlooking a countryside of breathless autumn beauty and drew their plans. They returned to New York in triumph. When the Château eventually rose in Newport, its cost was triple what had been estimated.

But La Pallice in Newport was worth every dollar Selby Adams lavished on it. The de Grelle party, Sara who knew France, her sister who did not, were enchanted with the house. It was outrageous. It stood in all its French glory, the noble stairways sweeping up to arras-hung landings. Suits of sixteenth-century armour stood glimmering ominously at the end of stone corridors. The great bedrooms were enhanced by the solemn presence of four posters. La Pallice lacked no single French detail except the seigneur. And at present this honour was being taken by a man who had been born on holy French soil – the better for that, the old imitation house might have breathed.

Alexander came into Lee's bedroom when she was already undressed. He'd discreetly chosen their rooms in an entirely different part of the château from the rest of the family. His room and Lee's were in a tower: both were circular and the walls slit for arrows.

'Who's going to shoot you, Alex?' said Lee lazily from her pillows, as he peeped through one of the narrow apertures in the wall.

'Old Thomas Kirby. He's still a power in the land. At seventy-five! Or Christie's in London? One or other of my hated rivals.' He hopped with agility into bed beside her. 'Do you know, I've always wanted to own a château. This little place would do nicely. Come to me, *ma belle*. I ache for you.'

'Well . . . that's nice.'

When they finished love-making, he said to her again, looking up at the four-poster's painted ceiling, that he'd wanted a château like this since he was a boy.

'One of my fantasies. Of course this is a replica and one prefers the real. You can't be in my business for thirty years and enjoy replicas. But there are not all that number of châteaux one might buy in France, and in any case . . .'

'In any case, you only want to stay here six weeks.'

'Precisely.'

'And what would I do with a château in France?'

'You'd sell it, Alex.'

'You know me too well.'

On the other floor and another side of la Pallice, Sara was asleep. She had knelt for a long time on a window-seat, watching the park across which the snow whirled, and thinking it curious to realize she didn't know what it was like outside. She knew only the interior of this absurd beautiful place. She felt happy. Or as happy as she could be with Perry in possession of her. He would be here soon and she was afraid of him. To be more exact, afraid he would hurt her. That was how it had been on board ship. It was enough for now. Sex was enough for now. Who knew what the future might hold? Maybe, she thought, it will be better than I imagine. She doubted it.

Three rooms away (she'd had her bedroom changed as she said the previous one was too draughty) Catherine took a long bath gratefully in hot water, did not once look out at the snow and climbed into the very large bed. She arranged her pillows.

Suddenly she went tense. There was a loud shuddering squeak from an unoiled lock. As she watched in alarm the medieval iron-studded door opened. A tall figure came in.

'Dudley, what's happened?'

'Ssh.'

He quietly locked the door and she said in a tense whisper,

'*What are you doing here?*' But the whisper shook with anger.

He padded across and sat down on her bed. He had never seen her in nightwear before; she wore an old-fashioned nightgown with lace and long sleeves and a high neck. Her fine hair was plaited into thinnish pigtails: she looked flushed, angry, and virginal.

'Now, Cath, don't pretend you don't know why I'm here. It's time we found out a bit more about each other. That extra important bit.' He pushed his hand through the fastening of her nightgown and clasping one full breast clipped the nipple between his fingers. She seized his hand, digging in her finger nails and dragging it out. While he was laughing – a token resistance excited him – she slapped him hard across the face.

'How *dare* you! How dare you try to seduce me! You're disgusting. Get out of my room this minute or I'll scream.'

His face slammed shut. He was angrier than she was. He stood up and walked to the fireplace where the remains of a log fire still smouldered. His back was to her.

'Please go,' she said, but less harshly. She felt safer now he was at a distance. But she was shocked, bitterly shocked. Somewhere inside her head a voice jeered – What did you expect? He's a vulgarian.

He turned round and came back, hands in the pockets of his dressing gown. His face had regained its composure but one cheek burned scarlet from the smack.

'Don't cower back, for Christ's sake, I shan't touch you. In

228

fact, I don't want to now. I've never laid a hand on a woman who wasn't ready, willing and able, even if she pretended she wasn't. You're a virgin, aren't you?'

She turned away in revulsion. She thought – am I mad to have accepted this man? Vague ignorant hideous imaginings about what could happen in sex came grimacing into her mind. She was angry and afraid. Of his brutal nature. Her own ill judgement.

'You don't need to tell me. Virgin's written all over you.'

Automatically refastening her nightgown her fingers discovered he'd wrenched off a pearl button. She was suddenly furious all over again.

'And I don't need to ask what kind of woman you've associated with – ' at the expression he gave a convulsive laugh, 'before you became engaged to me. Women of our class do not sleep with their fiancés before marriage. You're supposed to be so clever; I should have thought you'd know that.'

'I couldn't miss it, could I? All those horsey virgins. Don't you talk down to me. Not now. Not ever.'

Naive as she was about sex, she saw he was infuriated because she'd made him look a fool. She had occasionally met this male viciousness in the face of rejection before. At dances and parties. She had no sympathy with it.

He leaned against the post of the bed and she thought with astonishment – he's going to stay. Doesn't he know being here is an outrage? How boorish and ignorant he is. Catherine had not a shred of her sister's diplomacy despite all she had invested in hopeful affection, thought, plans. It was her Lytchett blood that spoke.

'Go. At once.'

Anger had faded from his face. He gave his usual grin, showing his teeth. Beautiful teeth.

'Afraid your revered parent will find me here, are you?'

'If Father came in, I'd ask him to make you go.'

He looked at her with something like respect.

'You're a hard woman, Cath, and no mistake. Ah well. Have to wait for a go until the wedding night, eh?'

She did not deign to reply.

'Worth a try, though,' he added impudently. He went over

and quietly unlocked the door. Then returned to stand beside her. Knowing she had won, she relaxed. When he squeezed her hand she actually smiled.

'Just one thing to spoil your beauty sleep – not counting the other, and you don't know what you just missed. Keep that beady eye on your sister. She's hand in glove with your father, in case you haven't noticed. You should have heard them a couple of evenings ago when I called in at Madison Avenue. In cahoots. If we aren't very slick indeed, who do you suppose will thieve the business from right under our noses when the time comes?'

William Thornbury and Perry arrived at Newport two days after the de Grelle party had settled into the château. The snow fell steadily for twenty-four hours, but now it had stopped. A sun like a flaming orange ball shone on an extraordinary landscape of wind-piled drifts, a kind of exquisite frozen peace. The woods were white and silent. The ponds covered with ice.

The two men travelled by train and when they arrived at the station Perry jumped out energetically and strode off down the snow-covered platform in search of a horse-drawn cab. There was one used by guests of the great houses along the sea drive, and Perry had taken it occasionally. Returning to the front of the station in triumph, he said, 'Hal Reilly's just told me the postman had to make his round this morning on snow shoes, over the tops of the hedges! But the snow plough's been out now, and the drive should be just fine.'

He swung their luggage effortlessly into the cab. William was not sure whether to be grateful at his courtesy or resentful that van Rijn thought the valise too heavy for a man of his age. The young man was very friendly to the cab driver too. Americans, thought William, treat every man like a blood brother.

But he'd enjoyed van Rijn's company on the journey. They had the pleasure of mutual interests, talking of the share structure of de Grelle's, for instance; the classic problems of wholly-owned subsidiaries and of long- and short-term finance.

As the cab moved briskly down a road scarcely marked by

wheels on the virgin snow, van Rijn pointed out many great houses. William glimpsed turrets, and lines of box trees smothered by snow.

'There's a deal of Old Europe down Bellevue Avenue and along Ocean Drive,' Perry said. 'I must take you walking along the cliffs one morning when it's thawed a bit. You'll see palaces and châteaux straight from Northern Italy and France.'

'Any English castles?'

'A sumptuous Victorian cottage or two – not cottages at all, of course. But our Newport taste runs mostly to Italian palazzos or the Grand Trianon at Versailles. And there's The Breakers on Ochre Point Avenue, that's the Vanderbilt mansion.'

'I'll be interested to see all these wonderful places.'

'I don't expect you will, sir,' said Perry, slightly smiling. 'Though Sara may coax you to take a look. There's a girl who can be very persuasive.'

William glanced at the young man thoughtfully. A widower himself, lonely except for his work which had replaced, in heart and mind, the gentle affections of domestic life, William often noticed the unseen shafts of attraction, mysterious and secret, which flashed and trembled between the young. They made him feel old and momentarily sad. He'd discerned something of the sort between Sara and this man. He almost envied them. His own sex life was intermittent: there was a woman he took to bed now and again but it wasn't much of a thing. She simpered and pretended after sex to be shocked at herself. And she was predatory and rather a bore. A pity, that.

The horse trotted along through the countryside hidden under blinding white, arched by a sky of icy blue; the shapes of more houses could be seen. They lay behind great iron gates beside which were pillars topped with lions or dragons clasping shields decorated with coats of arms. William scarcely noticed. He'd always been immune from beauty and strangeness except in women.

But to Perry the snow had a terrible enchantment. As he looked through the poky windows or ahead across the shoulders of the horse confidently trotting on a road cleared of snow which was heaped seven foot high on either side, Perry saw the pure white sweeps of drives, the winding road vanishing into a snow haze, the bumpy shapes of ploughed fields. Uninvited and dreaded came the memory of other snows crisping the edge of trenches. And a journey when he and twenty companions had carried the whitened bodies of the dead into a day as brilliant as this. He shivered.

'Cold? Have more of this rug,' William said.

'No, no, thank you. I am quite comfortable. I'm rather looking forward, by the way, to seeing your face when we get to La Pallice.'

'Is it very curious?'

'Outrageous is more accurate,' said Perry with a grin. He had the sort of expression which a smile changes and gravity noticeably darkens. An odd man, thought William.

The driver pulled at the reins, the horse slowed to a walk as they turned through open gates towards a château whose twin was in the Grande Auvergne.

'Alexander,' remarked William after a moment, 'has surpassed himself.'

The house party was now complete, the sunny weather held. The guests remained more or less together during the day and in the evenings. Everything was pleasant and companionable. To her surprise Catherine found her feeling for Dudley had not changed, in spite of his attempt to break her virgin knot. It was as if it had never happened. They joined the others on slippery invigorating walks in the château's huge park where there were lakes, bridges, follies, decorative ha-has to keep out the cattle, and a stretch of marshes towards the sea. Alexander made Perry their guide when they went sight-seeing.

'It's the only reason I invited you, my dear fellow. Tell us about the Vanderbilts.'

'But you know all about them, sir.'

'I know Cornelius paid fifty thousand dollars for Rosa Bonheur's *The Horse Fair* (which I've never liked, have you?) and presented it to your Metropolitan Museum. I know their taste in painting. You tell us about the family,' said Alexander, at his most charming.

With colleagues Alexander made friendly hoops of steel.

He was more than satisfied with van Rijn's bank, and was already considering new conquests. Washington? Booming Chicago? Such questions put him in a high good humour.

It was his idea, on the third day of orange sunshine and unmelted snow when the party collected for a large breakfast, to go shooting.

'Lee has discovered the gun-room. That long-faced caretaker chap gave her the key,' said Alexander, buttering hot toast.

'Surely the guns are in no state to *use*,' said Dudley, who was an excellent shot.

'Come and take a look. To my eye they've been kept in good condition. One or two are twelve-bore hammer guns. Pretty things, twenty or thirty years old.'

During the large family meal in a panelled dining room flooded with sunshine, Sara was next to Perry. She wished she wasn't. He had come to her room last night and they had made love for a long time. She now felt weak and languorous, and to a degree helpless, just as when she'd been on board ship. She seemed to know less and less about this man. He possessed her body completely and did not put a finger on her soul. He seemed to recoil against doing that. She didn't understand him and he deeply, violently, dreadfully affected her. This morning he was eating a hearty American breakfast of hot blueberry muffins and Canadian bacon while she could scarcely manage her croissant and black coffee.

'Your old French tastes still. Where's a good American appetite?' he said teasingly.

'Where indeed?' said Sara, thinking, leave me alone, Perry van Rijn. During the day, anyway.

'You spoke about shooting,' said Catherine to her father. She was at her ease in talk of sport. 'What sort of game is there at present in this part of the world?'

'There are the lakes. We might find duck. Black duck. Mallards and so on,' said Dudley, and Alexander said 'Excellent'.

'Poor ducks,' said Sara. '*Must* you?'

'Don't be stupid,' from Catherine. 'It's the season for duck. But naturally one can only shoot on the foreshore below the high-water mark.'

Sara ignored the arcane knowledge; she was in a disputatious mood.

'What'll you do with them when you've shot them? We can't pretend we're hungry. I went into the kitchens yesterday. Enough food for a siege.'

'Duck shooting is sport,' said Catherine in a tone of pity. 'I should have thought everybody knew that.'

Dudley enjoyed the disagreement. Alexander, who never listened when women talked to each other and not to him, spun the dumb waiter round to see which jams or marmalades he had not sampled. There were at least a dozen.

Perry said, 'Don't fret, Sara, we probably won't bag a single bird. They're quick at spotting movement and the Pallice lakes have little cover.'

'Oh good.'

'Well, now,' said Alexander, thickly spreading some peach preserve on more toast, 'who's for some sport?'

'I'll come, Father,' said Catherine, darting a look at her sister.

'Would you mind if I don't, Alex?' from Lee. 'The light is so good and I'd like to draw this morning.'

'And your weak stomach won't let *you* accompany us?' said Alexander, who had taken in Sara's remark about the château's kitchens. 'I don't believe you'll turn up that sentimental nose at duck *à l'orange*.'

Sara couldn't help laughing. But she did not go with them, and nor did William who decided to do some work which he had brought with him.

It was a morning of all mornings. The sunshine dyed the snow a radiant pink, the air was icy, the humps of earth and shapes of trees all disguised and hidden by the snow. They tramped across the blazing park and along a scarcely discernible path towards the lakes. The men carried their guns slung over their shoulders, and wore breeches, jackets and thick coats. Alexander's was made of sealskin. Catherine was wrapped in furs, none too new, with a fur beret pulled down over her ears. Her stout boots spoke of country walks in the Lytchett woods. The party, cheerfully joking, sometimes stumbled on the frozen path. Catherine, in her English boots, was as sure-footed as a deer.

Behind them was the fantastic shape of the château. Ahead were the lakes, not winking in the sunshine. The water was dull, steely and frozen.

'No game this morning,' exclaimed Alexander in disappointment as they came nearer. But just then, with a whirr of wings, a cloud of birds flew up from the east and landed in a swooping dark mass some distance away on the lake.

'Canada geese,' said Dudley. 'See their black heads and necks?'

'Good,' said his host, narrowing his eyes.

'Father, you must have the first shot,' put in Catherine.

'You'll need cover, Sir,' from Perry. 'They see anything that means danger at once.'

He went ahead towards some high rushes sugary with frozen rain and began to test the ice. It creaked but it was very thick and no starry cracks appeared.

He returned carefully.

'It seems okay but you ought to go slowly, sir.'

'Of course, of course.'

Alexander flipped the cartridges into the chamber and closed the gun. 'I've shot in weather like this all over Europe, my dear chap. On the lakes in Hungary. Austria . . . Now, let us see, my beauties.'

Walking gingerly towards the frozen rushes he left Catherine, Dudley and Perry standing immobile. They knew movement could frighten off the flock. Alexander watched the mass of brown and black. He enjoyed shooting – not the killing of creatures but the test of eye and hand. His own hand was steady and his sight, he was long-sighted, better than when he'd been young. He was on his mettle in the company of men thirty years younger than he. He made his way carefully, watching the feathery mass as it moved and fed in the icy distance. One goose wandered away from the main flock in his direction; but it was still too far off.

Set on shooting accurately, concentrating on the small outline of the distant bird, his gun at the ready, he took one long careless stride. With a hideous sound like smashing glass the ice split. He vanished into black water.

Catherine screamed.

Perry sprang heedlessly towards the growing gap in the ice until Dudley yelled,

'Test it for God's sake! Don't fall in too.'

Perry heard – and obeyed. He lay flat and began to drag himself towards the hole in the ice, calling, 'Pass me your gun, he can hold on to your gun –' He had dropped his own.

Catherine snatched Dudley's gun from him, lay clumsily down and managed to crawl towards Perry and push the gun barrel into his hands. Alexander's head appeared, then an arm. He gave a strangled sound as his shoulders and both arms came out of the water, then he horribly vanished again. Perry felt the ice shuddering. He pushed the gun butt foremost as Alexander came to the surface again, gasping.

'*Hold the gun. Take hold of the gun and hold it fast, We'll pull you.*'

His words must have reached the half-drowned man who somehow grasped the butt and Dudley and Catherine, bent almost double, gripped hands to make a chain. Dudley reached to Perry, who sweating and taut had both hands holding the barrel, as slowly, slowly, they pulled the dripping clutching figure dark with water and weed across the ice to safety. When he was on solid ground he could not speak or rise, and when Catherine tried to help him, he fell, taking her with him.

'Quick. Coats,' Perry said.

'Shall I get help?' Dudley spoke fast, 'or can we manage between us two?'

'Three. I'm strong,' said Catherine hoarsely. 'But how to make a stretcher?'

Perry stripped off his coat, took Dudley's, and Catherine gave him hers. Somehow they knotted sleeves and hems into a kind of enormous sling. Unconscious of the freezing air Catherine knelt in the snow chafing her father's hands, wrapping her scarf round his dripping hair. They rolled the now-unconscious man into the sling. His face was grey, bluish round the mouth. But he was breathing.

The mile back to the house was a nightmare. Alexander

became heavier with every icy step they took. Nobody could speak. Perry had given Catherine the end of the sling by her father's feet. The men each carried a corner by his heavy shoulders. Once as they came over a hummock, Alexander groaned.

Catherine gasped, '*Father.*'

No answer.

They crawled painfully on.

'Do you think he is dead?' Catherine said. Her voice was steady and Perry, his shoulders screaming with the pain of Alexander's weight, had a moment of admiration.

'He's still breathing,' Dudley said.

There was no further word until they reached the château and suddenly it seemed to Catherine they were surrounded by voices and – she fainted.

From the moment the trio arrived with their half-dead burden, there was a frenzied activity. Alexander, wrapped in blankets, was carried upstairs by four servants. An enormous fire was lit in his bedroom and, while Perry telephoned the doctor and Lee was with Alexander, Sara took Catherine who had revived up to her room for a bath and brandy.

Sara sat in Catherine's bedroom by yet another fire, the château glittered with them, waiting for her sister to emerge from the bathroom; she didn't feel it safe to leave her.

'Are you all right?' she called twice, to be answered by a scornful 'Of course'.

Catherine eventually appeared wrapped in a bathrobe.

'Lee said you must go to bed.'

'Rubbish. Just because I was dizzy for a minute or two.'

'You were flat out. You'd best do as Lee says, you don't want to upset her more. *Catherine, what happened?*'

Her sister, climbing with ill grace into the four poster, said briefly that their father had fallen into the ice. He'd forgotten to test it and it had cracked under him.

'But why is he unconscious?'

'Shock, I suppose.'

Catherine felt suddenly very tired. Sara passed her a glass of hot milk and brandy.

'Do you think you could sleep?'

'How can I sleep when Father may be very ill?'

'There's nothing we can do for him just now. They've sent for the doctor. And Lee is with him. You ought to sleep. You're suffering from shock too. Perry said so.'

'How does he know?' said Catherine, but she lay back.

'The war, I expect.'

Silence fell. The fire licked. In a short while Catherine's breathing was steady and Sara crept out.

Shock. She herself shivered with it. She had been appalled by the sight of her father, grey-faced, drenched and unconscious like a figure carried out of the trenches. She had almost shrieked aloud.

Going down the staircase she found Perry waiting for her.

'The doctor will be here in half an hour.'

'No sooner?'

'He'll have to crawl. Some of the roads haven't been cleared. How's Catherine?'

'Asleep.'

In the drawing room Dudley, foot on the fireplace, was drinking neat whisky. He, too, asked after Catherine.

'She's a real corker,' he said. 'Don't know how she managed to help carry him.' He was less strained than Perry. More resilient, she thought. Or more unfeeling?

They sat down by the fire. Sara broke a silence, exclaiming,

'But *why* is he still unconscious? I don't understand. If it's just shock, why isn't he better now?'

'Falling into icy water –' began Perry in a low voice,

'Can kill,' finished Dudley with brutal frankness. 'It used to happen on Russian convoys. The men who went overboard were dead the moment they went into the water. It worked like an electric shock.'

Sara looked at him in horror.

'You're saying my father may die. But Perry, you told me you all got him out at once –'

'That's not it, Sara,' he said, and his voice was gentle. 'He could get hypothermia in seconds. The clothes freeze. They were heavy as lead when we carried him home.'

'But he survived. He was breathing.'

'I know. I know. There's a good deal of hope still.'

She looked blank. She couldn't grasp it. Never for a single minute had she imagined Alexander could die. Alexander! The immortal one . . .

The doctor arrived, saw the patient, and left the château, saying he would come back bringing another colleague. There was no sign of Lee or William Thornbury. Catherine appeared, composed and dressed, by tea-time. The four sat by the fire pretending to read. William eventually appeared. When asked for news he said in a colourless voice, 'He's out of the coma. The doctor gave him something to make him sleep. That's all we know.'

'How's Lee?' asked Sara.

'As one would expect,' said William, and left the room.

Sara, with more energy than she'd shown since the accident, exclaimed, 'What does he mean? Doesn't he know how we feel? William is awful sometimes.'

Perry looked up.

'Of course he knows. He's under more strain than any of us. Except Lee.'

Both sisters stared at him. He looked from one to the other.

'And if you don't understand what I'm saying it's time you did. William has been like a brother to your father for thirty years. You don't know him as William does. And probably don't love him as much, either.'

'I think we should stop this conversation,' said Catherine, who thought it in revoltingly bad taste. She went to the window. Two lights like eyes were advancing unevenly down the snow-covered drive.

'That must be the doctor again.'

Everybody got to their feet.

An hour went by. The doctors eventually left, and it was not William who came down from the sickroom but Lee. She wore a shawl which she kept nervously wrapping round her shoulders, tying and untying its trailing ends. She was the colour of paper, the blue of her eyes more intense from shadows lying under them like smears of dirt. She looked old. Perry led her to the fire. She sat down, tying and untying the shawl.

'Both doctors say it's the arteries of his heart,' she said. 'It must have been building up for years. Without us knowing.'

Sara sank beside her.

'It was *there* all the time,' Lee said. 'But we didn't know and now the heart's had to bear extra stress. A violent shock –'

Her voice slurred and tears ran down her face.

'Oh Sara. Oh Sara. I think he's dying.'

Sara put her arms round her.

The door opened and William came into the room.

'He's regained consciousness. He wants to see Catherine and Sara. I'll take you both up now.'

A voice said respectfully,

'I think I ought to be with Catherine. I'll come up too.'

It was Dudley. Everybody but Lee looked towards him.

'I'm sorry. That's impossible. He only wants to see his daughters,' said William.

'But I am part of the family. I ought to be present!'

Dudley's voice had a roughness in it.

'I'm sorry,' said William sharply. 'Catherine? Sara? We'll go up now.'

Dudley took a step towards the trio leaving the room. Forgetting Lee huddled by the fire, Perry sprang after him and shoved him aside – Dudley was taken by surprise – preventing him from leaving with William and the girls. He slammed the door shut and leaned against it.

Dudley said in a voice of fury,

'What in Christ's name do you think *you're* doing?'

'What Alex wants. Letting him see his daughters alone.'

Dudley almost hit him. He thought – I'll crack him on the jaw and still have time to get out of here.

'Were you proposing,' said Perry with contempt, 'to force yourself into his room? God, man, the sight of a stranger could kill him.'

He moved away from the door. It would be easy now to wrench it open and run up the stairs. But Dudley couldn't.

The turret bedroom was hot as a boiler room, the fire had

240

burned all day and the air was heavy with the smell of woodsmoke mingled with ether and antiseptic. Sara saw the nurse by the four-poster bed with a dazed surprise; she hadn't known there was a nurse in the house. As they entered William said quietly, 'Nurse, Mr de Grelle wishes to see his daughters alone.'

The woman looked at her fob watch pinned to the bib of her apron.

'Five minutes. No more.'

She and William went out.

Alexander lay propped on many pillows, his reddish grey-ish hair brushed and silky, his eyes shut. He looked beautiful and strong and struck down like a newly-slaughtered tree which still trembles with the leaves of its life. His daughters, dark head and auburn, stood on either side of the bed; the fruits of his two unions, neither of which had been true or blessed. Catherine took his right hand, Sara his left. At their light touch, he opened heavy eyes.

'Dear children. Kiss me.'

They leaned forward enveloped in the scent of eau de cologne and that particular smell which was Alexander's own. His eyes closed again as Catherine, then Sara, pressed a kiss on his cheek.

He gave a long sigh.

They stayed, each holding his hand, staring at the broad face, the thick lips, the red beard, the closed eyes with sandy eyelashes. They almost held their breath.

'I'm afraid you must go now,' said the nurse, slipping back into the room.

Why must we go, thought Sara as she and Catherine went out into the empty landing. Can she save him? Of course she can't. He is lost to us already.

She turned to Catherine, and suddenly they ran into each other's arms and both began to cry.

CHAPTER FIFTEEN

The snow lasted. It did not melt into slush and vanish from the streets of New York as it did in Paris and London. It fell again heavily on the day of Alexander's funeral. The winds coming round corners were like sharpened knives. Alexander, that most lapsed of Catholics, had left instructions that there was to be a Requiem Mass before he was cremated. It was like Alexander to choose both ways of dissolution: the solemn prayers and the modern use of fire.

His ashes, he instructed, should be sprinkled in the graveyard of 'Saint-Sauveur, the church at the end of the rue des Cordeliers in Paris, by Lee Becker, the greatest friend of my life.'

Catherine raised her eyebrows.

'Surely it ought to be –'

'Lee, do you feel you can do it?' cut in Sara.

Lee looked very ill. Her fair middle-aged looks were gone, she had lost fourteen pounds and her clothes were too big for her. Yes, she said. She would go to Paris and do what Alex asked.

Of the three de Grelle women, Catherine recovered the most quickly. New York suited her. She had not approved of a Roman Catholic funeral but when she attended it (she'd never been inside a Roman Catholic church before) she did not dislike it. The choir sang the De Profundis. Orange-coloured candles burned at the four corners of the bier. There was a nobility about the Latin prayers. She liked the tributes sent by colleagues, friends, collectors, dealers, all the motley yet distinguished members of Alexander's international world. The flowers heaped on her father's coffin were more like symbols of plenty than of death. The letters, telegrams, cablegrams which poured into the hotel and the galleries satisfied a deep instinct in her, a pride in lineage and inheritance. She felt herself the daughter of a great house. Her manner was stately and matched the snowbound funeral, the long Mass and the short (to Sara ludicrous) ceremony of the cremation.

Sara was not a Catholic but found herself wishing she was when she heard the Latin prayers. They had mystery, and faced with death you needed that.

With the funeral over, limbo descended on Sara. She, Catherine, Dudley and Lee, at William's insistence had returned to the Ellsworth Palace. They occupied the same suites, were waited upon by the same servants, sat at the same table, as if Alexander had just stepped out to meet a client and would be back directly. His presence was so strong that Sara's brain refused to accept that she would never see him again.

Reports and newspapers articles from the American press came in every morning. His face, confident, half smiling, stared out at her. More and more papers arrived from England, France and Germany.

The day after the funeral New York was still in a frozen spell, the tops of the skyscrapers wreathing themselves in mist and gradually disappearing like the crests of mountains. Sara took a taxi to Madison Avenue. She felt in need of work. Wasn't it supposed to be a cure for grief? But Cheriton Spencer was out, and of course there was nothing for her to do.

Returning through the icy streets she thought about Perry. She had scarcely spoken to him since the night her father died. She remembered how she and her sister had wept in each other's arms. Had that really happened? Later, she wasn't sure how much later, William had come down into the drawing room, to say Alexander was dead.

She thought she would never forget the sound Lee had made. A dreadful, choking groan. Lee had started to her feet and rushed out, running up the stairs calling 'Alex, Alex,' as if to stop his spirit leaving, to halt its flight and take the invisible beloved thing into her arms.

Perry came into Sara's room very late that night, locking

the door and getting into her bed without a word. He wrapped his arms round her and held her. She lay, glad of his warmth, his physical presence and so far from the act of love that her body and his could have been strangers. He did not kiss her. He said nothing. He simply held her and they lay awake until the dawn. Then he left.

Now she felt a sudden desperate longing to see him. He had been beside her at the funeral and afterwards when they returned to the hotel, Catherine had said, 'Won't you come in and have tea with us?'

He had refused, very kindly, given Sara's hand a hard pressure, and was gone.

That had been yesterday.

When she returned to the hotel she was told that Lee was in her bedroom and would like to see her. Sara went up in the gilded lift. Lee's bedroom and Alexander's were on a different more expensive floor than his daughters'. Lee was sitting on the bed surrounded by clothes, portfolios, canvases and open valises. A litter of opened and unopened letters lay about.

'I know,' Lee said looking up. 'It's a mess. *I'm* a mess.'

'Darling, why are you already packing?'

'I'm sailing on the *Mauretania* tomorrow.'

'Let me come with you,' said Sara, filled with pain and pity.

'How I wish you could. But William needs you and Catherine here awhile. Something to do with the will. Big stakes.'

Lee gave a wintry smile.

'But wills usually take months,' said Sara, frowning.

Shattered by the first deep sorrow of her life, Sara had not once thought of the future. She'd only known that it was important, it was necessary, to grieve.

'William says the New York lawyers have to see you both before you return to Europe,' Lee said. 'I suppose –' she paused, 'you *are* going back?'

'My work is in London.'

'Perry isn't, though.'

Sara was silent for a moment.

'You've never mentioned that before.'

'I was myopic when Alex was around. He filled the whole

244

canvas. You're sleeping with Perry, aren't you? I knew it yesterday when he looked at you.'

Sara could think of no answer. It seemed brutal and wrong to talk of her sex with Perry to this woman with death in her face. She sat down among the debris on the bed.

'Yes. Sure. We do. Or we did, I suppose I should say.'

'It isn't over, Sara. Unless you want it to be.'

Sara began to pick up the opened letters, seeing a sentence here and there: 'Your great loss . . . so brilliant . . .'; 'incomparable charm . . .' 'Enormous respect and affection . . .'; 'that competitive and eager spirit . . .'

She gathered the letters carefully, the opened ones in one pile, the sealed ones in another.

'No, Lee, I don't. Want it to be over, I mean. But I don't understand Perry and he certainly doesn't understand me. What I need now is work. Work.'

'Alex's daughter,' said Lee.

The most independent of women, she accepted Sara's offer to help her pack.

With Lee gone from New York there remained the coming interview with the lawyers. Catherine and Dudley had been out almost all the time since the funeral. Catherine, not Sara, accepted condolence dinners, lunches and all the other occasions at which New Yorkers showed the warmth of their hearts. She and Dudley were telephoned and sought after. Flowers arrived, filling Catherine's and Sara's room with colour and scent. Sara knew her compatriots' love of flowers as messengers. Catherine thought it all most odd, unsuitable and flattering.

The meeting with the New York lawyers, Reinhardt and Kimber, was arranged and William called at the hotel to collect them one morning at midday. Both girls were in mourning, he noticed with old-fashioned approval. That sad female darkness, *de rigeur* in Victorian times, had ended during the Great War when – had it been worn – there wouldn't have been a woman in France or England not clad in black. Today the gesture was curiously correct. It showed a sober spirit and quenched their youth.

Catherine wore black velvet, but Sara, who possessed no

black clothes, had to visit a salon on Fifth Avenue. The vendeuse showed her 'some really chic mourning, worn by all the widows in Paris, you know.' With an inward shudder, Sara asked for the clothes to be sent to the hotel. They drained her face and hair of colour: she looked frail. Catherine's cheeks were rosy again. She looked dignified, countryfied, self-possessed.

'You may bring Mr Forrest if you wish,' said William, greeting her.

'Oh, I don't think so. Dudley would feel it rather unsuitable,' said Catherine.

The suite of offices belonging to Reinhardt and Kimber was in a skyscraper block and the bright girl in reception might have known them for years.

'Good morning, Miss de Grelle, Miss Sara, Mr Thornbury. Mr Reinhardt is expecting you.'

In Paris or London they would have waited half an hour.

Joseph Reinhardt, white-haired and with the air of a statesman rather than a lawyer, greeted them warmly. He and William had met before, and spoke the same language, despite his being pure New York, and William's an English faintly flavoured by his native Bristol. The girls sat by windows which looked out on to the clouds. It gave Sara a curious sensation: she had lost the trick of New York. You had to think in the sky, not on the ground.

'It's my pleasure to see you, ladies,' said Reinhardt. 'We would not have worried you at this sad time, but William here, and I, both agree that for the sake of de Grelle's it's of the greatest importance you should know the contents of the will right away. William?' The first name was cordial, 'would you explain?'

William opened the leather case he has used since he was twenty years old.

Just then Sara emerged from the carapace of grief. They were going to hear Alexander's voice again for the last time.

William cleared his throat.

' "Last will and testament of Alexander Marc de Grelle . . ." and so on and so on. We don't need all this.' He turned the pages. ' "First, the bequests. A hundred thousand dollars to Mrs Becker." '

246

Catherine gave a slight start.

'And so on,' continued William. 'Now. Here we are. I must first tell you that the total shares in de Grelle's number four thousand five hundred. Alexander owned three thousand and the remaining fifteen hundred (which of course stay unchanged) belong to Sara's mother.'

Sara looked astonished. Louise owning an interest in de Grelle's! It was utterly unlike her father. Why on earth had he let Louise keep the shares after the divorce; surely he could have commandeered them.

'Sara's *mother*,' repeated Catherine, also astounded. 'What has *she* to do with de Grelle's?'

At the tone Sara blushed and said nothing.

William gave Catherine a fatherly look. He was accustomed to people showing their teeth over money.

'You could not have been aware of it, Catherine, but Sara's mother put a considerable amount of money into de Grelle's before Sara was born. The shares were part of the arrangement.'

Sara took this in; a thought struck her.

'But William, surely you . . .'

'I possess no de Grelle shares, Sara. It was an early decision of mine which I've never regretted. My investments are elsewhere. Not being a shareholder gave me a certain freedom; Alexander understood that.'

'Now we get to the matter in hand,' prompted Joseph Reinhardt. Auctioneering was high finance; it had been since the upsurge of negotiable culture during the Elegant Eighties. Reinhardt had actually met the legendary Thomas E. Kirby, Father of Auctions, who had sold sixty million dollars' worth of art in his extraordinary career. Kirby was about to retire now, people said he'd become very whimsical. And here was a new auction house which had opened in a blaze of public interest – with Reinhardt and Kimber as its lawyers.

'The section of your father's will which affects you both, the heart of the thing, is simple,' William said. 'Sara, he left you one thousand shares. Less than your mother owns but a very fair amount which should pay handsome dividends. As for you, Catherine, your father states: 'it is my wish that

Catherine Fulford de Grelle as my heir and elder child shall inherit two thousand shares.'

He looked up at her.

'You own the controlling interest, my dear Catherine.'

The sisters did not exchange a word on the ride back to the hotel. William, sensing the atmosphere, kept up a pleasant conversation as they drove through the fjords between the skyscrapers. The snow was fading at last, the streets were heavily gritted.

Sara spent the afternoon answering letters of condolence which continued to arrive daily. She'd persuaded Lee to give her all her letters, and she answered these as well as her own. She forgot to switch on the light and sat in a greyish dusk, still writing, when Catherine wearing her black velvet came into the room.

'Shall we have tea? I'll ring.'

'They don't serve afternoon tea in the States, Cathy.'

Her sister smiled.

'They do now. I spoke to the manager and gave them my supply from Fortnums. They have grasped the fact that for us it is an accepted meal.'

She picked up the telephone.

After ordering she sat on Sara's bed, arranging her velvet skirts. It was unlike her to be so informal, she usually chose a chair with the straightest back. Now she leaned against the bed and looked across at Sara who suddenly thought – *What's coming?*

'How does it feel to be de Grelle's new boss?' said Sara, managing a smile.

'I always expected it. After all, I'm the heir. If I'd been a son there would have been no question. It's the same with English titles.'

'I hadn't thought.'

'Father was very generous to you too.'

'I suppose he was.'

In the last few hours Sara had known the hideous emotion of being angry with the dead.

'Dudley tells me you're not sailing with us on the *Majestic* tomorrow,' said Catherine, 'but taking the *Olympic* at the end of the week.'

'Yes. Guy's written to me and wants me to see Cheriton Spencer at Madison Avenue. Before Father died he gave me some stuff to do here in New York. I'll be glad to start. They say it's a cure when terrible things happen.'

'Quite.' Catherine hadn't heard a word.

She said thoughtfully, 'About your work in de Grelle's. The fact is I've been thinking it over and talking to Dudley. I won't mince words, Sara. I know you prefer the truth. I suppose it was all right, you working at de Grelle's when Father was alive. He thought so, although I'm afraid I didn't. But now I'm the head of things you must see how unsuitable it is. How could I possibly,' said Catherine appealing to her sister's good sense, 'take the reins when my sister is in some minor position as a sort of clerk? It simply won't do.'

The silence which followed was broken by a waiter's knock. He wheeled in a trolley of tea. Catherine would not allow him to go until she had checked that there was both Indian and China tea, hot water and was the toast – she lifted the silver lid – hot enough? The waiter bowed and left, privately cursing Limeys.

The interlude gave Sara time. Her father was gone. She was to be robbed of her connexion with de Grelle's. And because she loved it with such passion she knew the danger of making an enemy of its new owner.

'If that's your decision, Cathy, I must accept it.'

Catherine gave her a friendly smile.

'Do have some toast. Thanks to me, it's piping hot.'

The moment her sister had gone Sara's control broke. Walking up and down, she used every filthy word she'd picked up long ago from soldiers at the Roumaniev. For one moment, suddenly aware that she only knew how to swear in French, she gave a kind of laugh. Then back flooded her fury. How dared Catherine. How dared Catherine take away her work. Alexander had been proud of Sara working and had once said, 'There'll come a time when you, *mon enfant*, may inherit the crown.' The crown! She was being thrown out like a porter caught stealing some spoons.

Hugging her shoulders, walking to and fro, she felt mortally wounded. Twice wounded. By her father's death and her sister's cruelty. The room was dark and outside New York sparkled with a million man-made diamonds. She thought – Perry will help me. And at that moment, longing for him, she knew she loved him.

She telephoned his office.

'Good to hear from you,' he said, with the formality of somebody who is not alone.

'Can I see you? This evening?'

He was very apologetic. Alas, he couldn't make tonight. There was a late board meeting this evening, an investment proposal he had to present. The matter was urgent. What about tomorrow?

'Why not come here to the office? I'd like to show it to you. Then we'll dine.'

Bruised, anxious, Sara was so disappointed that tears stood in her eyes. She pulled herself together, thanked him and rang off.

Catherine and Dudley were leaving at noon the following day and Sara stayed at the hotel to say goodbye. There was an intense bustle of packing, for it was Catherine, not Lee, who was taking all Alexander's trunks back to London. When she left the entrance hall for the second time to check that nothing had been forgotten in any of their rooms, Dudley spoke to Sara.

'Look, I hope that decision about you wasn't too much of a shock,' he said sympathetically. 'It's Cath's nerves, really. She's not as cool as she looks. Very unsure of herself in business, you know. And that's the trouble. Give her time. I'll try and get her to be more reasonable about you, I promise.'

It was unexpected and Sara had a rush of gratitude.

'That's *very* kind of you.'

'Of course it isn't. You're my sister now, aren't you?'

'If you could make her see –'

'Leave it to me. Oh, hello, Cath. Find anything the chambermaid missed?' said Dudley. 'Your big sister fusses, Sara. Heiresses shouldn't fuss.'

Sara did not know how to get through the rest of the day.

Everybody was gone from the Ellsworth Palace. Lee. Catherine and Dudley. Even William. She was the only one left.

She went out into the cold street, wrapped in furs, to look at the shops. She felt she couldn't bear to go to her father's new galleries. In the end she took a steamer trip round Manhattan, something she hadn't done since Louise had taken her as a child.

A dense mist hid all the buildings, high and low, it did not seem like New York at all. The mist was different from sulphurous London fog, it smelled freshly of the sea, and when it lifted it still hung in the air like a veil. She stared at the great misty canyon of Broadway, whitish, reddish where the sun tried to get through. As the steamer moved away, the mist began to disappear, and she watched docks and piers go by, the great liners, every kind of ship, tugs, steamers, busy or anchored. In the distance a ship was swarming with tiny figures loading or unloading. They passed the fish market, and Brooklyn Bridge, the first and oldest of the world's wonderful suspension bridges. She stared at the intricate pattern of bridge and city. Perry is somewhere there. Living. Breathing. Being.

The long half-misted day made her thoughtful. She felt at home in New York as she'd never done in the cicada-whirring land of the Midi or even in London, apart from the sharp pleasures of work. London was a place of secret squares and guarded people, but New York tingled with life, it was in the very air. I could be happy here. I am American. Father is gone and so are all my European ties. Mother gave me up when I escaped from the Villa des Roses. Cathy has taken away my reason to be in London. Surely I can work in Madison Avenue. She can't object to that. William will persuade her and so will Dudley.

There was a stronger reason than a desire for work. She would be where Perry was.

But while she was dressing in a dark chiffon she'd bought before her father died and never worn before, Sara remembered Fay. The girlish face came accusingly into her mind. I'm being selfish as hell, she thought. Fay will never forgive me.

The van Rijn bank, elaborate and handsome, was in a 1910 building on Wall Street. It was built of curious dun-coloured bricks and faced with tiles. Sara was taken up to the twenty-fifth floor by a messenger, the building had regiments of them, and shown into an anteroom. A secretary pretty enough to have been hired by her father took her into Perry's office. He was sitting at a desk on which there was nothing but a silver ink-stand and a clean blotter.

Springing up he came over to her and, when the secretary had shut the door, immediately kissed her. Sara, standing inside his arms, shut her eyes and thought – I have come home.

The kiss ended and he pulled up a chair for her, then switched on a lamp which made the large room seem intimate. She thought – oh you do love me. I can see it.

'I've felt so guilty, not calling you up since the funeral, Sara.'

'It was only five days ago.'

'It seems a month. How *are* you?'

'Not used to it. I keep thinking I never will be.'

He nodded as if expecting that.

'When are you and Catherine sailing? Wish I could come too.'

He looked at her in the way he had done during the desolate days after Alexander's death. Sara did not interpret the look. The knots of misery had been untied when he kissed her.

'Perry – they've gone. Cathy and Dudley, William too. I – I'm the only one who's in New York now.'

And then she told him the story. It poured out. He listened in silence, only once exclaiming 'How *bloody*!' She finished by saying, 'The only good thing is that Dudley was so kind this morning. He said he'll try and help me. Get Cathy to change her mind!'

'Good.'

'Don't you believe him?'

'I have reservations about Dudley Forrest. Don't trust him.'

'Perry. What do you mean?'

He shrugged. 'I don't know what I mean. That's the trouble.

I'm just bothered by him sometimes. Sorry.'

She felt a slight chill, not because of Dudley but because of Perry's manner. She thought, I'm nervous. I care too much. I must stop.

'Let's go and have a meal, shall we, Sara? We'll talk more then.'

He took her hands and pulled her to her feet, and in his face she saw what he was thinking. They would make love. We'll solve everything together, she thought. I'm safe. I shall make a new life. Here. With him.

Instinct told her not to ask for help during the meal they had together. He wanted to talk about her father and she wanted him to. There was a special joy in that. After dinner they walked to the Ellsworth Palace down the cheerful crowded streets. At the hotel the desk clerk bowed as Sara took her key. They went up in the gilded birdcage lift and along the quiet corridors. Sara fitted her key into the lock.

As they went into the room she thought – Cathy was here, taking away part of my life. Now here is someone who'll give me back so much more.

He locked the door, picked her up and carried her to the bed.

It seemed an eternity since they had made love at La Pallice. They threw off their clothes, joined, lay together. They moved, first he was above her, then she rode above him. They were skilful in their sexual union, knowing how to drive each other to a point of bliss like a madness. When their love-making ended they stayed joined, wet with love and sweat.

The familiar feeling that her body knew filled Sara with well-being. She'd often thought after their sex together it was as if they'd come through a forest fire. Behind them the burned trees fell. They were safe on the other side. Free just then of sorrow she said without looking at him, 'Perry.'

'Mmm?'

'You know what I told you. About Cathy stopping me from working.'

'Don't feel bitter about it. You'll make out. You're a clever creature.'

'What would you say if –'

'If what?'

'If I could fix to work for de Grelle's in New York?'

She waited, the rich sanguine hope of the young filling her as love had just done.

The silence was curiously long.

'Oh, I shouldn't do that, Sara. All your friends are in London. Your connexions too. What on earth would you do here in New York? Much better to get another job in London. I'm sure Guy Buckingham will help you.'

Part Five

CHAPTER SIXTEEN

On a summer morning in June 1923, William Thornbury took a train from Victoria Station to Lewes, travelling first class, and the only occupant in his compartment. An early freshness was everywhere. In the green of the hazel woods, the daisy-studded embankments, the little back gardens brimming with roses. William did not attempt to read his folded copy of *The Times*. He stared out of the window at the flap of washing or the gleam of a duck pond. He was in a troubled mood, and the small sights of the English countryside were soothing. At least they hadn't changed.

Everything else was changing so fast that William, who prided himself on a sense of balance, felt the instability almost under his feet. Alexander, dearest friend and colleague, had been dead for over two years. That loss one must bear. But what distressed him deeply now was the effect that the tragedy had had on de Grelle's. Every night when William returned to the Kensington house where he lived in sedate bachelorhood, he went to his study to think over the de Grelle problems. Every night they were marginally worse.

They resembled modern life, he thought. Where were the days of high style which he and Alexander had enjoyed? The formality, the magnificent experts, the ruthless yet elegant auction fighters? Bernard Quaritch. Sir Joseph Duveen. Of course there were still some of the old guard left; but in truth they were getting old.

He remembered Alexander on the rostrum, fresh pink carnation in his button hole, his face brilliant after a hard-won battle over some heroic and famous canvas. Before the war Alexander had auctioned an Alma Tadema, *Homer Reading the Odyssey*, for thirty thousand pounds. It had been the highest price for a painting that season. Tadema was a joke now. Yet the paint and canvas hadn't changed. Was it that only money and not beauty – suppose there *was* beauty – had any meaning?

As for the younger generation springing up like plants in new-turned earth, he found them incomprehensible. This craze for dancing. The madness had seized all classes, new dance halls were opened weekly, people shuffled on tiny floors in embraces which quite shocked him. And the night clubs. Young Sara talked about those. She'd been dancing, she said, and had 'gone on' to Mrs Meyrick's. People called the lady the Night Club Queen, and at her club in Gerrard Street, said Sara, all the 'topping' people went: painters and actors and jockeys and foreign royalties. You had to ring the door in a special way to get in. Fun!

'I'll make you take me there one evening, William,' said Sara.

His friend's younger daughter was also changed. She was no longer the beautiful eager girl in a dark overall who worked for Gilbert Travice, and put de Grelle's in the way of that Parisian auction. Since her father's death, William scarcely recognized her. Her skirts were short, the fashions extreme, and her manner was most changed of all. William had been shocked to be told by Catherine that she intended to sell up her father's Park Street house. The contents could go under the hammer at de Grelle's, she said firmly. There were naturally things she wished to keep and 'Sara can choose some. But please let me know which, William, I don't want any unpleasantness.'

William disliked the idea of the sale. Unsentimental himself, he preferred sentiment in women.

He had been at Park Street on the afternoon that Sara came to the house, walking from room to room with a set face. She finally appeared carrying a small cardboard box.

'Tell Cathy I want this.'

'What is it?' he asked, smiling and hoping to soften her expression.

She opened the box without replying and gave it to him. It

contained what were apparently the remains of dead flowers, brown, papery, falling almost to dust.

'You don't know what they are, do you? They're the first pink carnations Father wore at his first de Grelle auctions. There are four. He told me he'd kept them, and I found them at the back of his bureau. There are the auction dates on the inside of the lid.'

William put on his glasses.

'Why yes. Yes. How well I remember . . . and what have you decided you want from the house, Sara?'

'This.'

'But which paintings? The little Gainsborough? The Turner water colours? And I know you've always loved your father's jade.'

'This is all I want. People going round valuing everything make me sick.'

'My dear child! You do the same thing with Guy Buckingham often enough.'

'I make myself sick too.'

She flung out of the room and the house. He had not seen her again for months.

On the other hand he saw Catherine every day. How she worried him. He had not lost his affection for her, there were still in Catherine traces of the stiff little girl who had come into his office the first time and arranged his pin cushion to spell her own initials. But the main emotion she roused in him now was sheer alarm. He'd never dealt with such inflexibility, from the daughter of the most flexible man William had ever known. He had not realized what damage an authoritative and inexpert hand could do to a thriving business.

Catherine simply did not understand what she held in her thin, iron grip. She took no advice except possibly from that questionable Dudley Forrest. She did not listen to William himself, or to the men who made up Alexander's brilliant team of experts. Her only concessions were to people of her own class. There were a growing number of titled families feeling the pinch, and Catherine began to find employment for some of these. By the simple means of getting rid of the professionals. Her decisions never came from reflection, they were sudden and subjective. She developed theories. God knows where she got them from, certainly not from Forrest busy making his gallery larger while taking a salary from de Grelle's at the same time.

One of Catherine's first acts after selling up the contents of Park Street was to get rid of de Grelle's expert on the early nineteenth century, Alban Tucker, and give the post to Dudley. William was horrified. It was true that Alban Tucker moved to a position in a smaller auction house at a higher salary. That was not the point. Alban, chosen by Alexander, was a classical scholar with a wonderful grasp of his subjects, a humorous thoughtful man, a pleasure to work with. And William did not forget that Dudley Forrest had once walked into his office in the role of blackmailer for Lady Lytchett.

William's journey today was the result of a letter from Lee Becker:

'I'm in Sussex right now painting my head off, but I need to see you about something. And I'd rather not talk about it in the office. Could you spare a morning? I promise not to complain if you leave after luncheon.
Gratefully, Lee.'

At Lewes station William took an antique Daimler taxi-cab and instructed the driver, older than his motor, to take him to Enstone village.

'A tidy way out of the town, Master.'

'I know that. Hurry up, man. We haven't got all day.'

Reflecting that Londoners were all mad, the old man swung the starting handle with such difficulty that William expected him to fall down in an apoplectic fit. The car shuddered and they ground away up the hill towards the Downs.

Lee had set up her easel under an apple tree in full blossom. She wore a pale pink smock, her hair was bleached by the recent spell of sunshine, and when the maid showed William into the garden he paused for a moment, pleased with the traditional picture of a pretty woman in a garden. No short skirts. No jazz. Lee ran towards him.

'William.'

'My dear.'

260

He kissed her cheek warmed by the sun. She had arranged deck chairs near her easel.

They looked at each other with cordial curiosity. He thought she seemed older. There were little fans of lines round her eyes, her mouth was less generous and less easily smiling. She looked strong and tired. Perhaps we turn into our real selves as we grow older. Who was it said we simply get more so, he thought. But Lee, looking at him affectionately, found him unchanged, the silvery hair as sleek, the figure as spare.

'It's good of you to come all the way down here. I knew you would,' she said.

'Because I am fond of you,' he said and smiled. 'And more to the point at present, I know you. You wouldn't haven't sent for me if it wasn't important.'

'Yes. I was sure you'd guess that. It's so good to see you. Oh William. You do remind me of when Alex was alive.'

'Those were good times.'

She nodded, rubbed her nose and said that Sara had been to stay and had left yesterday.

'She's another member of the family I have not seen for a long time,' said William. The words were those of some benevolent uncle. But the eyes were penetrating.

'You aren't much on Sara's side, are you?'

'My dear Lee, are we playing Oranges and Lemons?'

'Of course we are. It's like divorce. No good fooling yourself you can be on both sides at once. You have to choose. I'm for Sara. You for Catherine.'

The maid, a country girl, came out with some home-made lemonade. William had not realized that the train journey had made him thirsty. When he put down the empty glass he said, 'I suppose I am here to talk about Sara?'

'Afraid so. She's told me about her job.'

He disliked the modern word, particularly when applied to women. Slang grated.

'But Sara has no "job" as you call it, since she left de Grelle's.'

'You are out of date! She's working with Guy. After he left too, following some ill feeling with Catherine one gathers, he set up as a dealer. Haven't you heard? It's going like a house on fire and Sara's with him. Which brings me to something I've wanted to say to you for ages. I couldn't after Alex died. It was too soon and I felt slightly crazy. But now I'd like to say it, William. Alex did Sara a terrible wrong, leaving those controlling shares to Catherine. I can only suppose he never rewrote his will. He always hated even talking about that. But when one sees the result . . . *Catherine* at the head of Alex's business! She doesn't know the difference between a Roman flask and American glass from West Virginia. The only thing she knows about de Grelle's is the money. And a chance to give her classy friends jobs. I hear she's making an almighty hash of everything.'

William's face closed like the shutter of a camera.

'I trust you did not ask me down, Lee, to discuss de Grelle's. And disclose confidential information.'

She gave an angry laugh.

'I'd forgotten how pious you are. All I am doing is repeating gossip which is all over London, and I gather in Paris too. It's certainly talked about in New York, but I hear Cheriton Spencer's too shrewd to let her mess up *his* side of the business. No, William, I did not ask you here to gossip. I have to tell you something you are not going to like.'

She lifted her head and looked straight at him with her intensely blue eyes.

'Sara wants to contest her father's will. She maintains it was unjust – I agree – that he made it long before she began to work for de Grelle's – which could be true – and that control of the firm should be split into two. Three, counting Louise. But *she* wouldn't want any part of the responsibility, of course.'

William, his face now as sharp as an animal's, said shortly, 'I take it Sara has had advice.'

'Of course. She's been to a very smart solicitor who took her to a leading King's Counsel. They're both, what was the phrase she used – not unoptimistic.'

He sat clinking the ice in the empty glass. Clink. Clink. What went on behind that impassive face? It was one of the things Alex enjoyed in you, she thought, you're so cool. His opposite. His counterpoise. He needed that.

'Sara has not a chance of winning such an action if she were foolish enough to bring it,' he said finally. 'You must prevent her from trying.'

For a moment Lee was dumbfounded.

'Prevent her! Why in hell should I do that?'

'Because, as I've just said, she cannot win.'

How emotional women are, he thought. He held up his hand.

'Lee, you must believe what I say. Not because I work in de Grelle's and Catherine is now its head. I am thinking of what is best for both Alexander's daughters.'

'That's rich. It's just fine for Catherine who scooped the pool. What about Sara? All she got was the push.'

He looked at her outraged expression, her bright, angry eyes, and sighed. There was nothing for it.

'I wish it hadn't come to this. I would very much prefer not to tell you why Sara cannot win an action brought against her sister. However if there's no other way to persuade you . . .' He paused for a moment. 'If I do not tell you, Dudley Forrest certainly will the moment the news gets out about a lawsuit. Sara could not win any legal claim against the will, Lee. She could never get parity with Catherine, never obtain a new apportionment of de Grelle shares. For the unfortunate reason that Sara is illegitimate.'

Lee's eyes grew enormous.

'But – but – do you mean Alex –'

'Married Louise Goodier? No, Lee, he did not. Why didn't he? And why indeed did he not marry you, so infinitely more suited to him than either of his women, the mothers of his two daughters?'

'He did not wish to marry again.'

'But you never asked him why, did you? You are a woman of pride. I knew you hadn't. I was glad, for he would not have told you. He was ashamed of the reason when he saw how his life had turned out, I suppose. The only woman he married was Verena Lytchett. And since, despite the divorce, she was still living and he was a Roman Catholic, he would not remarry. The fact that Louise, poor child, was pregnant at the time didn't make a jot of difference. He was adamant. She was forced to make up some fairytale about their wedding in France. Alexander didn't care about that if it made her happy. But marry her – no. It was the same with you. I broached the subject (forgive me, this is impertinent but I was very fond of him and I saw how he felt about you). It was years after he and Louise had separated, the first year you and he –'

'Became lovers,' she said in a thin voice.

'Yes. You were both so discreet. Well . . . I asked again. And got the same answer. "I am a Catholic. I can live in sin. But not remarry". "What's the difference since in your faith adultery is also a sin?" I said. He shook his head. I told him it was an upside-down kind of religion which made such a rule. He said the Church knew its business and so it should after two thousand years, and while he lived in sin as he called it, the Church believed there was a chance he might repent. If he had two wives living, Rome would excommunicate him. Of course after Verena died –'

'It would have been too late,' was all she said. 'Too late. Everything was settled between us then.'

She went to the easel and lifted the cloth to reveal a blue and green landscape without a single figure. Peaceful. Luminous. She turned round, grimly smiling.

'It seems Sara and I both have our come-uppance,' she said. 'Am I supposed to tell her, then?'

'It would be wise.'

'I'm not. I'm not. I never was!' she burst out, and ran away through the orchard.

Lee finished the painting, left her Sussex cottage in the care of some neighbours (glad of the loan of the little maid) and went to London. She could not settle until she saw Sara.

The wound of Alexander's death was aching again. It had seemed healed this summer in the garden, but what William had told her almost reopened it and made it bleed, and she was in pain. Why couldn't Alex have told her the truth, had he thought she would try to dissuade him? That she wasn't somebody who could respect his unforgotten and flouted Faith? In the letter he had left her, filled with love, he asked her to take his ashes to the Church of Saint-Sauveur 'at the end of the rue des Cordeliers, where I lived as a boy with my parents. I was born at Number 109, mignonne. I should have taken you to see the house, but I was ashamed. Which is why you never met my parents either, who went back to Alsace when they were old.'

Lee had gone to Paris on an April day when the wind was fierce and the Channel rough. Paris seemed dark and sad. She found the church without difficulty, having travelled by the Métro. There it was, an ugly nineteenth-century church in a city of exquisite medieval ones. Black and grey brick, a wrought-iron decoration of lilies round a board with the times of Masses. Somebody had repainted the lilies, spattering white paint on the board which was a cracked and peeling brown.

In the church she found an old man wearing a surplice.

'*Monsieur le Curé?*'

'You would like Confession, *madame?*'

Lee thought – I wish I could.

She thanked him, saying she was not of the Faith, but had brought this. She was carrying the marble box, vulgarly shaped like a miniature urn, which contained Alex's ashes. Or what the New York crematorium people claimed them to be, thought Lee. The curé listened and nodded. Of course. He would just fetch a spade.

Lee was surprised. She had imagined one sprinkled ashes like compost on a garden. The curé came back, walking briskly, with a small red-handled spade.

'Where shall we put him? What about a good position near the gate?'

He put his foot on the spade, drove it into the rough grass and dug a small hole into which Lee poured the silky sticky ashes. The curé said a Latin prayer and, with a gesture beautiful in its antiquity, blessed them. Lee sprinkled some earth, he filled the hole and stamped it down.

When she left the church, she thought about the priest's choice of site. Did he think it easy for me to find a place by the gate? Or does he imagine Alex's ghost may wander sometimes down the rue des Cordeliers and know where he is and be at home?

London was at its early summer best when she let herself

into her dusty mews cottage. Letters lay all over the floor. Invitations. Art shows. Bills. A de Grelle catalogue.

She telephoned Guy Buckingham.

'Lee. Nice to hear you. And you want young Sara.'

Sara sounded happy enough, which to Lee's mind was not sufficient. They arranged to meet.

'I will have to leave you before ten –' said Sara.

'Because you're dancing.'

'Yes. With Fay and her lot.'

'I thought she was in Egypt.'

'She's back. For Ascot.'

'Still selling up the happy home?'

'Anything that isn't nailed down.'

When Sara arrived at the studio and pulled off a small straw hat, Lee whistled. Sara had cut off her long red hair.

'Sara! What a shock!'

'Fay and I took the plunge last week. We went to a brand new Mayfair place where the man's an expert at short hair. You should have *seen* our hair all over the floor. It was like harvest time.'

The short hair bobbed to her jawline made her look like a young Renaissance page. Lee was not sure she preferred this rakish boyish creature to the girl who had fled from France four years ago.

Sara prowled round the studio, turning canvases which faced the wall, inspecting them and replacing them. Once she said 'this one's unhappy'. Lee, who disliked people looking at her work without permission, said nothing. She was waiting for the right moment. When's the right moment, she thought, swearing inwardly, to tell a girl she's a by-blow? A bastard. That her father hadn't had the grace to make her mother his wife.

Sara, having finished looking over the paintings, sat down on a table and swung her legs. Her skirts, like her hair, were very short and fashionable. Twelve inches from the ankle and showing yards of silk-clad leg.

'I saw my sister yesterday,' she said. 'She asked me to tea. Guess what. She'd heard the rumour about my seeing a solicitor or two.'

'Only fools go to law, Sara.'

'Unless they win, then everybody says how brave and clever. Well, Lee. I am not going to waste my father's money in the law courts after all. Though it would have been fascinating, wouldn't it?'

Her long eyes had a speculative look. They were like Alex's when he was in competition with another auction house. Before Lee could speak, Sara went on, 'Cathy trumped my ace. The King's Counsel told me I might have won, you know. And get Father's will altered fairly. I saw him again on Monday. The fact that Cathy sacked me would count against her, he said. If she'd been clever,' added Sara in her new casual voice, 'she'd have kept me on and given me work worth doing. But she won't have even a minor rival. With her it's all or nothing.'

Lee was silent.

'What she doesn't know,' went on Sara, 'is that if you pour a cocktail too quickly it slops over. If you pour carefully and slowly, you can fill it right up to the brim. However, that's in the past. My sister gave me a cup of tea and some bad news.'

Lee did not know where this conversation was leading.

'Cathy informed me, more in pity than in spite, that I am illegitimate,' said Sara brightly. 'It seems Father never married my unfortunate parent. Imagine, poor Louise. I did feel sorry for her. I must say I was also rather surprised.'

She looked at Lee, daring her not to accept the modern flippancy.

'I see,' she added, 'that you know all this anyway.'

'Yes. William told me. And I think I understand why it happened,' Lee said slowly. For selfish reasons, as well as to alter the girl's glittering face, she began to speak about Alex's religion. Sara said nothing. She was remembering her visit to Catherine, who had shown her round her new house in South Moulton Street. Sara had seen nothing of her since Alexander's death when the sisterly tie had been hacked to bits by Catherine one winter afternoon in New York. Sara saw it die without regret. I cannot bear her, and she certainly cannot bear me.

Since then Sara had cobbled together a life of her own. The

visit to Catherine, after so long, put her on her guard.

Catherine sat complacently in a drawing room of the old-fashioned style, her taste never budged, and said, 'There's something I must speak to you about, Sara. I've heard rumours about a proposed law suit. A friend in the Temple told Dudley.'

Sara was unabashed.

'Yes. I'm thinking of challenging Father's will,' she said, eating a biscuit.

She noticed that Catherine looked very calm.

'It's over two years since he died, Sara. What on earth made you think of such an extraordinary idea?'

As a matter of fact it had been Fay who had recently acquired a stout solicitor to challenge her own tied-up fortune. Fay and the solicitor had the bright idea about Sara.

'One's sense of injustice is apt to grow,' Sara remarked amiably.

Catherine gave a short laugh.

'There wasn't a word of injustice about the will. You have a generous portion of shares. Too generous, I consider.'

'And *you* have the control. Unjust, I consider.'

'No. I am Father's heir.'

'You're not a *son*,' said Sara, suddenly vicious, 'and we're not fighting over some footling English title. We're talking about de Grelle's which Father built and I understand. *You're* messing it up like a kid with a sandcastle. Why, if I had the chance –'

Catherine interrupted.

'You could scarcely have any chance. Since Father never married your mother.'

Sara recoiled as violently as if her sister had thrown a snake into her lap. She was quite speechless.

'It's true. What's that word at de Grelle's? Provenance. I have the provenance. Ask William. Ask your mother, though it seems unnecessarily cruel to dig it all up. He treated my mother cruelly too. But he never replaced her.'

She studied Sara for a moment, and added in a kinder tone,

'Dudley and I would never have breathed a word of this if you hadn't threatened to go to law. You couldn't win, Sara.

Who would give judgement for you, and not for me?'

The contrast between the two young women was at its strongest just then. Catherine cool, virginal, on the edge of old-maidishness despite the ring on her left hand. Snobbish. Upper class. And winning. Sara, modern as the London day outside, clever, brilliant, tempered by sadness. And with nothing for her future but thwarted talent and a ruined love affair . . .

Lee tapped her with the end of a long paint brush.

Sara roused herself.

'Sorry. I was thinking it would be useful to understand Cathy and I can't. I understand nothing about her. Do you? Her engagement, for instance. Why aren't they married by now, for heaven's sake?'

'I can answer that,' said Lee, feeling she had been let off too lightly. 'She enjoys being engaged. A lot of girls of her sort have long engagements. She wants everything arranged down to the minutest detail. She has a new house. Business interests. Dudley's enlarging his gallery. And incidentally, I gather her grandmother is not well, so that would be another reason for postponing the marriage.'

Sara shrugged.

'Tell me a single trait, Lee, one single family characteristic we've both inherited from Father.'

'Your will. Determination. Persistence. In a game of cards, I guess you'd be well matched.'

'Oh, very amusing. What single card in the pack is left to me?'

'You'll find one.'

It was true that Sara had managed to re-make her life after Alexander died and Perry had rejected her. Fay became a figure of destiny again.

When she returned to London that winter, Sara had thought painfully about Fay. She'd betrayed her friend yet had still lost – or never possessed – Perry's love. It served her right. Unable to think straight during the last days of her stay at Park Street, she did not telephone Fay. Totally unexpectedly Fay appeared. She found Sara alone in the library, sitting on the floor among piles of books which were to be sold.

Fay looked round the door and said in a voice unlike her own, 'I want to see you.'

She came in, shutting the door. She was shivering.

'I came to say I'm sorry about your Papa, I *am*, but – but I can't not tell you that I know about you and Perry.'

Sara made a sudden movement towards her and Fay backed away. She wore something short and white. A diamond arrow piercing a heart was on the shoulder of her dress.

'Don't say you're sorry. I should hate it. I wish I could hate you too. One of my cousins saw you with Perry on the *Aquitania* and – and she said anybody could see about you both and I ought to know. I wish I didn't. You *knew* I loved him. I still do. You knew he was the one I dreadfully wanted. Just because you're clever and know everything and I'm so silly doesn't mean I haven't any feelings. Oh, how could you, how could you?'

She ran sobbing from the house.

Sara wrote to her. Tore up the letter. Wrote again. Then remembered how seldom her friend read letters in case they were from her lawyers. The letter in any case wasn't worth writing for there was nothing to say but to be sorry. Am I only sorry Perry's gone, thought Sara. She hated herself for that sexual slavery. Or was it love which still lay in a dead weight inside her.

In the end she went to Chester Square on a spring evening, the day after the Park Street auction. Lee had been away and had lent her the mews cottage. Sara, throwing suitcases into Lee's studio, took a taxi to Chester Square. When the parlour maid let her into the house, she heard music.

'Toot toot tootsy goodbye,' sang a voice.

There was a burst of clapping.

'Miss Fay's upstairs,' said the maid unnecessarily. 'Shall I announce, you, miss?'

'No, thank you, Gladys. I'll just go up.'

It took a good deal of courage to climb the stairs down which many couples had danced. Sara was so nervous when she came to the open door that her heart was thudding.

Fay, wearing a dress so short that it only reached to the top of her legs and was edged with white feathers, was dancing. The gramophone blared. The audience was of two, Eddy and Tommy.

'Sara!' cried Fay, not stopping her dance, 'this is the shimmy. Mae Murray does it, you turn in your knees and wiggle,' shaking her bottom in a tremble of feathers. 'Can you do it? Tommy, you and Sara shimmy together. Oh toot toot tootsy . . .'

There was no mention of Perry during an evening which went on until dawn crept over the London chimney pots.

Two days later Fay telephoned the cottage.

'Guy said I'd find you at Lee's. Has that horrible Catherine really sold up Park Street? I've had a ripping idea, Sara. Say yes. Come and live in Chester Square. I have all these bedrooms which people only use to throw their coats around or do naughty things. Be my lodger. Oh do.'

Sara protested, arguments followed, in the end she said yes. Fay at first refused to accept a penny, but Sara at last persuaded her to let her pay some rent. Fay received the money with delight on Fridays, exclaiming, 'Hooray. I needn't sell the Lalique', or 'This'll pay a teensy bit of the Harrods bill.'

More men than ever called at Chester Square. At present Fay was also occupied with the arrangements for a charity ball at which she had promised to appear, out of a cardboard wedding cake, dressed in a bathing suit.

Perry's name never crossed her lips, and Sara loved her for the generosity of her forgiveness.

It was not long after Sara moved to Chester Square that Guy also made a move. He left de Grelle's.

'A small argument with your sister,' he said to Sara, meeting her at Chester Square. 'I'm too old and too fat, young Sara, to cope with her whims. Now we are both unemployed. What about a little work together?'

'Oh Guy. How I wish . . . but I'm so ignorant. What use would I be to you over silver?'

'You are a beginner and I'm very lazy. A perfect combination.'

It was Sara who found them a dusty office at the top of an

old house in Bruton Street. Here, where (Guy said) maids used to sleep in rows like pickled asparagus, they set to work. Sara learned fast. She fell in love with silver and gold as people have done since ancient Babylon.

Sara said to Lee Becker that in any game with Catherine, she hadn't a card in the pack. She had been working a few months for Guy when he came lazing into the poky attic office with a rumour. What did Sara think of this? He'd heard from a client that her sister was thinking of selling the London branch of de Grelle's.

'*Guy, how awful.*'

Guy was comforting. Rumours floated about London and Paris all the time. Sometimes started by rivals who hoped a nervous atmosphere would unsettle a firm. And lower the price when they thought about selling.

Sara was not convinced. The more she thought it over, the more she thought that it was exactly like Catherine. Somebody must have offered her a lot of money. Catherine was rather awe-struck by money, Sara had noticed that since they were children; she'd discovered later that it was a trait in the upper classes. Tracing their families back hundreds of years, fiercely proud of great deeds in the past, they bowed to money's power. Catherine was on the way to ruining de Grelle's and she would not enjoy the failure. What she would enjoy would be large sums paid to her by a greedy rival.

There was only one way to stop her, thought Sara.

CHAPTER SEVENTEEN

It was the deserted month of July, and Louise was irritated to the point of screaming that she was still in Antibes. The weather panted with heat. Every shutter was closed, and although the gardener drenched the roses every morning, by nightfall they drooped, exhausted.

Jean-Claude was responsible for chaining her to the Villa des Roses at such a time. Everybody of note, American, English, an Indian rajah or two, had gone on the eighth of April. On the seventh, Jean-Claude developed a sore throat and a temperature. The throat remained somewhat inflamed, the fever left him. But Louise's lover then caught something worse – a fretful hypochondria. Louise, reverting to her Spartan New York girlhood, thought him despicable.

'I cannot travel, *adorée*. Not until I am well,' he said peevishly.

'Switzerland will cure you. The air is so pure.'

'And so much colder. The train journey could re-infect my throat. Doctor Brunelli agrees I must not travel yet.'

Throwing her beautiful eyes to the ceiling, Louise submitted. As the weeks went by, she was convinced he had become bored with Montreux and preferred to remain here.

After her daughter ran off in that disgusting way to London, Louise, determined not to offend socially, made Jean-Claude move to a hotel. He hated that. It was his idea later that Louise must have a 'companion'. Louise agreed. She fancied a Russian. 'It is so chic to engage a former lady-in-waiting to the Czarina. Grace Haveling hired a Russian princess for her children as governess.'

Jean-Claude preferred a French girl, deciding that Louise

provided quite enough temperament at the Villa des Roses. A young French girl, Denise, was employed and Jean-Claude promptly moved back into sex and comfort with Louise. Denise's duties consisted of airing Louise's two yappy little dogs, doing some sewing, having tea with the lovers, and making herself scarce. A reserved young woman, with a face like Marianne on the French stamps, she appeared satisfied with her curious employment.

Meantime Louise was fettered at the Villa in the horrible month of July. Jean-Claude would not move an inch.

The sun poured down. The beaches were empty save for a few Americans who'd taken it into their crazy heads to stay on at cut rates in Juan les Pins and swim in the sea. Louise, who never swam, remained in cool rooms, reading, sighing and ringing for iced champagne.

The years and the champagne were not treating her well. Her looks had slightly but definitely deteriorated. Her chin was heavier, her lovely hair, once a raven's wing, was touched up as she called it. Jean-Claude made her have it cut, which alarmed her. Gazing at herself in many mirrors afterwards she thought, 'I look ten years younger.'

But Jean-Claude did not say so.

It was afternoon and she lay on her *chaise-longue*, resenting the heat. In the garden even the leaves of the eucalyptus trees had turned so that only the edge of their long blades faced the pitiless sun. Upstairs, Jean-Claude was in bed. He sent a message saying he would not get up today.

Louise lay staring at the ceiling, deeply, irritably bored. Not only from being trapped in this unfashionable heat but at the prospect of her daughter's arrival.

Sara had telegraphed the housekeeper, asking for the address of her mother's hotel at Montreux. When the telegram arrived Jean-Claude insisted that Louise should reply at once.

'Make it affectionate, please,' he said, adding that she must invite Sara to stay at Antibes.

Louise was not looking forward to seeing her in the least. She had enjoyed being a mother when the child had been a pretty little red-headed moppet whom it was fun to dress.

She'd even enjoyed buying her clothes when Sara was fifteen – Poiret, Worth. Clothes were clothes then. But as she
grew older, Sara's character was so unattractive. She had not
inherited Louise's beauty, she was thin, with dark grey eyes
and that thick white skin like her father's. And like him, she had
strong nerves. Louise disliked dealing with a second Alexander
and regretted she had chosen the first one. I could have married
anyone, she thought. All those proposals. Aunt Emily was
right.

The villa dozed. So did the servants in shadowed rooms.
Louise's eyelids drooped . . . the magazine slipped from her
lap. The southern summer flowed into the room . . .

One of the window shutters creaked. A voice said:

'Mother?'

Sara, blinded by the glare outside, came into the room.
Although she could see nothing, she knew Louise was there by
the scent of *Je Reviens*.

'I can't see a thing. Ah, there you are. Sorry. Did I wake you?'

Crossing a room striped in light and dark, she bent to kiss her
mother's cheek.

'I didn't hear a taxi,' yawned Louise.

'I walked up from the gate. I wanted to see what had happened to the garden.'

'Nothing's happened to the garden or anything else. It's the
Saison Morte. Sit where I can see you.'

Louise looked her over.

'You're too thin. It must be the disgusting English food.'

Sara bore the none-too-admiring look with philosophy.
Louise looked older, but not much, fatter, but not very. She
was as transparent as the water by Eden Roc. She lay there
resenting that she wasn't in Montreux. She was not fond of her
only child. She was spoiled and difficult and obscurely sad, and
Sara had a moment of passionate fondness for the ruined
beauty of her mother's face.

Hearing of Sara's arrival, Jean-Claude felt a little better and
appeared for dinner, handsome in a white jacket. He greeted
Sara with delight, and during a meal of Mediterranean dorade
with fennel asked her all the questions about her London life
which Louise had forgotten to do.

Free of Louise's power, Sara liked Jean-Claude very much. And did not miss the fact that although her mother still drank a good deal, he had almost nothing but two glasses of wine.

'He bothers about his figure. What kind of man thinks about that?' said Louise, when he refused a drink.

'Any man with sense in his head,' said Jean-Claude, mockingly. 'I do not wish to get fat and bloated, like most of our friends on the coast.'

As Louise drained her glass Sara thought – *Mother, don't say it*.

'Fat and bloated like me, you mean.'

Both Jean-Claude and Sara answered at the same time – What nonsense she was talking! How could she say such a thing, it had only been a joke.

Louise condescended to accept their exclaimed flatteries.

She'd taken in Sara's appearance closely. Those short skirts and that daring style of hair. For the rest, she considered Sara's presence a duty paid too late, but a tribute all the same. Jean-Claude wasn't sure. When they were alone that night, he hinted there must be another reason for Sara's sudden visit to the Midi. Louise, brushing her hair, criticized her, putting Sara in a bad light and herself in a good one.

'When I was twenty-five I'd never have worn such a hideous colour.'

'Did you notice she dodged the question when I asked about her beaux. One takes it there aren't any.'

She ended by referring to her daughter's 'nickel and dime work.'

Jean-Claude muttered what to his tone-deaf lover sounded like agreement. He was privately glad of a lively girl about of his own age. But he thought her presence ominous.

As for Sara she decided not to raise, just yet, the thorny subject of de Grelle shares. She wanted Louise to get more used to her before she did that.

The morning after she arrived, Sara, wearing her thinnest turquoise and grey voile, walked through the pine trees to the Antibes road on her way to visit Carl. The elderly should never be taken by surprise, and she had telephoned him the previous evening.

His front door on to the ramparts was open and he was sitting in the sun, looking at the sparkling sea below the high walls when he saw her.

'Sara!'

'Carl. Such ages.'

He kissed her hand and they went into the house and into the sitting room. It was utterly changed. An oil painting of a young woman stood on an easel. She had enormous dark eyes and an expression of melancholy seduction. In the corner on a costume stand was a green silk robe draped with a black lace scarf.

'*Ma Belle* wore that when she was very ill,' said Carl, touching the lace. 'The scarf was thrown over her plaits.'

Sara stood in front of the portrait.

'How beautiful she is. But so tragic.'

'Yes . . . yes . . . but she was quite a butterfly, you know. Costume balls in her immense house in the rue Trudon. A magnificent bedroom, Louis XV, she said that was the right style for love. That little chair is from her salon. And the painted Etruscan panels from her bathroom. Napoleon's son, remember? the Count Walewski, paid for all those costly rooms of hers . . .'

Sara looked about, played a chord on the piano which had belonged to Rachel's sister, touched the green silk robe. And returned to the tragic, alluring, girlish face.

'Where, oh where, is the Emperor?' she said, to tease.

'Bringing me in a regular income. Sit down, my dear child, let me look at you.'

She sat smiling very differently from the way she smiled at Louise. And he looked at her differently from Louise's jealous glance.

'You've changed. One must allow – more beautiful.'

'But?'

'But harder, I think. I thought it a little in Paris. More so, now. Was your father's death a great shock? I did write but letters are useless sometimes. Tell me about your life. There is nothing in mine but *La Grande Rachel*.'

Sara, released and relaxed more even than with Lee, talked. She took his love and admiration for granted, there was room to move inside it. She spoke of her father's death, her weeks in

New York, her sister's rejection. She explained that she now worked with Guy Buckingham who was a silver dealer. She skimmed across why she was in Antibes.

'But you have a plan in your head about de Grelle's. And you don't give up easily,' he remarked when she finished.

'Aren't there animals who cling on for too long. Crocodiles? Bulldogs? Isn't it a sign of stupidity?' she said gaily.

He reflected. Age suited him. His big nose and lined cheeks had distinction and he looked very spruce. He had Napoleon to thank for that.

'We'll leave de Grelle's for the time being. Something else is missing in your tale, Sara. What about the country of the heart?'

'Oh, there are one or two men about.'

'Or a dozen. Including Monsieur Buckingham about whom you speak so kindly. But he is not the one for you.'

'Oh Carl.'

'Oh Sara. Is there nobody, then?'

'Carl, you're a romantic. You've always been my father confessor and . . . yes . . . there was somebody. I didn't talk about him because it was reprehensible, in a way. And I always want you to admire me and not disapprove or give me lectures. You won't, will you, if I tell?'

'I expect I will, Sara.'

She laughed.

'I shall tell you anyway. It was a man I met, years ago, on the last night at the Villa Roumaniev . . .'

She talked about Perry then, using her flippant manner, new to Carl. It seemed to him to reflect the cynical dance-mad people with whom he supposed she spent her time. Yes, the man had been her lover. And had been in Newport when her father died. And that was all there was to it.

'I'm like that stupid song. Forever blowing bubbles. If I'm serious, which I prefer not to be, about Perry van Rijn, *he* was a pretty bubble in the air. He sure didn't want to come down to earth and be with me, Carl. There it is.'

She met his eyes, daring him to be sorry.

'You were in love with him,' Carl said, finding the words gave him a dull pain.

'Is there a test. How does one know?'

'By sleeping badly when alone. Waking at four in the morning as if with agonizing indigestion, but it isn't the stomach which is hurting. Seeing visions.'

'What visions, Carl?'

'The beloved. In the street. In crowds. A ghost in empty rooms. A scent of tobacco or human hair. Having the terrible delusion one hears his voice, only to realize a stranger is talking. Lovers are pursued by the Furies. Were you? Are you?'

'I was. It's over.'

'*Ah bon,*' he said in disbelief. 'And now let us talk about Rachel.'

It was midday when she left, promising to come back very soon. There were no shadows on the dusty ground and the walk home was exhausting.

She felt uneasy. Only Carl, not Lee, had made her tell the truth about Perry. And what was Perry to her now, after all?

When Fay had asked her to live at Chester Square and never once again reproached her, Sara knew one day she must speak about Perry to her friend. You couldn't just leave it or it would never heal. And since Fay was obviously happy, one evening when they were dressing, Sara said, 'Fay. I saw Perry when we were in Newport and New York.'

'Of course you did. You – well – you did the same as me with him, didn't you?' Fay buttoned the shoulder of a pink taffeta dress and wriggled to make it set properly.

'It didn't mean much.'

Fay nodded. 'We are alike, aren't we? The same man. I was quite quite crazy over him, wasn't I? Miserable when I knew you'd done it with him too. You being so clever and –'

'Fay, have mercy!'

'But you are, darling. Anyway, what I was going to say is, isn't he peculiar? My boyfriends all tell me about their lives and times, one just can't stop them. Well, I once asked Perry the teeniest question about if he had brothers and sisters and he closed up like a clam. Slam, wallop. He was rather nasty, too. He doesn't give, does he? It took me ages to get him back to being fun. Of course he was marvellous at love and all that,' said Fay, grinning, 'but you haven't met Robert. He's coming round tonight, and he really is a thrill. I've sort of moved on now.'

And that, thought Sara, is what I must do. Fay had put her scarlet finger-nail on the truth. Perry did not give. Never spoke of his friends, worries, hopes, those human things. Never told her a word about the war. That first night at the Roumaniev he'd told her he had been on the Italian Front as a liaison officer. Had fought on the River Piave and was only at the Roumaniev because an American friend was convalescing there. What had happened to him during the war? She had never felt she could ask. He kept her out. Why, then, did she mourn for him still?

Now and then her body still longed. There was no other lover among the men who took her out and about.

Fay, shimmering into her bedroom one night, all in silver fringe, had said, 'Bobbie and I think you're a goody at heart.'

'Of course I'm not.'

'All the boys swear you are.'

'Oh help, I must do something about it at once.'

Fay burst out laughing.

I wish I hadn't talked about Perry to Carl, she thought, reaching the drive of the Villa des Roses at last. She thought instead of why she was here, and tried to imagine what her mother would say about the sale of de Grelle's. Sara would need to explain, in a way which attracted Louise, that between them she and Louise could vote against Catherine. Why should Louise want to do that? Sara's hope now was that Jean-Claude might be an ally. But there were rocks ahead.

She scarcely noticed the Italian roadster parked under the trees, except to wonder vaguely if it belonged to the doctor. A dashing kind of doctor, apparently. Perhaps her mother was trying to persuade him to make Jean-Claude leave the Midi after all. I haven't much time . . .

As she went towards the drawing room, she heard a man laugh. It was not Jean-Claude's chuckle, but a laugh that was too loud and too long, a positive roar of determined amusement. Sitting on the shaded terrace, drinking champagne with his hostess, was Dudley.

'My dear Sara.'

He sprang up, bent to kiss her, said how delightful it was to find her 'here of all places.' The kiss and the warmth to Sara, who was summoning her wits not to look dismayed, caused Louise's expression to change. Dudley saw it and returned to her.

'I've been telling your mother, Sara, what a wonderful place she has. Why haven't I invited myself before? It's a thrill to meet you, *madame*.'

'Call me Louise.'

'Yes. I will,' agreed Dudley, and had his glass refilled.

Sara sat down and Jean-Claude explained to her that Dudley had sailed to Antibes this morning from Cannes.

'I'm here on business, but I've hired a twenty-footer,' said Dudley. 'It's an age since I sailed. In Melbourne I was more on the water than on dry land.'

'I can't imagine why you hired a yacht,' said Louise, dimpling. 'The season's over. Nobody goes in a boat except the fishermen. Jean-Claude and I are always in Switzerland at this time; all the *beau monde* are gone.'

'Not all,' said Dudley.

'I think it could be amusing to sail,' said Jean-Claude. 'You must also come, Sara.'

'Of course she will,' said Dudley breezily. 'I'm here on the look-out for pictures, of course. Prints. Water colours. My usual line.'

'There are some exciting new French painters about,' said Jean-Claude.

'I agree. But my customers don't seem ready for them. The best thing for me to do is to sniff about for something in their line. Maybe I'll find a sale or two. Or there are those shops in the old quarter at Nice, with the word "*brocante*" outside. Always a good sign.'

He could have lived in the Midi for years.

But, apart from a few hours sailing in the bay at Cannes, Dudley never went to Nice or to a sale but spent his time at the Villa des Roses. Louise asked him to stay and, with exclamations of protest, he moved in. Even Sara who became very thoughtful about him had to admit his charm when he wished to please. He told stories of his gallantry in war and his

281

shrewdness in peace; but his way of boasting was boyish and enthusiastic. He made them smile. He sat with Louise on the terrace, walked with her in the garden in the evening and picked her a great yellow rose. To Jean-Claude's amazement, he taught her to play chess.

Dudley decided to take them driving along the Grande Corniche, the highest of the three roads between Roquebrune and Nice. Jean-Claude never chose that road, much admired by visitors and built by Napoleon. He drove along the Lower Corniche which ran most of the way close to the sea at the bottom of the cliffs. But the Grande Corniche rose fifteen hundred feet at La Turbie, with many sheer cliff drops and sometimes no roadside walls. Dudley drove fast, and Jean-Claude who sat in the back of the car with Sara clutched her hand. His own was wringing with sweat.

Catherine's fiancé was with Louise all the livelong day. Jean-Claude grew morose and Sara was not surprised.

But Louise was drenched and dripping with the life-giving liquid of male attention. Recently Jean-Claude had not been the young adorer as in the past, and Dudley treated her as men used to do.

Why is he *here*, thought Sara. And how could she, with him present, have any kind of business conversation with her mother? The first moment she had seen him at the villa she had been sure he had come to talk her mother into selling her de Grelle shares to Catherine. But upon reflection she decided that was impossible. Why should Louise, who had detested Verena without knowing her, give Catherine anything? God, I wish he'd go, thought Sara. Longing to be back in London and at work, there was nothing for it but to put up with his presence and laugh at his jokes.

One morning when they were planning to go to Cannes and sail, Sara breakfasted alone on her balcony. A breeze shook the pine trees and made a sound like the sea; the sky was tender cloudless blue. Even Sara could not deny that this was one of the most beautiful places on earth. Painters came here and could not leave. Lovers too. Smelling the resinous scent of the trees, she remembered lying with Perry in the dark on the pine needless. In this very bedroom she'd looked into the mirror at her naked back and buttocks, and seen them scarred and criss-crossed as if she had been beaten. How they had loved, that night. She could not remember how many times, but only that he had whispered, 'I want you again.'

And when she woke, and ran to the Roumaniev, he was gone.

It is always like that. He is in my arms. Taking me. Giving me such bliss. Then he's gone. I must stop thinking of him. *I will*.

Dudley left early 'to get the craft ship-shape', and Jean-Claude, who was being difficult, said he wasn't well enough to drive the De Dion to Cannes. François must drive. When Sara came downstairs, dressed in white with a shady hat, Louise and Jean-Claude were actually ready. Jean-Claude was in pale shantung which showed off his slim figure, Louise in Parma violet chiffon. Jean-Claude carried a cane with a silver top which he flourished gaily at Sara.

'I telephoned La Galette. Late luncheon on the terrace – the food is passable. *Petites fritûres*.'

Louise looked dubious. Why was La Galette open when the Carlton and even the Gonnet et de la Reine were shut? She couldn't imagine the luncheon would be worth eating.

·La Galette will give us,' said Jean-Claude coldly, 'a little luncheon not to be despised.'

'There's a breeze,' said Sara when the drive started. The De Dion's hood was down and soft air brushed her cheeks.

Jean-Claude lit a cigarette, shading it with his hand, and when it was drawing satisfactorily said,

'Lou-lou. Have you told Sara the news?'

Louise sighed loudly.

'Jean-Claude, you are so stupid; it was supposed to be a surprise.'

'Perhaps she would rather not be surprised.'

'Oh, very well.' Louise was pettish. 'I've asked somebody else to spend a few days with us while Dudley is here. Guess who. Your sister!'

'*Catherine?*'

Louise looked pleased at the effect of her bombshell.

'Certainly. It's ridiculous, all that feuding and fighting now poor Alexander has been dead so long. And Dudley's such a pet. We talked it over and he wrote to her. He heard from her yesterday,' finished Louise, with a little laugh.

The car nosed its way round the point of the Croisette and Jean-Claude could not resist showing Louise that there were some yachts in the bay, and not only fishing boats. The season wasn't dead after all.

Dudley was skilful in a yacht and they had an enjoyable trip as far as Saint-Raphael. Luncheon, on a terrace shaded by a thick-growing vine, was a success. But to Sara it seemed a day of endless talk and she was relieved when it was over, and she was blessedly alone in her room at last with her troubled thoughts. It was extraordinary of her sister to swallow the old hatred of Louise and actually accept the invitation. Why had she changed? Why had Louise changed? In her mother's case it was obvious. Louise was putty in the hands of a man as attractive and clever as Dudley who had clearly persuaded her that the financially advantageous thing was to sell Catherine her shares. As for Catherine, it seemed she was also willing to put the past behind her – for money. The old upper-class reverence for hard cash.

Sitting by her window, Sara remembered another time when she'd been here in exactly the same frame of mind. So anxious that she felt desperate. And, as she'd done four years ago, she again thought – who can help me? She stared out unseeingly at the pine trees, and then she recalled her father's words: 'Always remember, *mon enfant*, that William is the heart and conscience of de Grelle's.'

The villa was quiet when she slipped out and almost ran down the hill towards Carl Bauer's house. And the privacy of a telephone call which her mother could know nothing about.

The Cannes-Calais express which brought William Thornbury to the Riviera had another voyager whom he'd spotted the moment she was on the London platform. Sara had said her sister might travel that day and William, glad of the warning, took care not to be seen. He was fond of Catherine, his favourite, but there were reasons why he should not speak to her at present.

For a man untrained in the art of remaining invisible, he was agile at keeping out of her view. He saw her alight from the boat train at Dover, saw her up the gangway, a slim figure in a travelling coat and cape. Then she was shown into a private cabin. On the express, he had his dinner served in his sleeping compartment. And on Cannes station, fussing over her luggage in schoolgirl French, she did not notice a dark-suited Englishman at the far end of the platform.

Knowing William was on his way, Sara walked in the garden, returned to the terrace, and jumped nearly out of her skin when a car drew up at the villa. She was thoroughly unnerved when, instead of a man's voice, she heard her sister's flat tones. Why was Cathy here first?

Catherine climbed out of the taxi and looked at the Villa des Roses almost with the eye of an estate agent; it must have cost a mint of money. A flock of servants hurried out, she was welcomed, briefly kissed by Sara, smackingly embraced by Dudley. Louise shook hands with her, both women wearing the same smile. And Jean-Claude kissed her hand and bowed. There was a buzz of conversation when they were settled on the terrace. A maid brought coffee and fresh croissants, Dudley told his fiancée about the yacht, Jean-Claude enquired about the visitor's journey, Louise too. Sara simply sat, wondering if she heard a second car coming up the hill. Then she was sure.

'Was that a car?' exclaimed Louise suddenly. 'The Villa des Roses is very popular this morning.'

'Might be one of my artists,' said Dudley, finishing his coffee.

'Oh Dudley, have you yet found –' began Catherine, just as the maid reappeared to say there was a gentleman to see madame. A Monsieur Thornbury.

Sara had never seen more dismayed and astonished faces. Quickest to recover, Dudley got to his feet as William was shown on to the terrace.

More introductions followed. Louise said prettily, 'William, what a wonderful surprise! Are you in the Midi looking for painters too? What years since we met. I suppose,' she could not resist it, 'I am quite, quite changed.'

'My dear Louise, you are as handsome as ever,' said William. He was given a seat. As if by a spell, conversation stopped.

How will he cope, thought Sara. He had scarcely looked at her, except to give her a non-committal nod.

'I know what we need,' cried Louise, clapping her hands as if to dispel the curious chill the visitor had brought with him. 'Champagne. Jean-Claude, ask them to fetch some from the cellar. William, you won't refuse to drink my health, when we have not seen each other for three hundred years!'

William smiled courteously. Champagne arrived, and the curious combination of breakfast and the cold sparkling drink was sampled by the five people on the terrace.

'Very nice, and very unfamiliar,' said William, putting down his glass. 'I must apologize, Louise, for being here without letting you know in advance. But the fact is, well, I'm afraid we need a meeting with the family. Something unexpected to be discussed. When I gathered everybody was here together, it seemed a most convenient opportunity.'

Louise giggled.

'A meeting. I've never attended a meeting in my born days.'

'It won't take long,' he said, in his old-fashioned manner with a pretty woman. 'But we need to talk. You and I and the girls.'

He looked from Catherine to Sara.

'Oh well, if we must,' sighed Louise.

'I'd appreciate it if I could also be present,' said Dudley. William had heard that said on another, fatal occasion; he crossed his legs. His dark suit looked out of place on the sun-checkered terrace, among women and men in pale clothes. He was a city beetle who had arrived among the white roses.

'I am sorry. But it has to be just Louise, Catherine and Sara. Do you think' – looking at Louise – 'we might manage it now?'

Jean-Claude stood up and went into the house without a word. Dudley did not follow. He was angry. And smiled.

Louise, saying she supposed they'd best go into the drawing room, led the way, adding to Catherine,

'Such a bore, ruining your first morning. I'm amazed at William being such a pest.'

'So am I,' said Catherine. She was deeply offended that

William Thornbury, an employee of hers in a way, should appear out of nowhere and behave as if he, not she, were the head of de Grelle's. She gave him a quelling glance before Louise took them indoors, leaving Dudley with the ice melting in the bucket, and the bottle empty.

In the drawing room, everybody sat down in silence. When they had spoken last night on the telephone, Sara had wondered at William's insistence that he must come at once. She waited to see what would happen with a dull and grateful curiosity. The game was lost before it was begun. But he was Alexander's friend.

Louise spread a lace handkerchief on her knee.

'I suppose it's quite good you are here, William. There's something to be settled. It concerns Catherine –' She did not look at Sara. 'And I may as well take the chance to tell you now. I have decided to sell my shares to Catherine. Don't try to talk me out of it,' she continued gaily. 'I have absolutely made up my mind. Catherine and Dudley have offered me a thrilling price. Besides, what do I want with Alexander's business now? I only gave him the money because he wheedled it out of me. So. Fix it all up, would you, William dear?'

Flirtation was never far from her voice when she spoke to a man.

William said,

'I'm afraid it is not as easy as that. I have been planning this visit for some time, Louise, but I had to wait for some papers. They came from Valbonne two days ago. From a Maître Ardisson.'

Sara, mystified, looked towards her mother. She had never seen anybody blanch before: the rouge stood out on Louise's cheeks.

'I don't know what you are talking about,' she began.

His voice was extraordinarily kind.

'It's no good, Louise, the truth is out. Maître Ardisson sent me a copy of the certificate of your marriage, four years ago, to Monsieur Jean-Claude Tournamy.'

'It isn't true!' burst out Louise with a sort of desperation, but William leaned forward to take her hands. She pulled them furiously away.

'Don't bother to deny it, my dear. You and the young man are married. He is your husband.'

Sara simply gaped, but Catherine said angrily,

'I'm sorry to intrude on what is a most private matter but I consider my presence most improper. This has nothing to do with me.'

'But it has, Catherine,' he said slowly, picking his words. 'The de Grelle shares were made out to Louise by your father with one proviso. They were hers unless she married. If she did, his responsibility to her and her connexion with de Grelle's would be at an end. The company would repay her the sum she lent him. Louise agreed to all this, and signed a document to that effect.'

'I can only presume, Louise,' he went on, his voice again very warm as he looked towards her, 'that you remembered it very well, my dear. Which is why you kept the marriage a secret.'

She said nothing, but looked at him with her white face.

Neither Sara nor Catherine spoke.

'Alexander left a codicil about this in his will,' added William. 'That if Louise married, and of course the shares would be paid for when she returned them to us, they would go to Sara.'

CHAPTER EIGHTEEN

News arrived before her. She was recognized by the salute of the doorman, the good mornings of her old friends the porters, and the way Miss Tomkins stood up when Sara came into her office.

It was less than a week since the meeting at Antibes. Catherine and Dudley left the Riviera the same evening. When Sara herself returned with William, a letter was waiting for her.

'In the circumstances, Dudley and I are going to Lytchett. I shall not be in London for some time.

C.'

Sara thought Miss Tomkins looked apprehensive. She wondered how much the girl had put up with during Catherine's reign. She enquired if her sister had called into the office.

'No, Miss de Grelle. I've tried to tidy up.'

This proved an understatement. In the next three hours, seated at Alexander's desk, Sara went through unanswered letters, newspaper cuttings, catalogues, schedules and incomprehensible notes on the backs of envelopes. And she saw what she had inherited. She eventually walked down the corridor, knocked and went into William's office. He, too, stood up.

'Did you wish to see me, Sara? You only have to tell Miss Tomkins and I'll always come –'

'No, you won't. I shall come to you.'

She sat on the other side of his desk.

He regarded her politely. But warily. Here was a second de Grelle girl all set to take on work utterly unsuited to her sex.

He had seen what harm could be done by a strong will reposed in a female bosom. This girl was as much an unknown quantity in business as his favourite had been. And possibly worse.

'I need your help,' Sara said. 'De Grelle's needs it. I've only looked through some papers, but I think I can see how things are. Tell me truthfully. Is de Grelle's weaker since Father died?'

He paused for a moment.

'One could say that.'

'How exactly?'

'In connexions. In the number and quality of our auctions. Failures when we've set prices too high. And the spirit of the place.'

'What does *that* mean?'

'Too many clever people have left.'

'Replaced by lords and honourables.'

'Well . . . your sister has a penchant for her friends and a kind heart towards them.'

'What you're saying is that they're no good.'

She was with him for the rest of that day. They talked. But it was actually William who talked because she wanted him to. She wanted his advice and in the end he gave it to her. He was for a quiet revolution.

'But could you do it? *You* would have to be involved in every single thing that happens,' he said.

'Yes. I will be. With you.'

The partnership of the fifty-five-year-old business man and a young woman suddenly enriched by authority was curious. They were nurses in a sickroom, working to restore health to a noble business almost mortally damaged. Only Sara and William set the course of action. He saw, in their first day together, that her instincts, like her father's, matched his own.

She was a subtle creature. As the days went by she never made, with her large and at present discontented staff, definite Noes or Yeses. She seemed to leave specific problems to their own cleverness, brought out the best in them. But they soon learned not to see her without solutions. Then, only then, she and William helped. There were times when the de Grelle experts, including her old tutor Gilbert Travice, found it difficult to make out what Sara de Grelle actually did think. She listened so eloquently.

One of William's harder tasks was to shed the titled hangers-on, the so-called experts in Old Masters, Antiquarian books and so on. In every case Catherine's friends had owned such things themselves, bought by their families in the past. 'Amateurs,' said William, after yet another unpleasant interview.

'Cathy's an amateur too,' said Sara.

She was charitable about her sister. She could afford to be. Like an acrobat who has longed to fly higher, and discovers the rope will take him to the sky, Sara flew. In the months of the 1923 summer she found her *métier*. She was excited and exhausted, triumphant and alarmed. With William's sober figure beside her, de Grelle's began to revive.

Late one summer evening Sara drove to the mews cottage and rang the doorbell. She found Lee in her painting smock, interestingly smeared with green, at work.

'Hi, stranger,' said Lee. 'I hope you're not working too hard.'

'I enjoy it. Lee. I've come for a favour.'

Lee put down her brushes and thrust her smeared hands into her smock pockets. She raised her eyebrows in enquiry.

'Don't faint,' said Sara, 'but do you think you could possibly recreate Park Street? Make it look the way it used to do when Father was alive.'

Lee laughed. Sara could not possibly be serious. Why, the house had stood empty since its contents had been auctioned. William was still trying to sell it but it was a white elephant, much too big for present fashion. Besides, how could one *recreate* a house!

'Oh, I knew you'd say that at first,' agreed Sara. 'I've been there five times, wandering about. Ghostly, it is. Especially the blanks on the walls where his pictures were. The bookshelves haven't been taken down. Guess what. In one corner I found a funny old book, *the Paris Fire of 1871*. Pictures of Saint-Cloud with flames coming out, and a menu of what the people ate . . . ragoût of cat and roast donkey. Ugh! Did Father really eat those? I have thought my idea over seriously, Lee, I promise. What do you say?'

'I don't know,' said Lee, mystified, 'but I'll be darned if I can see why you want to live there. It's too big and it's out of style. I thought you enjoyed being with that crazy Fay Nelson.'

'I shan't lose Fay. That's not the point. Father's clients loved Park Street. Some of them used to stay, the important ones. And we had dinners for special people, and piled into cars and went to St Charles Street for private viewings. It worked, Lee. Park Street was part of de Grelle's. Could you take it on? Would it drive you mad and stop you from painting?'

Lee continued to raise objections. Sara must see how old-fashioned Park Street, the Park Street that used to be, would seem to them now. Present fashion was for Spanish things, leather, a lot of white . . . Sara would naturally want the big house up to date.

'No, Lee. Not up to date at all. I want it to *feel* like my father's house. If you only would . . .'

She looked at her and slowly smiled.

'You *will*! How wonderful. Could it be soon?'

'Sara. You are very sudden.'

'No. That's what I am not.'

During supper Sara asked if Lee had news of Catherine. 'I haven't set eyes on her,' she said pensively.

'I telephone now and then,' murmured Lee.

'To talk about what?'

'Cathy's life and times. I went so far as to say how well de Grelle's is doing now. She'll notice that, won't she, when her dividends come in. She ought to be pleased.'

Sara grimaced. 'I hope you're not thinking of getting us together again. Cathy may like money but she sure doesn't like me. Come to think of it, Mother doesn't like me much either. Imagine,' with a grin 'her marrying Jean-Claude. Even odder, him marrying her. All that nonsense about the French girl living at the villa to make it respectable when all the time . . . poor Louise. It's lucky Jean-Claude has money. What do you think will happen to them?'

'I can't imagine he will be exactly faithful.'

'No. But I hope he won't hurt her. He's clever and kind, you know. I like my new stepfather.'

Sara leaned back, reflecting. Lee wondered what about. The power that the girl now wore, a kind of invisible iridescent aura, suited her. But she had lost two angry and difficult women when it fell round her shoulders. Louise. Catherine. Both had had dominion over her and both had misused it. No wonder they wouldn't forgive her.

The night was hot and airless. On nights like this, thought Lee, one's mind goes towards love.

'How's Guy Buckingham?' she asked, à propos of nothing.

'Working in a huge place in Wiltshire. They're selling an eighteenth-century dressing-table set, silver gilt. Rococo. Thirty-two pieces . . . rouge pots, pin cushions, a wonderful looking-glass. Guy rang, yawning with exhaustion and being very canny about the reserve.'

'I wasn't talking about work, Sara. Can we give that a rest?'

'I shouldn't think so. What you mean, then, is something about Guy. Is he in love with me? The answer is perhaps a bit. And if you're then asking if we go to bed, the answer is we don't.'

'Poor Guy Buckingham.'

'Poor Sara, more like. I can't love him, though. I *love* him, of course,' said Sara obscurely.

'And where's Perry van Rijn in all this, since you've inherited the crown?'

'He writes about one or two of our millionaire clients who haven't paid their bills. Oh, sorry. Work again. Goodness, it's late. I've stayed too long. Thank you, dear dear Lee, for saying you'll give me back Park Street.'

She put her arms round Lee and hugged her. Lee felt needed, admired, honoured.

And that, thought Lee as the car drove away through the quiet mews, is how she runs de Grelle's.

It was autumn before Sara saw Perry again. Lee magicked Park Street out of its dusty trance, breathed it into life, it was painted and decorated and furnished. Lee herself, affected by the big task, was happier. And every time she came to the house, into which Sara had gratefully moved, Lee saw new things which would make it more its old self again. Sara had also persuaded Georges and Maria to come back. The little Frenchman, who had been working in a hotel, returned to his old home like a nesting bird.

As Sara had said to Lee, Perry wrote to her in a friendly, businesslike manner. She was affected by the sight of his handwriting – he wrote from his apartment on Beekman Place and not from his office. Hungrily reading the letters, she always ended by thinking he might as well have dictated them. She passed them to William, saying 'Don't bother to send this back to me.' Her own replies were typed by Miss Tomkins.

Early in September she wrote to Perry to say she was coming to New York. It was her first trip since she had taken over de Grelle's. She was looking forward to it.

'I want to talk to Cheriton Spencer about making our premises larger in Madison Avenue. He has some ambitious plans. And I have to see the auditors. Much more fun to see you. Shall we have dinner one evening?'

She had a moment of glad surprise when a cable came back, naming the evening of her arrival and adding, 'If not okay cable another date which suits. Don't forget. Warm regards.'

She felt happy, reading that. Until she realized that merchant bankers have diaries full of appointments. And . . . what New York girl had replaced Fay or herself in Perry's bed?

Working, playing, with colleagues or with Fay's wildly entertaining friends, Sara could keep Perry at bay more or less successfully in her thoughts. But during the five days on board ship, repeating that same journey when they had made love, when Alexander had still been alive, she thought of her love affair constantly. Perhaps it was time to end it. The idea of escape kept coming to her. If I were strong enough I'd stop seeing him. She was strong – in everything else. Where was pride? More to the point, where was self-preservation? Each time he took her and later, each time she was cut off again from joy, she suffered the same familiar, excruciating pain.

The ship docked at last. The band played. The towers of

New York touched the sky. And when Sara was in a taxi speeding to the hotel she had the impression she remembered, of a great city in great haste. People rushed across the street almost under the taxi wheels to save a few seconds. At a traffic light the cab revved its engine, straining, in a hurry; she thought, so am I. Springing from her cab, she paid the driver and almost ran into the hotel.

There were a number of telephone calls. Cheriton Spencer. A Fifth Avenue dealer who had recently been to Paris. And her great-aunt.

'Good evening, Sara,' said the elderly lady. 'It seems you are taking after Louise.'

'Aunt Emily, I'm so very sorry I haven't written.'

'So you should be. One letter since you were back in England, and what kind of letter? A child would have produced something more interesting. I take it you are in New York right now.'

'Yes. On business. Did you hear about –'

Sara paused, wondering how to put it.

'If you mean do I know you are now head of your father's business, yes I do. I read it in the Wall Street columns. I congratulate you.'

Sara had never heard good wishes filled with more mockery.

'Thank you, Aunt. May I see you? What about tomorrow?' she said, with more warmth than she thought her elderly relative deserved.

'I'm afraid that won't suit. I have another visitor from Europe. You may telephone at the end of the week.'

Sara meekly agreed. She did not expect much would come from the cool invitation. And she was right.

Wearing silver and blue and a diamond band on her forehead, she stepped from the lift to find Perry waiting. He was watching each of the lifts as the doors opened and shut. He was carrying a gold box.

'Perry. Have I kept you waiting?'

They did not kiss.

'Sara. Good to see you. I just don't know how you manage to be so punctual. And to look the way you do.'

He gave her the box in which were two white camellias.

'How beautiful.'

'Are they all right? I went into the florist's ice room to choose them.'

She fixed the waxen flowers across her wrist in her bracelet.

They had dinner and danced and Sara, moving in his arms, remembered other times. We'll make love, I suppose. She longed for its pleasure and recoiled against its pain.

'I was wondering if you'd like to see my apartment, Sara.'

'Very much.'

Her heart lifted. Their love-making had been in ship's cabins, hotel bedrooms, in that deserted London house. And all night in a garden, lying on the pine needles. He had never taken her to his home. She knew the address on Beekman Place and nothing else.

Broadway ran across the city like a river of jewels, rubies and diamonds for windows, clocks like pearls suspended in the sky. The faces of the crowds were drained of colour by the brightness above and on every side, crimson and purplish blue and a harsh diamond white.

In Perry's apartment, she had a sense of anti-climax. It told her nothing about him when they walked into the spacious lounge. There were pieces of American colonial furniture which might have come from his home: unless they merely showed a taste for nostalgic simplicity. There was a terracotta bust of a woman which could have been his mother: unless he simply liked its tranquil regard. She didn't walk around or examine things: she was here on sufferance. Settling her on a large settle, he said he would make coffee.

So this is where you live, she thought. Who comes here? What girls know the way into your bed?

She sat looking at her buckled satin shoes and thought – how long can I bear this? I am in love, and the more we *make* love the deeper I fall into a sexual slavery. Apart from the wonderful sex it's second best, tenth best. Near him I feel I'll die if we don't do it again and again. I must end it. Every time I see him the bond gets worse.

Looking across the room with its unspeaking history she thought of another room. Carl's, on the ramparts. Napoleon

296

used to be there standing in corners, staring from walls, tripping you up when you moved. Then Carl had coolly replaced his Emperor with a melting actress who now reigned there instead. Over Carl's heart too . . .

Breaking into her reverie, Perry came back with a tray and sat beside her.

'Will you take it black? It may keep you awake. Might be a good idea . . .'

'I don't need coffee to do that. I guess you're confusing me with somebody else,' she said with irony.

The laughter died in his face.

'Don't be tiresome, Sara.'

They made love for a long time, and when at last it ended he did not roll apart from her as he usually did but cradled her in his arms. She did not want that. To lie in what should be a loving, not a sexual, embrace hurt her. When he was asleep she moved away and lay wide awake in the half dark. People in New York did not shut away the shining drama outside the windows. She could see pyramids of diamonds. She listened to Perry's gentle breathing, then slid out of bed and walked naked into the sitting room.

The coffee was still on the table. His cup, only half-finished, was where he had put it before he kissed her. The sight of it filled her with a moment of passionate fondness.

She sat down on the sofa and thought, perhaps that was our last time. Her body was moist from him, her senses sated, her heart pierced. She was still a slave. The man asleep next door, who gave her such pleasure, did not give a straw for her. What did she know of him? Some empty facts about his schooldays. His parents had died when he was young. A good deal about his banking, the only subject apart from de Grelle's which he liked to talk about. What of the interior man whom Browning said had two soul sides, one to face the world with, one to show a woman when he loved her. Perhaps that part of Perry did not exist.

She thought about other men she had known. Her powerful father. Carl Bauer. Dudley Forrest, oh, one knew all about *him*. Guy. William. Even Jean-Claude. Only Perry was closed to her. He lived in the glare of work like the bright city

297

outside the windows, or in his own chosen dark. Europeans lived in a sort of silvery gloaming. A man on board ship had said to her, 'In America if the bathwater isn't hot at first, boy, it stays cold.'

So the decision is made, she thought, and gave a long shuddering sigh. It was like a burn, a soon-to-be-excruciating burn. The moment it happens you feel nothing. Pain comes soon enough. Tender, nervous and sad, she stood up and wandered idly across to a desk in the corner, simply because it was his.

How tidy the desk was. Embossed writing paper which she recognized. Envelopes, and a small silver snuff box for stamps. A postcard of a fat lady with a monstrous bottom, busy digging a sandcastle. She turned the card over.

'Oops. Next time you appear, darling, I'll look just like this. What news? Luv, luv, Fay.'

She put the card back. Then in the corner of the desk almost out of sight she noticed a shabby leather-bound book. With her bibliophile's interest in any book which looked old, she reached for it. The leather of the spine was flaking, the book water-stained. She opened it curiously. It was a diary in Perry's writing in faded washed-out brown ink.

She began to read:

November 8, 1917.

I walked in the pine forest this evening. The trees were silent, not a breath stirred. I kept feeling they were waiting for the war to end.

Uncle writes from N.Y. to say Janet is ill again. Worse, he says. Uncle never overstates and, when I saw that, I was frightened. I wrote to her at once but found it impossibly difficult. How do you tell a sister you adore her? My dear one, looking at me with bright eyes like a bird. She was so thin before I embarked. Her hand a bird's claw. Little Janet.

November 20.

Haven't written this for many days since I heard the news that Janet has died. Death is all around the moment I am writing this. Trench coats on chairs, trench boots creaking with dried mud. And up the line the troops go today or tomorrow – how many to be slaughtered by the Boche machine guns. They don't know why they must throw their lives away. The war goes on, threatening to continue until we are all dead.

I feel stunned that my sister's little life, always frail, horribly gallant, is over. And that it affects me more than those poor stout creatures shuffling through the dusk outside my tent. But you can't love the world, only a few people. Janet and Dick Daniels are mine. Even writing Dick's name makes me superstitious. Where is he? Oh Janet, Janet, my poor little Janet, are you really gone without a word?

Sara turned the pages slowly. The months went by, recorded in the pale ink: 'this damned ink, I have to water it, there is scarcely any left. Will it fade completely? But does that matter to anybody, least of all to me?'

In December, Sara saw his friend's name again.

Dick Daniels writes from the Front that he's fine.
Still at Amiens. I don't recall feeling 'fine' since I came to Italy. I envy his nature. He'll always laugh.
As for me, I don't even dream of anything but this place.
The grey landscape fringed with splintered trees.
Straggling trench-grey ruins which were living villages.
Silence, then the sound of feet. A lark singing. An aeroplane droning. And all the open space broken by rusty tangles of barbed wire. New troops arrived today. They look young and cheerful, just as Dick always does.

She turned more pages. Then she saw it.

June 15, 1918.

A battered copy of the N.Y. *Times* in the mess. I always look at newspapers fearfully and what I've waited for was there at last. Daniels. Richard. Killed in action. For a moment like an idiot I thought – they've got it wrong. It is impossible.
There was a poem in the paper called 'The Fallen'.
The filthy words they used. Being mown down on the wire is to perish like a hero. Dead men rotting in No Man's Land are the fallen. It makes me vomit. Dick is – was – my one irreplaceable friend. As Janet was my only irreplaceable sister. Both belong to the time when we were young. Was there ever such a time? Janet's voice in the garden – she's sitting in a hammock. Butterflies on tall

pink flowers. Where did you walk today, Janet, what flowers did you pick? She won't answer. She's dead. Dick and Janet.

I've discovered the fatuity of love. It makes the stinking mess of life worse. To cling to the living or the dead is a despicable weakness. Last week I saw a heap of earth thrown up by an exploded shell. Two hands stuck out of it. I climbed up to see if they were warm. No. The man must have been dead for days. That's all we are. If I survive, I won't ever love again.

She shut the book and put it back. She thought of the millions of living men who had been called the lost generation, the ruined generation. Her friends at the Roumaniev. Perry. They still tried to forget that they had come from the deadly landscape of Armageddon. But their souls were changed.

She went back into the bedroom and climbed into bed, looking down at the man who had escaped into sleep. She moved close, abandoning herself to his shoulder, pressing against his naked body. In sleep he did not put his arm round her again.

CHAPTER NINETEEN

One stormy October night Lady Lytchett died in her sleep.
Called next morning by a sobbing maid, Catherine found her
grandmother in the curtained four-poster, looking like a marble of the old Queen Elizabeth. White and hard, hawkish and
immobile. When she was alone, Catherine touched her grandmother's hand.

'You could have waited. You could have waited a little
longer, my dear, my dearest Grandmother.'

It was the first time she had used an endearment to the old
woman who loved her.

At the funeral Dudley was much in evidence, subdued but
energetic and with a great attention to detail. The service and
the music must be right, their friends written to and received;
the elaborate ceremony, the weight of flowers, the correspondence on writing paper with black edges, occupied him for
days. He seemed more a Lytchett than Catherine just then.

When it was over, Catherine began to try and reassemble
her life. Her grandmother had told her many times that she
should stop putting off her marriage. It was true that long
engagements among people 'of our sort' were not unusual but
this was invariably because of money. Which Catherine did
not lack. Yet *was* it money, Catherine asked herself, which
had made her procrastinate? In a way yes. She disliked a man
taking more than he gave. When she had been head of de
Grelle's, Dudley had been quick to point out that she ought to
make him a director, and pay him a handsome salary. He
would be able, he told her with cheerful effrontery, to buy
some of his future wife's shares. She had spoken to William,
but it had been his turn to postpone. And when she lost de

Grelle's Dudley was still a man with a small gallery and an overdraft.

She missed her grandmother painfully. So did the servants. The very house itself seemed bereft. The routine of Lytchett had been laid down by its mistress years and years ago: the time the dogs were taken out, the regular replacement of flowers, which day the silver must be cleaned, the daily choice of menu. The servants no longer needed to spring up in answer to the constant peal of a bell from whichever room the old lady happened to have entered.

Dudley was in London a good deal and Catherine, feeling lonely, tried to plan. Yes, she and Dudley must marry. Her life as a Lytchett was over.

Needing to talk to an old friend she telephoned William Thornbury and asked if he could come down to see her. He was cordial. He wanted to see her too, and it would be an excellent chance to talk things over. Catherine imagined this must be good news about money and was pleased. Dudley had told her all about de Grelle's recent successes and although half of her resented these, her commonsense did not. In any case Sara was not responsible for the improvement; it must be the increasing number of profitable country-house sales. Death duties had started to bite; and although Catherine was sorry for her friends, she saw that these were good for business.

Driving down to Lytchett the night before William's visit, Dudley was tired and drank and boasted too much.

'I made a thou' last week. Remember the engravings I picked up in Arundel?'

The rain and wind which had heralded Lady Lytchett's death had gone, the autumn was soft and tawny. The drawing room windows were still open and light shone out into the fragrant dark.

Dudley picked up a copy of *Country Life* and began to do sums on the front cover.

'Let's see my profit for the last six months. Pretty good. The water colours of Egypt – fifteen of those. Stuff I bought in Brighton. The show of mezzotints, I sold seventy-five per cent of those. Four hundred . . . five hundred . . . I think I'll

302

include the Bouchers your grandmother bought. They're a good buy for you as well as for me.'

He finished his arithmetic and showed her the total. Catherine paid him the expected compliments, but more absently than usual. After a moment she said, 'Dudley.'

'Mmm?' He was checking his figures.

'I've been thinking. Shall we set the date for the wedding, when my mourning is over, of course.'

He looked up. A lock of hair fell in a crescent on his forehead. He was handsome. He looked so – so male, she thought. He was the only man she'd ever been sexually drawn to and tonight something in him, an exhausted look, the very lines which proclaimed him years older than she, stirred her. Without realizing it she made her voice more inviting.

'What do you think, Dudley?'

Since the night in Newport when he had tried to seduce her, his caresses had been chaste. She wished he would go further, while telling herself that his control showed respect. But she was vulnerable since her grandmother's death and suddenly needed to embrace the man scribbling those tedious columns of figures.

'How long is mourning?' he said, after a moment. 'I thought that old stuff went out during the war.'

'It did but *we* still do it. Three months.'

'Let's see, that would make a February wedding. Sounds fine to me. Start making your plans, Cath. You know that's what you enjoy.'

She thought, with pleased relief – so it was easy after all.

When she woke next day and went to the window to see the October sunshine, she wished William was not coming. There were so many interesting things to think about now. Then she remembered that *he* wished to talk to her. Apart from the one hideous day in Antibes, Catherine felt affectionately about William. She was at home with him more than she'd ever been with her father. She knew he was fond of her, and had never been sure Alexander was. But how could one tell with a foreigner?

During breakfast Dudley told her he was going out. He had

a prospect, as he would call people with something to sell. He would not be back at Lychett until the afternoon.

'But if you want any help with that cold fish Thornbury, don't worry. I'll be home by four.'

'I thought you liked William.'

'Did you, Cath?'

Climbing into his open roadster he drove showily up the drive.

It was midday when Catherine was walking by the borders of massed purple and orange and the maid came to say Mr Thornbury had arrived. A cityfied figure came round a corner of the old house.

'My dear Catherine.'

'William. How nice to see you.'

They shook hands. Nobody watching them would guess they had known each other since Catherine was born.

In the drawing room filled with flowers and silver-framed photographs they drank some sherry. There was an exchange of banalities, a throat-clearing before they arrived at the reason for the visit. She put down her glass.

'When I rang you yesterday, I was going to ask for advice. But as it happens, things were settled last night. The fact is – well – I wasn't quite sure –' for once she was at a loss for words, and finished hastily with, 'Dudley and I are getting married in February when my mourning time is over.'

She expected approving congratulations. When he said nothing, she was very offended.

'You don't seem very pleased,' she said coolly. 'I know we have been engaged for far too long. Grandmother never approved, and I don't really know why I kept putting off the wedding –'

'Perhaps it is a good thing you did.'

Catherine sat very straight. She frowned with displeasure.

'What do you mean?'

Again he did not answer for a moment and she waited, increasingly annoyed and offended.

'Are you sure,' he eventually said. 'Are you absolutely sure about Dudley Forrest?'

'Sure? That he – cares for me,' she said. It was so vulgar to mention emotion. 'Of course.'

'I'm not talking about his affection for you or yours for him. But of the man himself. His quality. His probity.'

Catherine stared.

'What are you trying to say? That Dudley is not honest? What possible evidence –'

'My dear girl, we are not in a court of law. This is difficult for me to say, and more so now you have told me you plan to be married soon. I can't be precise at present. Painful as it must be to you, and believe me I do realize that, all I'm here to ask is that you postpone this marriage once again. For the time being. Is that very difficult?'

She swallowed. She had a trait, Sara had it too, of keeping very still in moments of crisis.

She said slowly, 'I suppose I could find an excuse to put it off for a while longer. But –'

'But,' he repeated, 'but which of us do you trust? Dudley? Or me? That's the nub of it.'

'Yes,' said Catherine, 'it is.'

Nothing more was said. They had luncheon. They went for a tour round the gardens. William had a townsman's interest in this plant and that, and admired the burnished discs of the marigolds. Catherine called them by their Latin name. When they walked past the strongly scented bushes of roses she gave them their English names: Gertrude, Snow Queen, and Prudence.

There was no set plan to the Lytchett gardens which were of many dates. There were walled gardens, some enclosed by high hedges, long borders and in the misty autumnal distance hills fringed with beechwoods. The couple sat down in the last of the sunlight by an unlikely statue of the god of Love.

'Will Dudley be back soon, Catherine?'

'I'm surprised he isn't home already.'

Just then a figure appeared at the end of the path. Dudley gave them his Australian army salute. He was cordial to William, and launched into an account of an entertaining day.

'I think I've struck gold. Pictures to make your mouth water. Good, eh, Cath?'

She nodded automatically, noticing a fan of chickweed round the lupins, and knelt on the grass to pull it up. Taking the opportunity William said quietly, 'Could I have a word, Dudley? On our own?'

Dudley looked brightly interested and said to Catherine, still on her knees, 'William and I are going to the study for a parley. Won't be long.'

She continued to drag at the weeds shallow-rooted in the dry soil.

William remained in the old Earl's study for some time after Dudley had slammed out. The interview had not been pretty. He was accustomed to difficulties among a three-hundred-strong staff, but the men who stood in front of his desk had a sense of self-preservation. To save face, keep the chance of a reference, even a ghost of goodwill. Not so Forrest. He had behaved like a wildcat. The easy manner vanished after the first two minutes, replaced by a snarling rage. He had used obscenities and threats. As William grew colder, Forrest grew hotter and William had thought – for two pins you'd hit me. Violence was in the man's furious eyes, and just when William thought the control was about to snap, he'd rushed out, slamming the door so roughly that the windows rattled.

William went slowly out through the French windows on to the terrace. He did not want to see Catherine just yet. He was very conscious that she was waiting. But he wasn't satisfied. The last very unpleasant ten minutes had achieved nothing. He'd faced Dudley Forrest with one crime (if infidelity was a crime) and had implied, he was too canny to do more, that Dudley's honesty was in question. There were a lot of rumours. Dudley shouted, used oaths, denied everything. But he did not promise to get rid of the women he was associating with, he did not admit the affair. And he said nothing to clear himself of suspicions over his business dealings. The interview had been a mess. William should have forced decisions. Things must be straightened out. Again, his thoughts went anxiously towards Catherine.

He walked up and down the terrace for longer than he

realized. The shadows from some cedar trees had begun to stretch across the grass. When he had waited on the terrace a while longer, he went indoors and rang the bell.

The elderly parlour maid, with her respectful manner and air of authority, appeared. William asked her to find Mr Forrest. He wanted a word with him.

'But the gentleman has gone, sir.'

'You mean he's in the garden with Miss de Grelle?'

It was what William had feared. He shouldn't have remained here.

'Oh no, sir, not in the garden,' said Ada, her Sussex accent more pronounced than usual because she was intrigued. 'Mr Forrest had Davis pack his trunks, and he's gone. In that of a hurry, sir. Just drove off down the back drive a good twenty minutes ago.'

A pause.

'I see. He did mention he might have to return urgently to London. Thank you, Ada.'

There was a light of incredulity in her eye. She went off, rather fast, to her tea in the servants' hall.

Out in the garden the evening was full of the smell of tobacco flowers. William looked for Catherine in one hedged or walled garden after another, even going as far as the duck pond. At last, opening he saw her in the kitchen garden. She was sitting on a rustic bench by some dahlias grown for cutting, great mop-headed garish things, purples and lemon yellows.

She smiled as he came up. He wished she wouldn't.

'I saw Forrest,' he said, standing beside her, hands in his pockets.

'What happened?'

'I'm afraid he was angry.'

'Of course he was.'

He looked for a way to break the news кindly and didn't find one.

'Catherine, he has gone.'

'What do you mean? Driven off in a huff. You must have been very unpleasant to him, William. He never does things like that.'

He hated his role in this.

'He has left Lytchett. Packed his bags twenty minutes ago, Ada told me. Took his car and drove away.'

'Drove away. *You* drove him away!'

She was perfectly furious.

'I did no such thing. I was attempting to clear the air.'

'By dragging up lying rumours about him. People are jealous because he's a success. That world he works in is full of scandal. You faced him with a pack of lies and he blames me too for believing them. How dared you! Do you think I can't look after my own life? I'm twenty-eight and I intend to marry Dudley and oh – how dared you!'

He had faced two different kinds of rage in the last half hour. From a snarling dog. And a queen.

He sat down by her. The bench was small and his shoulder brushed hers. She did not recoil, but simply turned and looked at him as if at an enemy.

'I presume you're now going to tell me some rigmarole about him which I shan't believe. I shall go straight to London and undo the harm you've just done.'

'Please don't go to London, Catherine.'

She stood up.

'Please. Not until you've heard me out. It's damnable to be in this position, it's my duty and I loathe it. I've tried to keep the truth from you, I thought it would hurt you too much. Now I see you could hurt yourself more. You would be right to be loyal to Forrest except that, to put it bluntly, he has a mistress. He's keeping her in the flat above the gallery. Her name is Kitty Croft. You may have met her, she works in the gallery now and then. Good-looking in a common sort of way.'

'I don't believe you.'

He saw that she did.

He waited a moment.

'I can't tell you how sorry I am. I won't go into details but the evidence is unequivocal. He denied it, naturally. The rumours about the couple's dishonesty are another matter and I have no doubt more will come out now he has gone. He'll go quickly because he knows we're on his track.'

She took the blow without flinching. She sat upright, looking across the kitchen garden towards the house.

She was thinking about the sexy lounging man who had walked into her life. She had disliked many things about him and admired and wanted many more. He'd been her spirited companion, her attempted seducer, the man she had chosen as a husband. The centre of her planned life. All her affection, her disturbed consciousness of his male attraction, her form of love, suddenly withered up, as if weed-killer had been poured over her emotions. Nothing for him was left in her heart but scorched brownish dust.

She stood up.

'Will you stay and dine?' was all she said.

Sara returned to England, one of the seventeen hundred passengers on the *Majestic* sailing out of New York. Most of the first-class passengers were American, and went ashore at Cherbourg to arrive on the Riviera in good time for Christmas. The Côte D'Azur was in fashion again, as Jean-Claude recently wrote to tell her.

She had no intention of being caught up in the social life of the *Majestic*. She'd brought from New York a large amount of work and stayed in her stateroom. When she needed exercise, she walked round the deck after breakfast. People looked curiously at the red-headed girl, a silk scarf streaming behind her.

If they tried to be friends she was pleasant, even charming. And escaped, not to be seen again for hours.

But however much she dived into work, Perry was in her mind. Since the night when she had read the diary, she saw him differently. She no longer believed he did not love her. She was like a woman kneeling by a tree after an icy winter, willing and willing the branches to put out leaves again.

When the Rolls set her down at Park Street, she smiled to see the house shining with lights. Georges and Marie behaved as they used to do for Alexander. She knew they regretted that their mistress was a single young person living alone in the huge great place. Any occasion for a dinner party, for expected or unexpected guests, was greeted with sober French approval. But the words '*Ah, les beaux jours du passé*' hung about.

With a smile of welcome, Georges took her coat and said in a tone of satisfaction,

'Miss Nelson is here, Mademoiselle Sara.'

The door burst open and Fay stood framed, round-eyed, teetering on high heels. Her brief beaded silver skirts shook as she ran to throw bare arms round Sara.

'I was afraid you'd be late. We've missed you *all the time*. Georges, Georges, I can't wait a sec' longer for a teensy drink. Sara, my one chum, come and tell me everything.'

Tugging her into the drawing room, she bubbled on, 'I've all kinds of thrilling things to tell you. Georges, what agony, all that waiting.'

'But why didn't you have a drink while you waited, Fay?'

'How could I? Not the same thing.'

When Georges had left them, Fay picked up the shaker, shook it musically and poured out two ice-cold drinks.

'Two parts gin, one part Vermouth, ice, lemon and an itsy-bitsy dash of Curaçao . . . Tarah! A White Lady.'

'Rather a fierce White Lady,' said Sara, wrinkling her nose.

'You have to get tuned to them. Inoculated, really. My news. Then yours. Darling, Bobs Tyrone is taking your friend Guy and me to Paris *tonight*. What do you think about that? From Croydon aerodrome. You know Bobs was a pilot, well, you didn't, but he was and he's converted an Avro reconnaissance war-plane.'

'Fay, you've become very technical.'

'Haven't I, though. He says we'll go at sixty miles an hour and fly four thousand feet up and land at Le Bourget in two and a half hours. I am so excited. The Avro only has two seats, for Guy and me, and Bobs will be outside in the cockpit. Guy's coming 'cos he can't resist it and he's going to do something or other at your Paris place, and Bobs is taking me to the rue de la Paix to buy me a Chanel dress. Then dancing, with Guy as well. Always better, going out with two men, don't you agree?'

'Not really . . .'

Fay looked pitying.

'You go in for the *dîner intime*, don't you, darling. A mistake. One should have lots of men about. *Vogue* says the best jewellery for a girl is a string of men. How's New York?'

'Beautiful. Busy. I didn't stay long.'

'And how's horrible Perry van Rijn? I hope you told him he broke my heart.'

'*Did* he, Fay?'

'I suppose you think that'd be impossible,' said Fay, lifting the shaker enquiringly to Sara. 'I did get over him quite fast but that's because I do. I missed him *hideously* when you came to live here, darling, but I'm better now. It's like my colds, they suddenly go. Remember at school when we all gave each other the measles and had such larks being ghosts with sheets? How cross Mademoiselle was. I got better before any of the other girls. Madame Bonjean said I had "*une facilité inouïe de récupération*".'

'So she did. So you do.'

'You're very quiet tonight, Sara, and I'd say a wee bit boring if I didn't know you're worn out being important,' said Fay without a shred of sarcasm. 'Anyway, I came round to say Guy's coming back by boat but Bobs and me and the Avro may stay in Paris a while. I sold that stupid painting of the horse so I'm bursting with thousand-franc notes. It's so cheap in France now! Oh, another reason I'm here. Lee rang. She's going to the country and mightn't catch you, she said, and I was to tell you the news about your poor old sis.'

Sara gave a start. Fay's stories went from comedy to tragedy in the same airy voice. Even death was fair game for a joke. Sara had seen her cry and laugh at the same time. Fay sipped her cocktail.

'Dudley Forrest has disappeared. Think of that, Sara. He vanished like the demon king in the panto, green smoke and all.'

Questioned by an incredulous Sara, Fay knew no more. The gossip was that Dudley was bankrupt. Maybe he was in prison, added Fay hopefully. But would Sara telephone Catherine who was probably feeling poorly. (Sara recognized Lee's long-distance hand). And that, said Fay, was how things were. Interesting.

311

Exclaiming she was now late, Fay bent forward to kiss Sara and almost ran out of the house. A long open Riley, gleaming with polished aluminium, was patiently drawn up at the kerb.

'Haven't time to introduce you to Bobs,' called Fay, gesturing to the man at the wheel who smiled and shouted,

'Bobs Tyrone, how de do?'

Fay jumped into the car, which was piled with luggage. Fay had never been known, in hail or storm, to travel in a closed vehicle.

'Think of me tonight, darling. Flying over your head like an eagle!'

She blew some kisses and the car roared away.

CHAPTER TWENTY

Sara's drive through quiet roads, still tunnels of green (the leaves had not yet fallen), gave her time to think. She was going to a sister who would not be glad to welcome her, just as she was going against the grain of their tie, thick with shared blood and thin with lack of love. But she was on her way, driving an open yacht of a car like the one Fay had vanished in earlier this evening. I don't care if she doesn't want to see me. I want to see her, she thought.

Driving through Sussex villages not exactly asleep, taking small side roads, consulting her map, Sara eventually found the lane which led to the manor's gates. The headlights showed stone pillars, a curved drive described by William who, when she telephoned him, made no comment about her proposed journey. Also, she had not told him she was driving down this evening.

She slowed the car down by the door of the old house.

The parlour maid showed no surprise when, taking Sara into the drawing room, she announced for the first time in her life, 'Miss Sara de Grelle, Miss Catherine.'

Catherine stood up rather suddenly. Sara apologized for the unexpected call but gave no reason for it. Catherine, showing as little surprise as the maid, accepted her appearance with hospitality. She asked kindly if Sara had dined, surely not? And when Sara admitted that she hadn't, rang for Ada.

'Would chicken sandwiches and a glass of milk do?' said Catherine. 'My mother always had that left for me when I came back from hunt balls. I think she suspected I was too shy to eat when I was there.'

'Were you?'

'Oh yes.'

The small meal arrived and the sisters talked: of the things which strangers might discuss when intent on being pleasant. Catherine spoke of her garden, Sara of Fay flying in an aeroplane to Paris. Looking at her sister, she thought her night drive had been a mistake. Catherine wasn't in trouble.

But as the talk continued, something stirred in Sara's memory and it came to her with a pang that she was at last inside her sister's home. This was Lytchett, about which Cathy would never talk, the house where her mother had lived and died; it was a jewel. Was it possible that Cathy, shining in her own setting, might cease to regard Sara as an enemy and a rival?

'I believe you just returned from New York,' Catherine said, and Sara thought – I suppose this is my chance. After all I have come here, and in the end I must say why.

'Yes, I only got back this afternoon. Cathy, I'm sure you think it very strange of me to turn up like this. But I heard about Dudley. I am so sorry. It must have been a horrible shock for you.'

Catherine gave a grim smile.

'I wondered if that was why you came. Yes, it was a shock. A surprise too. That I was such a bad judge of character. William said he's always had a feeling something wasn't right about Dudley. I never did.'

'So you don't exactly –'

'Feel too upset. No. Imagine finding oneself married to a swindler.' She shuddered slightly. 'It was good of you to come rushing down. But I am quite all right. As you see.'

Sara finished the hunt ball supper, thinking the impulsive journey had been stupid. What had she expected? A sobbing Catherine in a darkened room? An enraged sister vowing revenge. The quality in Catherine was that she sobbed over nobody. The Lytchett pride of which Sara did not have a drop would refuse the indulgence of tears. If Catherine was hurt she'd die rather than show it.

'You will stay, won't you, Sara? It's after eleven o'clock.'

'But it only takes –'

'Don't go,' Catherine said. 'You've never been here before. I can show you round. The garden too. I'd like you to stay.'

When Sara was in bed in a low-ceilinged beamed room, with a harvest moon floating between distant trees, she thought that tonight had been full of surprises.

The two young women spent the morning in and out of the manor. Catherine never once started up the old game of gaining points and showing off. They went into room after room of the Tudor house. Sara knew English mansions, she and Guy had visited so many, but this place was more than just old and beautiful, it provided the missing parts of her sister's nature. In the nursery with its sentimental pictures, where Catherine had done her lessons, and in the conservatory where the Lytchetts used to grow orchids 'white ones, like butterflies'. There were stately, named bedrooms.

'This is the Monkey Room. I always loved that monkey swinging on that branch. He looked like one of my great uncles.'

The tour ended in a smallish picture gallery where rows of Lytchetts, red-coated, silver-armoured, white-wigged, and in Verena's case floating in grey silk taffeta by Sergeant, looked out of their frames, painted eyes full of a quiet serene certainty.

'Now you've seen it all,' Catherine said.

Deck chairs had been placed in a deckled mid-morning shade under some trees. In the distance a gardener worked in the borders. Autumn hung like a bubble in the blue air.

The girls sat down and Catherine ran her finger up and down the wooden arm of the chair.

'William thinks Lytchett's too big for just me. Both of us alone in huge houses now. Odd, isn't it? But William says you've opened up Park Street because of business. It's not like that with me. I am simply landed with Lytchett.'

'Cathy, it's your home!'

Catherine gave her metallic laugh. She actually seemed amused.

'Now you *don't* sound like Father. Think of the country-house sales going on at present. Staying here isn't much good, Sara. Some of the servants would love to retire, and the others, including Ada, would come to town. Since Dudley Forrest went' said Catherine with the disdainful addition of his surname, 'I've been doing my accounts. I know the de Grelle shares bring in a good income, but Lytchett eats money. I can't afford to stay, even supposing I wanted to.'

Sara looked at her.

Her sister's oval face wore the same expression Sara had seen in the faces in the paintings. It was confident and calm. Sentiment, sentimentality, had no place.

'William thinks you and Guy may want to spend some time here at Lytchett. And anybody else you think ought to look over things. I've made a rough list of the various items I don't intend to put into the auction.'

Catherine had started to plan again.

Alexander once told Sara that preparing an important auction in a country house reminded him of a production at a theatre. Sara remembered that during the weeks when Lytchett was being arranged and re-arranged.

The news that the contents of the historic Sussex house were to be sold created much interest in the auction world. Collectors and dealers knew Lytchett's past, knew there would be beautiful and valuable possessions to be sold – and when the catalogue arrived, they were right. Local people in Sussex eagerly – rather angrily – looked forward to attending the sale as well.

The manor was being organized by Sara, Guy, Gilbert Travice and two other members of de Grelle's as well as by Catherine's staff. When the job was finally completed, the rooms were exquisitely arranged, furniture perfectly placed, pictures lit. Catherine said that Lytchett looked better than it had ever done since she was born.

'My grandmother would not have been pleased.'

Sara had seen the portrait of Lady Lytchett (which wasn't to be auctioned) and agreed with her. The old lady looked as if she would have despatched Sara and her friends straight to the Tower for execution.

William came to Sussex the day before the sale and spent the afternoon with Catherine in a little study, her favourite room overlooking the lawns and clipped yews. Autumn was nearly winter now, and they sat by a pine-log fire. William thought Catherine looked tired but pretty in her upper-class way. She was glad to see him and showed it.

They remained together all afternoon, while the rest of Lytchett buzzed like a reverberating glass. People worked and hurried, carried and polished. Guy groaned aloud.

'Why did we take this on? We should have moved it, lock, stock and Georgian silver chocolate pots, to St Charles St.'

Peter Merrick, the auctioneer for tomorrow, had not yet come. He was late and Sara, as the afternoon waned, grew nervous. Taking a sale herself was something she never did, and did not intend to do. She knew where she was in this thrusting male world. She spoke at board meetings, briefly. She conducted her business, after much thought, with one man at a time. She used William almost every day, consulting, deciding. She had no wish to try her hand at the exposed, actor's job on the rostrum. Peter Merrick did it well. He was relaxed, rather aristocratic in manner, yet he had wit. He managed to be almost detached but never so much that it discouraged. Sara approved of him. But she wished he were here and, until he arrived, knew she'd go on feeling twitchy.

Leaving Guy in deep conversation with Gilbert Travice, who wore his usual air of fussed self-importance, Sara went down some passages and slipped through a side door which led to the front drive. She had not been alone, except to sleep, since she'd come to Lytchett weeks ago. Outside, the night was chill. The shock of the cold air, the silence after the house's bustle, the lights falling in squares on to a terrace slightly smeared with frost, gave her a sense of relief. Catherine was not the only one whose life was being changed. She had not heard from Perry since they had said goodbye in New York. She had actually thought she had the key to his mystery. And they would meet again, and somehow she would unlock his love. It had not happened. He had seen her to the ship – and that was all.

I suppose I know my fate now, she thought, looking back at the old house which was waiting for its own. I felt in my soul I was the one to follow Father, I longed for de Grelle's and by almost unaccountable chance it's mine. Why am I not happy? It was like the Grimm story of the man given three wishes for his heart's desire. Each wish wasn't enough. Hearts were greedy.

The headlights of a car came nosing down the drive in the frosty dark and she thought – Peter Merrick and about time too. It's so cold. I ought to get a coat.

She walked towards the car. It was a taxi, the door opened and a man stepped out. In a split second of non-recognition – expecting Merrick's short slight figure, she saw the man was tall.

'Sara, what are you doing out here? You'll freeze to death.'

'Perry!'

The taxi drove away. He took her in his arms. She thought of nothing. Nothing. She abandoned herself to the kiss: but it was so brief.

As they walked into the house he said, 'Look, I need a word with you alone. Can we slip off somewhere. Jiminy,' he added, hearing the noise of footsteps and slam of doors, 'this place sounds like Grand Central.'

'The auction's tomorrow,' she said. All the amazed pleasure left her. 'We can go into the breakfast room, nobody will bother us there. Perry, what *is* this? I am very surprised to see you.'

'Of course you are.'

His manner was strange. She took him into a deserted room without a chair or table, empty as a barn. The air was so cold that their breath was like smoke.

'You said you're surprised to see me. I wasn't sure I could get to England. Get away. Then something happened and I had to take the *France* and come at once.'

'You could have cabled.'

'I didn't want to alarm you. I thought we had more time, I must have got the auction date wrong –'

'Perry, what are you talking about?'

'You changed the date of the auction.'

She raised her eyebrows.

'So we did. By a day or two. Catherine wanted it. What on earth is all this about?'

'The two Bouchers in the catalogue. They must be withdrawn.'

'*What did you say!*'

It was clear that he'd expected her horrified reaction. Her pale face went crimson.

'What's all this nonsense, you come here out of nowhere –'

He took her shoulders and held her hard, but without affection. Almost as if he wanted to shake her.

'Listen. Don't talk. Listen. By God's grace Cheritree Spencer picked up this information, you know how many people he deals with. Somebody told him about it who got it from the Louvre. They're on your tail about the two Bouchers which Forrest sold to Lady Lytchett. They were stolen from the Louvre five years ago.'

'Impossible!'

'I didn't think you'd believe me, Sara. It is true. Forrest was a receiver. Not in a big way, apparently, but now and then when there was a good slice of profit to be made without too much difficulty. I've no idea how he came by the Bouchers. From some shady dealer, I suppose. I don't doubt he charged Catherine's grandmother a swingeing price. He thought he was perfectly safe. The pictures were here, quietly hanging in a house in Sussex, without anybody likely to pay them much heed from one year's end to the other. He couldn't know Catherine was going to sell the contents of Lytchett, could he? That the Bouchers would be featured in your catalogue and land up, many such catalogues do, in the Louvre. You must withdraw them. It's more luck than judgement that I'm in time.'

He gave her a sharing smile of somebody as involved as she was.

Sara had listened with growing fury. She was outraged. It was utterly impossible for de Grelle's to make such a mistake. The provenance had been checked and rechecked. Who was Perry van Rijn to appear the night before the auction and tell her what to do?

'I shan't withdraw them,' she said and walked out.

She ran up the stairs to the picture gallery. Most of the paintings, the portraits, seascapes, battle scenes, had been taken downstairs and rehung in the saloon, drawing rooms, ballroom. The drawings were still being arranged by Gilbert. Some had gone, others were ranged along the far wall on the floor. Porters went to and fro.

Shivering with cold – God, Lytchett was freezing – she squatted down and stared at two pictures side by side leaning against the wall. The two Bouchers. Both were of nudes. In one a graceful female reclined on a *chaise longue*, her face in profile, delicate, frivolous, a baby boy curled against her body. In the other, two buxom girls were by a pool, one sat on a rock, her rounded leg stretched out to touch the water with her toe . . .

With a set face, Sara went to look for her sister.

Catherine and William were still by the fire in the small parlour, but Perry had joined them. All three turned as she came into the room. It was obvious what they had been talking about.

'I refuse to believe what Perry's just told me,' she said at once, her voice as hard as even Catherine's could be. 'The provenance was gone into. We know our business, for God's sake. This is all just a lot of despicable gossip.'

'Sara, Sara,' William said quietly. 'This sort of trouble is new to you, but not to de Grelle's. Alexander had to put up with some very difficult situations now and then. Once he auctioned a James II goblet in St Charles Street and an Irish nobleman recognized it. It had been stolen from his house in County Down. It was all most unpleasant. De Grelle's are not infallible. And we can't knowingly sell stolen property.'

'As if I'd suggest –' burst out Sara, angrier than before. 'What I'm saying is that I don't accept this – this cock-and-bull story. I do *not*. What do you think, Cathy? You were there when your grandmother bought the damned things.'

Catherine was silent for a moment.

'I can only say it sounds like the Dudley Forrest I've been learning about recently.' She grimaced, as if she'd turned up a stone with her foot which had lice and slugs crawling under it.

'But what about us? What sort of auction house is taken in by –' began Sara. William cut in.

'You're forgetting that these pictures are your sister's property, Sara. The decision must be hers.'

They looked at Catherine.

'He was peculiar about the drawings,' she said slowly, 'now I come to think about it. Dead set on selling them to my grandmother. He said they belonged to a Count Ginestière, they'd been at the family château for years and years. They were absolutely authentic Bouchers and the Ginestières had known the painter in the 1750s. He pressed Grandmother very hard. She wasn't keen on naked women but he showed her a book about Boucher and said anything by him was an investment. And brought down the Davies Street catalogue with the Ginestière provenance printed in it. Well ... Grandmother agreed. She paid a lot but she said if I eventually sold them (I'm not overfond of them either), I would get much more than she paid. She said,' finished Catherine acidly, 'I ought to sell them through de Grelle's.'

There was silence for quite a long time. Then,

'Withdraw them please, Sara.'

'As you wish.' For the second time that evening, Sara walked out.

Late that night a call came through from Paris and a man with great courtesy and in bad English said he was from the Musée du Louvre. Two of their experts would attend the auction tomorrow, and might they have the pleasure of meeting Miss de Grelle?

Which one, thought Sara, agreeing that they could.

The old house was more crowded on the first morning of the auction than it had been since the grand Victorian days of balls, weddings and funerals. Cars lined the drive and were parked all the way down the lane. It was still bitterly cold and the country roads were fretted with ice.

The house was lit at breakfast time and lights shone all day long. The sale lasted three days. Buyers and dealers, friends, rivals, county grandees, stayed all over Sussex. They occupied every room at both the village inns and went to stay at hotels as far away as Lewes and Brighton. Every morning they arrived like flocks of hungry birds.

In Sara's experience, and even more in Guy's, there were invariably country-house owners who changed their minds about some items to be sold at the last minute. It was human and understandable and damned inconvenient when that heartache, that realization of impending loss, came over them. Not over Catherine. For three months she had been making decisions on every item she wished to keep, some of great value, some of none. For an auction house, Catherine was the ideal client.

When the ballroom began to fill up (it was soon so crammed that people could scarcely fit in), Catherine and Sara sat together with William and Guy. Perry had left for London. He would soon be returning to New York. He and Sara had not parted friends.

At the start of the sale when Peter Merrick announced the withdrawal of the Bouchers 'on instructions from the Owner,' there was a spontaneous noise. Something between a sigh and a groan.

It was always the same when an important sale was over; there was a sense of exhausted anti-climax. Sara was worn out. Even William's quiet satisfaction, when he told Catherine and herself the princely total of the sale, did not make her spirits rise. But Catherine laughed and actually blushed. Refusing Guy's offer to drive her home Sara invented an excuse and took the train. Winter had come and when she rang the bell at Park Street, a flake of snow landed on her sleeve. Georges greeted her with concern. There was a fire in the study, it had been kept in all day, he would serve tea at once.

Sara walked into her father's old room and sank down in a leather chair, staring at the logs which glowed and sent out a strong intense warmth. In her head she heard Merrick's voice: 'One thousand pounds. More?' And saw the porter holding up a Regency epergne, the dishes shaped like shells swinging. All the booty of her sister's family sold and scattered. Catherine is tough, she thought. That's what made the upper classes get where they did. They pushed and stayed steady. She thought of Catherine and William, consulting, conferring, now and then exchanging glances. Another de Grelle link.

And then she forgot the drama of the auction, the Tudor house crowded and exciting, the noise and silences, the arrogant faces in the portraits, and thought of Perry. She had been angry with him because of de Grelle's. She'd been wrong.

When the two Louvre experts had arrived William suggested he might deal with them, 'as it is a legal matter as well as a financial one'.

Knowing he was protecting her, despising herself, Sara accepted. Afterwards, William presented both sisters to the two Frenchmen. One was elderly, with a beaked nose and dark eyes. The other handsome, Byronic-looking, about forty. Both had the French air of authority Sara recognized. Just like Alexander's.

'Mr Thornbury has arranged things most satisfactorily,' said the eagle, pressing first Catherine's hand and then Sara's.

'You have done the Musée much service,' added the younger man.

When the sale ended at last, Sara had wandered back into the ballroom. It had already been swept clear of chairs and tables and the rostrum was gone. The larger pieces of furniture stood in corners, sheeted like ghosts. She sat on a window ledge.

Catherine came into the room. She said dryly,

'William's just told me how much the Louvre paid for the Bouchers. Less than half what my grandmother paid.'

'Oh Cathy. I am so sorry.'

'The blessing is to know it is all cleared up,' said Catherine. And that was all.

Home in Park Street, Sara was too tired to work. She felt drained and desolate. She had a life which any young woman in Europe or America must envy: an extraordinary life dealing with beautiful, curious or terrifyingly valuable things. But Perry did not love her and her hope was gone. I shall never be able to change anything between us now. It's my fault. Why did I behave like that the other night? It was pride, which is only a puffed-up word for vanity. She had resented his dramatic last-minute rescue, had shown it and behaved like a fool. Nothing had tied him to her but sex and, strong as it was, that could be split to pieces by a wrong word.

When the telephone rang, she supposed it was Guy. The American voice was a shock.

'Sara? I'm glad you're back. Was the journey difficult?'

She didn't understand and when she asked what he meant he laughed.

'My dear girl, I'm talking about the snow. You must have got home just in time. Apparently you haven't looked out of your window. Would it be okay if I came round? Now?'

When he rang off, with a feeling of nervous happiness she went to look out and saw the snow floating down in huge flakes, covering the pavement with unmarked white. The distant sound of traffic had gone, muffled by the cold counterpane.

When Georges showed Perry into the study, Sara went to him with her hands outstretched.

'I'm *glad* to see you.'

Georges returned thoughtfully to the kitchen. It worried him to see the girl looking like that. It was the first time he'd noticed such an expression on her face. *Enfin* . . .

Perry took her in his arms and they kissed. She thought – it's not like it was at Lytchett. Everything is mended, it's as it was, no, it is going to be better. When he drew away from her he said, 'William called me up with the total of the sale. Good news for Catherine and for you. I'm sure you're both very pleased.'

'Yes, yes, and he told you about the Bouchers?' said Sara, luxurious in defeat. 'You were right. I should have been grateful. I behaved stupidly.'

He grinned. 'I'm sorry I upset you. I'm a tactless bastard sometimes.'

He drew her on to the sofa.

'You look very beautiful.'

Reaching up, he switched off the lamp and in a glow full of shadows began to embrace her.

'Oh Perry. We can't. Not just yet.'

He let her go but his eyes were heavy.

'It's your fault. So exciting, you are. I suppose we'll have to wait. How long?'

'We could have dinner early.'

'We must.'

They waited for what seemed a long moment. Then Sara laced her arms round his neck and looked at him. At his dark eyes and thick lashes, his flat ears, the even olive of his skin. He returned her look, raising his eyebrows in amusement.

'Shall I tell you something, Perry.'

'And what is that?'

'I think I've started to understand about you. I never did before.'

He listened with an idle affection which had replaced desire. Putting up his hand he touched her short bright hair.

'So what is this mystery you've finally solved?'

'You remember in New York when you took me to your apartment.'

'Of course. I found something of yours afterwards. Guess what. Guess where. An amethyst heart in my bed.'

'Perry, what a relief! Father gave it to me and I was certain I'd lost it. I've been looking everywhere.'

He fished in his pocket and produced the little jewel edged with seed pearls. He put it into her hand.

'It has a flaw,' he remarked.

'I know. It's one of the reasons I like it so.'

'Naturally,' he said, as if she much amused him. 'And the mystery?'

'It was when you were asleep. I mean really asleep after we'd made love. I got up and wandered around.'

'Mother naked?'

'It was quite warm that night.'

He chuckled.

'And what did you think about, haunting my apartment without a stitch on?'

'Oh, that this was your home which I'd never seen before and how glad I was to be there. I went into your sitting room, all the lights were glittering outside, it looked beautiful. And then, what do you think? I found your old diary. I know you'll understand,' she went on, speaking impulsively, 'how I couldn't resist taking the quickest look. What a sad time it was for you then – I read about when your poor sister died and about your friend Dick Daniels. And I felt grateful to read it because it explained you, Perry. Explained everything about you.'

It was only then that she saw what she had done.

'It didn't occur to you that you had no right to read it.'

'But I only quickly looked,'

'Quickly looked,' he repeated savagely. 'Enough to discover things I won't speak about to anybody. Anybody.'

'Surely you can't be angry just because –'

Her voice trailed to a stop. He had stood up. Looking away from her he said, as if to himself,

'I can't stay here.'

She heard the front door slam. For a moment she couldn't move, then with a dry sob rushed to the window. The street was empty. His footsteps must have been instantly covered by the snow.

To Georges's concern and, in the kitchen, Marie's louder dismay Sara would eat nothing. She lay on the sofa in the place where Perry had sat. Two hours went by. Three. Now and then she went to look out into the whirling dark. Like the woman in the myth nightly visited by the god of love and forbidden to know who it was or to see his face, she'd been unable to bear the secret any longer. Taking a lamp she had bent to look at the sleeping god. Scalding oil had dropped on him. He had woken – and was gone forever.

She lay by the dying fire too unhappy to revive it. Georges came in at last to pile on some logs and coax it back into flame.

'May we bring you something?'

From pity for him Sara said she would have tea.

'Is it still snowing, Georges?'

'It is worse, Mademoiselle.'

She gave a shudder and remembered La Pallice.

As he turned to go the front door bell rang loudly, and Sara looked at Georges, her eyes enormous.

'Are you out, Mademoiselle?'

'Yes. No. I don't know.'

He came back to say it was Monsieur van Rijn.

Before she could reply, Perry came through the door and Georges frowned, taking his overcoat, the shoulders and sleeves thickly smothered with snow. He draped the wet coat gingerly over his arm.

'Let me get you some dry shoes, sir.'

'Thanks, Georges. Yes, they are pretty soaked.'

Georges went out and returned almost at once. Perry merely stood. He did not look at her.

'If I could have your shoes, sir, I can fill them with paper and put them somewhere to dry. These are going to be too small, I think.'

Perry gave something like a grin as he fitted his large feet into small morocco slippers, and thanked him. Georges took the wet shoes and left the room, shutting the door.

There was a curious waiting pause.

All Sara managed was,

'You must be cold.'

'It was deep in the park.'

'In the *park*?'

'Sure. And drifting. I had the whole place to myself.'

'Come to the fire. It's horrible to be cold.'

Her heart was dully aching. She did not understand why he was here looking at her with that iron face. It must be to reproach her, as if he'd said to himself – I'll go back and finish that row. At the idea of what he might say to wound her more she began to feel sick. She had broken into a place he had sealed, he would never forgive her. And what made it worse was that she did not believe trespassing into the past was wrong. But to make him suffer, yes, that was a sin, and for the first time in her life she saw that to hurt somebody by mistake could be worse than deliberate cruelty. It was a coarseness of soul.

He sat, scuffing off the slippers and leaning slightly towards the fire. The silence filled up with the ticking of Alexander's clock as its cherub swung to and fro.

'You're right,' he said at last.

'What do you mean?' she asked fearfully.

'That it's horrible to be cold.'

He began to rub his feet. With a faint look of himself returning to his grim face, he said,

'Frost bite. They're just coming back to life. When I was in the park I fell over twice, once into a drift. That's a laugh, isn't it? Nobody to share it with, though. And I thought that place without a living soul in it, freezing and silent, was like me. Yes, Sara, exactly like me. Don't look at me so sorrowfully. I'm sorry I left you like that. I was stunned for a bit. I don't give a goddam that you read the diary, I haven't opened

327

it since the Armistice. It was because, hell, somebody actually spoke about Janet and Dick and how I'd felt. It was as if you'd put your hand on a scar and I was sure your finger nails would rip at it. Sara. You're shivering.'

'I'm so brutal. I hate it in myself.'

'You're not brutal,' he said detachedly. 'You just have more guts than other people. I've treated you badly.'

She still trembled and wished she could keep her body still. She saw then the moral dangers of two different natures locked in sexual embrace and parted only to find mystery and terror. She knew if she touched him she would no longer understand. And this moment it seemed that she did.

'Why are we together, Sara? Is it for sex? Only for sex?'

He spoke as if the words hurt him, his voice seemed to have lost its guard. The tears stood in her eyes, thinking how he'd trudged in the snow, how he had fallen down. It was why she loved him. That he cared for her, treated her to a passion full of selfishness, and was sorry.

Without knowing what she was doing, forgetting the instinct to keep physically away just then, she took his hand and began to rub it between her own and her tears fell upon it. He made a sudden start forward.

'I'm sorry,' she said, weeping like a child, 'I'm so sorry, I am a fool to cry. It's only that you got so cold out there in the snow and you're not getting warmer and your hand is freezing . . .'

When she looked up with a streaked desolate face, he was staring at her. He said slowly,

'Oh Christ. How I love you. Worship you. I wish I didn't. I wish –'

'No, no, no,' she gasped, and kneeling down beside him held out her arms.

328